PRAISE *for* BARBARA WOOD

"Wood crafts vivid sketches of women who triumph over destiny."
—*Publishers Weekly*

"Entertainment fiction at its best."
—*Booklist*

"Absolutely splendid."
—Cynthia Freeman, *New York Times* bestselling author of
A World Full of Strangers and *Come Pour the Wine*

"Wood creates genuine, engaging characters whose
stories are fascinating."
—*Library Journal*

"A master storyteller."
—*Tulsa World*

"[Wood] never fails to leave the reader enthralled."
—Elizabeth Forsythe Hailey, author of *A Woman of Independent Means*

THE SERPENT AND THE STAFF

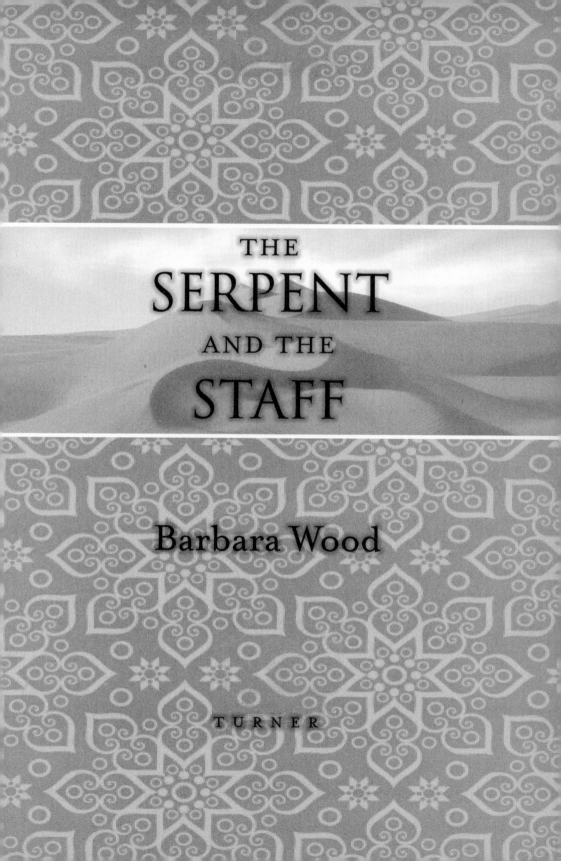

THE
SERPENT
AND THE
STAFF

Barbara Wood

TURNER

Turner Publishing Company

424 Church Street · Suite 2240
Nashville, Tennessee 37219

445 Park Avenue · 9th Floor
New York, NY 10022

www.turnerpublishing.com

The Serpent and the Staff

The Serpent and the Staff is a work of historical fiction. Although
some events and people in this book are based on historical
fact, others are the products of the author's imagination.

Cover by Gina Binkley
Jacket design by Mike Penticost
Cover photo by Getty Images
Author photo by Gabriel Acosta
Interior design by Glen Edelstein

Library of Congress Cataloging-in-Publication Data
Wood, Barbara, 1947-
  The Serpent and the Staff / Barbara Wood.
    pages cm
  ISBN 978-1-62045-461-9 (hardcover)
1. Forced marriage--Fiction. 2. Extortion--Fiction.
3. Betrayal--Fiction. 4. Syria--Ugarit--Fiction. I. Title.
PS3573.O5877S47 2013
813'.54--dc23
                          2013024463

Printed in the United States of America
13 14 15 16 17 18 19 20—0 9 8 7 6 5 4 3 2 1

To my husband Walt, with love.

OTHER BOOKS *by* BARBARA WOOD

The Divining
Virgins of Paradise
The Dreaming
Green City in the Sun
This Golden Land
Soul Flame
Vital Signs
Domina
The Watch Gods
Childsong
Night Trains
Yesterday's Child
Curse This House
Hounds and Jackals

BOOKS *by* KATHRYN HARVEY

Butterfly
Stars
Private Entrance

THE SERPENT AND THE STAFF

PROLOGUE

I remember two things about the night Jericho fell.

I remember that I was sixteen years old, and that I was in love.

Thoughts of war were the furthest from my young mind as I tossed and turned in my bed, hearing the sounds of the city beyond my balcony—Jericho on the Jordan River never slept—because I could not put Benjamin's handsome face from my mind.

I heard distant thunder that night. A spring storm rolling in from the Great Sea, I thought. Black clouds tumbling over the coastal towns, over Jerusalem, soon to quench Jericho's thirst. Thank the Highest One, I silently prayed. My father's date groves needed the rain.

He was at that moment in the Temple, offering a fat spring lamb and asking the Most High for relief from the drought. His brother, my uncle, and a physician in high standing, was in the poor quarter where the drought-fever had struck the hardest. He was a familiar sight among the poor, who called him "beloved healer."

But my thoughts, on that fateful spring night, could not remain on the charitable deeds of pious men. Benjamin came into my vision as I closed my eyes and treated myself to his smile, his laugh, his broad shoulders, the way he walked. I was a girl dreaming of marriage. Benjamin was the son of a wealthy family who monopolized Jericho's rich textile trade. His father was close friends with the King.

We were betrothed.

That evening, Papa had kissed me good night, promising to speak to Benjamin's father on the matter of the wedding date. It was to be a summer wedding, for there is no luckier time to wed. My life was perfect. My father was one of Jericho's wealthiest citizens, and my mother the descendant of a king of Syria in the North. We lived in a palatial house with marble pillars within the high walls of a fortified town. Jericho was the safest city in the world, and our house—which was elegant and second only to the King's palace—stood in the protective shadow of Jericho's formidable southwest tower from which soldiers had defended the city through the centuries. We had servants and fine furniture, my sisters and I dressed in gowns of the softest wool. We wore gold. We ate off silver plates. And so I saw before me, like a feast laid out on a table, a life of abundance and joy and possibilities.

No girl in the world was happier than I.

The thunder drew nearer, that night, rolling over the western hills. And when I heard shouts and screams in the streets beyond my balcony, I wondered why someone would be afraid of a spring rain.

And then I heard a cry downstairs. A crash. Feet stamping across the polished limestone floor. I flew from my bed to the inner balcony that ran around the inside of the second story of our house. I looked down at the main hall below, where we received guests and held fabulous banquets. My eyes widened in shock as I saw soldiers rudely striding in. They were not wearing the green tunics of Canaanite troops but white kilts, leather breastplates, and close-fitting helmets. From their speech, as they shouted orders at the panicked servants, I realized they were Egyptian.

I realized, too, that the thunder I had heard was not the sound of rain coming to Jericho but the rumble of war chariots racing across the plains surrounding the city.

I stood frozen as I watched a soldier seize one of our female servants by the hair and drag her along the floor as she kicked and screamed. A nursemaid appeared below, carrying a baby. My youngest sister, who had yet to be named. A soldier plucked the infant from her arms, grasping its little feet in one mighty hand to swing it against the wall. I saw the soft skull split open. Brains and blood flew out.

When I heard footsteps behind me, I whipped around. It was Aunt

Rakel, holding a lamp. Her sandals whispered across the marble floor. Her white robes floated around her like a cloud. Her face was pale.

"Quickly, Avigail," she said. "Get dressed. We must seek safety."

I dressed hastily, and we left the upper floor by a back stairway. I found the rest of my family gathered at the door to a secret passage. My mother had her arms around my two younger sisters. Her eyes filled with fright. This alarmed me. My mother was a beauty and of royal blood. Everyone marveled at her poise, her elegance. But in that moment she was an image of panic.

We trembled and shook as we heard screams fill our house, the sound of things being smashed, men shouting in Egyptian. Surely I was dreaming. It was a nightmare from which I would soon waken. The King had assured us of peace between Jericho and Egypt. A treaty had been signed.

The house steward appeared, his long black robe disheveled, the red sash hanging loosely. His name was Avraham and he had been with our family for two generations. "The house is not safe, my lady," he said to my mother. "The Egyptians are invading all homes. We are safer outside the walls. I will take you to the hills."

"But my husband—"

"Quickly, my lady."

Aunt Rakel took me by the arm. "Come, Avigail, we must save ourselves."

Her face was white. Fear burned in her eyes. Her husband—my uncle—was in the poor quarter. My father was at the Temple. Would the Most High protect them?

We followed Avraham through a narrow passage that had been built into the walls long ago as a means of retreat because Jericho had been raided many times in its long history. We ran in fear, our hearts pounding, our ears filled with the cries of our servants.

We came out into a night of chaos and mayhem. People were running in the streets. Foreign soldiers galloped after them on horseback. We huddled together as we waited for Avraham to find a way to get us to the fields beyond. The city gates were open, and there we saw a horrific sight . . . blazing torches, soldiers in hand-to-hand combat, generals in gilded chariots, unearthly screams, and blood, so much blood . . .

We ran.

The citizens of Jericho were fleeing every which way, down the roads, across fields of spring crops, carrying children and possessions, some half-dressed, while Egyptian soldiers gave chase with swords and spears.

As our group ran across an onion field, the glow from the full moon lighting our way, an Egyptian cavalryman on a mighty horse came from nowhere, galloping toward us. I veered away, just escaping the thundering hooves. My mother darted the other way, safe from the hooves, but the soldier's sword came down in a horrifying arc. The blade sliced through my mother's neck as cleanly as a scythe slicing a sheaf of wheat. I saw her head fly into the air, a look of astonishment on her face. The warhorse galloped past and I watched my mother's white-robed body go down like a toppled statue.

I stopped. My mouth dropped open. I could not, in that moment, understand what I was seeing, what had happened. I looked around for her head. Why I did this I do not know. But in that moment it seemed important that I find it.

All I remember after that is being swept up into strong arms and then blackness enveloped me.

When I regained consciousness I was among a group of refugees in the hills west of Jericho. It was still dark out. A large number had fled to the safety of caves and thickly wooded groves, there to hold onto one another and watch in horror as Jericho fell to Pharaoh's mighty forces.

Out of the darkness a tall, lean figure appeared. Praise the Most High, it was Rakel's son, my cousin Yacov. I learned that it was he who had carried me to the hills, and then he had made his way back to the city, to learn what was happening. "Say a prayer," Yacov said. "The men are dead. They were rounded up and taken to the Temple of the Moon and slain. I saw this with my own eyes."

"Papa?" I said.

Yacov's eyes were bleak. "And my father, pulled from a patient's bedside and taken to slaughter. But now they are gone to the Most High, praise His name."

Aunt Rakel covered her face with her hands and murmured, "Most High, take their souls into thy loving Presence." Her veil had slipped, revealing rich auburn hair. Yacov's hair and beard were the same color.

"It is the end of Jericho!" the others cried. "It is the end of the world."

But Yacov said, "Pharaoh will not destroy the city. That is not his intent. He wishes to occupy Jericho, a rich center at the crossroads of many profitable trade routes. But we cannot return to our homes, for they will be given to Egyptian citizens." He added bitterly, "Thus Pharaoh expands his empire, by conquering the towns and cities of Canaan and making them Egypt's vassals."

My sisters, who were aged nine and eleven, rocked back and forth, wailing into their hands. "What can we do? Where shall we go?"

Aunt Rakel said, "Can we wait, Yacov? Can we stay here until hostilities have died and perhaps negotiate to regain our house?" I saw how tightly she clasped her hands together as she fought for self-control. My parents dead. Her own husband slain. It was up to Rakel and her young son to see that the rest of us survived.

He shook his head. "The Egyptians are raping the women. They do this to spread Egypt's seed and further ensure loyalty to Pharaoh—through their half-breed bastards. Mother, you and the girls can never go back."

"But why, my son?" Rakel cried, needing to make sense of this calamity.

"They say Pharaoh needs workers to build his new city. His troops are raiding the lands south of here, to round up prisoners for a forced march back to Egypt. Mostly, they are Habiru, for the Habiru are nomadic shepherds without defenses and are easily captured. But a few Canaanites have been taken as well."

"Pharaoh must be mad," I said bitterly as I gathered my two young sisters into my arms. "The Habiru are an uncivilized people who know only how to erect goat's hide tents, not stone buildings."

"Avigail, say a prayer!" Aunt Rakel said. "You must never speak disparagingly of a people you know nothing about."

Cousin Yacov said, "The Habiru will be taught how to build."

When tears rolled down my aunt's cheeks, Yacov said, "Fear not for Jericho, Mother. Kings come and go, kingdoms rise and fall. But Jericho will be eternal. No force on earth can bring down those mighty walls."

As he turned his eyes to the city, where already the fighting was

5

dying down, while he spoke of "surprise attacks" and "broken treaties" and listed all the treacherous ways Egypt had betrayed their peace with Jericho, I searched the dark plain for my mother. Beautiful, loved by all, brutally cut down. I wanted to cry, but could not find the tears, the emotion. It was as if the mounted soldier had struck me down as well and my body lay next to my mother's, leaving me an unfeeling wraith.

And where was Benjamin? My beloved, my betrothed.

"We must leave this place," Yacov said, rising to his feet. He was only eighteen, but as he towered over us in his knee-length brown tunic, sashed at the waist, a black cloak over his shoulders, he seemed a giant. He produced gold rings from his sash. "I have money. We will join together with other families for protection."

"We cannot just walk away from our home!" Rakel cried.

"Mother, after the city is secured, Pharaoh's troops will comb these hills for those who fled. We have no choice."

She considered this, then said, "I had a dream that foretold this night. When I voiced it to my husband, he said it was nothing, to ignore it. But I know now that dreams are messages from the unseen world. Perhaps from the Most High, even, and they are not to be dismissed. I will never underestimate the prophetic power of dreams again."

She turned to her son. "We have cousins in the north." She spoke gravely. She kept her composure for she was older than the rest of us and although now a widow, could not enjoy the luxury of giving in to her emotions.

That is what I remember most about that night. Aunt Rakel's solid presence. Her strength. "Avigail," she said to me. "I charge you with the care of your sisters. We have a long journey ahead of us. We must look out for one another. Do not lose faith. The Most High will guide us to a new home in the North. Now we will pray, and then we will depart for Ugarit in Syria."

I looked down on the city of my birth, where I had known only happiness and security, and I felt my heart cleave in two. The pain was unbearable. My father and uncle, dead. My mother, lying in a field. And where was Benjamin, my beloved? Although Aunt Rakel assured us that the cousins in Ugarit would take us in, I knew I would not be happy in that distant city, in a house that was not ours.

And so we turned our backs on Jericho and began our sorrow-ful exodus, holding onto one another, weeping, leaving our ances-tral home with just the clothes on our backs. We formed a human river of homeless refugees, not knowing what the future held. But although we left behind our precious possessions—furniture made of cedar and pine, vases of alabaster and malachite, jewelry handed down through the generations—we all nonetheless carried with us a precious commodity: the histories of our families, names, events, tragedies, and triumphs—secrets, too, for every family has those—carefully remembered and stored away in our minds and hearts. For although our houses might be lost, our identities would never be. We would always remember we were Canaanites, descendants of Shem, son of Noah, and therefore we were the chosen of El, the Most High.

As for me, Avigail Bat Shemuel, it was not on that night, when Jericho fell to Egypt, nor during our flight to Jerusalem where friends took us in and gave us provisions for our arduous journey ahead, but somewhere on the Plains of Sharon and Jezreel, somewhere in the hills west of Galilee, as we camped with nomads and shepherds—old Avraham, my widowed Aunt Rakel, her son Yacov, my two sisters, three servants and I—as I sent prayers to the Most High for the souls of my father, my uncle, my mother, and my beloved Benjamin, as I slept beneath cold and impersonal stars, wondering about my uncer-tain future, as I wept into my arms, thinking that my broken heart would never be whole again, I whispered an oath—silent, secret, private, known only to myself. I vowed that never again would my home be taken from me. Never again would I allow an enemy to harm my family. For the rest of my life, wherever my path took me, into whatever foreign town, whatever strange land I entered, I would put down roots, I would claim a place for myself and my family and never again would we be driven out as we were on the fateful spring night that Jericho fell . . .

PART ONE

CHAPTER ONE

W hat do you think, Grandmother?"
    When she received no reply, Leah turned around. "Grandmother?"

Avigail drew herself out of her thoughts. It was a spring night and thunder rumbled in the distance. Every year, when spring storms came to Ugarit, that terrible night came back. The fall of Jericho. So many years ago, yet so vivid in her mind, as if she had fled the city yesterday.

Avigail looked at the object in her hand—a small fertility amulet made of finely hammered gold and engraved with a woman's face above two breasts and a pubic mound, the familiar features of Qadesha, the Sacred Prostitute, goddess of procreation and sexual pleasure. It was a good luck charm guaranteed to arouse lust in unsuspecting men, and Avigail prayed it worked on Jotham the wealthy shipbuilder tonight.

The citizens of Ugarit were goddess-worshippers and although El, the god of Jericho, was revered, the Most High was not Ugarit's sole deity. Having long ago married a follower of Baal, Avigail had gradually learned to pray to the many gods of northern Canaan.

"When you are in our guest's presence, Leah," she said to her granddaughter as she tucked the amulet into Leah's belt, "keep your eyes cast downward. Jotham will be looking you over, and if your eyes meet his, he will take it as a bold gesture and will be offended. Do not speak, do not fidget. Keep your hands still and your face hidden."

Leah murmured, "Yes, Grandmother," while her heart raced. To be singled out by one of the wealthiest men in Ugarit! Especially when her parents had worried no man would ask for her. At eighteen, Leah was past the traditional age of betrothal. She had been promised to a young man from another family, and would have married last summer had he not died of a fever that swept through the city. Leah had feared she faced a life of spinsterhood until the unexpected communication had come from the House of Jotham.

And now the House of Elias was alive with industry as the family and servants hurried about in anticipation of the arrival of so esteemed a guest.

Leah and her grandmother were in the women's quarters of the palatial villa, a sequestered feminine world of softly glowing lamps and diaphanous hangings stirring in the spring night, the sweet scent of flowers mingling with women's delicate perfumes, and the music of bracelets jingling on slender wrists joining that of trickling fountains.

Sharing in the festive preparations were two other women and two girls: Leah's mother, Hannah, elderly Aunt Rakel, and Leah's two younger sisters, Tamar and Esther, assisting Leah with her wardrobe, jewelry, makeup.

"When you serve our guest," Leah's grandmother continued, "demonstrate by your posture your servitude and humility. Show him that you will be an obedient wife. Remember that a good wife never speaks unless spoken to."

Avigail paused to take a sip of wine to calm her nerves. Marriage had not yet been agreed upon. Through a series of communications from Jotham the wealthy shipbuilder to Elias the prosperous vintner, the former had let it be known that he was interested in marrying the latter's eldest daughter. This visit had been arranged so that the esteemed Jotham could get a better look at Leah, whom he had seen on several occasions in Ugarit's bazaars in the company of her mother, sisters, and female servants. Halla! Avigail thought now as she fussed with the folds and hems of Leah's long skirts and veils. If Jotham marries Leah, the binding of our two houses will create the most powerful family in Ugarit, perhaps in all of Canaan! With our vineyards and Jotham's ships, we can monopolize the wine trade from here to the headwaters of the Nile.

She restored a stray lock of thick hair under Leah's veil and said, "I have told the honorable Jotham that your mother conceived seven times—and that even now she is well along with her eighth. That will tell him our women are fertile." Avigail had not mentioned that all Hannah's pregnancies had resulted in girls, and that only three had survived infancy. She glanced at her daughter-in-law who was seated in a special chair because of her pregnancy. Everyone was praying for a son.

Suffering the ministrations of her grandmother, who continued to make adjustments to her gown and veil, Leah bit her lip as anxiety joined the myriad emotions that were making her heart gallop. She knew about the ways of men and women, and what went on behind bedroom doors. And she vowed to be a good, obedient wife and do her best to produce sons. The achievement was not only for the sake of the family, but necessary to Leah herself. Canaanite women were never addressed by their own names, but by their relationship to their male protector. Leah was known as "Bat Elias," daughter of Elias. If today went well, she would become "Isha Jotham," Jotham's wife. And the birth of her first son would bestow on her the honorable title of "Em," meaning "mother of." Women who did not give birth to at least one son were pitied, for their status never changed from wife, no matter how many daughters they had.

"I remember," Avigail said as she took another sip of rich, red wine, "when my Yosep came to inspect me. There were girls in other families he was considering, and he took a long time with me. When he reached out and boldly pinched my buttocks, as if he were buying a fat-tailed sheep, I squealed. I believe that is what made him choose me. We were married for thirty years and he only took two concubines. May he sleep in the bliss of the gods."

Avigail sighed and marveled at the long path she had traveled these past forty years since her flight from Jericho.

After an arduous trek of five hundred miles, suffering hardships and setbacks, they had reached the city of Ugarit, where cousins took them in. News came from the south. The Egyptians had collected all the corpses of the slain Canaanites and burned them on a massive pyre. They said the smoke could be seen as far away as Jerusalem. Benjamin and his family were slaughtered. Egyptians took the houses of the rich, to discard Canaanite pottery and furniture and gods, installing their own pottery and furniture and gods. The king of Jericho was allowed to stay on his throne, but he was a figurehead, nothing more, while Pharaoh's agents took over the government of Jericho and surrounding districts.

Two years later, eighteen-year-old Avigail caught the eye of a wealthy vintner named Yosep. Although she herself was penniless, he wanted to marry her. Despite her lack of personal wealth, Avigail did have one valuable possession: her royal blood. And the fact that it was the blood of a popular king of Ugarit, named Ozzediah, made Avigail all the more desirable as a wife. When Yosep brought Avigail into this villa tucked against the foothills and embraced by sweeping, green vineyards, Avigail knew she had found her home, her roots, and vowed she would never leave.

She frowned at her granddaughter. "Your hips are woefully slim, Leah. Tamar, darling, hand me that veil." Avigail rolled the length of cloth and slipped it under Leah's dress. "That's better," she said, eyeing her handiwork.

"But won't Jotham be angry when he discovers the deception?"

Avigail laughed. "Trust me, dear child, no man on his wedding night is concerned with measuring his wife's hips. Now listen, Jotham will ask you a question, for he will want to assess the quality of your voice. When you reply, address him as My Lord, as if you were already his wife." Avigail readjusted Leah's veil. "You have such beautiful hair. So thick and long. I wish you could show it off to Jotham. He would not think twice to take you for his wife."

Avigail stepped back to admire her granddaughter. Leah was beautiful. Tall and slender, with a clear complexion and large, luminous eyes. She possessed a fine forehead that Avigail hoped someday to be festooned with gold rings to show off her husband's wealth as Avigail's own forehead did. "Say a prayer, Leah. If all goes well tonight, you will soon be the mistress of a fine house overlooking the harbor. You will have many slaves and servants at your command. And when you bear your first son, you will be the envy of every woman in Canaan."

As she spoke these words, Avigail felt contentment fill her heart. For the first time in years, she was at peace with the world, and secure in the knowledge that her family was going to survive.

Because the nightmare of Jericho had never left her, Avigail had worked hard and with determination to make sure her family knew only safety and security. To that end, when she came to live at this villa as a young bride, she began her methodical campaign to ensure such safety. The House of Elias was now protected by a strong and loyal security force, made up of sturdy guards who stood sentry and patrolled the outer walls at regular intervals. They were armed and had sworn to fight any invaders to the death. To further ensure that they would indeed protect her family, Avigail had promised each guard a generous reward after such an event. She had also cunningly made sure that each of the guards had a family member working either as a slave or servant inside the house—additional incentive to fend off attackers.

Further safeguards included a house hidden up in the hills, stocked with provisions—a place for her family to flee to should invaders come to Ugarit. Gold was buried on that secret property, so that if she and her family became refugees, they would have money for food and shelter. It had been her obsession in the years since Jericho to make sure her family would never have to go through what she and her sisters and Rakel went through.

And now, tonight, she saw the culmination of all her hard work and determination. Leah would be betrothed to one of the richest men in Syria, her future secure and guaranteed. After that, Avigail would find a husband for Tamar. For the first time in years, the sound of thunder would not make Avigail think of war chariots and fill her heart with fear. She would know it was only the sound of rain and her soul would return to that long-ago night when she had lain in bed thinking of her beloved Benjamin.

She smiled. She had come full circle. Life was good, her family was blessed.

Perhaps she might even take a trip to Jericho. Her sisters had gone to the gods, and Yacov perished long ago in an accident. Avigail and Aunt Rakel were the only ones left from that terrible night. Jericho was Canaanite again. No more raids came after that terrible one. It was said that Egypt had enough Habiru slaves to build its monuments. In the time since, scattered citizens had returned to their homes, and many of the Egyptians went back to Egypt, until all that remained were a few agents to see that tribute was paid in full and annually to Pharaoh's coffers. It might be nice, Avigail thought nostalgically, to see the old house again.

A slave came in and murmured something to her mistress. "Asherah be praised," Avigail said with a smile, "Jotham has arrived and is already drinking his first cup of wine. We can go in now. Ask for the blessings of the gods and remember to keep your veil up to your face."

"Wait!" twelve-year-old Esther said. She lifted up on her toes and slipped a white jasmine, freshly bloomed and sweetly fragrant, over Leah's ear.

"Thank you, Esther," Leah said. Poor Esther, born with a cleft lip that made her so ugly she was fated to become the family spinster who would take care of her parents in their old age.

Beautiful Tamar, sixteen years old and not to be outdone, said, "This is for you, dear sister," and she removed a ring from her hand and slipped it onto Leah's.

Avigail looked at her second granddaughter, known for her selfishness, in surprise. "That is most generous of you, Tamar."

"It's only for tonight. I will want it back."

For an instant, Avigail's thoughts strayed to her least favorite granddaughter as she grasped the motives behind Tamar's show of generosity: she could not marry until her older sister did. And Avigail knew that Tamar had her heart set on the son of an olive grower. It would be another brilliant match, Avigail thought, although she suspected Tamar would never be happy no matter whom she married.

"Time to go," she said, returning to Leah, her favorite. "Ask the blessings of the gods."

The villa was built around a central courtyard that was open to the sky, to admit daylight, the sun, and rain that periodically filled the cistern in the center. Around this paved courtyard ran a colonnaded loggia, with doorways leading to rooms. In the western half of the house, daily activities were conducted and visitors received. The kitchens, laundry, food storage, and, in an enclosed yard, animal pens and slaughter shed were on the eastern half of the residence so that the prevailing winds off the Great Sea swept the smells away from the house.

Originally, the residence had been one story, but over the generations rooms had been erected on the roof so that it was now a complete second story. Here were the private chambers of Elias the head of the house, with empty bedchambers waiting to be filled with sons and grandsons. On the other side of the open space stood the bedchambers of the women, and their protected courtyards and gardens where men were forbidden to enter.

Above this second story, a flat roof planted with gardens looked out upon the family's vineyards that grew up the slopes of the mountains, and beyond, the city of Ugarit. Elias the Canaanite's house was one of the tallest and most spacious in the land; it was also sumptuous and the envy of many wealthy families.

Avigail accompanied Leah into the hospitality hall, where her son Elias was entertaining their guest. In the glow of shining bronze lamps, the two men lay upon rich carpets with thick cushions at their backs, while slaves were setting before them golden platters hot from the kitchen: sea scallops in shells, sculptured bread loaves, fried asparagus spears artfully arranged. Pork chops, suckling pig, and a favorite in Ugarit: blood sausage. Leah's entrance into the hall at the same time as the food symbolized her role as one who serves her master.

"Shalaam, Em Elias," Jotham said to Avigail, his eyes flicking briefly to the silent girl at her side. Unlike his host who wore a brown tunic under a conservative coat sashed at the middle, Jotham had arrayed his corpulent body in a flamboyantly red tunic with a striped coat over it. He was barefoot, having left his sandals at the door, but his dark brown hair and beard had been oiled and curled, and his thick wrists were encased in gold sheaths. On the low table before him, his gift to Leah's family glowed in the lamplight: five balls of a fragrant gum resin called frankincense. A generous gift.

"Shalaam. The blessings of Dagon," Avigail replied, and tried not to frown at the second guest seated on a stool: Jotham's sister, Zira, wearing a long black dress with a black veil draped over her head and shoulders. Avigail had not known the woman would be accompanying him. Behind the pair were Jotham's scribe and a lawyer, both prepared to record the meeting and draw up a contract. Occupying a stool behind Elias was his own private scribe, also prepared to record the meeting on clay tablets.

"Welcome to my son's house, Em Yehuda," she said to Zira, thinking that the woman's display of gold rings across her forehead, with not a copper or silver one among them, a trifle ostentatious. Zira did not resemble her brother, who might be considered handsome were he not so fat. Zira was thin with sharp cheekbones and an unfortunate overbite.

Surprised at herself for taking such an instant dislike to Jotham's sister—Zira might be a very kind woman—Avigail excused herself and retired to the other side of an intricate privacy screen, where she joined Hannah and Aunt Rakel and the two younger girls so that they could watch the proceedings without themselves being seen. As Avigail took a seat, she heard elderly Rakel murmur, "Asherah save us, I don't like the looks of Jotham's sister. Her mother must have been frightened by a donkey."

As Avigail and Rakel turned their attention to Leah and the guests, Hannah suddenly leaned forward, hands protectively on her belly, a worried look on her face.

Last night she had been visited by a disturbing dream: She is awakened by a raven that flies into her bedchamber which she shares with her husband Elias. The raven perches at the foot of the bed and speaks to her. "Two hundred amphoras of your finest vintage will be satisfactory."

In the next moment, a girl who resembles her daughter Leah comes into the chamber carrying a bowl of steaming soup. Hannah detects the aroma of clams. As the girl takes a step toward the bed, the raven suddenly flies up in a frenzy of screeching and flapping of black wings. The girl screams, drops the clam soup, and collapses to the floor in a seizure.

Hannah cannot move in the dream. Elias does not wake up. She watches in horror as the girl writhes on the floor, foam and spittle flying from her lips, her arms and legs going rigid, flailing, while a high keening sound comes from her throat.

Hannah woke up then, and had been filled with dread and fear all day as she had wondered what it meant.

The dream came back to her now, in all its realistic detail and horror, for Jotham's sister resembled a great black bird in her widow's robes, and her nose that was like a beak. Hannah pressed her hand to her bosom and felt the sudden racing of her heart.

As Leah started serving, deftly keeping her veil to her face while offering plates of food to her father and his guests, Jotham selected an oily black olive stuffed with garlic and, popping it into his mouth, declared, "I tell you, my brother, the Egyptians are perverse. Imagine—the most powerful country in the world, the wealthiest and most advanced, ruled by a woman!"

"Then I would say they are not the most advanced," Elias replied, choosing a raw oyster swimming in vinegar. In his late thirties, and bearded like all Canaanite men, Elias the vintner was a robust man with a likeable personality and known to all in Ugarit as a fair-minded man.

"Women haven't the capacity for complex thought nor are they capable of ruling a country. Hatshepsut must have many advisers."

"The boy who inherited the throne is too young," said Elias, always a man to see both sides of a situation. "Thutmose needs a co-regent. His stepmother is merely guiding him until he comes into his own."

"Elias, my friend, I can accept a Dowager Queen. But that outrageous female has declared herself to be king! Hatshepsut wears men's clothing and even sports a false beard! What weaklings are the people of Egypt that they would tolerate such an obscenity? Hmmph! Egyptians care only about where their next mug of beer is coming from. No woman should be allowed that much power. It is dangerous."

"Nonetheless, Queen Hatshepsut is smart enough to extract an annual tribute from Ugarit under the guise of friendly trade."

"Yes, and Canaanites everywhere grumble about this and swear to rebel someday."

"Enough of politics," Elias said. "Let us drink until the grape lifts us into the air!" And he then invited Jotham to try a new wine. The shipbuilder looked into his goblet and frowned. "You serve me water?"

"Not at all! Taste it!"

Cautiously. Then: "It is wine! But such color, or no color really."

"It is white wine, my friend, a special vintage that I have been working to perfect. It began with an experiment in which I removed the skins from the pressed grapes before the fermentation began. It was simply an exercise in curiosity. This was the result, praise the gods!"

Another taste. Jotham smacked his lips. "Light. Crisp. Slightly sweet. I believe it will be a great success. You know, my friend and brother, that I am planning to open a new shipbuilding yard in Cyprus. From there, I will open new trade routes across the Great Sea. What a profitable business union we could have, with your legendary wines and my swift ships. Soon, all the world will be enjoying this remarkable vintage."

His eyes slid to Leah as he said, "union," and slightly emphasized the word.

Elias grinned and lifted his goblet. "Here's to wine and ships, my friend and brother! The gods are with us tonight."

Jotham echoed the toast and then drained his goblet, murmuring, "Delightful," as he looked at Leah, his eyes on her hips.

As Elias and his guests enjoyed selections of roast pork, scallops in sauce, and giant crab legs, they heard the beginning of a spring rain whisper in the night. A delightful sound at the start, but it soon became heavy, so that rain splashed in the empty pool in the open courtyard, and cold drafts found their way into the house.

Jotham's sister Zira dabbed her lips with a cloth and spoke for the first time. "You should be glad we are willing to take Leah off your hands, considering her age."

Elias frowned. "My daughter is not so old."

Zira lifted her chin. "Still, people will wonder what is wrong with her that she is eighteen and not yet married. We have to think of our reputation, you know."

Elias said, "My house is well known in all of Canaan. Anyone of means and status knows my daughter's story."

"That she is to be pitied?" Zira said.

Behind the screen, Avigail hissed, "Halla! The woman twists my son's words. And look how Jotham says nothing! He does not correct her."

Avigail had known Jotham's widowed sister lived with him, but as Zira was younger and without a husband, Avigail had assumed she had a lesser status in the house. But now Avigail was seeing something different. While Jotham was a powerful man among his peers, and a wealthy businessman, connected to all the wealthy men in Canaan, in his own house it appeared he was under his sister's thumb.

"Halla, Mother Avigail!" Hannah whispered. "I do not like that woman." Avigail looked at her pregnant daughter-in-law, a likeable woman from the North whose father was a date farmer. Hannah's tense posture alarmed her, the way she leaned forward with her hands on her swollen belly. Avigail had gone to the temple of Asherah every day for twenty-eight days to pray for a male child. "Quickly say a prayer, daughter."

The sharp-voiced woman spoke up: "Is your daughter a hard worker, Elias? I do not tolerate laziness under my roof."

"Halla!" Hannah whispered again, pressing her hands to her abdomen. "She will work my daughter like a slave. Leah will not have a life of ease."

"Hannah, go to your room quickly. Say a prayer. You must protect the baby."

But Hannah stayed. "I do not like the way Jotham is looking at my daughter," she fretted in a soft voice. "May the gods protect her."

Avigail patted her daughter-in-law's arm. "He is a man. He is supposed to look at her that way."

"See how he licks his lip. His lust is so obvious it is disgusting. They say his previous wives died from too much work in the bed-chamber."

"Calm yourself, Hannah." Avigail said, marveling at the power of Qadesha's fertility amulet, for Jotham truly was eyeing Leah with naked desire. "You are distressing yourself needlessly. Invoke the gods. Think of your unborn child."

"He is so old. Forty-five, and none of his male children survived! It is a bad-luck house."

Avigail could have pointed out that it was the same in the House of Elias, and that it was through prayer to Qadesha and Asherah that she hoped a union between the two houses would change that luck. But, wondering at her daughter-in-law's sudden alarm and what had caused it, she said, "Do not worry, Hannah, dear. I shall see to it that Leah is treated fairly in Jotham's house. You must think of the child in your womb. He has two more months of sleep. Do not give him bad dreams. Invoke Asherah's blessed name."

But Hannah grew more agitated. Her face drained of color. The nightmare filled her thoughts—the raven, speaking of amphoras of wine, while the girl who resembled Leah writhed on the floor . . .

And now Leah was about to serve Jotham a bowl of clam soup. "Mother Avigail—" Hannah began in a voice so breathless her mother-in-law did not hear.

"You will have to bring something more to the marriage," Zira was saying archly, while Elias and the women behind the screen waited for Jotham to silence her. But the fat shipbuilder occupied himself with a blood sausage and allowed his sister a free tongue.

"Why do you say that?" Elias asked, unaccustomed to discussing business with a woman.

"My brother will be marrying a girl who was passed over. What will people think?"

"Passed over?" Elias said sharply. "The young man died."

Zira shrugged. "My brother will want compensation for taking her off your hands. Two hundred amphoras of your finest vintage will be satisfactory."

Elias said, "What!" And behind the privacy screen, his wife Hannah whispered to Avigail, "Mother Avigail, the dream I told you about this morning—that is exactly what the raven said to me! And then I saw the girl who looked like Leah fall to the floor in a seizure. I know now what the dream is about. It is a warning that the falling sickness is in Jotham's blood. The girl resembled Leah. I believe she is Leah's future daughter, and the gods are warning us that if Leah marries Jotham, her children will inherit the falling sickness."

Avigail stared at her daughter-in-law. Everyone in Ugarit had heard the rumor that Zira's son suffered from seizures. But Zira had political ambitions for her son and in politics one could never believe what one heard. But ever since their flight from Jericho, Aunt Rakel had instilled in Avigail a respect for the prophetic power of dreams, and now she worried that perhaps it was a warning from the gods.

"Mother," Hannah said, "the girl in the dream was serving clam soup. Look at Leah."

Avigail nodded gravely. Patting Hannah's hand, she said, "We will clear this up at once."

To the shock of her son and his guests, Avigail emerged from behind the privacy screen to stand before them, drawing herself up straight and tall. "Forgive the interruption, my son," she said, "but there is a vital question that must be answered before negotiations go any further."

She turned to Zira and said, "Many pardons, Em Yehuda, but before I hand over my granddaughter in marriage to your brother I must ask a delicate question. Forgive the inquiry, but you will understand that this is of the utmost importance. It is whispered that your son, Yehuda, suffers from the falling sickness. Is this true?"

"Mother!" Elias blurted.

Zira shot to her feet. "How dare you!"

"I dare because if it is true, then I must reconsider giving my granddaughter to your brother. It has been said that the falling sickness is in family blood. If this is so, then Leah is at risk for bearing children who have the illness. So I ask you, Zira Em Yehuda, does your son suffer from this affliction?"

Zira pressed her lips together in a tight thin line. "It is a vicious rumor, nothing more."

Avigail met the woman's eyes, saw how she clasped her hands, how she trembled. "You will swear upon Asherah that your son does not have the affliction?"

Zira opened her mouth, while Elias and Jotham watched and Leah stood with a bowl of soup in her hands. And then Zira closed her mouth, saying nothing.

"Halla," Avigail whispered. "Then it is true. Yehuda suffers from the falling sickness."

A shrill cry came from behind the privacy screen and Tamar called out, "Grandmother! Something is wrong with Mother!"

Avigail turned to a male servant and said, "Tell Baruch he must go at once and fetch the physician. Tell him he is needed for childbirth. Hurry! The gods speed you." And then she ran to Hannah's aid.

Hearing her mother's cry behind the screen, Leah turned sharply and the bowl of hot clam soup slipped from her hands and into Jotham's lap. He shouted and leapt to his feet. Slaves rushed forward with linen towels. Elias stared in horror while a furious expression darkened Zira's face.

Leah froze as she watched the privacy screen. And then she heard her mother's sobs and moans gradually fade as the women hurried Hannah to the other side of the house.

"Daughter!" Elias said sharply.

She spun about and was startled to see Jotham's scarlet tunic covered in clam soup, slaves frantically wiping him off. Her father was on his feet and glowering at her. "Apologize to our guest."

But as Leah was about to say she was sorry, she heard another scream, and she knew her mother was in labor. But it was too soon!

She spun on her heel and, before the astonished eyes of her father and his guests, fled the hospitality hall.

Leah arrived in the birthing chamber to find her mother lying on the bed and crying out as Avigail and female slaves tried to make her comfortable. Leah went to her mother's side, to kneel beside the bed and take Hannah's hand. "Are you all right, Mother?"

Hannah rolled her head. She was pale, her face glistening with sweat. "There is too much pain," she whispered. "Something is wrong."

Leah watched as Avigail lifted Hannah's gown to expose the swollen abdomen. "Halla," she whispered when she saw the taught skin ripple with contraction.

Tamar and her younger sister hung back with fearful looks on their faces.

Avigail spoke calmly to those around her. "Bring spiced wine and a hot poker to warm it. I must have water in a basin, and fresh linens. Quickly! Tamar, make yourself useful and light the incense at Asherah's shrine. Esther, pray for your mother." Although she spoke calmly, Avigail was filled with terror. Everyone knew that words when spoken took on a life of their own with a power to bless or to injure. Zira's words had created bad luck and sent it through the air, like an evil wind, entering through Hannah's ears to swim down to her belly and begin its demonic work on her unborn child.

She bent over her daughter-in-law and, placing her hand on her forehead, said, "Quickly, invoke the gods, Hannah. You must calm yourself. We must stop these contractions. The baby cannot be born yet. He will not survive."

"That horrible, horrible woman," Hannah said through clenched teeth. Veins bulged at her neck. "I will not let her have my daughter. She is a raven who will give my grandchildren the falling sickness." Hannah screamed, and water appeared between her legs, to spread over the bed.

24

"Halla!" Avigail whispered, and traced a protective sign in the air. She looked around the room. "Where is the wine? Where is that girl with the basin and linens? Esther and Tamar, do not stop praying. Invoke Asherah and Dagon. Quickly! Bring the gods into our presence."

Lifting a taper from a candlestick, Avigail went around the room lighting incense so that the air was soon filled with sweet smoke designed to keep evil spirits away. Then she went to the outer corridor to look up and down the torchlit columns.

As Leah listened to the rain that was now coming down harder, she felt a hand on her arm. She looked up into the wrinkled face of Auntie Rakel, whose veil had slipped to expose wispy white hair. Rakel was the oldest resident in the House of Elias, where she had lived for twenty years. "Mera darling, run to the kitchen and fetch the Elixir of Asherah."

"What are you talking about, Auntie?"

"Go quickly now. My husband gave me the recipe. He was a physician and he grew all sorts of bushes and flowers, even a few trees. That was in Jericho, where I was born. People came to our house for my husband's cures. If he were here, he would give Hannah the Elixir of Asherah."

"What is the Elixir of Asherah?"

Rakel placed an ancient hand, white and blue-veined, on Hannah's abdomen. "By the grace of the gods, it stops labor contractions. My sister was seven months pregnant when a falcon flew into the house. It could not find a way out. We tried to catch it. The bird flew from room to room until it hit a pillar and fell dead. My sister went into labor and we almost lost the baby, but my husband gave her the elixir and the contractions stopped and the baby stayed in the womb until full term. He is alive and healthy today, my nephew Ari."

Avigail came back into the room, frowning. "What is Aunt Rakel going on about? Who is Ari?"

"Mera, you must go to the kitchen," the older woman cried. "We cannot lose Rebekka again!"

"Rebekka?" Avigail gave her a perplexed look, and then her face cleared. "Ari, Rebekka. Halla, they died years ago. Mera was a servant, I think, when I was a child. Leah, go out to the road and see if the doctor is coming. Rakel, come along dear and go to your room. You will frighten Hannah with your talk."

"But the Elixir of Asherah will help her! It will save the baby."

"Come now, be a dear and go lie down. Pray to the gods. Ah, here is the wine."

Avigail took the cup and hurried to the bed. Sitting next to her laboring daughter-in-law, she held the wine to her lips and said, "Drink as much as you can, dear, and invoke the gods as you do. It will slow the contractions. It will calm you so that you can keep the baby inside you."

"Asherah help me, I cannot!" Hannah screamed. "The child comes!"

With a trembling hand, Avigail set the cup aside and moved to the foot of the bed. Her veil had slipped from her head so that auburn hair streaked with silver caught the lamp light. With her lips set in resolve, she leaned forward, hands ready. "We cannot stop this. It is now in Asherah's hands. Leah, come help me."

Her eyes wide with fear, Leah went to her grandmother's side and watched in horror as the baby came, quickly and with much blood.

"Praise the gods, it is a boy," Avigail said as she wrapped the mewling infant in a blanket and handed it to Leah. But there had been no joy in her voice, and then she returned her attention to Hannah.

While Avigail severed the umbilical cord with a sharp copper blade, Leah looked down at the little life in her arms, red-faced, eyes tightly shut, his body covered in the fluids of birth. His mouth was open to release kitten-like cries and he shuddered with each intake of breath.

He is so small, Leah thought, so helpless. Her tears fell on him as she silently prayed to Asherah to spare his life.

The house steward came in then, breathless, his robes damp from rain. "The physician was not at home, mistress," he said to Avigail. "His servant directed me to a nearby doctor who was available and said he would come at once."

"Not at home?" Like all wealthy families, Elias's household kept a physician on permanent retainer. He was supposed to be available at all hours so that they never had to resort to seeking out one of the practitioners at the House of Gold, as ordinary citizens must do.

She winkled her nose and watched the door. "Well? Where is the man? We are in dire need—"

Her voice caught as she made a choking sound. Her eyes widened at the sight of the stranger who came quietly through the doorway, tall and white-robed, wearing a long black wig, with a box hanging from his shoulder by a strap. Avigail could not for the moment speak, she was so shocked.

The she turned to the steward and said, "You brought an Egyptian into our house? Halla! You bring a curse!"

She shot a dismissive gesture toward the unwanted visitor, but he stepped forward and said in heavily accented words: "I was trained in the House of Life at Thebes. I can help."

Avigail shuddered. Sickness rose in her. Outside, the spring rain brought rumbling thunder and now an Egyptian stood before her. It was Jericho all over again.

Standing in the shadows, holding the baby in her arms, Leah watched the exchange and thought the physician seemed harmless. He was clean and polite, and seemed genuinely desirous of helping. But she knew of her grandmother's ingrained prejudice against the man's race, and watched as he gave Avigail a curt nod, turned, and left the chamber, while Leah wondered what miracle cures might be contained in the box on his shoulder.

"My baby," Hannah whispered. "Please give him to me."

But Leah looked down and saw that the baby had stopped quivering. His arms were flaccid, his tiny mouth, slack.

"Grandmother!" Leah said.

Avigail hurried over and took one look. "He has gone to the gods," she murmured and traced the sacred sign of Asherah on his forehead.

"Halla!" cried a masculine voice, and they turned to see Elias in the doorway, a large man looking useless and clumsy in so feminine a room.

"Elias," Avigail said in alarm. "You should not be here. It is bad luck."

"Hannah's cries stopped. I waited for news but no one came to tell me."

"My son," Avigail said, going to him. She drew him into an embrace and said, "The child died. We could not save him."

Elias knelt by the bed where he kissed his wife and let his tears fall on the lifeless baby. Then he pressed his face into his wife's bosom and wept without restraint. "My love, my love! I thank the gods that you are alive! Smite me for being grateful that, if one of you must die, it was the child! I cannot lose you, my love!" And he wept some more.

Lifting a weary arm, Hannah stroked her husband's thick hair and whispered, "Please do not send Leah away to live with that horrible woman. Our grandchildren will be afflicted as Zira's son is afflicted."

Avigail stepped in, grave-faced. She trembled as she said, "You have left our guests all alone, Elias. You must rejoin them. I will be along as soon as I can."

With a heavy heart, Elias returned to the hospitality hall where he apologized that the dinner was interrupted and that he must ask his guests to leave. "We are now a house of mourning. My son has gone to the gods."

"This is intolerable," Zira said sharply. "When my Yehuda was born, we were entertaining Princess Sahti and her family at our home. My water broke during dinner and I politely excused myself without saying why. I went to my bedchamber where I delivered my son on my own. Our guests were not even aware of the event, I was that respect-ful of them. Not only did your daughter Leah show extreme disobe-dience, you yourself abandoned us. And do not forgive how your mother insulted me with her lies about my son."

Elias could not reply. Seizing the neckline of his tunic, he tugged sharply until it tore. Later, he would shave his beard and scatter ashes in his hair.

Grimly, Jotham said, "I am sorry for your loss, Elias, and pray that your son is with Dagon. But you caused me great offense. You have made me lose face. If you give me your daughter, I will consider it restitution."

Elias gave him a startled look. They had not yet discussed marriage. He shook his head and said wearily, "I am sorry, my friend, but I cannot."

Jotham's face darkened. "You will regret this, Elias. Your daugh-ter and your mother have shamed both our families. What kind of emasculated man are you?"

"By the gods!" Elias shouted. "I have just lost my son. Do you think I could suffer more than this?" He rubbed his face. He felt a hundred years old. "The only shame here, Jotham, is upon you for not showing this house respect in an hour of mourning."

Jotham tilted his head in indignation. "You caused me to lose face in front of my sister. How will I rule my house now?"

Elias wanted to say, *You never ruled your house.* But he bit his lip. He felt the weight of the world on his shoulders. He could not think straight. His firstborn son, dead . . .

Jotham leaned forward and said, "Mark me, Elias, the day will come when you will beg me to take your daughter. And I promise you now before Dagon and Baal, that I will have Leah, or no man will."

CHAPTER TWO

The situation is becoming intolerable, Elias. Something must be done or your daughters will be without husbands."

Avigail and her son were visiting in the sunroom of the women's quarters. Men who were not relatives were forbidden to enter this part of the villa, and male relatives could enter only with permission from the women. It was a tradition begun long ago by ladies of the house who wished to live in their own realms, to retreat to a world not dominated by men, where they could move through their cycles and nurture their families beyond the tempests of the outside world. Avigail ruled this private domain, her son was here as a guest. He had in fact been summoned.

Elias twisted the heavy signet ring on his thumb. It was made of chalcedony and carved with Elias's identifying mark: A man seated beneath a bower of grape vines, his arms lifted up in praise of the gods. He used it to sign contracts, letters, receipts, legal documents. "I do not know what to do, mother. I had not thought Jotham would be so vindictive."

Avigail, too, was surprised at the extent of Jotham's vitriol. But not Zira's. Avigail had exposed the truth about her son and his affliction. Even though she had assured Zira afterward that she would never say a word about Yehuda's falling sickness, the fact that Avigail had uncovered Zira's secret at all had brought retribution upon their heads. Jotham's vendetta had wide reach. While Elias's friends sympathized, they feared Jotham's wrath.

Avigail had hoped that, because of her own ancestry, Elias would be immune to Jotham's campaign of revenge. She was descended from Ozzediah, one of Canaan's greatest kings, and therefore her granddaughters enjoyed a special prestige. But no. Prospective husbands stayed away from the House of Elias.

And now she was worried. Avigail had worked so hard to secure her family's future, had been so certain she had achieved her goal, that she had forgotten the vagaries of fate. She had thought a house hidden in the hills, a place of refuge, buried gold, security guards—she had concentrated on the physical security of her family, never imagining an attack such as this! And now the house of Elias the vintner was a house of women. The only man who resided here was Elias himself. Rooms intended for beards and deep voices stood empty. Blessed Asherah, Avigail prayed, bring sons to this house or our bloodline will die out!

She brought herself back to the moment. The family in crisis. Because Jotham could not have Leah, neither could any other man. A word here, a vague threat there, and Jotham saw to it that the men of Ugarit decided it was wiser to look elsewhere for a wife than to be on the powerful shipbuilder's wrong side.

Avigail looked at her youngest granddaughter, Esther, who sat quietly beading a necklace. A sweet-natured girl, obedient and modest, she would have made a good wife. But with her split lip that left her teeth permanently exposed, the thirteen-year-old would never marry or have children. Her course was set. Avigail did not have to worry about Esther.

But then she looked at Tamar, her seventeen-year-old granddaughter, who sat in the sunshine weaving upon a loom. Avigail worried a great deal about Tamar. Fire burned in that willowy body. So young and yet she already possessed a healthy sexual appetite. "Tell me again, Grandmother, how it will be on my wedding night." Of course, there was nothing wrong with a woman having a strong libido. In Ugarit, a wife could legally divorce her husband if he did not satisfy her in the bedroom. But such curiosity was not proper for a maiden.

And the way she looked at men in the marketplace, letting her veil slip! Avigail had seen how they looked at her, for Tamar was an astonishing beauty. The sort of beauty that could be a burden to a woman, but Tamar knew how to use it to her advantage. Even when she was a child she enjoyed sitting on men's laps, tickling their beards, receiving sweets in return. Avigail knew that Tamar would need to marry soon, or her nature would lead to her ruin.

However, Tamar could not marry until her older sister did. Thus the urgency to find a husband for Leah. "I will write to my cousin in Sidon," Avigail said at last. "She has five healthy sons. One of them will do for Leah. Send Shemuel the scribe to me. I will dictate a letter at once."

As Leah combed her mother's hair, she tried to recall what she knew of her grandmother's cousin in Sidon—especially the five sons. Leah had overheard the dictation to Shemuel the family scribe: "Leah is a strong healthy girl, obedient, good with her hands." Leah wondered which of the sons the cousin would send. She prayed he was decent looking, and kind. At nineteen, Leah knew she could not be choosy.

She and her mother were sitting in the spring sunshine, listening to the larks on the other side of the high wall that protected the courtyard. Two women separated from the world by mudbrick and sorrow.

They were not alone in the sunroom. Tamar was at her loom and Esther was making a necklace of blue and red clay beads purchased in the marketplace. Aunt Rakel sat at a low table, using a wooden mallet to shell almonds for cakes she would later bake in the kitchen.

Leah drew the ivory comb through her mother's thick tresses and thought about the terrible night a year ago that had resulted in unexpected consequences. She had heard her mother's cries and had known where her devotion lay. She did not regret her actions of that night, but she was sorry for having caused her father such distress. His friends were starting to shun him and his business was beginning to suffer as once-loyal customers were turning to other vintners for their wine. Leah had even told her father she would marry Jotham if he would still have her, but her father had said no. A promise made to her mother . . .

"Which veil will you wear today, Mother?" she asked, thinking how comely her mother always looked in pale blue.

"Just my house veil, dear. I have no need of the others." It was Hannah's monthly retreat, during which she would not leave the house nor receive visitors. A sacred time, one that baffled and frightened men but which put women in touch with the moon and the Goddess. The same ancestresses who had decided half the house should be theirs alone had also decreed that during her monthly moon-flow a woman must rest. This was her time for meditation and reflection. No work could be demanded of her, no visiting, no responsibilities. It was a time women looked forward to, when they gave up the cares of life and household duties to restore their bodies and spirits and engage in leisure activities. Men called this time taboo, women called it sacred.

But Leah knew that, for her mother, this was also a time of sadness and a poignant reminder of loss. Hannah had celebrated twelve cycles since the night the baby died. She had welcomed Elias to her bed many times. But she had not conceived. Hannah was almost forty years old. She knew—the whole household knew—that her fertile days were coming to an end.

And she had failed to give Elias a son.

Sensing her mother's sorrow, Leah could not help her own feelings of guilt. Even though it was Zira's harsh words and the prophecy of a dream that had sent her mother into labor, Leah had been grossly disobedient that night. And everyone knew that the gods punished disobedience. Was she responsible for the loss of the baby?

Avigail came into the sunroom with a satisfied smile on her face. "I found a family traveling to Sidon for a wedding, which means they will journey at a good pace with only brief stops. They assured me they will take my letter to my cousin as soon as they arrive." She picked up a basket of mending. Although the family was wealthy and could afford new clothes, Avigail was frugal and did not believe in waste. "Leah, dear, tomorrow we will begin work on your wedding dress."

"Yes, Grandmother."

"And with the blessings of Dagon and Asherah, once you are married Jotham will abandon his evil assault on our house." Avigail chose the frayed hem of one of Elias's ankle-length tunics, and paused to watch Tamar at the loom. Affixed to the top of a simple wooden frame, the warp threads of black wool hung straight and taut, anchored by stones at the bottom, while Tamar guided brown weft threads in and out with a smooth guiding stick. Avigail saw that Tamar's hand moved quickly, missing threads, while the girl herself kept glancing at the sun dipping low over the garden wall. She is in a hurry, Avigail thought. She is marking the time. For what? Avigail prayed that the cousin in Sidon sent a husband for Leah as quickly as possible, and then she could concentrate on marrying Tamar to a man who would control the wild girl.

As she inspected the frayed hem, Avigail said, "I encountered Keena in the lane as I was coming home. She said that Zira's son had another of his attacks last night. Three physicians were called to treat him but they could do nothing."

"He has the falling sickness," Aunt Rakel said as she placed an almond on a round flat stone and deftly cracked it open with a single strike of the mallet.

Avigail said nothing as she selected a bronze needle from the mending box. The memory of that disastrous night a year ago was still fresh. While she was glad she had saved Leah from a terrible fate, she was upset about the unexpected repercussions. "How can she expect her son to rise to the throne of Ugarit when he suffers from such spells?" Avigail said with bitterness. "They say he drops to the floor and shakes and foams at the mouth. There is no cure for it." How dare Zira keep such a family affliction a secret while negotiating a marriage contract?

"Oh, there is a cure," Rakel said as she plucked the intact nut from the broken shell. "My husband cured the falling sickness with a remedy grown in his garden. We had wonderful gardens in those days. I have begun one of my own you know," she said, selecting another almond from the basket. "I found a neglected patch of ground at the southern wall, just below the kitchens. Do you know it, Avigail dear?"

"I have things on my mind, Aunt Rakel. Leah's wedding clothes. Halla!" she said suddenly, snapping her head up. "Will her husband live here with us, or will he take her back to Sidon? I did not think of that!"

"If there is a husband," Tamar said fretfully at her loom.

"Invoke the gods, child," Avigail snapped. "Words are destiny.

35

We have enough bad luck in this house without you creating more."
Asherah! Why was the girl so mean spirited?

Aunt Rakel looked up from her task and said with a smile, "I have
a way of guaranteeing a husband for Leah. A magic potion that we used
in Jericho. All of our women found good husbands using the potion."

"Is it true, Grandmother?" Leah asked in sudden excitement, her
mother's veil momentarily forgotten in her hands. "Is there such a
potion?"

Rakel said, "Of course there is. You remember, Avigail. We mixed
good-luck potions for all kinds of occasions. Our family was very well
protected."

"I suppose so, but potions do not replace prayer," Avigail said,
wishing her elderly aunt would retreat for an afternoon nap. She had
too much to think about, too much to plan, without Rakel's words
buzzing in her ears. Especially bringing up unwanted memories of
the past.

"Leah, dear," Rakel said as she laid the mallet down and rose to
her feet. "Help me harvest the herbs for the good-luck potion. I even
remember the spell that must be recited when you drink it."

Leah turned to Hannah. "Mother, may I go with Auntie Rakel?"

Hannah looked at the older woman and felt a stab of envy. Rakel
had entered her "wise" years, and had lived for so long that everyone
revered her simply for her age. Nothing was expected of Rakel other
than to keep living, to remind others that a long life was possible.
Hannah thought: I have been reduced to my womb, for that is all I am
now. And once my womb is empty what will my purpose be? Will I live
the rest of my life as Isha Elias, never to be called Em Ari, or whatever
my son's name might have been?

But she smiled and said, "Of course, dear. Run along. I believe I
will take a nap."

Leah followed her elderly aunt whose head veil had flown off to
reveal white hair going every which way. Despite her advanced age,
Rakel was energetic and spry. Leah knew that it was because of the
tonic—her aunt's morning drink, which she consumed every day for
breakfast and had done so since she was a child. Rakel declared that
it was this special concoction that had enabled her to live such a long
life and to reach such an advanced age with no pain in the joints, no

digestive problems, and with eyesight and hearing still keen. It was a very old recipe, handed down through generations, but no one in Elias's house drank it. Avigail declared the drink revolting, having tasted it once. It was expensive, too, as one of its ingredients was difficult to grow and had to be imported. Mostly, however, Avigail's distaste for her aunt's morning drink was that the main ingredient— the one that was expensive and difficult to grow—was a plant native to Egypt and which one could purchase in Ugarit only at the Egyptian market, which Avigail refused to patronize. Rakel had no qualms about taking her gold rings to Egyptian merchants. These were not the same Egyptian as those forty years ago, she would declare. Besides, she would not do without the juice of the rare plant, which was called celery. She mixed it each morning with pressed juniper berries, parsley, and carrot juice. She also added poppy seeds and cumin, another Egyptian import! The exact formula—the amount of each ingredient—was known only to Rakel. And Avigail was happy to leave it at that.

"Where are we going, Aunt Rakel?" Leah asked.

"To my special garden, dear. You did not know about it, did you? No one does. I have been cultivating it this past year. In memory of the precious little one who went to the gods the night that loathsome Jotham and his donkey-faced sister came to the house. And now I am going to let you see what I have created."

Leah was pleased to see her favorite aunt so lively and robust, and relieved that the strange memory lapse on the night the baby was born had not lasted. In the time since, Rakel had been her normal self, weaving at her loom, overseeing the large kitchen staff, taking a broom to all thresholds to keep evil spirits out, believing that no woman, however wealthy, should be idle.

And Rakel always seemed to have answers. There was nothing she could not solve. Years ago, Leah bringing home a stray cat, wanting to keep it, but the cat being wild would run away. Auntie Rakel saying, "Pour cream on its paws. It will stay."

Leah had wondered why creamed paws would make a cat stay where it did not want to be, but she did as told, and as she watched the cat clean itself fastidiously, taking hours to lick the cream from its paws, Leah understood a truth: that by the time the cat had thoroughly cleaned itself it would be familiar with the smells and sounds of the house and think it had lived there all its life. The cat stayed for eight years, fat and content, until its death.

Another time: Esther in agony because of something in her eye. Their mother and grandmother attempting, to no avail, to remove the speck until Auntie Rakel came in with a freshly sliced onion. Waving the onion before Esther's face had triggered a waterfall of tears, painlessly washing the mote from the eye.

How wonderful, Leah often thought, to have such a storehouse inside one's head.

"The good-luck potion is an Egyptian recipe," Rakel said now as she led her great-niece through the villa, down corridors, around columns, past doorways, making Leah wonder where they were going. She was familiar with the various gardens in and around her house, but now they had bypassed them all. "The Egyptians have the most powerful magic in the world. Did you know that, dear? I will show you how to properly crush the leaves and steep them in hot water. Everything must be just so for the good-luck magic to work. The wonders that my garden holds, dear child! I went to the marketplace and bought seeds and cuttings from far-away places. Dittany from Crete! Sandalwood from Indus! Papyrus from Egypt! I brought workers in from your father's vineyards and had them create a pool for lily pads and golden fish. They built a fountain for me that runs continuously. Trellises for climbing flowers. A stone bath for birds. Benches and statues. It is a garden fit for the gods, my dear!"

As Rakel described the healing herbs and fragrant flowers she had planted, tending the secret garden on her own, Leah pictured the verdant paradise and wondered if Rakel would let her bring her mother there, Hannah who was grieving, to draw solace from so much life.

As they arrived at the eastern edge of the villa's protective outer wall, which abutted fallow pastures and foothills beyond—a neglected corner of the compound which Leah had rarely explored—Rakel said, "Medicinal recipes have been in my family for generations, handed down from mother to daughter. And of course I was married to a physician. But I fear so many have been forgotten. And I am the last of my line. I will pass them on to you, dear child, as you help me harvest and mix and store away the precious cures."

The tall wooden gate was set within a high stone wall. It had been grown over—Leah could see the trails left by vines that had climbed up long ago. Rakel had pulled them away herself, she said, with her own hands so that the spirits of the garden would know who their new mistress was.

"Remember, dear child, the skill lies not just in identifying the plants. One must know when to put the seed into the soil. How much rain to allow in. Which phase of the moon is the best harvest time. Some plants bloom only at night, did you know that? Others scream silently when you pull them from the earth. And of course, the spells one must chant during planting and harvesting. Oh, there is much to be learned from my garden, dear child."

The gate creaked open on ancient wooden hinges. Leah held her breath as she widened her eyes to gather in as much as they could hold. Her heart raced with hope—a good-luck potion that would guarantee a husband from Sidon!

And then her mouth fell open. She stared at the dust, the gnarled roots, the dried scattered leaves. The scrap of barren earth littered with rubble. A withered tree trunk in the center. It was all dead. Not a paradise at all.

She looked at her aunt who was beaming with pride. Rakel handed Leah a basket with a hole in it and said, "So, Rebekka, shall we begin?"

Tamar made sure Esther was asleep before she quietly slipped out of bed and, donning her sandals, seized an outer robe and hurried from the bedchamber.

The olive groves stood off the road that led to the city, and so it was but a short trek in the moonlight, where she knew Baruch would be waiting. Tamar ran with the joy and excitement of a girl deeply in love. She and Baruch had been meeting secretly for a year. Tonight she was going to pledge herself to him. A husband was coming for Leah—from Sidon! Leaving Tamar free to marry.

There he was, among his father's olive trees, pacing in and out of the moonlight like a stallion eager to begin a race. Tonight we will make love, Tamar thought as she ran to him. We have been chaste for a year. I can wait no longer.

"Hold me," she said, delivering herself into his eager arms. The feel of a man's body! Shoulders so broad, muscles as hard as rock! Unlike a woman's embrace, with narrow shoulders and hands barely felt.

I was supposed to be a boy, she thought. Leah was, too. But Father loves her anyway. When I came, he said, "This time the gods will give me a son." They did not. After me, a girl-baby that did not thrive. When Esther came, with her deformed mouth, Father's heart moved for her. Two more short-lived girl babies after that, and then the boy, at last, a year ago that came too soon and died. Father is still hopeful for a son, but when he looks at me there is always a shade of that first disappointment.

Tamar had known Baruch all her life. Their fathers had been boyhood friends, and today Elias and Baruch's father were proctors at the Temple of Dagon, highly esteemed ranks outside the official priesthood. She did not know when she first fell in love with the olive grower's middle son. Had it been during a feast of Asherah, or at one of his family's many weddings, namings, birth celebrations? One day, Baruch had felt like a brother, and the next he had awakened sexual hunger within her.

They began meeting secretly, at first simply to talk, and then to hold hands. Of late, they had begun kissing and exploring each other's bodies outside their clothing. When he pressed his hardness against her, Tamar burst into flame. But lately the fire did not go out when she left him. It burned day and night, and she knew of only one way to douse it.

"Grandmother sent a letter to a cousin in Sidon, who will send a husband for Leah. You and I will be free to marry."

"Tamar—"

She could not stop kissing him, her hands devouring his body as she pressed herself against him. She felt the delicious hardness beneath his tunic. "Please . . ." she hissed against his ear. "I must feel you inside me."

"Wait," he said in a strangled voice. "We must not."

"I burn for you. Please show me you love me."

"I do love you but—"

"Show me, show me."

He groaned. His young, beardless cheeks flamed with heat. "Tamar, we must be strong. You must be a virgin on your wedding night."

"I am weary of being strong! And this is our wedding night. If Leah had not disrespected Jotham, she would be married to him now, and you and I would be betrothed."

"But—"

She silenced his protest with a kiss. And when her hand went down to his groin, and her fingers curled around his erection, he gave a strangled cry and sank to his knees, bringing Tamar with him.

Suddenly all thoughts of reason and rationality left him. Baruch burned as Tamar did, and all he was aware of was the delicious body squirming beneath him, the feel of silken skin as he lifted her skirt and explored her thigh. To his shock, she wore no modesty undercloth. His ardor grew until he thought his entire body was going to explode. And then he was inside her and her legs went around him, tightening, pulling him in deeper. She gave a little cry of pain and then she kissed his neck, ravenously, sinking her teeth into him. Animals sounds came from her throat and he, too, grunted and groaned as he thrust into her.

He was young, and this was his first time, and so it was quickly over. He let out a strangled shout, and then he collapsed onto her, and Tamar released a deep, satisfied sigh. She herself had experienced no climax, but she knew that with practice and experience, their love-making would be sublime.

He finally lifted himself up and, looking down at her face in the moonlight, murmured, "Tamar, Tamar, my beautiful wicked Tamar."

She giggled. He stroked her hair while she ran her hand under his tunic, to explore the muscles of his thighs. Nothing felt so good as a man's body. She could not wait to be his wife, to experience this every night.

He lifted up on an elbow and looked down at her with a grave expression. "Tamar," he said in a tone she had not heard before. "By Dagon, I am sorry to have to speak these words. But I must. Tamar, I love you, but I cannot marry you."

She blinked up at him.

He said, "My father does business with Jotham. My father's olives and oil are transported all over the world on Jotham's ships. If I marry into the House of Elias, Jotham will no longer carry my father's oil."

She struggled for breath. "You jest!"

He sat up, his eyes filled with regret. "Dagon have mercy on me, but I have no choice, Tamar. Your sister and father offended Jotham and Zira. They did not apologize. All of Ugarit speaks of it."

"But I cannot help that! I love you, Baruch."

"And I love you," he said as he rose to his feet and adjusted his clothes. Tamar stared up at him, adoring this youth who had filled her dreams and thoughts, who made her burn with desire. And who had just taken her virginity.

Halla! What have I done? "Please," she began, tears rolling down her cheeks.

"I am sorry, Tamar. As Dagon is witness, I am. But I must do as my father tells me. I cannot see you again. My mother has arranged for me to marry a cousin in Ebla. I leave within the month."

Dropping down on one knee, Baruch impulsively took her face in his hands and said in a thick voice, "Your heart will hurt for a while, but as time passes, you will forget me, Tamar. You will forget me because other men will come along who will fall under your spell."

She held her breath as she fell under Baruch's own powerful spell. "I swear upon my ancestors, dearest Tamar, that what I say is true. You can hear it in my voice, you see it in my eyes. You will know it when you sleep and dream. You are beautiful, Tamar, although no one in your family has ever told you so. You were not born a boy, and so you have thought yourself insignificant. But I swear by Dagon and Baal, Tamar, that you are more than beautiful. You are powerful, more powerful than you know. Men will fall at your feet. They will offer you riches. The world will be a round, plump fruit in the palm of your hand. And Baruch will be forgotten."

He rose to his feet and turned away. Tamar remained kneeling on the leaf-strewn ground and watched Baruch with his straight back and broad shoulders and strong thighs disappear through the olive trees. She thought of what he had just said—words burned into her brain. Her power. Her beauty. Was it true? Will men fall at my feet?

No, she thought in a maelstrom of sadness and anger. I do not want other men. I want Baruch. And I swear by Asherah, I will see to it that he does not leave me. By the power within me, I will make Baruch defy his father and come back to me.

Shemuel the scribe lived in his own house with a wife and a staff of servants. Elias was his only client because the wine business was a full time job—labeling jars, labeling the vines themselves, cataloging inventory, taking care of shipping documents and receipts, acting as bookkeeper, balancing Elias's many accounts, knowing who owed and who needed to be paid, keeping track of the lists of slaves and servants, wages paid, hours worked, writing and reading correspondence, personal and business.

Part of Shemuel's duties was taking letters into town to place them with outgoing caravans. But the letter Avigail had dictated that morning and which he had impressed carefully onto clay, she had taken herself to the caravanserai. That spoke of her desperation to find a husband for her granddaughter. Avigail did not trust Shemuel to find a swift enough caravan to Sidon.

He suspected the letter was an exercise in futility. By the time the cousin received it, Shemuel feared the House of Elias would be no more.

Which was why he had decided to tender his resignation and leave the employer for whom he had worked twenty-five years.

A man had to think of himself. Call him a rat deserting a sinking ship, Shemuel thought. He did not care. It was time for him to retire anyway. He knew what Jotham was really up to—something far more sinister than merely hurting Elias's wine business and reputation. The family faced certain ruin and Shemuel wanted to be well away when it happened.

He briefly considered warning Elias of the disaster that was coming, but it might start a legal feud that would end up in the courts with lawyers, with Shemuel detained as a witness and it could take years! Best keep silent and sail quietly away from trouble.

He found his employer in the fermenting room, a stone building that was part of the winery behind the villa. It was cool inside, and reeked of yeast and spoiled fruit. Here, the crushed grapes lay in great wooden vats overseen by special wine stewards who stirred the mixtures, tasted and tested them, a time-honored profession. Elias was over-seeing the first filling of amphoras of a young vintage when Shemuel came in. Respectfully, he removed the skullcap that protected his bald crown from the sun and said, "I must submit my resignation, dear friend. You have been good to me, but the years have caught up with me and I desire a peaceful retirement."

Elias looked at him in shock. "You have always said you would die with a stylus in your hand."

"Alas, my eyes are not what they used to be." A lie, but a believable one. Shemuel was almost fifty years of age. "I have purchased a villa on Cyprus."

"Cyprus! But that is across the Great Sea. I shall never see you again."

They locked eyes and then Elias's shoulders slumped. "I under-stand, old friend. It is not your fault that I offended Jotham and that since then he has systematically waged a dishonorable war against me and my house. I do not blame you for wanting to leave."

But Shemuel was not totally without feelings. "I have arranged for someone to take my place. I wrote to a friend in the Brotherhood in the city of Lagash on the Euphrates, where there is a plethora of good scribes and not enough open positions for them all. I asked him if he knew of any young scribe looking for employment and he wrote back that he could highly recommend a very capable young man who was willing to come and live in Ugarit."

"Fresh out of school?" Elias said with a frown.

"Elias, you would be hard pressed to find a scribe of my years and experience to come and work for you."

"When does he arrive?"

"He is already on his way and should arrive within a few days. Elias, my friend, do not look so dejected. This could be a boon for you, considering your strained circumstances. A young scribe would be willing to apprentice for just his room and board. And you would benefit from his eagerness to please you."

Another lie, but a small one. Shemuel's friend in Lagash had cautioned him that the new scribe, Daveed, was in fact a prince, and quite arrogant, full of high ambitions. No need to mention that now. Once Elias learns the truth, I shall be comfortably settled in my villa across the sea.

CHAPTER THREE

I hear the Queen of Ugarit is insatiable," Nobu said as he pulled a lamb chop from the coals. "They say she takes a different lover every day, sometimes one in the morning and another in the evening. She prefers her lovers to be well endowed. They say the Queen has candidates brought before her, naked, so she can inspect their privates."

Daveed took a sip of wine and murmured, "Do not believe everything you hear about a queen."

Nobu munched on the crispy meat and eyed his master across the glowing campfire. Twenty-four years old, Daveed was handsome, dark-eyed and big-nosed, as suited the prince of a royal house. Nobu wondered if Daveed's dismissal of what he had just said had something to do with his own mother, the queen of Lagash, whose high morals were well known. They said that she kept chaste even within her marriage to the King. After giving him twelve children, she had announced that she was "done with all that," and moved to a separate bedchamber.

Nobu shrugged and pulled his cloak more tightly about himself against the cold spring night. Daveed seemed not to mind the cold as he wore only a woolen tunic—in the fashion of Lagash that left one arm bare. Upon that exposed arm, a sheathed dagger was strapped, symbol of Daveed's membership in a secret, elite fraternity called Zh'kwan-eth.

"Let us pray Ugarit's queen does not set eyes upon you, master. She would forget all other men and keep you in her bed until your testicles shrivel to raisins." He tossed the bone aside and plucked another greasy chop from the coals. He and Daveed were the only two at the campfire as they were traveling alone with just two horses and a pack mule. Tomorrow would see the end of their long trek from Lagash to Ugarit.

Nobu crunched crispy fat between his big strong teeth and shook his head at the thought of a woman who had sex possibly seven hundred times a year. But he kept silent, knowing his words would fall on deaf ears. His young master was preoccupied as he gazed into the flames of the campfire, his hands clasping a golden goblet of wine.

The paunchy slave knew what exciting thoughts filled his young master's head. Nobu had been a palace slave when he was assigned to the young prince who, at age seven, went into the School of Life to learn the scribe's profession. Nobu had taken care of the boy since.

"Just think, my friend," Daveed said now, lifting dark eyes that were filled with passion and vitality. "When the great king Gilgamesh went in search of the herb of everlasting youth, the one that is called Old Man Grows Young, he found it on a seabed. But while Gilgamesh slept, a serpent came along and ate the herb. And that is why the serpent is immortal, for it sheds its skin and is born anew, but humans die because they lost the herb of immortality. I have heard, Nobu, that in the library at the House of Gold in Ugarit, there is a map of that seabed, showing the way to the place where Gilgamesh slept, and where the herb of eternal youth still grows!"

Nobu's heavily lidded eyes widened in interest. "Will you look at the map, master? Will we go to that seabed? I rather fancy living forever."

"Shubat protect you from your sacrilege, my foolish friend. The herb is sacred. But there is more, much much more in Ugarit's library. By Shubat, it is said that more than twenty thousand books are stored there! And written so long ago that it is said the gods themselves wrote them. And in them, my doubting friend, lie the answers to every question any man has ever asked."

Nobu sniffed and scratched a buttock. As far as he was concerned, the only question any man need ask was where his next meal was coming from. But he did not voice this, allowing his young master his ideals, for soon enough, Nobu was certain, they would be shattered and Daveed would be as jaded and skeptical as any other man.

A voice whispered in Nobu's head: Perhaps, but do not forget that your master loves his profession, is very dedicated. He places honor and integrity before all else. The day when he was seven and the first letter suddenly came clear, he "heard" a calling. To do what? Daveed had said he was not sure but he knew that his god would give him a sign, and when word came from Ugarit, a wealthy vintner in need of a private scribe, Daveed said that this was the sign. And look at him now. Excited, filled with vitality and vision, like a child on the eve of Winter Festival, unable to sleep, thinking only of the sweet cakes that would greet him upon waking. A young scribe eager to get to Ugarit and begin service to his god.

The voice continued its relentless whispering: But it isn't good for a young man to be so religious. It narrows his choices in life. Daveed should be visiting taverns and bedding as many women as he can. Instead he visits libraries and lays his hands lovingly on books! And when he did have physical yearnings, he went to the sacred prostitutes of Ishtar!

Nobu reached for his wineskin and drank deeply until the voice in his head went away.

He understood his master's excitement. Tomorrow they would arrive at the House of Elias on the outskirts of Ugarit, where Daveed would begin his year of apprenticeship as personal scribe to the prosperous vintner. After that, the Brotherhood.

It was not easy to enter the Brotherhood, but Nobu knew that Daveed was confident he would be accepted because the highly respected Shemuel, whom he was replacing, was going to sponsor him. In fact, it was the only way to gain admittance, through a connection. But Nobu knew that Daveed's ambition did not end there. He planned to someday run the Brotherhood, an elite fraternity of men who were the guardians and protectors of the great Library of Ugarit, where tens of thousands of tablets were housed, an archive that was rumored to contain the story of how the world began, the very spells that created life on Earth, the secrets to immortality, the whereabouts of the divine herb that restores life to the dead and youth to old men. A trove of arcane and sacred knowledge gathered from the four corners of the earth, because of Ugarit's central placement on trade routes and shipping lanes. Nobu suspected that it was not so much the treasure that the fraternity protected that called to Daveed as the chance to serve his god. Daveed so loved his profession, was so passionate about the written word, that he felt a higher calling than to be a mere scribe—and there was no higher calling than serving as Rab of the Brotherhood.

The Rab, which meant "master" in Canaanite, was the senior priest and teacher of the Brotherhood of Scribes. This was Daveed's goal. And there was no reason he should not succeed. Nobu was proud of the fact that his young master could speak four languages and write in all of them—including the incomprehensible Egyptian hieroglyphs! Once he entered the Brotherhood, nothing would stop his rise to the loftiest position.

Nobu got up from his stool and made his way to a collection of boulders where he could relieve himself in private. "Yes, yes," he muttered beneath the spring moon. "I know."

At forty-four, Nobu was twenty years older than his master, and wore his brown hair short, to signify his status as a slave. Although he had a protruding belly, he was not fat, but he was funny looking. His nickname was Turtle because he walked with a slouch, his head thrust forward. Heavy lids drooped over squinting eyes, and because he had to lift his brows to get a good look at something, he had a deeply creased forehead. But Nobu was most well known, not for his comical looks, but for the god-voices in his head. He sometimes muttered replies to them. People said it was a gift from the gods, but Nobu didn't think so, although there was one side benefit: women wanted him to father their children. He was special to the gods, and they hoped that maybe their children would hear voices, too. Everyone was used to Nobu's muttering, when he was at tasks, or staring into a fire, even when others were speaking. They knew he was answering his inner voices.

But what no one knew, not even Daveed, was that Nobu did not wish to hear the voices—whether they came from the gods or not. He wished for silence in his head. And the day he had discovered that alcohol muted the voices was the day he had embraced wine with singular devotion.

But he saw to it that the wine never interfered with his duties as Daveed's personal slave, keeping his master's extensive wardrobe in good repair, caring for his scribe's kit, accompanying Daveed everywhere. One of Nobu's most complicated tasks was dressing his master's hair, about which Daveed, like most young men, was quite vain. It required special skill, supplies, and time to create perfect ringlets, coiling the long black hair on a bronze poker hot from the fire, oiling each long curl so that it shined, fastening each with a gold ring, making his master look indeed like the prince of a very noble and royal house.

While Nobu emptied his bladder and pondered many things, five pairs of eyes watched him.

The bandits grinned to one another as they eyed the small camp with but two men. They owned horses—a sign of wealth—and wore finery. Especially the young one who had gold in his hair! The leader of the ragged bandits laughed softly. It served them right, those lonely travelers. Teach them a lesson about going abroad with not even a single guard for protection.

Arranging his robes back into place, Nobu returned to the fire and took another drink from the wineskin to stare into the dying flames of the fire. He hoped they were going to a sumptuous house—a man who owned vineyards and shipped wine all over the world must certainly be rich! There would be young and lovely slave girls to be found there, or at least a decent brothel in the city of Ugarit. It was after all a harbor and therefore a sailor's town.

Hearing footfall, Daveed looked up to see five burly men in filthy tunics and grins on their bearded faces enter the camp. "Look what we have here," one said to his companions. "A rich man and his slave." The intruder looked to the right and left. "And no protection."

"Friend," Daveed said in a calm voice. "You do not want to do this. Go in peace with the gods."

The first one, whom Daveed took to be the leader, threw back his head and laughed. "You've got me quaking, friend. Me and my brothers don't stand a chance against such a giant as you."

"Trust me," Daveed said wearily. "I wish only to be left alone. I ask you again to turn away and go in peace. I will not ask a third time."

"Then don't. Just hand over all the gold you've got. We take silver and copper, too. And we'll relieve you of those fine horses. And I quite fancy that handsome cloak you're sitting on."

Daveed slowly rose to his feet. "Nobu, seek safety."

"Yes, master," Nobu said, and stepped back, out of reach.

The bandits laughed. "What kind of rich man are you? Traveling alone with no guards, and not even your pot-bellied slave will fight for—"

They did not see Daveed move, did not see the lightning-swift grasp of the dagger on his left arm, nor the flight of the crooked stiletto as it flew through the air to lodge into the meat of the leader's shoulder. The man gave a startled cry and fell backwards from the impact.

As the fellow's companions blinked in surprise, Daveed's hands shot down to his waist, and before the bandits could advance upon him, two more daggers flew through the air and found: an upper arm, a thigh. Both men shouted out as they, too, staggered backward beneath the impact of the weapons.

With three men down and writhing in pain, the remaining two closed ranks and strode, shoulder to shoulder, toward Daveed, their big arms ending in massive ham-fists, ferocious looks on their faces. They saw no more weapons on the nobleman. He was smaller than they, and alone.

Daveed shook his head. "You should learn to listen, my friends. Learn to heed warnings."

"We ain't your friend!" one of the two shouted, and they bolted forward, arms and fists flying.

Daveed sidestepped them. Caught the first alongside the head with a jab of his hand. Then he spun on one heel and kicked the legs out from under the second. In an instant, he was standing over both, with yet another dagger in his hand, retrieved from his belt behind his back. "I have only the one left," he said, "so I leave it to you fellows to choose which one gets it."

Behind him, one of the fallen bandits was struggling to his feet, wincing as he pulled the stiletto out of his shoulder. Before the blade was all the way out, Daveed spun around and shot the remaining dagger directly into the man's chest. When the bandit fell backward, blood gurgling in his throat, Daveed ran forward, pulled daggers from the other's thigh and arm and, dropping to his knees, held a dagger inches above each man's chest. He looked at the two who were getting back to their feet. "I gave your friends the benefit of the doubt with my first three daggers," Daveed said. "I could have killed them where they stood, for my aim is so perfect that even now I can throw one of these daggers and trim the hair over your ear and you wouldn't even feel it. I have no desire to kill you or your friends. But I can, and I will, if you do not leave me and my slave in peace."

The two whom he had felled with a punch and a kick were breathing heavily. But they saw that the young nobleman hadn't lost even a breath, no sweat adorned his brow. And his hands were dangerously steady over their companion's vulnerable chests.

While one of the two wanted to surrender, his companion only grew more surly. "Your boasts fall on deaf ears, young lord, for while you might throw a dagger, that leaves one of my friends able to reach up and tackle you."

"If your ears are deaf, then choose the one you will miss the least."

"What?"

Daveed shrugged. "Very well, the left."

"What're you—" The man felt the pain before his eyes registered that Daveed's hand had moved. A sharp, searing pain on the left side of his head. As he whipped about to cup his ear, Daveed threw the second dagger at the second man, slicing through his right calf. Both men went down, while Daveed pinned the first two with his knees, their blood pouring onto the desert sand.

From his place of safety, Nobu shook his head. *They never learn,* his god-voice said. *But from now on, it is certain these lumps will never again dare cross a warrior-scribe.*

"You cut off my ear!" one protested while the other wailed as he pulled the dagger out of his calf. They looked sheepishly at Daveed, their moaning and bleeding companions, and then they looked at each other and, with slumping shoulders, said, "You are favored by the gods." And they held up their bloody hands to show surrender.

They helped their wounded friends out of the camp, dragging the dead one behind them, and when they could no longer be seen or heard, Daveed set about to cleaning his special daggers. Nobu returned to the fire after kicking the severed ear from his view and said, "From

Lagash to the Great Sea, in all areas of population, people recognize a warrior-scribe. They see the famous dagger on your arm and know you are skilled in the ancient martial art of Zh'kwan-eth and know to let you go unmolested. But not these louts who clearly had no idea whom they were accosting. I pray that this was the first and last of such encounters in our journey, master, and that the people of Ugarit respect your elite station. For surely, master," Nobu added as he rubbed his belly, "the sight of such combat is hard on one's digestion."

We must find a vendor of green mint, Rebekka dear," Rakel was saying as she and Leah made their way down the crowded street. "Your Uncle Yacov is suffering from hot stomach."

Yacov was Rakel's son, who died years ago when he fell out of a chariot during a lion hunt. Although he was gone, Rakel still retained the respectful title of Em Yacov. Unfortunately, there was no one left to address her as such, for all of her peers and friends had gone to the gods, and her family called her "aunt." The punishment, or reward, for having lived so long, Leah supposed. But Rakel did not seem to mind. In fact, she seemed to think they were all still alive, which was why Leah, in her concern for her aunt's state of mind, did not take the problem to their family physician. She was afraid he would report back to Avigail, and then poor Rakel would be subjected to endless examination, with priests and magicians brought in, and rituals performed to drive out the demons that were clouding her mind.

This was why Leah had brought Rakel to the House of Gold in secret, in the hope of finding a medical man who knew of a simple and painless cure.

Long ago, when Ugarit was a small town, a stone vault had been built into the western wall of the palace to hold the royal treasure. Over the centuries, more structures were added: a School of Life, a hall of records, a court of law, and the headquarters of the Brotherhood of Scribes with its library of twenty thousand books. But it was still called the House of Gold and here, in the center of this complex of buildings, a large public courtyard was laid out, and every morning the doctors, lawyers, and scribes of Ugarit came to wait for business. Any citizen could come to the House of Gold and find a professional man to help with letter writing, bookkeeping, legal problems, and health matters.

But as Leah neared the massive gate set into towering stone walls, with people coming and going and creating a din, she had no idea where to go. Keeping a protective arm around Rakel's shoulders, with their two companion slaves close behind, Leah joined the crowd entering the courtyard. She was overwhelmed by the sight of so many people, the rows of columns that went on forever. And so many men in fine robes! Arguing, gesturing, or sitting cross-legged with clay and stylus, papyrus, and pen.

"Halla," Rakel whispered. "The gods protect us. What is this place?"

"We will find what we need here, Aunt Rakel," Leah said, although her voice was filled with uncertainty.

How did someone find a doctor in this chaos?

"There, mistress," one of the slaves said, an older man who also served as a bodyguard in a harbor town that could be dangerous for two women on their own. Leah followed his pointing finger and saw, in the shade of a loggia, a row of men sitting on stools, with people clustered in front of them. Each was with a patient, listening to a chest, inspecting a mouth, applying a poultice, extracting a tooth. One knelt over a supine child. Another opened a cloth and inspected its contents. Leah saw tiny jars or pouches, retrieved from wooden boxes, being handed over for payments of copper and gold rings. She saw how those who waited coughed, sneezed, limped, winced, cradled an arm, held wool to a nose. All waiting to see the men sitting on the stools.

The doctors.

As she and her three companions drew near, Leah wondered how she would choose a man to consult with about Rakel. The courtyard was nearly deafening with noise—not only from the ailing patients, but from voices lifted on the other side of the courtyard where lawyers heard complaints and gave advice, and citizens loudly dictated letters, contracts, sales receipts to seated scribes. It seemed a disorganized way to conduct professional business.

But she had no idea where else to turn, and so she led Rakel forward, closer to the doctors, where she now smelled the odors of illness and diseased bodies. As she tried to decide which to choose— perhaps the one extracting a tooth was only a dentist and knew nothing else, and the one setting a broken bone knew nothing of ailments of the mind—a tall man in long white robes, with a box hanging from his shoulder, stepped toward her and said in heavily accented Canaanite, "Shalaam, Lady. Perhaps I can be of help?"

Leah turned to him and almost fell back a step. The stranger stood out from the others in that he wore a long black wig and painted his eyes, something Canaanite men did not do, and he was clean-shaven whereas the men of Canaan were proud of their beards. The man was Egyptian and even though Leah knew her reaction was from having grown up within the sphere of her grandmother's prejudice, she could not help herself. He was not the same doctor who had come to their house the night the baby died. Egyptian physicians did not stay long in Ugarit, so deeply ingrained was the hatred of their race among Canaanites. He had no patients—the sick and injured preferred to stand in line than go to a despised foreigner—and so Leah knew that he too would soon leave Ugarit.

Before she could turn away, Aunt Rakel suddenly spoke: "You look like a nice young man," she said with a smile. "My mother sent me to buy some poppy milk and I cannot find the merchant who sells them."

He pursed his lips and looked at Rakel from beneath eyelids laden with green cosmetic. "Your mother?" he said, taking in the white hair, plump wrinkled face, curved spine.

"My aunt," Leah said quickly, "is having a lapse in memory. She is otherwise quite well."

He returned Rakel's smile and Leah felt her aunt's shoulders relax beneath her protective arm. "And what use have you for poppy milk, Madam?" he asked.

"For an eye ointment to prevent dryness and sun-blindness. One must grind equal amounts of acacia leaves and flowers, mix them with poppy milk and apply with a bandage. If the mixture is too thick, it can be thinned with small drops of acacia juice."

"This is so," the Egyptian said, visibly impressed, "you have the correct formula, Madam. Many of my countrymen suffer from afflictions of the eye."

Rakel giggled in a girlish way. "You remind me of my Uncle. He's a tanner in Jericho. Tall and handsome, like yourself."

Leah could not believe it. Her elderly aunt was flirting!

The Egyptian's smile deepened and then he addressed Leah. "I have seen this before. In some elderly people, for reasons unknown, they begin a reversal of memory. It is believed that when the soul is preparing to return to the gods, it divests itself of the cares and woes of the flesh and of this life. In some people, like your aunt, that shedding of years of experience and memory exposes earlier memories long forgotten. It is as if she were traveling back in time. Soon your aunt will think she is a child again, and everything she tells you will be as it was years ago. The process is neither painful nor distressing, and can in fact be quite pleasant. But the condition cannot be cured. Your aunt will regress down through the years until there are no more years to relive."

He ended the sentence with a lift of his eyebrow, and Leah knew the rest: No more years, and Rakel would die.

Hastily thanking him, and wondering belatedly if she should have paid him, Leah escorted Rakel out of the crowd and back onto the lane where foot traffic was lighter. "What about the mint, the poppy milk?" Rakel said fretfully.

Leah did not respond. Rather than producing a remedy for her aunt's mental state, this visit to the House of Gold had merely deepened Leah's worry. She knew that a reply from Sidon would arrive any day now—word of a husband. While the family hoped that the new son-in-law would live in the House of Elias, it was his right to set up house elsewhere, and if that happened, then Leah would have to leave, and Auntie Rakel would slip into a mental prison from which there might be no return.

I have to help her.

And an idea came to Leah. Something that might stimulate her aunt's mind and perhaps stop the regression.

Securing her arm through her aunt's, Leah gave it a squeeze and said with a smile, "We will grow them ourselves! We can grow anything we wish, dear Aunt. Would you like to grow celery for your morning tonic? That way, you would not have to come into the city and buy it from Egyptians."

And if I should be forced to leave my father's house, Auntie Rakel will be safe and secure in her own healing garden.

What is keeping him?" Nobu muttered impatiently. "How long are we supposed to stand here?"

Daveed and Nobu had arrived at the palatial villa tucked against the foothills of the mountains that embraced Ugarit and its harbor and announced themselves to the armed guards standing sentry at the gate. Beyond the high walls that surrounded the main house were outbuildings, gardens and animal pens, lush vineyards climbing the slopes, miles of rich grape vines, with slaves laboring among the rows, pruning, weeding, keeping birds away from the vulnerable fruit.

One of the guards went inside, and when the house steward arrived, Daveed requested that they be taken to Shemuel the scribe. They were escorted into the reception atrium, where they now waited for Shemuel to appear.

Hearing footsteps, the two visitors turned, expecting to see a dignified gentleman. Their eyes widened at the sight of a young woman hurrying through in a most unladylike fashion, her skirts caught up in her belt to reveal bare legs and feet. To their shock, her face was smudged with dirt, her head was bare with hair tumbling over her shoulders, and in her arms she cradled what looked like a basket of rocks. She looked wild, and rendered Daveed and Nobu speechless.

Leah stopped abruptly in her hasty shortcut through the house, and stared back at the two strangers standing in her father's entry hall. Foreigners, she deduced, from their fringed robes and the excess of gold ornamentation in their hair. Especially the younger man, who was dressed so ostentatiously she wondered if they had come to the right house.

"You there, girl!" the older one called. "Tell your master that Daveed of Lagash will not be kept waiting!"

Leah's eyes locked with those of the younger man, whose tunic was draped over only one shoulder, leaving the other shoulder and arm bare—definitely foreigners! And then, remembering her own disarrayed appearance, she murmured, "I will tell them," and hurried on.

But not before she heard the older one say in a loud voice, "This

Elias cannot be a very sophisticated man to allow his slaves to go about looking like that."

Daveed watched the girl go, thinking there was something unusual about her—her clothes were too fine to be a slave's, and her hair, though unkempt, was shiny and groomed. But it was her eyes—in that brief moment, Daveed had seen the spark of intellect, and perhaps a glimmer of a strong will.

And then a dignified gentleman did enter the atrium, saying, "Shalaam, I am Elias. Welcome to my house, the gods are with us. You are the new scribe? We have much work to do. Can you tell me what this is?" Elias thrust a clay tablet at him.

Surprised at the lack of formalities or offer of refreshment after so long a journey, Daveed composed himself and took a moment to inspect the small clay tablet that fit in the palm of his hand. He saw that it was covered in cuneiform symbols, and the language was Canaanite. "Yes, I can read this. But may I meet with Shemuel first, so he can explain my duties?"

"Shemuel is no longer here. He has retired to the island of Cyprus."

Daveed stared at his new employer. Shemuel not here? Then how was he supposed to learn his new duties? This was highly irregular. An apprentice always went through an assistance period with a senior scribe.

He glanced at Nobu who returned a quizzical look.

"Well? What is it?" Elias said. He had only a rudimentary skill in reading, but he knew enough to recognize the tablet as a bill of exchange, and it was signed with Jotham's seal. But he didn't owe Jotham any money, so what was it?

"It is a collection notice, sir," Daveed said. "Money is owed for the purchase of amphoras."

"Amphoras! But I made no such purchase from Jotham."

Daveed frowned. He was certain he had read it correctly. "This receipt describes the goods as amphoras with pedestals, and the number delivered to you was five hundred and fifty."

"Nonsense! For years I have been buying my export vessels from Thalos the Minoan. He supplies me with them from his factory and I pay him at grape harvest. So we have always done it. Why is Jotham

57

presenting me with—" Elias stopped. "Did you say five hundred and fifty amphoras with pedestals?"

"That is what it says."

"And that is the number I ordered from Thalos! And all with pedestals! By Dagon, what is going on?" He took the tablet from Daveed. "I must pay the man a visit. You will accompany me."

The factory of Thalos the Minoan lay south of Ugarit, a sprawling settlement of workshops, kilns, warehouses, showrooms, and housing for the many workers who labored over clay and pottery wheels. When Thalos saw his old friend Elias stepping down from a carrying chair in the middle of potters working outdoors, with the smell of ceramic dust and hot fires in the air, he lifted the hems of his long blue robes, exposing sandaled feet, and rushed forward to greet his visitor.

"Shalaam, my friend and brother!" he said, clasping chubby hands together and bowing energetically at his ample waist. Like all Minoans, Thalos wore his hair drawn back into a long pony tail. "I trust you and your family are well and enjoy prosperity."

Elias was in no mood for pleasantries. He held out the clay tablet and said, "This note arrived today. It says I owe Jotham for the amphoras I purchased from you."

Thalos wrung his hands as sweat dripped down his beardless face. "Dear friend and brother, the gods are my witness, I could not refuse! As you know, I have four daughters entering marrying age and I must come up with dowries for each. When Jotham offered to buy your note at one and a half times its value, I could scarcely turn it down!"

Elias felt anger shoot up within him and then die just as quickly. He could not blame Thalos. Four daughters needing dowries! Elias sympathized. He wondered, too, if Jotham might not have applied pressure as well. This vast ceramics factory crafted bowls, cups, jugs, pitchers, and amphoras that were bound for other lands. Should Jotham refuse to carry them on his ships . . .

As Elias turned to go, Thalos laid a hand on his arm and said with gravity, "Beware, my friend and brother. Keep the protection of Dagon close."

"It is Jotham who will need Dagon's protection," Elias growled and hurried back to his carrying chair.

* * *

The magnificent home of Jotham and Zira stood on a promontory overlooking the harbor. From here, Jotham could keep an eye on his fleet of ships, and also gauge the mood of the sea. Ugarit was a major shipping hub, and Jotham sat on its pulse, ever watchful over a fickle sea that could be cruel or beneficent. Therefore, Jotham was diligent about making daily sacrifice to Yamm, the Canaanite god of the sea, and, just to make sure, to Baal, god of sky and rain.

He was lighting incense in the household shrine when the chief steward entered and announced the arrival of Elias the vintner.

The shipbuilder grinned. It had been a year since the two had laid eyes on each other, but he had known that the bill of exchange—gold for the amphoras—would bring Elias to his door.

In the months since the night of the great offense, Jotham's desire for the vintner's daughter had grown. It was not love he felt for Leah, or any sweet sentiment of the heart. His lust was basic and carnal. He wanted Leah in his bed. And the longer Elias held out, the more Jotham burned for her. And now, he knew, she would soon be his.

"Have him wait in the atrium," Jotham said to the steward, and then he left the shrine to go to his own chambers that opened onto a vista of blue-green sea, white clouds, fresh breezes, and the sounds of a prosperous harbor below.

Jotham took his time adding heavy gold rings to his fingers, oiling his beard with perfume, setting a gold circlet upon his head and brow— all the adornments of an extremely wealthy man. Draping a purple cloak around his shoulders, he felt he looked like a king. He was going to enjoy this victory over Elias.

As he hurried down marble halls where slaves quickly stepped aside for his passage, Jotham was glad Zira wasn't home. His sister had a way of meddling in men's business. It was not entirely her fault. Their mother died when they were children, and Zira, though younger than Jotham, had taken over the role. He didn't mind her bossiness. Sometimes it even relieved him of burdensome decisions. But in the matter of the vintner's eldest daughter, Jotham wanted to be in control.

Besides, Zira's desire to have him marry Leah was motivated by very different reasons. Zira did not like the House of Elias, but Elias's mother Avigail came from an undeniably prestigious bloodline, being a descendant of legendary King Ozzediah. Jotham's marriage into that bloodline would catapult him and his family into a higher status, opening the way for Zira's son to rise to the very throne of Ugarit. Because Ugarit's kings did not ascend through lineage but through the vote of the rich and powerful families of Canaan, campaigning was necessary. At that moment, Zira was at the home of a wealthy and influential friend, spinning her web of politics and persuasion.

It was all his sister lived for—working night and day to see Jotham's good-for-nothing nephew wearing the crown of Ugarit. Never mind that King Shalaaman was wildly popular with the people, that his name was praised on every street corner, Zira believed her son could do a better job. Let her have her dreams and schemes, Jotham thought, as long as she left him alone to enjoy Leah.

"You go too far," Elias barked when Jotham entered the atrium, forgoing formalities and etiquette. Daveed and Nobu stood a discreet distance away, sensing that a drama was about to unfold.

"Dagon is my witness, I warned you," the perfumed and gold-laden Jotham said. He spoke breathlessly because of his girth, which had grown in the past year. "You should have heeded my words. You should have shown me the respect I was due. You insulted me. You allowed your daughter to insult me. Your mother insulted my sister. I demand satisfaction."

From the folds of his purple robe, Jotham produced the original clay tablet for the amphoras, with Elias's seal impressed in the clay and which Jotham had purchased from Thalos at a high price. "You will pay me this gold at once, or I will take you to court."

Elias eyed the tablet through a red veil of fury. He could barely speak. Finally he said, "Very well, I will send my steward to the counting house. We will reckon this today and be done with it."

"Before you get to feeling too smug," Jotham said, producing two more tablets incised with cuneiform script. "You owe me for these as well."

Elias was thunderstruck. And then he understood the full meaning of Jotham's intent: to buy up all of Elias's notes and call them in. It would bankrupt him.

"Elias, who used to be my friend," Jotham said gravely. "I will cancel these notes if you bring Leah to me as my wife. I caution you to be wise, Elias. For if you do not agree to my terms, I will ruin you. And when you are completely broken, you will be forced to sell yourself and your family into slavery. And at that time I will purchase Leah. She will no longer be my honorable wife, but my object of pleasure. The choice is yours."

Avigail stood nervously at the threshold of her son's estate, watching the road for Elias's return. He had bolted from the house that morning the minute the new scribe arrived, to clear up a matter with Thalos the Minoan. He should have returned by now and Avigail was anxious to make use of the new scribe's skill. A letter had just arrived from Sidon and she was desperate to learn its contents.

She prayed it was good news, and that a husband for Leah was on his way! They would announce the betrothal at once, and not wait the traditional year for the wedding. A respectable amount of time, three months perhaps, and then a feast fit for Elias's and Hannah's firstborn.

And then Avigail would see about Tamar. She was worried about her middle granddaughter. The girl had been uncharacteristically silent and moody of late, weeping while insisting there was nothing wrong.

As Avigail looked up and down the road, where soldiers rode by on horseback, and families on donkeys, shepherds driving sheep, members of the nobility in curtained carrying chairs on their way to pay visits to friends, she sighted a ragged group, recognizable by the familiar red and brown striped robes that identified their tribe.

Avigail had never known where her distaste for the Habiru had come from, but she had always felt strangely uncomfortable around the desert wanderers who lived in tents, calling no place home, following a faith so paltry they had only one god. And he hadn't even a face! Imagine, just one poor invisible god. It was said that the Habiru prayed to a burning bush, and their only symbol was a seven-branched tree. They had no roots except for a distant ancestor in ancient Ur. They kept to themselves and practiced secret ways. Avigail knew the root of her prejudice against Egyptians.

But the Habiru . . .

It was almost as if she had been born with a dislike of the wilderness nomads, because it felt more like an instinct than a conscious thought. And try though she did not to feel revulsion at the sight of them, she could not help it. They rarely came into town, but when they did, citizens shunned them and closed their shutters.

Oddly, Canaanites shared a language with the Habiru, although no one knew why. According to myth, a man named Shem survived the Great Flood that the gods had sent to punish mankind. Shem rode in an ark with his brothers, and when the waters receded, he came to the Land of Two Rivers and fathered a new race. They were called Shemites, from which the Canaanites descended. Avigail did not know how or why the Habiru adopted the Shemitic language, but it enabled them to sojourn among the cities of Canaan.

There it was! Elias's carrying chair! Supported on the shoulders of six strong slaves and followed by his bodyguards and the new scribe's personal attendant.

When Elias and the young scribe stepped down from the chair, Avigail ran to greet them, eager to hear what had transpired with Thalos the Minoan. When Elias reported the grim news from Jotham, she held out the newly arrived letter, impressed in cuneiform on a clay tablet, and said, "This will be our saving! A husband from my cousin's house in Sidon will be a great impediment to Jotham's plan, for my cousin is rich and has many loyal friends here in Ugarit."

They hurried inside and assembled in the same hospitality hall where Leah had spilled clam soup in Jotham's lap. Avigail called for wine and honey cakes. She sent for her daughter-in-law and the three granddaughters. Everyone must be present to hear the reading of the cousin's letter.

When Leah came in to take a seat on a large cushion, dressed now in clean clothes, a veil over her perfectly coiffed hair, she saw the new scribe staring at her and heard his friend mutter, "Look who I called a slave. A daughter of the house!"

Her eyes locked with Daveed's, and she felt a sharp curiosity about him.

Daveed, too, was curious about her. On the way back from Jotham's, Elias had filled him in on the family crisis. "You are now our private scribe and must be made privy to our secrets. I trust that the scribes of Lagash swear oaths of confidentiality as do the scribes

of Ugarit and that you will speak to no one of our family business."
Daveed now looked at Leah across the hospitality hall and thought: So
this is the cause of such venomous enmity, and what might very well be
the ruin of Elias the vintner.

Recalling Jotham's loud declaration to "make the girl mine,"
Daveed suddenly felt sorry for her.

They all turned their attention to Avigail when she took the seat of
honor. Since everyone here was family, or family servants, there was
no need to retreat behind the privacy screen. Once Hannah, Esther,
and Tamar were there, and slaves were pouring the wine—the only one
not present was Rakel, who was resting from her visit to the House of
Gold—Avigail handed Daveed the letter.

On the road from Jotham's house, Elias had filled Daveed in on
the family members. He knew this was the grandmother, Avigail. She
was short and plump, but the mother—Elias's wife Hannah—although
also plump, was tall, a trait which her three daughters had inherited,
especially the oldest, Leah.

Daveed studied his new patron's wife. There was sorrow in
Hannah's eyes, a permanent sadness, he thought, as though painted
on with cosmetic. A handsome woman with a proud bearing. He
would imagine that she was a quiet, obedient wife, but one also who
counseled her husband softly and wisely. Elias's wife was no shrew,
Daveed guessed. She did not dominate this family.

It was Avigail, Elias's mother, Daveed decided, who ruled this domain.

Silence filled the hall as he scanned the impressions in the hard
clay, identifying the language and writing system, familiarizing
himself with special symbols and the cadence of the "voice," of the
letter writer. While they waited, Nobu took it upon himself, as he
always did, to take the measure of his master's hosts.

The vintner seemed affable enough, if a bit naïve in his dealings
with the angry shipbuilder. The three young ones would be his daughters. The eldest, which Nobu had thought was a slave, and a young one
with a deformed upper lip that left her teeth grotesquely exposed. But
the middle one caught Nobu's attention in particular. He had heard
Avigail address her as Tamar. She was an extraordinary beauty, but
that was not what arrested Nobu just now: it was the way she looked at
Daveed—with an almost scheming eye.

This family has more than its share of trouble. If they think the fat shipbuilder is going to give them grief, they should look to the girls of the house.

"What is wrong with your slave?" Elias said.

Daveed looked up. "He is a god-listener. He hears voices."

"Please tell him not to reply to them."

Daveed sent his companion a disciplinary look and Nobu was suitably chastised, sucking in his lip to keep from muttering. Then Daveed closed his eyes for a brief prayer to Shubat, his personal god, something he did whenever he was about to deal with written words. Like everyone else, Daveed knew the power of words. An impulsive or misspoken word could bring calamity upon the head of one who spoke it. Even more potent were written words, for they possessed a permanence not found in the spoken. Therefore, he treated writings with respect and caution. Shubat guide my eyes and tongue, he prayed silently.

Then he cleared his throat and his rich voice filled the hall as he read: "Cherished cousin, peace and the blessings of Dagon upon you. My sons are all married. I can send you no one. Please accept my regrets. The family is well."

When his voice died, silence rushed in. No one moved. And then Avigail whispered, "Halla!" and traced a protective sign in the air.

Elias looked at his mother. "What do we do now?"

She stiffened her chin. "I have another cousin. In Damaska. If she cannot send a son, she will find someone who can. But now I will send for two, as Tamar must marry as well." To Daveed she said, "I will dictate a letter."

"If I may, my lady," he said. "I prefer to bathe and to pray before I take dictation. As my slave and I have just come from a long journey, it is disrespectful to my profession that I handle stylus and clay with the dust of travel still on my person."

"There is no time. We must do this now so that I can take the letter to the caravanserai before the sun is down."

Masking his displeasure, Daveed gestured Nobu, who came over with Daveed's box of instruments and supplies. Everyone watched as he reached in and brought out a small statuette. Carved from a single small block of dark green diorite, the statuette was the length and width of a man's hand. The god was seated, his arms crossed over his chest. He wore a long robe inscribed with wedge-shaped symbols identifying him as Shubat, the god of wisdom, knowledge, and writing. He was bearded with a turban on his head. His staring eyes were wide and unnaturally large, denoting his divinity. Daveed never took dictation without Shubat's watchful presence.

"Shall it be clay or papyrus, Em Elias?" he asked. "And which language do you wish?"

"Clay," she said. "Canaanite."

Daveed asked for water. When it was brought, he prayed softly to Shubat as he retrieved a sealed packet from his box. Cutting it open, he produce a lump of moist clay. Adding water, he molded the clay until it was a convenient shape lying in the palm of his left hand, and was moist enough to receive impressions.

Choosing a sharp-edged reed from his collection of writing implements, Daveed readied it in his right hand, murmured "Shubat guide my hand," and gave Avigail an expectant look.

She began to dictate and Daveed's hand moved swiftly over the damp clay, pressing the stylus into it, producing vertical, horizontal and sloping lines that terminated in triangles. At times he upended the reed to press only the triangular end into the clay. His hand moved so swiftly that when Avigail paused, Daveed's hand paused only a second later. Elias was impressed with his new scribe's skill, but others in the hall were not so delighted. As Avigail said, "Please send us two sons. There is no bride-price. We will pay whatever you demand . . ." Leah burned with humiliation and Tamar raged in silent fury.

Their grandmother was buying husbands.

I am sorry, master," Nobu said, "but without fire to heat the curling rod, that is the best I can do."

Daveed studied his reflection in the copper mirror. Nobu had had to resort to curling the drooping ringlets around his finger and invigorate them with oil. Turning his head this way and that to make sure the gold clips that anchored his ringlets to the nape of his neck were in a straight line, Daveed examined the crimped black hair that swept back from his high forehead and over his skull. It, too, could do with some livening. His beard needed tending as well, but no water had been brought with which to make a lathery shampoo.

"And where is your bath?" Nobu muttered as he restored the grooming implements to his barber's box. "Cleanliness is a matter of self-respect, which is something Canaanites clearly lack. Courtesy, too, and etiquette, virtues which we men of Lagash pride ourselves in. This entire household seems to have forgotten that there are newcomers among them!"

Daveed rose from his stool and went to a wall niche containing an oil lamp. "Bring me the god," he said. "I must pray."

After Daveed had finished inscribing the letter on clay, the tablet had been baked to hardness in the kitchen's bread oven, allowed to cool, and then the lady of the house, Avigail, had departed with it, declaring that she would find a swift caravan who would carry the letter to Damaska. A distracted Elias had explained Daveed's duties to him and said that the chief steward would show him to their quarters, where they would be living for the next twelve months. But Daveed thought of the shipbuilder's financial assault on Elias and wondered if he and Nobu were even going to have a patron a year from now, much less a place to live.

Daveed looked around his new quarters. It was but a small chamber, the width and breadth of which he could cover in six strides. The bed was narrow, the wooden storage chest plain and unpainted. And only four pegs in the wall on which to hang his garments. He did not mind. All newly graduated scribes must serve a year of apprenticeship before going out on their own, just as doctors and lawyers, fresh out of school, must humble themselves in service to others before hanging up shingles that told citizens they were in business.

"I'm hungry," Nobu grumbled as he removed Shubat from his special carrying case and brought the statuette to Daveed. "Do Canaanites not understand hospitality?"

"Have some compassion," Daveed said as he took the god from Nobu. "We have arrived at a misfortunate time. And after all, we are servants, not guests."

"But what about you, master? The man who would sponsor you into the Brotherhood is no longer here. And your new patron seems to be rapidly accruing enemies!"

"I must come up with a new plan," Daveed said as he reverently placed the statuette of Shubat in the wall niche. "I must find a new sponsor before my year of apprenticeship is done." But how? Daveed was a stranger to Ugarit, and getting into the fraternity of scribes depended on whom one knew. Making friends in this climate was going to be difficult.

If only he had not had the terrible falling out with his father. The King of Lagash had friends and connections here in Ugarit, but after their row, Daveed knew he dared not call upon any. And he knew the situation would not change until he apologized and that would never happen. The argument was over his status as a warrior-scribe.

From earliest childhood, along with his book learning, Daveed had been trained in the ancient form of close combat, Zh'kwan-eth, which had its roots in the mists of time when military men took scribes into battle with them for their conquests to be recorded for all time. Since the scribe was one of the most valuable members of an army, and the loss of him meant loss of a king's prowess in the historical record, such scribes had been trained to defend themselves—especially as they were also privy to the army's secret strategies and plans and the capture of a scribe meant torture for the information. No one knew the origins of Zh'kwan-eth, but it was a rigorous and demanding form of combat that people greatly admired. Daveed had made a name for himself in his precise and daring skills at throwing daggers. With such swiftness and accuracy that citizens had come from miles around to watch the games.

But Daveed had not wanted to join his father's army. He had no taste for fighting, did not desire combat or the recording of it. He had a higher calling. And this was what they argued over before Daveed left for Lagash. He had not only let his father down, but the King claimed his son had also dishonored him and their house.

"Did we hear correctly," Nobu was saying, "what the shipbuilder said? Was your new patron's daughter promised to him and then they backed out?"

Daveed did not reply. It was not Nobu's place to know the family business. But in the carrying chair, on the way back from Jotham's, Elias had explained that Jotham was angry that a marriage agreement had not been arrived at. However, Elias had assured Daveed that no contract had been broken, no promise had been retracted. There were no legal grounds for Jotham's complaint.

Still, the shipbuilder's ire and threat of revenge were great. Something more must have happened. No legal grounds, but perhaps personal ones?

Nobu said, "Master, did you hear that letter the woman dictated? She is begging for sons! This is a house of women! Do they think we have no pride? This would never happen in Lagash where fathers have authority over their children and daughters obey! My voices tell me that we should leave this place as soon as possible!" He resumed unpacking their travel bags and laid out his master's tunic and cloak for the coming evening. He himself would occupy the smaller room next door, sleeping lightly as he always did, in case his master needed him. Nobu moved slowly and methodically, head thrust forward, thick-lidded tortoise eyes blinking. He muttered sporadically, finding the god-voices to be as loud in Ugarit as they had been in Lagash. "Although, how you will find another position that offers a place to live is beyond me."

Daveed had the same fear. But he said, "I will figure something out," wondering where to even begin.

Nobu laid his hand on his paunch. "When will we be called for dinner? Wine would be nice right now, too." With a grunt he laid Daveed's spare sandals by the bed and said, "I will find someone."

"No, I will go." The lamp in the niche was out of oil. He could not pray to Shubat without a purifying flame. Throwing his cloak over his left shoulder, leaving his right shoulder and arm bare, he strode from the room while Nobu muttered responses to his whispered voices.

The villa was a vast maze of corridors, doorways, columns, sudden gardens, and paths that led nowhere, as if the various owners through the generations had added willy-nilly. Daveed thought: it is a large house for so small a family. In Lagash, they had heard of the illness that had swept through the port town of Ugarit. Daveed's father, the king, had made daily sacrifice to their gods, pleading with them to stop the evil spirits of that fever from traveling down the Euphrates. His supplications had worked. Cities east of Ugarit had been spared, but they had heard of loss in every family in Ugarit. Daveed understood the grandmother's desperation to repopulate this house.

As he was about to call out for help, Daveed heard voices—one deep and masculine, the other feminine and high.

Following them, he turned the corner onto a colonnaded portico, the crowns of the columns painted like flowers, and realized the voices were coming from an open doorway. Recognizing the voice of his new patron, Elias, Daveed stepped up to the door, intending to ask Elias to send a servant to his quarters.

He stopped. Elias was seated in a chair, and at his feet knelt the girl, Leah, her face lifted like a flower. Daveed held his breath. They did not see him and he found himself unable to move.

"Daughter," Elias was saying in a voice laden with sadness, "in the thirty-nine years that I have been on this earth, I have learned one thing. Love is more precious than gold. Without love, we are nothing. We are like the beasts in the field. And I speak not just of the love of a father for his daughter—which in my heart is bountiful beyond measure, for you are precious to me, Leah. But also of love between man and woman. My love for your mother goes beyond the stars. It will outlast time itself. And I pray that someday, Leah, you will find such a love. You will meet a man and know in your heart that your two souls are one. And when that day comes, you will understand how I can never break a promise to your mother. No matter what Jotham does to us, it is nothing compared to the tremendous wrong that I would do if I broke my word to the woman I love."

Daveed could not pull himself away. Elias was a man of proud bearing, and sat in the armed chair like a statesman or prince, while the girl kneeling on the floor seemed so small, vulnerable. Her willowy body molded itself to her father's strong legs, bent at the knees. Her upturned face, Daveed could see, was wet with tears. "But Papa, I will go gladly to Jotham's house. You need not break your word."

"Dear child," Elias said as he tenderly laid a hand on his daughter's cheek, "I promised your mother I would keep you here. If I let you go, then I am breaking that promise. Besides, your grandmother fears the falling sickness is in Jotham's blood. Do not fear, Leah. Have faith in the gods. Everything will be all right. Jotham cannot keep this up forever. Even he is limited financially. And I still have friends. Do not argue," he said, putting a finger to her lips. "I am your father,

Leah. It is up to me to protect you and keep you safe. This is but a storm that will pass. You will see."

When Leah broke down and wept in her father's lap, Daveed silently backed away. Now he knew the truth of what had happened in this house. Elias had made a promise to his wife, out of love. Daveed also understood now that his new patron, a proud man, was torn between family honor and his love for a woman.

As he continued along the portico, Daveed thought of his sisters, the four princesses of Lagash, spoiled and pampered women whose marriages had been arranged. Although they had gone willingly into the houses of wealth and privilege, for the royal family could only marry into noble families of excellent blood, he doubted they would find the love Elias had spoken of, doubted they would make personal sacrifices for the sake of their families.

Turning into another corridor, Daveed wondered why he should suddenly be thinking of sisters and wives when such thoughts had never before entered his head. He thought of Avigail's desperate plea for husbands. What if the cousin in Damaska couldn't deliver? What would Elias do then? With Jotham like a wolf at his door, and three girls of marrying age unable to find men, what desperate measures would the Canaanite take? What would his wife, mother, daughters do?

A word he was not accustomed to now came to mind: self-sacrifice. Elias sacrificing his wealth and reputation to make his wife happy; and the girl, offering to marry the odious Jotham to save her father.

Daveed had only known his own father as "My Lord," a man seated on a high throne and who had expected his son to bow in his presence. Mother, aloof and preoccupied with her leisure, her many friends, her hours at the vanity table. Between the palace at Lagash and the dormitories in the House of Life, Daveed had known no other home. This was his first taste of a real house and a normal family.

And suddenly he thought: Is there some way I can help them?

He crossed a courtyard with a whispering fountain, down a cool passageway, and when he came out, found himself facing an old wooden gate set in a stone wall. Wondering what lay on the other side, he pushed and it swung away to reveal an enclosed space that must have once been a garden. He judged that it was ten long strides in width, and twenty in length, with a high wall all around. This place had not been visited in a long time, he deduced, eyeing the dried leaves on the stone paths, the broken marble benches, the withered tree in the center, and over there—

He brought his head back. But no, not entirely dead! There was a green patch. A small square of freshly turned earth and baby shoots sticking up through the dirt. The ground was wet, as if it had been recently watered.

"Halla!"

He spun about. She was standing there, her eyes red and swollen, her face still damp.

"My servant is hungry," he said. "I went in search of someone and I ended up here."

"I am sorry! I had thought my mother or grandmother would have—" She wiped her eyes with the back of her hand. "What must you think of us?"

He took in the eyelids puffy from tears, a girl willing to sacrifice herself for her family. He thought: she is very pretty, and softly spoken. Under other circumstances she would have no end of suitors from which to choose. She would even be married by now. And it struck him as a crime that Jotham's vindictiveness should put such an unfair curse on the girl.

"It is not my place to judge," he said in a kindly tone. "But if you want to know, I see a family suffering unfair misfortune, and I pray that the gods deliver you from this adversity."

Although Leah had thought the garden large and roomy, it suddenly seemed small. This broad-shouldered stranger filled it with his masculine size and power. Leah wondered if a man had ever set foot within these private walls. She doubted it. And then she was struck for the first time by the fundamental differences between men and women. She felt herself smaller in his company, more vulnerable, and yet strangely, she liked the feeling. She tried not to stare at the one bare arm in the late afternoon sunlight, muscles too large for a man who spent his days writing letters. It was the arm of a dock worker, or a stone mason. He could overpower her and she would not be able to fight him off.

Even more intriguing was the sheathed dagger strapped to his bare arm. Was he a fighter as well as a scribe?

She was impressed with his long hair coiled into shining black ringlets that draped over his shoulders, each curl held to his scalp with a gold clasp. It was an elegant and intricate coiffure and she imagined it must take a long time to create. His beard was sparse, having not fully grown in, and he kept it trimmed short. His clothes were foreign. His fringed tunic left one shoulder and arm bare, and his belt was wide, cinching in a narrow waist over strong thighs. The men of Canaan wore loose robes so that the physique could only be guessed at. The young men of Lagash must be proud of their bodies.

"It is all my fault," she said, suddenly wanting this handsome stranger to know about her secret pain. And then, embarrassed at her selfishness, quickly said, "Forgive me. Your servant is hungry. We are being neglectful."

Daveed smiled. "Nobu will survive an hour of hunger."

He adjusted his cloak, and sunlight flashed a brilliant red on his hand. When he saw Leah's eyes go to the flash, he held out his arm so that she could see the ring. To his shock, she lightly touched his hand as she bent for a closer look.

The carnelian signet ring was engraved with two humans facing each other as they stood with their hands raised, as if in salute. Giant wings fanned out on their backs, and Leah could not tell if they were male or female. But she recognized them all the same, for Ugarit's pantheon knew the same beings: angels, messengers of the gods. She realized it must be the royal crest of Ugarit, the stamp that Daveed signed documents, letters, receipts.

Her brief touch electrified him. It was but a moment, and yet with the power of a bolt of lightning. Unexpected. Exciting. He looked at the crown of her head as she bent to examine the ring. Her hair was shiny and gave off a sweet fragrance. She stood close. He could hear her faint respirations. The world went silent. A butterfly winged its way around Daveed's head and then Leah's, as if to trace an invisible thread binding them together. It was blue and gold and flashed like gemstones in its flight. And then it was gone and Leah was releasing Daveed's hand and stepping back to say, "It is a very handsome ring."

Daveed thought: she is very pretty, and her voice has an interesting quality. Dimples when she smiles. A graceful wave of her hand as she brushed a strand of hair from her cheek. Recalling the fat and oily

Jotham, Daveed found himself suddenly appalled at the thought of the man's lustful hands on this girl. He recalled the tenderness between father and daughter he had witnessed. Such naked love. His own mother addressed his father as "My Lord." Stiff, formal, cold, despite giving him twelve children. Daveed imagined the bedroom act to have been as stiff and formal and dutiful as if they were in the throne room receiving ambassadors.

He paused to look down at the barren earth of this forgotten garden and marveled at the green patch. "It is all my fault," she had said. He wanted to know, yet was too respectful to pry. So he said, "You are growing a garden." Daveed had passed a few gardens during his journey through the house, and he knew that larger gardens would be beyond this high wall, where the kitchens and animal pens were. What was the purpose of this neglected patch?

"It is for my elderly aunt. She is failing in the mind, and I think that perhaps growing things, making a garden like the one she had in her youth, will bring her back."

Daveed had never grown anything. He was not even certain how it was done, for he had spent his life in the hushed halls of books and scholars. His mind was filled with meaningful symbols and lines and drawings, yet he was baffled by the budding of a simple leaf. It is a gift, he thought, to be able to bring earth to life. "If we can keep our house," she added softly. "You met Jotham today. You know about our problems with him. It is all my fault. It was my disobedience a year ago, when Jotham and his sister came to visit, that has brought this calamity upon my family. Because of this, it is up to me to correct things. Only I can make things right again. But how? My father will not let me go to Jotham. I must wait for Grandmother to find a husband for me. How can I just stand by and let them all be ruined because of my poor judgment!"

"Your family will be all right," he said, wondering about the act of disobedience. She did not strike him as headstrong and defiant. "I am not without experience in these matters. Two of my uncles are lawyers and a third is a banker. I have been around legal and financial matters all my life. Your father is a wise businessman and will find a solution to his problems. He will seek out those creditors whom he thinks will be easily swayed by Jotham, and he will pay them now what he owes them. Those whom he believes will stay loyal to him, who will resist Jotham's attempt to purchase your father's notes, Elias can leave alone for now."

To his surprise, she shook her head. "It will not be enough. I must do something, but I do not know what."

Daveed gave this some thought. "What exactly was your act of disobedience, if I may be allowed to ask?"

She looked across beams of sunlight and saw dark eyes filled with kindness. I can trust this stranger. And so she told him a remarkable story about one fateful night filled with tragedy, sorrow, and umbrage. When she was finished, Daveed finally grasped the full drama of this house, and he thought: She wanted to be at her mother's side. She did the right thing. Jotham should understand this, and forgive. As should the sister, if the story of her afflicted son was true.

Daveed was suddenly furious with the arrogant shipbuilder, and felt an unaccustomed desire to protect this girl. "Perhaps your solution doesn't lie with Jotham. Have you considered the sister?"

Leah frowned. "Zira?"

"From what you have just told me, it would seem that Zira has influence over her brother. Was it not her harsh words that sent the bad luck into your mother? Jotham did not silence her when he should have. Perhaps Zira is the key."

Leah thought about this—Zira's son and his affliction, and Auntie Rakel saying that her husband had once known the cure for the falling sickness . . .

"Will you stay?" she asked, suddenly encouraged. Zira's ambition for her son was common knowledge. What would she give for a cure for his illness? I will start tomorrow. I will ask Auntie Rakel what the remedy is . . . "Even though our circumstances might fall below your expectations, especially after leaving your home and traveling so far? Will you stay with us?"

The question caught him by surprise. "I traveled far not for your father's sake, or even for my own, but to honor my god. And I made a promise to your father, which I will keep." He took a step toward her, suddenly needing to close the space that separated them. "Know this about me, Leah Bat Elias, I worship the written word, I live to serve the scribe's profession."

He spoke with passion now, and Leah was caught up in the intense emotion of his tone, the tension in his body, the light shining in his eyes as he said, "The miracle of one man writing something on a tablet so that another man, hundreds of miles away, or perhaps hundreds of years hence, can read those words and understand—two strangers connected by an invisible conduit, talking to each other through the magic of the writing that was given to humankind as a gift from the gods—it is because of this miracle that I wish to serve my cherished profession by being a member of the Brotherhood of Scribes, doing them proud, being an honorable example of their noble fraternity. It is the highest and best way I know to show Shubat my devotion to him. With each symbol I press into clay, I honor my god and that which is noble in man.

"Therefore, I tell you this, Leah Bat Elias, when I graduated from the House of Life, I swore an oath to my god to abide by the rules and ethics of my profession, never to use my arts to bring harm to another, to hold myself to the highest integrity and self-respect. Obedience to Shubat, and honor come before all else. In order to uphold my oath and fulfill my duty as an apprentice in this house, however, I must find a way to ensure that the House of Elias will still be in existence one year from now. I will do everything in my power to help . . ." His voice trailed.

She tilted her head. "There is something wrong?"

"I would have been more helpful if your prior scribe, Shemuel, were still here, for he was to sponsor my membership into the Brotherhood. Now I fear I must seek another sponsor, although how, being a stranger to Ugarit, I do not know. Still, I will honor my prom-ise to serve your father."

"Is there no one in Ugarit who can help you?"

"I am alone here. And although I am a prince, for personal reasons I cannot approach men who are friends of my father."

"There are people from Lagash who live in Ugarit. Perhaps you might know one or two of them." She paused, taking in his rich clothes, the jewelry and finely groomed hair. He was a man of wealth, a prince of Lagash, Shemuel had said. Thus he would know only men of the upper class. "I know of a family a mile south of here. They are very wealthy, owning almond orchards that are famous far and wide. The father's name is Izaak. And he is from Lagash."

Daveed fell silent, mentally traveling back down the years. But he shook his head. "I can recall no Izaak, a grower of almonds."

"Then there is a trader in gemstones who has a shop near the House of Gold. He, too, is from Lagash and boasts a blood connection to the royal house. His name is Manthus."

Daveed frowned. The name sounded familiar. He searched his memory again and suddenly: "By Shubat! My uncle's wife has a brother who lives here in Ugarit. He trades in precious stones, such as carnelian and lapis lazuli. And yes, I remember now—the name is Manthus. I had forgotten."

Leah smiled. "I can direct you to his shop."

Daveed stared at Leah for a long moment, and then he said, "I do not believe in accident or coincidence. Our personal gods guide our lives every step of the way. Therefore, it was not by accident that I came into this garden. Shubat brought me here so that you and I would have this encounter. For now I have a plan, I know what to do next, which I did not know earlier when I learned that my sponsor, Shemuel, had sailed to Cypress. Tomorrow morning I will pay respects to Manthus, the carnelian trader. He will help me, for we are related on my mother's side. Kin, no matter how distant, must always help kin. And perhaps, Bat Elias, in being connected to Manthus, I can in some way help your family."

"My name is Leah," she said softly.

He smiled. "I thank you, Leah, for helping me. I know I will be successful tomorrow, for Shubat will guide me. He is my protector and spiritual guide. He has never failed me. Now I leave you in peace. Shalaam."

But he hesitated, as if held in place by invisible bonds. It did not seem enough, he thought. To promise to help, to promise to stay. Daveed suddenly wanted to say so much more to this girl with eyes that seemed to see right into his soul. The spring day shifted slightly, as if the earth were holding its breath, as if magic had stolen into this neglected little garden. Had he truly only arrived here that morning? Had mere hours passed since he set foot in Ugarit for the first time? He felt different somehow. Daveed of Lagash had arrived at this new city with plans and ambitions and a definite path. But things had changed along the way—and in such a short time! Now there was this enchanting girl in his life. There had been others, in Lagash, pretty girls, charming ones, girls hopeful of marrying such a man. But Leah did not flirt the way other girls did, seemed not to be on the hunt for a husband—although her grandmother certainly was. Daveed had the distinct impression that she was interested in him for his own sake, not as marrying material. And it was a strange but flattering feeling.

"Shalaam," he murmured again with a nod of his head, and reluctantly left the garden.

As Leah watched him go, she felt the electricity in the air, an energy left behind, like a warm spot on the grass where the sun has shone but still warm after the sun has gone behind a cloud. Daveed's passion for his faith astounded her. People spoke of the gods, gave lip service to them, but she had never seen true devotion. It made her realize that she had not thought of asking the gods for help. But now, Daveed's deep faith in the divine inspired her.

She studied the old sycamore fig in the center of the garden, dead now and leafless, but a tree nonetheless and the tree was the symbol of Asherah.

Yes! she thought.

Turning to the decaying tree trunk, Leah held out her arms and prayed silently: "Blessed Asherah, I ask your forgiveness for my act of disobedience a year ago. I disrespected my father's guests, and in so doing, disrespected my father. For this I am truly sorry. From this moment forward, Blessed Asherah, I will be obedient to my father, to your will and to the laws of the gods. Never again will I disobey my father, my elders, or the gods. I ask only that, in return, Mother of All, you find it in your munificent heart to restore my family's honor and good fortune to the way it was before the night my defiance brought bad luck upon our heads."

But even as she voiced her oath, Leah knew that the mere vowing to be obedient would not be enough to save her family. The gods must witness her obedience and so, in this moment of trembling hope, her worst fear was born: that she would be put to a mighty test and that she would have neither the strength nor the courage to pass it. And as she had no idea what that test might be, or when it might come, she would not recognize it as such, and fail because of it!

And that, perhaps, was her biggest fear of all.

CHAPTER FOUR

The fugitive waited until the captain and crew were well away from the ship, their laughter rising to the stars. They were heading for the nearest tavern to enjoy local wine and women, and they had invited him to come along, but he had declined.

He had boarded the ship at the coastal town of Sidon, where the captain of the northbound vessel had had to make port because of the loss of crewmen in a storm. He asked no questions, being desperate for hands, and the fugitive had volunteered no information, being equally as desperate. He kept to himself doing what he was told, straining at oars, raising the sail, and, finally, in the harbor of Ugarit, offloading the last of the trader's Egyptian linen and papyrus. The captain would then fill his empty craft with cedar from the nearby forests and sail southward again.

The fugitive, a man alone in the world, looked around the harbor, where water craft of all sizes and nationalities were moored or anchored, some occupied and glowing with lights, others dark and deserted. The docks were illuminated by light that spilled from doorways where music and laughter poured out into the warm, humid night. Massive warehouses also lined the wharf, and in between them, lanes that led away into the town.

He had no idea where to go. He had murdered a family back in

Sidon and had fled with just the clothes on his back. A place to hide was his first concern, for the prince of Sidon would surely alert the authorities of other towns that a mass-murderer was on the loose. Should he be caught, they would ask no questions. Justice in Canaan was swift.

As he pulled his cloak about himself—a garment he stole from the marketplace on his flight from Sidon—he selected a tavern and scurried along the waterfront in the direction of its light.

He was in a hurry. To find a place to hide, and a new name.

The fugitive did not know his own name, or how old he was, or the place of his birth. His earliest memory was of living in a cage and being used sexually by several men. They laughed when he squealed, and so they called him Piglet. He didn't know if his mother had sold him, or if he had been kidnapped. When he was old enough, he escaped and had been itinerant ever since. He did not know where it was, that place of the cage, in which town or province, only that it was a place of wool dyeing and that when the men came to his cage to make him squeal, their bodies were dyed the indigo blue of the vats they worked.

That was when his Blue Devils were born—invisible demons that periodically invaded his body and made his life a torment.

He never knew what wakened the devils. But when they possessed him his skull thundered and he could not breathe. The only thing that drove them away was the sound of squealing pigs. Once, they had stayed away for a year and he had wondered if they had tired of tormenting him and left. But then they had wakened with a ferocious appetite and had not been satisfied until they had heard the squealing of pigs for seven successive nights. That was in the town of Jerusalem. He had found prostitutes, one each evening, and had taken them out into fields to make them squeal. On the seventh night, after burying the seventh "piglet," his head cleared, he could breathe again, and he knew the Blue Devils were gone.

At the farm outside of Sidon, he had stopped to drink at the well. The Blue Devils had come, suddenly and without warning. That was why he had slain the farmer and his family. It wasn't until the little girls, the farmer's youngest daughters, squealed beneath his assault that the devils left. And so he had had to run from Sidon, once again a fugitive.

Tonight, it was not the Blue Devils that drove him to search for a victim in a dockside tavern. He needed a new name, a new place to hide. He had gone by many names over the years, too many to remember. Tonight would be no different. He stood in the doorway and surveyed the few patrons in the dim, smoky light. He had to choose his victim carefully in order for his new identity to work. It was important that he fool as many people as possible, the authorities in particular. And so not only must he secure a change of name, but his appearance must change as well. The fugitive had let his hair grow over the years, or cut it short many times, shaved his beard or worn in full, gained weight, lost weight. It made him think of a marvel he saw once in a marketplace where street performers were entertaining the crowd for copper rings. A magician had produced a brown lizard that, when placed upon a green leaf, turned green! The magician had called it a chameleon. That is what I am, he thought as he scanned the patrons— some were too thin, too short, too swarthy—I am a chameleon.

The only thing he could not change was the scar over his left brow where one of his "piglets" had bit him.

Finally, his sharp, calculating eyes came to a loud braggart across the tavern and his lips curved in a smile.

I tell you my friends," the traveler from Damaska was boasting to a few bored tavern patrons, "there is no luckier man than I in the entire world! There I was, mourning the loss of my wife, and the loss I might add of my livelihood as it was her textile business and reverted to her brothers upon her death—anyway, I was bemoaning my sad fate when a letter arrived from this very town, asking my sister to send husbands for the daughters of a distant cousin! A very rich cousin, I might add," Caleb recklessly said as he signaled to the barmaid for more wine.

But the girl herself did not bring the pitcher and fresh cup. It was a bearded stranger with leathery skin and deep-set shadowed eyes, wearing a cloak that looked better than he could afford. "I like your story, my friend," he said to Caleb as he slammed the jug down and took a seat on the stool opposite. Between them, a low table was set with cheese, nuts, olives, and bread, which the dark stranger proceeded to devour.

Caleb of Damaska did not mind. Once he was settled in his new home in the foothills, he would have food to spare. He decanted wine from the fresh jug, took a long drink, and then said to the stranger, "My story is indeed remarkable! You see before you a man headed for a life of ease. All I have to do is marry one of the daughters, get her with child, and I reap the benefits of being a rich man's son-in-law."

The sailor listened. When Caleb ran out of wine, the sailor bought more with the last of his copper rings. Caleb resumed his rambling. "They do not even know I am coming! I persuaded my sister not to write back in reply. Why warn them ahead of time that I am a widower without prospects? Best just to present myself at their door and give them no chance to turn me away. I am told that the House of Elias stands at the edge of one of Canaan's richest vineyards, along the southern road. I will be there first thing in the morning."

As Caleb gulped his wine, holding the mug with two hands as he was growing shaky, the fugitive gave this tale deep consideration. He noted that the braggart was but a few years older than himself. Not as broad-shouldered but thick-haired and spoke the local language with an accent that was easily mimicked. The fugitive from Sidon grinned. "Tell me more about yourself, my friend, for you strike me as an interesting fellow."

The man from Damaska, Caleb the erstwhile vendor of textiles, spoke of this and that, mentioning names, places, and events, rambling to and fro in his narrative, his speech growing slurred, his tongue stumbling over words until he gave his new friend a cross-eyed look and said, "I'm drunk."

The sailor smiled and rose to his feet—a big man with shoulders like an ox and hands like haunches of venison, or so they seemed to Caleb who had started seeing double. "Thank you, sir," he said as he accepted an offered hand. Swaying on his feet, he said, "By good fortune, I am staying at an inn along the lane, four doors down. Upstairs. If you help me to my room, I shall reward you with a gold ring. After tomorrow, I will have gold rings in plenty!"

In the alley behind the tavern, a narrow space between two build-ings where no light from stars or moon could find its way, the fugitive stopped suddenly, causing Caleb to bump into him. "I must relieve myself," he said, and while Caleb swayed on unsteady legs, the man from Sidon—who had slain more people than he could count—withdrew a knife from his sash. Caleb blinked at it, seeing two knives. "Oh," he began.

"Where does one begin to slaughter a pig?" the fugitive said with a smile. No Blue Devils motivated him in this moment because he also liked killing just for the sake of it. The boy who had once been power-less in a cage needed to feel power now and then as a man. So he made Caleb kneel before him and beg for his life. And before it went on for too long and they might be discovered, the sailor slit the Damaskan's neck from ear to ear, slowly, so that the braggart could feel the full horror of losing his life.

Relieving the corpse of purse and rings, and taking Caleb's hand-some cloak, the fugitive continued four doors down and climbed the stairs, thinking: A man stupid enough to boast of his good fortune in a foreign tavern among strangers deserves to die.

In the upper room, Caleb's personal servant snored on a pallet. A quick snap of the neck and the man was dead.

The sailor took his time going through Caleb's possessions, admir-ing the fine clothes and jewelry. As he tried things on and liked the feel of them, he thought of the names and places and events Caleb had blathered about, and tucked them away for when they would come in handy. Who knew what Elias the vintner might inquire of distant relatives?

"They practically paid me to come," the man from Damaska had said. Sounded like the family was desperate. It meant an ugly or a defective daughter.

The fugitive didn't care. For a life of ease, for a roof over his head and plenty to eat—and a safe hiding place where no one would find him—for all that, he would marry a pig. He grinned at the irony of it. He would live a life of ease until he needed to make the bride squeal, and then move on.

Extinguishing the oil lamp, he bedded down for the night and thought: Caleb. As good a name as any.

Six miles from the harbor, across the city and down the southern road, the inhabitants of the House of Elias were likewise preparing for bed.

"It is called a love-fruit," Rakel was saying as Leah gently combed her long white hair. The hour was late. Rakel did not like having a slave girl prepare her hair for the night. She appreciated her niece's delicate touch, as Rakel's scalp was tender. "This is because the mandrake heats a man's blood and excites a woman's womb. But be careful when you harvest the mandrake, my dear. It must be drawn gently from the earth. If it is yanked out, it screams, and they say the screams of the mandrake cause madness in those who hear it. My Ari and I drank a potion of the love-fruit, and the result was my Yacov. He is studying law, you know. My son is going to be a lawyer."

"We are all very proud of Yacov, Auntie," Leah said as she laid the comb aside. She hated to lie, but when she saw that going along with Rakel's imagined world made the elderly woman happy, she decided the lies were forgivable. "But what can you tell me of the cure for the falling sickness?" Leah asked the question every day, with no results. She was growing anxious.

Two months and no word from the cousin in Damaska. It was the peak of summer, grapes were sweetening on the vine, and Elias's house was filled with tension and worry. Leah wondered why there had been no reply from Damaska. Were there no husbands to be had there, either? Or was Jotham's venomous reach that far?

A new man in the house, everyone knew, would help. How much, depended on the man. Elias was alone in his fight against Jotham, but a son-in-law at his side, especially one who was young and strong and possibly bringing wealth and influence to the family, would give Elias a chance.

In the meantime, Leah knew her father was not idle. As the new scribe, Daveed, had predicted, Elias had wasted no time in going around to friends, asking them not to sell him out, to be strong, paying what debts he could before Jotham seized them. Elias sold off assets to the few buyers who were not influenced by Jotham, and he kept working at the wine business, because after the harvest the older wines would be ready to sell, and Elias would have plenty of money.

If they could hold out that long. That was the worry. Three more creditors had sold their collection notes to Jotham, who was presenting them to Elias for instant payment. Leah feared her father might not be able to remain solvent long enough. Which was why she had offered to comb Auntie Rakel's hair for bedtime. She must find the cure for the falling sickness soon.

She was certain that Zira's devotion to her son was so great that she would agree to anything in exchange for a cure for his affliction—even convince her brother to cease his vendetta against Elias!

But that precious cure was trapped beneath the snow-white hair Leah now twisted into long braids.

As the Egyptian physician at the House of Gold had predicted, Rakel was spending more and more time in the past, speaking of bygone days as if they were the present. She also described remedies and shared folk wisdom. But there was no direction or cohesion to her thoughts. Rakel would speak one moment of the best place to plant peppermint and the next how to prevent dandruff using willow bark shampoo.

"I would like a thinner scarf tonight, dear," Rakel said when the braids were finished. "The winter one is too hot when I sleep. In that chest over there, dear. I keep my summer scarves."

They were in Rakel's chamber, which was furnished with a bed, pegs on the walls for clothes, niches for gods and lamps, and several large wooden chests that held the contents of one woman's lifetime. Leah lifted the lid of a cedar chest, but Rakel said, "No dear, none of those. I wish to wear my linen scarf tonight. The weather is so warm."

Leah went to a chest made of ebony and inlaid with ivory and lifted the lid to find beautiful garments neatly folded, with jewelry and cups made of gold.

"I believe it is at the bottom," Rakel said as she fingered her braids to make sure no strands had escaped.

Leah searched under dresses and veils and cloaks. She found no linen scarf, but came upon clay tablets tucked away under leather slippers. It was almost as if they had been hidden there. "Auntie," she said cautiously, lifting one of the tablets out of the chest, "do you know what this is?"

Rakel turned in her chair and peered through the soft lamplight. She shook her head.

"Might this be a medicinal formula?" Leah asked, trying to contain her excitement.

"I have no idea what that is, dear. Why don't you take it to your father's new scribe? Is it Daveed? He can read it for you. I would like to know what it says."

85

Leah was always pleased to have an excuse to talk to Daveed. Although he was legally a servant, Daveed was of royal blood, a prince, and more educated than the man he served! Apprentice scribes, like apprenticed doctors and lawyers, enjoyed a peculiar status in Ugarit's upper class homes. Servants, yet treated as members of the family, and so Daveed dined with Elias and his women every evening, took part in their daily religious rituals, and, by the very nature of his profession, was taken into confidences and shared in all the family news and business. And so Leah's path crossed that of Daveed's every day, and often several times.

At some moment in the past two months, the seed of mutual attraction had been planted, perhaps during their first encounter in her little garden, when they had stood among the weeds and dust, with the patch of new green growth at their feet, perhaps it was then that the seed had been sown. And over the days and weeks since, the seed had been watered by chance encounters, smiles, words of greeting, the two becoming more familiar with each other, turning from strangers into friends of a kind, more than acquaintances but less than family members, and a respectful affection started to grow, like a seedling becoming a sapling, so that Daveed and Leah would sit on cushions and help themselves to food platters on the low table, and their eyes would meet in silent communication—a shared joke, perhaps, as her father and grandmother shared gossip from the city, or Auntie Rakel would delicately break wind and Daveed and Leah would look at each other in amusement. Little moments over two months, strung together like a necklace, Leah thought, until suddenly she was thinking about him all the time, feeling the early seed growing and blossoming within her, and dare she hope, within Daveed, too?

Surely she did not imagine the joy on his face when they encountered each other in a corridor, by surprise, not expecting it, a sudden, "Oh!" a broad smile, an awkward hesitation, a slight blush above the beard. Surely his heart jumped as hers did at the sight of him. Did he think of her at night, too, as he lay in bed waiting for sleep? Did he pray to Shubat to keep her safe, as she prayed to Asherah to watch over him?

As Leah climbed the stone stairway to the roof, knowing Daveed was up there gazing at the stars as was his nightly habit, she hugged a secret close to herself: she prayed that no husband came from Damaska.

It was a disobedient thought, she knew, but such a small act of disobedience that surely Asherah would forgive it. And it wasn't really a wish or a prayer, Leah would never actually ask the gods to keep her Damaskan kin from sending a husband, it was more of a wonderful fantasy, one which played out in her mind when she went to bed and lay in the soft glow of the oil lamps that kept evil spirits away—a girlish dream about a handsome, dark-eyed prince from Lagash living under her roof, serving her father, falling in love with her, and asking her, at the end of his year of apprenticeship, to marry him. She knew about his ambition to join the Brotherhood, but scribes could be members and not have to live at the House of Gold. And they were allowed to marry. Daveed would find a house in the better part of the city and hang out his shingle, as professional men did, and write letters for wealthy clients, draw up contracts, witness weddings, record property deeds. Leah would be his wife and take care of his house, take care of him, give him many children. No, not a disobedient thought, merely a dream . . .

And yet, when she came out onto the roof and saw him there in the moonlight, and her throat tightened with desire, and her blood turned warm and she thought she might die from the ache she felt for him—and yet, she could not help the brief, disobedient prayer: Please let no husband come from Damaska.

Because what she saw now, in the moonlight, so overwhelmed her that her breath was taken away, and she could swear her heart had gone with it.

Daveed was not gazing at the stars. Stripped down to just a loin-cloth, he was putting himself through a strange and rigorous exercise. Leah stared as she watched him jump and crouch and spring, fly up and spin around. His lithe body glistening with sweat. Muscles rippling, contracting in fluid motion with startling grace. He sprinted across the roof, whipped about and flung both arms, as if throwing imagined weapons. He danced to the side, and bobbed and weaved as if fighting an unseen foe.

He looked wild, and yet restrained, and Leah thought she had never seen a more exciting, more beautiful sight.

When he saw her he stopped suddenly, breathing heavily, his eyes locked with hers across the moonlit roof.

"Forgive me," she whispered. "I intruded."

He could not take his eyes off her. Leah's gown and veil were pale pink, the color of dawns and sunrises, his favorite times of the day. She made him think of sculpted cypress trees, slender, willowy, and mysterious in a way. When did it happen? he wondered as he felt desire stir within him. When was the day, the hour that he had suddenly thought of her as something more than the daughter of his patron? One moment all he could think about was joining the Brotherhood, and the next all he could think about was Leah.

It had crept slowly, he realized, this new attraction for her, so slowly and tenderly that he had not realized what was blossoming in his heart until it came into full flower, and he could think of nothing else. Thoughts of Leah gave him sleepless nights and restless days. It divided his mind and his devotion, for now Leah had taken place in his life next to the Brotherhood. But what exactly was this emotion that had him in a grip? How did he feel about Leah? Was it attraction? Curiosity? The fond attachment of a brother? This was what kept him awake at night, trying to seize upon unfamiliar and elusive emotions, trying to analyze them and understand them, and find stability and purpose again.

"You did not interrupt," he said, remembering himself, reaching for his cloak to cover his exposed body. "It is a nightly exercise I engage in, to keep my skills up."

"It was beautiful. Like a dance, and yet warlike, too."

"It is called Zh'kwan-eth, an ancient martial art designed long ago by scribes to defend themselves. My father wanted me to be a warrior-scribe and ride into battle with his generals, to record Lagash's victories over her enemies. But I have no taste for war. I worship the written word. My father and I had a bitter disagreement and he told me that until I relent and join his army, he will not acknowledge me as his son. I love him, but . . ."

"I'm sorry," she whispered.

The moment stretched between them as each realized they had been drawn into a intimate circle that no other person could enter.

And then Leah broke the spell. "I found this," she said, marveling at how moonlight carved ivory hills and valleys on his arms and torso, as he wore his cloak over one shoulder.

His eyes lingered on her face even though she was offering him a clay tablet. He tore himself away, reluctantly she thought, and looked at the tablet. And she saw, briefly, worry or fear cross his face. "Is it from Damaska?" he asked.

"No," she said, and an expression of relief appeared on his face. Dared she hope that he, too, prayed no husband was coming? "I found it at the bottom of one of Aunt Rakel's chests. She said she doesn't remember what it is."

Daveed brought the tablet close to his face, to study the symbols and to determine the language it was written in. "It is old," he said. "Southern Canaanite."

"Can you read it?"

"I can." Leah kept her eyes on his bowed head, the thick black hair, the curls on his shoulders, as he read out loud: "'My love is like a cedar. He is hard and endures. He fills my furrow with his sweet cream.'" Daveed cleared his throat in embarrassment. "This appears to be a love poem."

Their eyes met. Leah said nothing. Unspoken words flew between them like invisible doves. She wanted him to continue reading.

Bending his head, Daveed said softly, "'My love's breasts are like two moons. They delight me. They are filled with honey. I await my lover beneath the tamarisk tree. I await her kisses and her embrace. She holds me all night long. And then she empties me. Her leaving is the coldest of dawns. I know only sorrow until she brings joy to me again.'"

Daveed continued to stare down at the tablet before lifting his head to look at Leah. She saw something in his dark eyes. Longing, she thought, hunger. They shared a secret. They were falling in love. She knew that now. Did he know it, too?

Dare we admit it to ourselves, to each other?

He handed the tablet to her, his fingertips touching hers, and he whispered, "I wish I had written this for you." And her heart leapt.

A perfumed breeze came from the nearby vineyards to swirl around them and embrace the two in breathless desire. They had reached a brink. Both knew they were at the mercy of forces more powerful than themselves, an ancient, a sacred force. Yet they were not free to surrender. Laws of men and gods dictated how they must act. Leah was waiting for a husband from Damaska. Daveed's destiny lay within the walls of the Brotherhood.

She stepped back. She wanted to say, I love you. Three simple words. She saw Daveed's lips part, as if he too wanted to say the words. He had thought the tablet was from Damaska. He had feared that it was. She saw it in his eyes. Perhaps, if no husband came, and her father was able to save his winery, his house, his reputation, if so many things happened in the coming months, then possibly, just possibly her girlish fantasy could come true.

"Good night, Daveed," she whispered. "May Shubat keep you as you sleep."

Daveed was immobilized. He was confused. This young man whose profession was writing, whose very life was words and meanings, could not speak as Leah walked away and disappeared into the night. Only when he heard her sandals descending the stairway, and then fade away until all he heard was the wind and the lone howl of a jackal, only then could Daveed the scribe and prince of Lagash murmur, "May Asherah keep you as you sleep, Leah Bat Elias . . ."

The fugitive who had named himself Caleb awoke and left his bed before dawn. He avoided the alley where at daybreak a murdered foreigner would be found—and the magistrate with his guards would be summoned—and he went to the docks where unemployed men hoped to find work. Keeping an eye out for city guards, holding his cloak over his head to hide his face, he selected a robust laborer and brought him back to the inn to load his shoulders and arms with the gifts the Damaskan had brought for the women of Elias's house: bolts of the beautiful cloth for which Damaska was famous; lavish necklaces of pearls, turquoise, and lapis; bracelets made of quartz, topaz, and amethyst; ivory combs and golden cups; jars of costly oils and ointments. They worked swiftly but with caution. Although Caleb had thrown a blanket over the body of the slain servant, the corpse would soon begin to smell in the summer heat.

The two men went wordlessly to the marketplace, with Caleb noting the city guards who patrolled and managing to avoid catching their attention. The first arriving merchants reaped the rewards of their early rising. Such treasures, and the man selling them did not even haggle! Caleb hastily accepted whatever gold and silver rings they offered in exchange for the goods, glancing frequently over his shoulder, paying special attention to the guards.

Paying the porter, he hurried back to the inn, creeping up to his room before the innkeeper could see him, gathering the last of the Damaskan's belongings, and setting off before the hue and cry went out over a man found slain in an alley (and his soon-to-be discovered dead servant). Passing through the city gates with little notice from the sentries, he struck off down the road to the House of Elias, a safe hiding place where an easy life and a willing bride awaited him. Until the day came when he had to move on again.

You would have loved our house in Jericho," Rakel said to Leah as she deftly worked the bronze needle through the fabric.

Rakel, a devout woman, was a patroness of the temple of Asherah, and as such saw to it that the priestesses were garbed in raiment befitting their holy office. Rakel purchased expensive angora wool, which was imported from a mountainous country far to the north and transported to Ugarit by caravan and ship. She took the fragile and luxurious goat hair to an expert spinner and weaver, who produced such soft fabrics from the wool that it was worth its own weight in gold. When these lengths of cloth were delivered to the House of Elias, Rakel and her grandnieces spent afternoons embroidering the vestments with finely spun woolen yarns dyed a rainbow of colors, decorating the hems and borders of the robes with flowers, butterflies and imaginative designs. On Asherah's feast days, Rakel and the girls took them as offerings to the priestesses of the temple.

Esther was not with them on this sunny afternoon, as she had accompanied her grandmother Avigail to the caravan terminus, to see if a letter had arrived from the cousin in Damaska. Nor was Tamar helping with the sewing. No one knew where she was. And Hannah, the girls' mother, who had a delicate hand and sewed a fine stitch, was lying down with monthly cramps.

Leah did not reply as she finished a pink rose and used a small copper knife to cut the thread. Her thoughts were on Daveed. It seemed there was no room in her head for anything else, nor did she want there to be. Thinking about Daveed brought a giddy joy. Picturing him in her mind sent sweetness through her body.

She loved not only the man but also the idea of him. And the power of his body as he went through the motions of Zh'kwan-eth! When she was alone, she whispered his name, relishing the feel of it in her mouth, the sound of it in her ears. She would whisper, "My Daveed," and her lips would lift in a smile. Leah laughed softly at the surprising and undeniable pleasure of being in love.

Not long ago Esther had asked her, "Leah, how do you know you're in love? Truly, truly in love? How do you know that he is the one, that there will never be another no matter what happens or how long you might live? How do you know, Leah?"

At the time, Leah had not known the answer. But last night on the roof had changed everything—Daveed said he wished he had written the love poem for her!—and so today she would say, "You know when you are truly in love when you look at him and you suddenly realize how little time we have on this earth. Because now you want to live forever." Poor Esther who was almost a beauty. Men looked at her in the streets, in the temples and marketplace. When she wore her veil, they looked at her with interest. But Leah knew that if her sister were to lower her veil there would be shock on their faces, revulsion and pity. "I want to fall in love, Leah. I want to know what it is like," Esther had said, and now that Leah knew what love was really like, the excitement of it, the focusing all her thoughts on her beloved instead of on herself, living for the moment she would glimpse him, a chance to touch, or share a kiss—she wished this joy for Esther as well. But what man in all the world would fall in love with her?

"We were happy in Jericho, before the Egyptians took our home and drove us out," Rakel said as she brought the cloth close to her face to examine the stitchery. While she loved the feel of angora fabric, she would have preferred to give the priestesses linen. But as linen came only from Egypt, and as Avigail refused to allow anything "of that despised race" into the house, Rakel had to settle for angora. She resumed her embroidery. "We had Habiru slaves when I was a girl," she said. "They were very clean. Unlike other races, the Habiru have laws about bathing. The laws come from their invisible god. He has no name, which is very strange, for how can you pray to a god that has no name? How can you invoke his power and blessings?"

"Halla! What are you doing?"

Leah turned to see Avigail standing in the doorway. Quickly setting aside her sewing, she said, "Is there news, Grandmother?" Please, no husband from Damaska so that I will be free to marry Daveed.

"No letter from Damaska," Avigail said with a frown. "Child, what are you and Rakel talking about?"

Hiding her joy, Leah said, "I think I can help Father, Grandmother! Zira's son suffers from the falling sickness and Auntie Rakel knows a cure. Father can offer it to Zira if she will persuade Jotham to leave Father alone."

Avigail pursed her lips as she studied Rakel's head, white-haired and bent over a noble labor. "There is no cure for the falling sickness, Leah. Everyone knows that. Your father will work things out with Jotham. It is not for you to think about. No more questions."

"But Grandmother—"

"Quickly say a prayer and do as I say, child. I forbid you to pester your aunt about the past. It is unkind to make her suffer through painful memories. No more questions, do you understand? Invoke Asherah for your impertinence."

As Avigail hurried back to the kitchens to see about dinner, her mind tumbling over the disappointment of no word from her cousin— and now this business of Leah probing Rakel's memories!—she felt a niggling doubt flirt with the edge of her mind. Why had she felt such alarm to learn that Leah was asking questions? Was it truly concern that Rakel might be exposed to painful memories? Perhaps. But there was something else, too . . .

Avigail was dismayed by Aunt Rakel's faltering mind. Where was the strong woman who led them from war-torn Jericho, keeping them together, bartering in villages along the way, telling them stories at night as they camped under the stars, her own grief fresh and searing but keeping it buried for the sake of the others. Without Aunt Rakel we would have not survived . . .

Thinking of the past, going back many years to Jericho and the house where Avigail herself was born, suddenly filled her with a vague, undefined fear. But fear of what? She shook her head. There was too much else to worry about. Jotham and his collection notes. Zira spreading poison among the upper class ladies of Ugarit. Avigail's family in peril. Leah was a good, obedient girl. She would leave her Auntie alone. The past, and whatever it held, would stay in the past.

Leah watched her grandmother go, staring after her in disbelief. She had thought Grandmother would be happy to hear of a possible solution to their problems. Why had she forbidden her to ask Auntie Rakel about the past?

Leah turned to Rakel, who seemed oblivious of the recent exchange. Staring at the white hair shining in the afternoon sunlight, Leah thought: the solution to all our problems lies in that fragile skull. If I could but find a way to reach it.

But Grandmother has now forbidden me and I made a vow to Asherah to always obey . . .

"Leah, dear," Aunt Rakel said. "What were we talking about? Oh yes, the cure for the falling sickness. The medicine calls for the leaves of Moloch's Dream."

Leah stared at her in astonishment. So many times she had asked Rakel about the cure for the falling sickness, and each time the elderly woman had said she didn't remember. Now she did, just when Grandmother had forbidden Leah to engage in any more talk about the past!

But here was the very thing that might solve the family's current crisis. An offering to Zira so priceless that she would do anything in exchange for it.

"Moloch's Dream?" Leah said, wondering if she was committing an act of disobedience. "What is that?"

"A sacred plant that was used long ago by our ancestors when they sacrificed their children on the altar of Moloch. To prevent them from suffering in the fire, the children were given Moloch's Dream, which took their souls from their bodies so that they floated like little angels as they watched their flesh being consumed by fire."

Leah had never heard of it. "Does the plant go by any other name?"

"That is what we called it in Jericho. I do not know what name people know it by here in Ugarit. The plant grows tall with long spiky leaves that sprout from a single, central point."

"If we do not know its name here in Ugarit, how will we find it?"

Rakel's smile widened. "I will know it when I see it. Moloch's Dream resembles common weeds that have no value, and so we look for ourselves. We must go into the city, my dear, and visit the plant market."

Leah's excitement grew. "Aunt Rakel, can you show me how to make medicine from Moloch's Dream?"

"I know the recipe. But we must take care. To use too much of the plant makes the soul travel too far from the body and it cannot come back, leaving the patient trapped in the sleep that is like death." She patted Leah's hand. "Tomorrow we will go into the city and purchase the seeds. And now I wish to take a nap."

Leah's garden, no longer a secret as it was discovered weeks ago by an inquisitive Esther, was greener, with more shrubbery and foliage. She had stolen moments from her household duties to bring seeds and cuttings to the neglected sanctuary, plant and water them. But there was still the old sycamore fig in the center, a gnarly dead tree bearing not a single leaf or piece of fruit. Unsalvageable, her father's master gardener had said. Leah had asked him for advice. "Cut it down and pull out the stump," was his reply.

It was peaceful here, out of the way of household traffic, where slaves bustled to and fro, with Elias receiving important visitors, Grandmother arguing with her son, worried about her home and family. Here, within these old walls, Leah could spend time alone with her thoughts.

What should I do? she wondered now as she sat on the bench beneath the old tree. To obey or disobey her grandmother. The cure for the falling sickness would rescue the family, but in order to find the cure I must disobey Grandmother and therefore break my vow to Asherah!

"Great Goddess Asherah, Strength-of-All-Things," Leah whispered, lifting her hands to her face, covering her eyes in reverence, "please tell me what to do. My family is in trouble. My sister Tamar is filled with bitterness and anger because of me. She no longer speaks of Baruch, the boy she loves, because he was sent to Ebla to get married, and she blames me. Father is in danger of losing his vineyards and his reputation because of me. And Grandmother is losing friends because of Zira—because of me! This is all my fault and so it should be my responsibility to set things right again. If I continue to pursue the search for the falling sickness cure from Auntie Rakel, we can make peace with Zira and her brother. But to do that I must defy my grandmother, and it was my defiance that caused all this trouble to begin with! Blessed Mother of All, what am I meant to do? Which road should I take? Please, Asherah, send me a sign."

With her hands still covering her face, Leah listened. She heard sparrows in nearby trees, and the voices of slaves in the animal pens, the rumble of wagon wheels as a dray headed into the vineyard. But there was no whispered message from Asherah.

Drawing her hands away, Leah searched the garden for a sign. She scanned the summer flowers where bees buzzed. She searched the mulberry bushes that she had planted and had yet to bear fruit. Seedlings and saplings full of promise. The patch of clover which Daveed had noticed that day he had accidentally stumbled upon this garden.

Daveed . . .

Halla! Her mind was wandering! How could Asherah take her prayer seriously if she entertained thoughts of the young man she had fallen in love with. She should not be thinking about him.

But do not forget, her conscience argued, it was Daveed who gave you the idea of appeasing Jotham through Zira!

"Blessed Asherah," murmured Leah who, until a year ago, had thought only of motherhood and being a good wife. She was unused to complex thinking and decision-making. Issues dealing with ethics and morals and consequences were the province of men, not a girl whose brain should be taxed by no greater problem than which veil to wear with which dress!

Her shoulders slumped. There was no sign from Asherah. Leah was no closer to solving her problem—

She froze. Her eye caught something she had not noticed before. In the dry soil that surrounded the crumbling trunk of the dead sycamore fig something green shone in the afternoon sun.

Leah blinked, leaned forward on the bench, stared.

There, in the barren dirt, in a place where Leah had planted no seeds or cuttings, a young green shoot struggled toward the sky. The seedling had broad green leaves with jagged edges, three and four lobes per leaf. Leah recognized them as belonging to a sycamore fig, and she realized in surprise that this must be the "daughter" of the dead tree. Had the seed lain dormant all these years, waiting to be wakened with water? For Leah realized now that water which she had carried in to nourish her other plants had spilled from the pot and moistened this neglected ground.

She smiled, thinking of the miracle of nature, how she had toiled to bring life to this forgotten garden and all the while, life was occurring anyway! She would tend the little seedling, water it, keep weeds and insects away, nurture it until, one day, she would pluck the first sweet, red figs from its branches. And the old dead tree would continue to live on, in its "daughter."

And then Leah saw how close the fragile green shoot was to the mother tree, protected from too much sun, wind and rain, yet allowed just enough sunlight and water to flourish. And she thought: it is a sign from Asherah.

The goddess is telling me that just as the old tree continues on in the seedling, so it is with people, the older generation teaching the new. Was that not what Grandmother had said so many times over the years? "We fled Jericho with only the clothes we stood in. But in our hearts and minds we carried the memories and knowledge passed down to us from generations before us."

Yes, she thought in rising excitement. The Goddess wishes me to receive Rakel's memories and wisdom. I will go about it in a way that does not upset Grandmother. I will find other paths into my aunt's mind. But first I will take Aunt Rakel into the marketplace, we will purchase the seeds of Moloch's Dream, I will bring them back here, plant them, cultivate them, and when the harvest time comes, I will ask Aunt Rakel to show me how to make the medicine that cures the falling sickness.

A gift for Zira. Our family fortune will be secure again. And then

Daveed and I—

"Leah!" Esther burst into the garden, her deformed face shining with joy. "Come quickly! Praise the gods! The cousin from Damaska has arrived! Your husband, Leah!"

D aveed had not come to Ugarit expecting to fall in love, and yet the fact of it was there, as inescapable as the blue summer sky. He had not slept the night before, after Leah left the roof. He had remained up there under the stars pondering the mysteries of a world where a man was certain of his destiny, of his priorities, of knowing himself so thoroughly that he expected no surprises in life.

And in the next instant, everything was turned upside down.

As he returned to the House of Elias on the southern road, he felt a spring in his step, as he thought: Leah is in there. The mere thought of her filled him with sweet excitement. He could not wait for dinner that evening, when Elias and his grandmother, and occasionally his wife, Hannah, exchanged gossip heard during the day, or discussed a new plan for thwarting Jotham's vindictive attack, or maybe merely talked about this year's vintage, how the long summer days without the usual fog off the sea was going to mean sweeter wine. And while this went on, with Nobu in the corner on his stool, drinking too much wine and muttering replies to his god-voices, and Esther and Tamar talking about a girl on the next property getting married to a cousin from out of town—as the family engaged itself in the usual mealtime banter, Daveed and Leah would look at each other across the table and share their secret.

There was no rule in the Brotherhood against a scribe getting married. Even the Rab himself was allowed a wife, and sometimes it was even encouraged, for a wife, it was believed, kept a man honorable. Daveed had never given thought to marriage, being so preoccupied with learning his profession, but now that he could think of nothing else but sweet Leah, he thought about being a husband and decided he liked the idea.

Getting to that point, however, was going to be a challenge. He could not ask her to marry him if he was a penniless scribe with no credentials. He would settle for nothing less than being a member of the Brotherhood, for that was prestigious. Unfortunately he had spent the morning in the city, trying to find someone to sponsor him but doors closed in his face when, in response to, "Who is your patron?" he replied, "Elias the vintner." How to get around the growing web of maliciousness Jotham was spinning against his sworn enemy?

Daveed walked along the main road beneath a warm summer sun. It was a busy road, going south, snaking parallel to the coastline down from Ugarit to cities such as Jericho and Megiddo, following a river that ended, ultimately, in a dead sea. An important highway for travel and trade, a lifeline that, it was said, would be the route that Egypt would take, should she ever decide to invade. For this reason, Ugarit's strongest walls, with guarded towers, faced south. Though Egypt lay a thousand miles away, the threat hovered always in the minds of Canaanites.

Two months ago, Daveed had gone to the Brotherhood to register his name, and to see if there was a way he could achieve membership without the help of Shemuel. But he had been told that a sponsor was required, there was no other way. Daveed had then sought the house of his uncle's brother-in-law, Manthus, only to discover that the trader in gems had gone on an extended trip to Goshen where it was rumored emeralds had been found.

But now, two months later, he had yet to come up with another plan. And now he had an even more important reason to join the Brotherhood—to be worthy of asking Leah to be his wife.

A slave came down the path to meet him. "Master Elias is asking for you," the slave said. "It is urgent."

Hannah emerged from her purifying bath, which signaled the end of her monthly sequestration. But the thought of rejoining the family and resuming her life did not fill her with the usual happiness. Another moon cycle, another disappointment. Little time was left to her, she knew, to give her husband a son. And no word from Damaska. No husbands for her daughters.

Hannah had asked Avigail if she could write to her sister in the north, for there were men aplenty on that side of the family. But Avigail had dismissed the idea. Hannah did not come from an impressive bloodline, and her people were common date growers with little money. Avigail would draw only from her own side of the family, which was connected, three generations back, to a beloved King Ozzediah. Hannah did not deny that her mother-in-law had an impressive pedigree, but under these desperate circumstances, could they afford to be choosy?

Unfortunately, in this instance, Elias sided with his mother. While he could not resist his wife's requests in other matters, on the subject of finding husbands for his daughters, Elias remained firmly under his mother's thumb.

"Mama!" Esther came running in. "Mama! A cousin has arrived from Damaska! A husband for Leah!"

In the hospitality hall, the fugitive from Sidon, garbed in robes stolen from Caleb of Damaska, a man he had murdered, was seated in the chair of honor while a slave washed his feet. The head of the house, Elias, was saying effusively, "Shalaam, and welcome to the family, my son!"

"Blessings of the gods," the false Caleb said with a generous smile. The villa was bigger than he had imagined. Spacious and sumptuous. From the road, he had seen vineyards lying like thick green carpets on the mountain slopes, a seeming army of slaves tending the ripening fruit. And now he was being treated like a king. The fugitive from Sidon could not believe his good fortune.

An older woman came forward next, plump and brown-haired, handsomely dressed with gold and silver rings festooned across her forehead. He deduced she was the matriarch the drunken Caleb had spoken about, named Avigail. "Shalaam, Caleb," she said, "The gods are with us. I trust your journey was uneventful. Tell me, how is my cousin?"

The fugitive dipped into the well of information he had gleaned the night before and said, "She sends greetings, Em Elias. Her gout is easing and her husband's date farm prospers."

Avigail beamed with happiness. "Please call me Grandmother, for that is who I soon will be."

She clapped her hands, gold bracelets jingling on her wrists, and slaves appeared with platters. Set out on a low table before the guest of honor, was a feast that made his eyes widen and his mouth water: fried ham steaks, warm bread smothered in honey, baked fish smelling of garlic and thyme, chickpeas and lentils stewed in oil, off-season pomegranate as good as fresh. All accompanied by generous goblets of sweet wine.

Tomorrow, Avigail thought with excitement, she would treat their new family member to Ugarit's favorite dish: blood sausage. And in his honor, Avigail herself would prepare it from her own personal recipe. She would dice the pork fat, mix it with pig's blood, onions and spices, and stuff the mixture into lengths of cut intestine, sealing the ends and boiling the sausages over a carefully tended fire. She would not leave the task to slaves, who might overboil and use too little onion.

"Please," she said. "Pay honor to the gods by enjoying our humble feast."

Caleb helped himself, scooping compote of pear, apples, and toasted sesame seeds into his mouth, loudly proclaiming to Avigail that her kitchen must be the finest in all of Ugarit. Though of rough upbringing, the man who thought of himself as a chameleon had learned the ways of the upper class, had taught himself manners and etiquette and how to ingratiate himself with the noblest of families.

He saw by the look exchanged between Avigail and Elias that they were well pleased with their cousin from Damaska.

While he munched and swallowed, three girls came into the hall, modest creatures holding veils to their faces, momentarily distract-ing him from the meal as he wondered which was his bride. Each was introduced to the honored guest, and they lowered their veils to softly welcome Caleb into the family. The youngest was certainly not his wife-to-be, with that lip cut in two. The one with fire in her eyes and a boldness to her look? And then he saw the tall one, clearly the oldest. He blinked. This was the girl the family had to buy a husband for? What was wrong with her? Some hidden defect, he decided. Or a sharp tongue. Disobedient perhaps. Well, he would correct those faults in short order.

A middle-aged woman entered the hall, greeting him, and bring-ing with her the scent of a recent bath. By her resemblance to the girls, he decided she must be the mother, named Hannah. Immediately behind her, a young man with dark looks and a prideful gait strode into the hall, followed by a slave who walked with his head thrust forward. Judging by the box that hung by a strap from the slave's shoulder, the young man was the family scribe.

"Ah, here is Daveed," Elias said. "Please do not take offense, cousin, this is but a mere formality. You understand."

Caleb nodded graciously. The scribe would be called upon to verify his identity and pedigree by examining a special tablet all men of means and commerce carried. The tablet listed his name, his father's and grandfather's names, his place of residence, profession, whether he was freeborn or emancipated, and place of birth, finishing with his own seal impressed into the clay while it was still damp. Daveed examined the tablet, recognized the royal seal of Damaska, and then compared the man's personal seal with the large obsidian ring on his right hand.

"All is in order, sir," he said to Elias, who handed the tablet back to Caleb.

While Elias called for wine to be served to everyone, and he proceeded to declare that this was the day of an official betrothal, Daveed took a seat and prepared himself to record whatever Elias dictated. He tried not to look across the room at Leah. His disappointment would show in his eyes. The asked-for husband had arrived. And Daveed thought this was the darkest day of his life. He saw how Leah sat with her hands modestly in her lap, studying the newcomer named Caleb from beneath her lashes. Daveed saw uncertainty in her eyes, and perhaps a little fear. He bitterly chided himself for a fool, for entertaining a fantasy that was written only on the wind. Leah was going into this man's care, to be forever beyond his reach.

Remembering his duties, he summoned professional detachment and brought the figurine of Shubat out of its case and placed it by his side. Though his heart was heavy, he murmured a prayer, selected a moist lump of clay and readied the stylus over it.

Sitting behind his master, Nobu's deeply wrinkled forehead grew even more wrinkled as he eyed the newcomer. Head thrust forward turtlelike, heavy lids blinking, Nobu thought: The man's clothes don't fit.

They look as if tailored for a smaller man. The hem of his tunic doesn't reach his knees. See how taut the fabric is across his back and shoulders. He wears rings only on his pinky fingers. The gold circlet seems to ride too high on his head. And there is something shifty about his deep-set eyes that flick this way and that.

"I do not trust him," Nobu muttered and, realizing he had spoken out loud, quickly drank some wine to silence the god-voice. He looked around. Thankfully, with everyone talking, no one had heard.

Aunt Rakel entered the hall at that moment, her face brightening at the sight of their visitor. "Yacov!" she said, and came forward with her hands out.

Avigail gave her aunt a worried look and was sharply reminded of Leah's desire to probe that venerable mind. Avigail did not want Leah stirring up Rakel's memories, and even though she trusted Leah to obey her order not to ask Rakel about the past, Avigail thought it best to have a plan. An idea came to her.

"Elias, my son, I think we should not wait a long time for the wedding. After all, Leah will soon be twenty years old. And we have Tamar to think of. A month from today would be best."

"A month!" Hannah blurted. "Mother, such a short betrothal?"

"A summer wedding," Avigail said with a decisive nod, "it is just what this family needs, after a year of sorrow. Girls," she said as she turned to her granddaughters. "We shall devote all our time to making Leah's wedding clothes. We will not be idle for a moment." No time to sit and probe Rakel's mind, no time to pull unwanted memories from the past where some things were best left buried.

"And now let us formally record the betrothal." She turned to Daveed. "Are you ready?"

"I am ready, Em Elias."

Elias gestured to Caleb and to Leah, holding out his hands and inviting them to come and stand before him.

Avigail and Hannah watched with happy smiles as the couple took their places, while Esther giggled behind her hand and Rakel nodded in satisfaction, pleased that her son Yacov was marrying at last.

Only one member of the family was not happy.

Tamar twisted her fingers until they were bloodless. She had never had a chance to experiment with her new woman-power and seduce Baruch back into her arms. His father had sent him from Ugarit in haste, so that Tamar had been left only with Baruch's words in her ears—that she possessed a power over men.

She had briefly considered seducing Daveed, but had ultimately decided he was just a family servant and Tamar wished to set her sights higher. Now she settled her black-lashed eyes on the newcomer in the room: Caleb of Damaska who was tall and smiled easily and wore expensive robes, with gold rings on his fingers.

She saw how her grandmother and father and mother were pleased with him, how they drank in his words of flattery, and were won over by his charming manner. So Leah was to marry such a fine man, while her disobedience a year ago had robbed Tamar of her beloved Baruch. She had hated Leah since, and now, on this momentous afternoon, a delicious new thought blossomed in Tamar's calculating mind: she would experiment with her newly found woman-power on this charming Damaskan, and at the same time punish her sister for what she had done.

Unaware of her sister's gleeful, poisonous thoughts, unaware also of the suspicions of Daveed's slave, of her grandmother's worry that only one husband had been sent, of her mother's silent prayer that a son comes from this union within a year—unaware of the disastrous contract she was entering into, Leah thought only of the fact that with this large and imposing man, obviously rich and of strong character, to stand and help Elias defend family and home, there was hope at last in their fight with Jotham.

Her heart was weeping at the thought of losing Daveed, but she swallowed back her pain as she told herself it had been but a foolish dream. She was glad now she had not told Daveed she loved him, glad he had not said the same words to her, for now she could put the handsome scribe behind her, let him finish his apprenticeship and move to the House of Gold, and she would do her best to forget him and her girlish love for him.

And now she could dedicate herself to growing and cultivating the cure for the falling sickness, for marriage would bestow on her a new freedom which she knew Grandmother Avigail would honor. As Isha Caleb, Leah would have the independence to go into the city without permission. She would be free to search for Moloch's Dream.

At her side, repeating vows of betrothal that Elias pronounced, promising to stand in this same place thirty days hence, beneath the marriage canopy and take this girl to wife, the fugitive from Sidon—liar, murderer, thief, rapist—marveled anew at his incredible luck and found himself, for the first time in his hard, lonely life, looking forward to his wedding day. After that, as Elias's legal son-in-law,

"Caleb" was going to ingratiate himself into the family and see to it that he reaped many rewards with his false charm.

And should the day come when the Blue Devils possessed him again, Elias and his family, like the farmer and his womenfolk outside Sidon, would provide enough squeals to satisfy even the hungriest of them.

CHAPTER FIVE

Jotham held the copper mirror between his legs and bent over to see the reflection of his testicles.

Were they shrinking?

With his free hand he explored himself, and wondered if it was only his imagination that his genitals were getting smaller.

Whispering a curse, Jotham picked up another mirror so that he held one in each hand. He twisted his fat body this way and that as he maneuvered one mirror over the crown of his head, the other catching the reflection. There!

He whispered another curse. The bald spot was growing.

Immediately Elias the vintner came to mind. Jotham and he were the same age, yet Elias possessed a solid, trim physique, a stride that did not render him breathless and, worst of all, a thick head of hair. At nearly forty, Elias wasn't even graying yet while Jotham sported two white wings at his temples. Reminders of his own diminishing virility while Elias, who used to be his friend, was still in full bloom of manhood.

Thinking that he would bet Elias's testicles were not shrinking, Jotham's vitriol grew.

Not only was his enemy a finer specimen of man, Elias had not capitulated to Jotham's attempts to ruin him. On top of that, Avigail had succeeded in finding a husband for Leah! A man of means from Damaska. A big man, too, from what Jotham's informants told him. And once the girl was married, Jotham could no longer have her.

Surely there was a way to prevent the wedding from taking place.

He not only still lusted after Leah, he also wanted her more than ever now that she was betrothed. It reminded him of the creation myth in which El, the supreme god and father of all humankind, created two humans in a garden paradise. They were to avail themselves of everything in the garden except for a tree that bore fruit reserved for the gods. Leah is that fruit, Jotham thought. Plump, ripe, luscious. Forbidden. The more he thought about her that way, the more he hungered for her.

Setting the mirrors aside, he signaled to his manservant, who brought Jotham's loincloth and robes and helped him to dress. As the valet was oiling his master's beard, the house steward appeared, to announce the arrival of a visitor. It was a man Jotham had been expecting.

He received the visitor in the hospitality hall and, after an exchange of the usual amenities involving peace and health and an invocation of the gods, Jotham said, "I need to know everything there is about this man Caleb." The visitor was a trusted man who had spied on people for Jotham in the past. "Find men from Damaska who live here in Ugarit, and find also those who are visiting. Ask around. Caleb dealt in textiles. Someone must know of him."

"Yes, my lord," said the agent, a tall, lanky man with sallow skin and drooped shoulders. "I will go to the caravanserais and make discreet inquiries about any traders and travelers who have come recently from Damaska. I will also find those who live in town. My many informants are very knowledgeable about the comings and goings of Ugarit's citizens."

"It is said that Caleb is also a widower. Find out what you can about his wife and her family. Find out his connection to Avigail, the mother of Elias the vintner. Above all, find a weakness. I must not let this man speak marriage vows."

"I shall be the wind and the night, my Lord. With the blessings of Dagon, I shall fill your wishes before three days are done." He grinned. "Every man has a secret. You will know Caleb's, I promise."

Jotham grunted and dismissed him. He both trusted and hated

the unctuous fellow, and never asked how he came by his information. The man had yet to bring erroneous information, and so Jotham knew that whatever he brought back about Caleb of Damaska, would be accurate.

Jotham reached for a sweet raisin tart and, looking out at his precious harbor where his ships loaded and unloaded cargo, smiled at the thought of striding into Elias's hospitality hall, interrupting the marriage ceremony and revealing the dirty secrets of the man who was almost Elias's son-in-law.

I hear that Egypt is requesting more tribute from the cities of Canaan," Hadar, wife of a wealthy dye merchant, said.

She and Zira were playing the popular game of Fifty-Five Holes. The board was round, made of ivory, and inlaid with gold and lapis lazuli. The pegs were made of polished ivory, as were the carved casting-sticks that determined a player's moves. Hadar was middle-aged with plump hands, and when she threw the sticks, the many gold bangles on her chubby wrists sounded like rattling swords.

"Requesting!" Zira said sharply as she threw the sticks and moved her peg five holes. "Demanding, you mean. Queen Hatshepsut calls it peaceful diplomacy and our cowardly King Shalaaman is capitulating. I do not care what the people say of our king, how much they adore him and sing his praises. We need a stronger ruler. When my Yehuda is King of Ugarit—and I know I can count on you and your husband when the time comes for the royal election—"

Hadar dipped her head.

"My Yehuda would not show such cowardice in the face of the Egyptians."

Hadar traced a protective sign in the air. "May the gods preserve us from that filthy race. They never bathe, you know, and it is said that Egyptian men urinate in the streets which Canaanite men never do."

"Like dogs," Zira said.

"Dogs indeed. My husband in his trade in purple dyes must perforce deal with local Egyptian exporters, and when he comes home each day he says he feels soiled." Hadar's husband held the monopoly in extracting rare purple dye from the murex shells found in local waters, and thus was a wealthy and powerful man. His wife was Zira's good friend and staunch supporter in local politics.

Zira cast the sticks, read the engraved numbers, and moved her peg on the game board. They were taking their leisure in Hadar's villa in the hills, where cool breezes kept the summer heat away. Despite the long days and high temperatures, Zira wore her habitual black veil and black dress, even though her husband had gone to the gods long ago.

"Speaking of distasteful things," Hadar said with measured speech. "I received a wedding invitation from the House of Elias." She said nothing further as she watched for Zira's reaction to this piece of information.

The two friends were snacking on crispy meringue biscuits filled with a sweet almond paste. Zira placed one between her prominent teeth that made people think of a donkey and bit down delicately. Munched, swallowed, took a sip of wine, and said, "That family has caused my poor brother endless grief. Can you imagine? Offering a daughter in marriage, and then backing out? After allowing the girl to show us disrespect, that is, and after not making the girl apologize."

"Insult upon insult," Hadar murmured. "What is society coming to when headstrong girls are allowed their own minds?"

Zira tipped her narrow, fleshless chin. "Asherah knows that Avigail herself should have at least apologized to me. Never mind what goes on between men. It was Avigail's obligation to seek me out and, in the company of other women, say to my face that she was sorry for the offense caused that night. Does she not realize whom she is dealing with?"

Zira was proud to be addressed as Em Yehuda, was even prouder that her son was next in line to be the Rab of the Brotherhood of Scribes. Had not the last two kings made their way to the throne through the Brotherhood? King Yehuda of Ugarit. She liked the sound of it.

Her face suddenly darkened. Last night, waking to the sound of her son's keening cry.

As a member of the Brotherhood, Yehuda was not restricted to the scribes' dormitory but was permitted to live anywhere he wished, and no one blamed him for wanting to live with his uncle, whose villa overlooking the sea was one of the finest residences in Ugarit. Last night, Zira had run to his room to find him on the floor, arms and legs flailing, spittle flying from his mouth. A slave specially trained in the care of such an affliction was kneeling at Yehuda's side, making sure he did not bite off his tongue or hurt himself. It broke Zira's heart to see her only child in the grip of such a seizure. Yehuda was thirty years old, tall, and in good health otherwise. But when the falling sickness came over him, he was as helpless as an infant, soiling himself, unable to control his limbs. And when the seizures passed, he slipped into a deep sleep from which nothing could wake him.

It is not fair! Zira wanted to cry. My son is noble and good. He should sit upon the throne of Ugarit. Why has he been cursed with this terrible disease? But she said nothing out loud, keeping her thin lips pursed over buckteeth as she watched Hadar move pegs on the game board. Zira worked hard to cultivate Yehuda's public image to make him a favorable choice among the voting families of Ugarit, reminding them that it would be advantageous to have a king who could read and write, a skill not even the well-loved Shalaaman possessed.

Picking up the casting-sticks, Zira said, "Of course, anyone who attends the wedding at the House of Elias will no longer be a friend of mine."

"Of course," said her friend who, although fond of Elias and Avigail, was more afraid of Zira and her brother.

They were in the women's quarters, the three ladies and three girls of the house, plus slave girls and female servants, all industrious and busy, creating Leah's wedding clothes. They had only fourteen days in which to complete an entire wardrobe.

As Rakel embroidered, she said to no one in particular, "To protect your garden from snails set out saucers of beer. The snails will go for the beer and drown."

The others paid no heed, but Leah listened and tucked the piece of information away for later experimentation. Holding to her vow of obedience, Leah was careful not to ask Aunt Rakel questions, but merely took the elderly woman to the marketplace to peruse the many medicinal offerings and see if she recognized Moloch's Dream. So far she had not. But in the meantime Leah had gleaned interesting and possibly valuable information ("Chicory mixed with rose oil and vinegar relieves headaches"), which she committed to memory each night as she lay in bed, whispering the formulas like prayers, over and over until they were firmly etched in her mind. When her garden was grown, she planned to harvest ingredients and make medicinal concoctions for the family.

"This is tedious work," Tamar said suddenly, complaining of an aching back. When masculine laughter drifted in on the breeze, she added, incongruously, "Caleb is too loud. I do not like him."

"Quickly say a prayer," Hannah said to her middle daughter. "It is bad luck to say such things about another's husband. You should be happy for Leah. And Caleb will soon be your brother. Invoke the gods, child, and show respect."

Tamar rolled her eyes and returned to her sewing.

Leah wished her sister took more kindly to Caleb, the way the rest of the family had. He not only laughed loudly and often, he possessed an affable, outgoing personality that made him a great ally for her father. Elias was pleased with how eager Caleb was to learn the wine business, and the interest and concern he expressed in their troubled finances. They all hoped that Caleb's involvement was a sign that he was not planning to take her back to Damaska and live with his family. As her husband, it was his right, and nothing in the marriage contract could forbid it.

"It is only envy," Grandmother Avigail had assured Leah more than once. "Tamar will come around when she has a husband of her own."

But when would that be? Leah thought as she worked on the embroidery of her nightgown—the one she would wear on her wedding night. Grandmother had set the date so soon after the betrothal that there was not much time to put together her wardrobe.

A slave entered and said to Avigail, "A message has arrived for the master." He was holding a clay tablet.

Avigail frowned. Blessed Asherah, do not let it be another declined wedding invitation! What if there were no guests at all? Not even Caleb's kin in Damaska were going to attend, for he had told Avigail that he had written to them, announcing the wedding, to be told that there was sickness in the family, and they had fallen on hard times. So no one from his family was coming. "Elias is in the city, and this message might be urgent. I will take the message to Daveed at once. I need to know what it says."

But Leah quickly set her sewing aside and said, "I will go, Grandmother. The day is much too hot for you."

She had heard Daveed inform her father that, should he be needed, he would be on the roof over the northern side of the house, working on a personal matter. As Leah hurried up a flight of stone steps, her heart raced with anticipation of being in Daveed's presence again. She knew it was wrong to think of him that way but she had no control over her wayward heart. She had been able to keep her feelings for him a secret, and once she was married, Leah was certain, and must focus on her new husband, her love for Daveed would fade away.

The sun stood at its zenith, beating down on the rooftops of Ugarit. The summer heat was oppressive, but necessary for the baking of clay tablets, and so Daveed had stripped off his cloak and tunic and toiled in the afternoon sunlight in just a loincloth and sandals.

Watching over the labor was Shubat, sitting on a low wall where Daveed had reverently placed the dark green statuette of the seated god.

This was Daveed's personal project: his pledge-notes, lovingly crafted and inscribed according to tradition and that he intended to take around to the upper-class citizens of Ugarit. The idea had come to him the day Caleb of Damaska arrived. When Daveed had authenticated the man's identity tablet, Daveed had recalled the pledge-notes that were ubiquitous in the world of trade and commerce, and among men of means and standing. He had made thirty, each as long as a finger and three fingers wide, all bearing the same message in cuneiform: "The Royal Family of Lagash owes the bearer of this tablet a favor. It will be honored." Daveed had sealed each with his signet ring, impressing the clay with the royal crest of Lagash—the two winged angels which businessmen everywhere would recognize. The buying and selling of favors was a common way of conducting business and creating connections, and Daveed's pledges in particular were valuable, for being owed a favor by a royal family was a precious commodity.

The favors could be sold, for instance, to caravaneers traveling east who would pay a good price for them. And he knew that, even though he and his father the King were estranged, his father would nonetheless honor them.

Daveed planned to use the pledges in his pursuit of a sponsor into the Brotherhood. And if the offer of one pledge-note didn't suffice, because of Jotham's threats, Daveed could offer two or three, making the prize something a man could not refuse.

Daveed would begin to make the rounds immediately among the wealthy and influential families of Ugarit, presenting himself to them, explaining his circumstance and offering royal favors in return for assistance. Someone, in all of Ugarit, was bound to help!

He frowned. What if these were not enough? What if the stigma of being Elias's scribe were too much even for these valuable tablets? What would he do at the end of a year if he was unsuccessful?

I will be like a priest who has disappointed his god. I cannot let it happen. By Shubat, I will find a way into the Brotherhood.

Hearing a sound, he turned and saw Leah standing in the sunlight, her white dress and white veil shimmering in the afternoon heat. She was staring at him, her lips parted. She held something in her hand.

The familiar ache of desire came flooding back. Every time he saw her, heard her voice, caught the sound of her laughter. He had thought he could simply by force of will divest himself of feelings for her, but instead they had grown. The thought of her being possessed by Caleb made Daveed's blood boil, and it made him desire her all the more. "Can I be of service?" he asked. To distance himself from her, now that she was betrothed to another man, Daveed made a point of being archly polite with her.

On this rooftop hugging the foothills of towering green mountains, breezes swirled as if they were spirits. Daveed watched as the mischievous wind tugged at Leah's veil, as if daring her to reveal her hair. He wanted to see that hair, to touch it, inhale its fragrance.

"This came," she said, showing him the tablet. "The messenger said it was urgent, and my father is not home . . ."

"I will read it," he said, holding out his hand.

She came forward, like a timid deer he thought, and when she placed the square of hard clay in his palm, it struck him that she was placing herself in there as well. He looked at her for a moment longer, aware of the sky that embraced them, that he and Leah towered over the distant city, that the world lay beneath them so that they might be gods, and so great a flood of conflicting emotions washed over him that he could not, for the moment, speak.

Then, forcing himself to look down at the tablet, he read the signature, recognizing it as belonging to a wealthy importer of African and Indian ivory, and then he read the text.

As she waited, Leah felt the heat of the afternoon penetrate her clothing. Baking her skin. Setting it on fire. Daveed's torso glistened with sweat. His arms, sculpted with muscles, shone in the sun. Once again it struck her that he did not have the body of a scribe but of a man who toiled at hard labors, a man who built chariots and bridges instead of pressing sticks into wet clay. The hot air seemed difficult to take in, she could not breathe, had to force her lungs to draw in air. Why was it so hard to breathe?

When he lifted his head, and dark eyes met hers in the golden sun, she felt a strange stab in her belly. Followed by a sweet ache. She knew it was desire. She knew it was forbidden. She tried hard not to love this man.

"He sends regrets," Daveed said. "The ivory merchant and his wife cannot attend your wedding." When Daveed saw the disappointment in her eyes, the pain that now filled them, he added, "I am sorry." Like Leah, like everyone else in the family, he wondered if even a single soul was going to be in attendance.

Daveed felt a sudden impulse to take her into his arms, to comfort her, to protect her from a cruel world. He was in love with her. A girl who was to be wed in fourteen days.

"Thank you," she said. "I will tell Grandmother." The guest list grew shorter each day.

But she could not move. Did not want to. Wished to stay in Daveed's calming presence for the rest of her life. She looked down at the tablets growing hard in the sun. She knew what they were. Her father also used pledge-notes, although lately they seemed to have little value.

"I will use them as a way to find a sponsor into the Brotherhood," Daveed said. "They are favors from the royal house of Lagash. Someone will appreciate their value enough to help me."

"Yes," she whispered, struggling for breath. The heat of the day, Daveed glowing like a god in the sun, and another declined invitation . . .

He watched her. She seemed unable to move, lost, as if the heat and this tablet from the ivory importer had sapped all mind and reason from her. His heart went out to her. But he suppressed his desire. She was intended for another man, and he was destined to be the Rab of the Brotherhood.

"I wish I could read," Leah said suddenly. "It must be a wonderful thing, to look at symbols and know their meaning."

He had never given any thought to women other than someone to bear sons and be dutiful to a husband. Women and their world were a mystery to him. He never wondered what they were thinking, what they talked about, what their opinions were. Until now. Leah had awakened a curiosity in him—he found himself wondering about her hopes and dreams, if she had ambitions, if she was happy even. For the first time it occurred to him that women might possess a mind.

"When I was a boy," he said, wanting her to understand his passion. Although he and Leah could never be more intimate than this, at least she would glimpse this part of his soul. "I chafed at my lessons. I did not wish to be a scribe. Other boys were playing, fishing, but I was a prince of the royal house and destined to become an educated man, and so I could not play, I had to keep at my clay tablets. The symbols meant nothing to me. I copied from master texts, I pressed my stylus this way and that as our teachers demonstrated. But there was no meaning in it for me. They were simply decorative wedge-shapes on clay. Every day I complained to my father until one afternoon he took me out in his chariot to the Stele of the Vultures, a boundary stone beyond the city, and he told me to look at it. I was bored. I watched a hawk fly overhead. I dug my toes into the sand. But my father was not going to leave until I had given the stele my full attention. So I finally did. I was hungry. I wanted to go home. He told me to tell him what it said. I couldn't. The marks in the stone meant nothing . . . And then suddenly! It all came together!" Daveed spoke rapidly now, smiling, gesturing, eyes filled with wonder. His excitement was contagious. Leah smiled, as if she had just understood a written symbol.

"I was reading words inscribed by men long dead and gone to dust. They were speaking to me! Thus was my passion born. And a new faith in the gods, for I learned on that afternoon with my father that words are sacred. They are not simply sounds a man makes, meaningless utterances formed by lips and tongue. Words are born in the heart. They are the poetry of the soul. What a man says, Leah—it is a part of himself and he is giving it away. Like a piece of his heart, a portion of his soul. I would never treat words lightly, or sully them, or betray them to another man if spoken in confidence. Confidentiality of another man's words are my sacred trust."

He paused to smile at her, and to marvel as this unexpected outpouring of his faith to a girl he hardly knew. Yet the way she watched him, as if mesmerized by what he was saying, taking in his words, holding them close, made him want to say more—so much more, to take her into his arms and somehow make her feel how he felt, and he thought, yes, it is a shame that she was never taught to read and write, for he knew his own life would be nothing without words.

"On that same afternoon I felt deep inside," Daveed added softly, tapping his glistening chest, "a calling. I cannot describe how I knew, but I left the Stele of the Vultures that day knowing that Shubat had singled me out for a great task. I believe that call is to the Brotherhood of Scribes here in Ugarit, and to someday rise to the position of Rab."

"I have never heard of Shubat," she said, wishing he would go on and on, tell her all the stories of his boyhood, fill her head with visions of his city, the palace, his parents. She was hungry to know everything there was to know about this prince.

He bent to test one of the clay pledge-notes, Leah's eyes riveted to the movements of sinew and muscle beneath his taut skin. "Before the Great Flood that destroyed mankind," he said, "people did not know how to read and write. They knew nothing of symbols and tablets, ink and papyrus. No man had drawn a single hieroglyph or pressed a wedge-shaped stylus into clay. The gods reasoned that this was why people had fallen away from the laws, why they had become sinful and unruly, and why they had to be destroyed and the world made new. A few men survived in a giant ark, and when the waters receded and the ark came to rest on a mountain, the gods conferred among themselves and decided to send one of their own down to earth to teach men the skill of written communication so that their laws would be inscribed in stone and they would never again fall from grace."

He pointed to the statuette. "Shubat was elected. He came to Earth and took the form of a mortal man. He walked the land, choosing good and honest men to be his students. When they had learned all the symbols and characters and hieroglyphs, and were skilled in the art of painting and inscribing them, he shed his mortal guise and returned to the land of the gods. Before he left, however, Shubat gave a special gift to each of the thirteen scribes: a secret symbol by which they would recognize one another as they went out into the world to teach men how to write. But down through the centuries, the secret symbol became lost. We are a fragmented and scattered brotherhood and cannot be reunited until we find that symbol."

"Perhaps you should create a new one."

He gave her a startled look. "That would be arrogant, for that is the privilege of Shubat." Yet even as he said this, Leah saw interest spark in his eyes.

"I must go," she said reluctantly. "Grandmother will be wondering."

"Wait," he said, not knowing why he had said it only knowing he wished her to tarry just a while longer. "How is your garden?" He had not been back since he had stumbled into the neglected corner of the villa three months ago.

She smiled. He had shared something personal with her, a part of him that was important. He wanted something similar in return. It made her heart expand. "I thought the sycamore was dead, but I found a seedling. It grew despite the fact that no one watered it or saw that it had sunlight. I believe it is a sign from Asherah that I pursue a personal goal, despite the fact that Grandmother has forbidden me to do so. I have been tending the seedling and it is thriving, and as I see it become a strong and sturdy sapling, I know Asherah is speaking to me, reassuring me that I am on the correct path. Someday, Daveed of Lagash, my seedling will grow to a large tree and bear sweet fruit. I hope . . . you will still be in Ugarit then, and come and taste our sweet sycamore figs."

Daveed was speechless. She had said so little, and yet so much.

"I really must go," she said, and as she stepped back, pointed to the tablets growing hard in the sun. "I wish you good luck with your pledge-notes, Daveed of Lagash. I have no doubt that there will be men in Ugarit who will be proud to sponsor you into the Brotherhood." She turned away.

"Leah—"

When she turned around, he saw the tears in her eyes. "Oh Daveed," she whispered.

He reached her in two strides. Taking her by her arms, he pulled her to him and kissed her hard on the mouth.

A whimper escaped her throat, and then her arms were around him, she held onto him as the kiss grew long and ardent, as they tasted each other and felt each other's heat. The warmth of the bay beat down on them, the sun bathed them in a hot golden glow, desire flowed from their skin, they reveled in the feel of their bodies.

And then Daveed forced himself to draw back. Tears glistened in his eyes as he said in a tight voice, "I have wrestled with my feelings for you, my dearest Leah, for you are forbidden to me. I should not even be saying these words to you, but I must, as I will never say them again. I love you, Leah Bat Elias, and even after you are Leah Isha Caleb, I will still love you and for the rest of my life. I will always be here for you, whenever you need me, wherever I am, I will answer your call."

Leah sobbed. She wanted to tell him she would not marry Caleb, that she would go away with Daveed and stay with him forever. But as the words came to her lips, she remembered her vow to Asherah, remembered that she sensed that a great test of obedience coming, and her biggest fear was that, unaware that the test was at hand, she would fail. But she was wrong. She recognized the test after all, for here it was . . .

And so she held back words that would doom her and Daveed, and doom her family. She kept her silence, knowing that this was their last chance together. After today, she would belong to another man.

M y son, we cannot afford it."
Elias rarely raised his voice to his mother, but he did so now. "The gods are my witness! The first wedding I give as a father will not be a paltry affair! I will not let Jotham rob me of this. We can be thrifty

with Tamar. But my eldest daughter will be given a wedding all of Ugarit will remember!"

"How can 'all of Ugarit' remember it when most likely no one will even be here? Oh Elias, my son, I wish I could agree with you on this, but the family fortune is shrinking, thanks to the evil Jotham. And you are starting to lose customers as well, men who would prefer to drink sour wine than to cross Jotham."

"My mind is made up, Mother. On this I will not be swayed. My daughter will have the wedding she deserves."

Avigail knew he was doing it more for Hannah than for Leah, and so she knew he would not be swayed. "Very well," she said with a sigh. "After all, there will only be one wedding after this. Esther with her deformed face will never marry. So we can be frugal with Tamar's wedding feast. If we still have a house to hold it in."

D aveed and Nobu arrived at the first house on his list of possible sponsors. Daveed had donned his finest robes of red and blue wool, with golden fringes and a wide leather belt studded with silver. Nobu was more humbly dressed, although his garments were clearly those of an elite slave. He stood beside Daveed with two bags hanging from his shoulders: one contained the statuette of Shubat, the other held the pledge-notes Daveed was going to distribute.

The man who owned this large house in the northern quarter of the city, near the royal palace, was very wealthy, with much influence. His sponsorship would almost guarantee Daveed's admission into the Brotherhood.

As he waited for a steward to come to the gate in answer to the bell, Daveed noticed the seal engraved in the stone gatepost. It identified the resident as a man who manufactured and traded in costly purple dye. Daveed recognized the seal because he had seen it on one of the tablets that had come to Elias's house, declining to accept his wedding invitation.

Daveed was suddenly gripped by a divided heart. These people were shunning Elias, they were causing Leah great pain. It would be disloyal of him to curry this man's favor and patronage. But his name alone would get Daveed enrolled into the Brotherhood.

At his side, with head thrust forward, Nobu muttered responses to his god-voices. What they were saying, Daveed did not know, nor did he care. When he left Lagash four months prior, he had been filled with self-confidence, determination, and a planned future. But now, not only was his future uncertain, he was filled with self-doubt and a divided mind. In truth, coming to this house seeking help made him feel like a traitor to Elias. And to Leah.

They were received by the wife of the house, a plump woman named Hadar who explained that her husband was at his workshops north of the city. Daveed knew of the factory, an odiferous place where slaves toiled over steaming vats and hot fires extracting a rare and costly purple dye from spiny marine shells. The slaves were carefully watched by guards to make sure none of the precious dye was smuggled out. It was a brutal existence, and death came early.

"Shalaam and the blessings of the gods, my lady," he said. "I have come to ask a favor of your husband." He handed her a tablet, which Hadar eyed with interest. Her husband was currently competing with dye manufactures in Tyre and Sidon, who fought to hold onto a monopoly in trade with Lagash. Pledge-notes from this young man, to be honored by no less than the royal family, would give her husband an advantage in that competition.

"What is the favor you seek?" she asked, thinking he might ask for lodgings, or an introduction. Possibly even a position on her husband's staff. All easily granted!

Daveed thought of the Brotherhood, the fine building where the dormitory was housed, the gardens, the fraternity of the brothers, the great library and archives said to hold humankind's most ancient secrets—above all he thought about the chance to serve his god in the highest and most noble way he knew, and suddenly his mind and heart were no longer divided, all self-doubts and uncertainty vanished as he knew beyond a doubt what he must do. He said, "I would like you and your husband to attend a wedding."

Thirteen-year-old Esther ran out to the end of the path to look, once again, for guests arriving from the city. But the road was dark.

Was no one coming to the wedding?

Elias's kitchen slaves had been toiling for two days over a wedding feast that he hoped would be talked about for years to come: green beans in vinegar, boiled turnips with pine nuts, cabbage in sour cream, crab salad, steamed scallops, suckling pig, fried fish stuffed with nuts and garlic, blood sausage, walnut pie, salted watermelon, honeyed fig tarts, date palm pudding. Bread loaves of various sizes and shapes served with pomegranate and pear syrups, warm olive oil, whipped goat's butter. And goblets were to be kept filled with Elias's most expensive wines and beer imported from the rich wheat fields of Jericho.

Against her better judgment, Avigail had hired a dance and acrobatic troupe, as well as musicians and singers. She bought extra lamps, candles, and torches so that every corner of the villa was bright with light. Costly incense perfumed the air. Tables and cushions were laid out with fresh roses and lilies for the guests. Upstairs, Leah was putting finishing touches on her wedding costume, while Elias and Daveed did their best to stand in as Caleb's male kin as he, too, dressed in fine robes.

They were ready. The villa hummed with light and excitement. All that was needed now were guests.

Esther came back inside, distressed. She wore her best saffron-yellow gown and veil, and had been allowed eye cosmetic and rouge. She hadn't been able to sleep for excitement. But now she saw the empty tables and cushions, lights burning low, musicians nodding over their instruments.

Tamar sat sullenly at the family table, fuming all by herself about this turn of events. She had overheard Grandmother's argument with Father. Leah was to get the best wedding, while she would have to settle for a frugal one! It wasn't fair. And now no one was coming and Tamar was glad. Leah would have no witnesses to her wedding ceremony beneath the canopy, where she would stand with Caleb and promise to obey him.

A frugal wedding for Tamar . . .

She had attempted to use her woman-power on Caleb, wanting to see if what Baruch had said to her on their last night together was true—that men would fall at her feet and do her bidding. But while

Caleb smiled and flashed his teeth at her, and seemed charmed by her, Caleb treated all the family members that way, so she could not be sure. As the wedding had drawn near, Tamar had decided to abandon her seduction of Leah's fiancé.

And now she changed her mind again.

If a frugal wedding lay in her future, then she would at least reward herself with the seduction of her sister's husband. To prove that what Baruch had told her was true, to prove to herself that she was not powerless after all, and to punish Leah for this wretched turn of events.

Clang clang! Clang clang!

Tamar snapped her head up, causing flowers to fall from her veil. The gate bell. It was heard all over the house. Avigail, in the kitchen, froze. Leah, upstairs with her mother and Aunt Rakel, paused to listen. Elias stepped away from Caleb to look over the balcony.

Had a guest finally come?

The steward swung the gate open and gawked at the large gathering on the threshold, beautifully dressed men and women who had arrived by chair and horse and chariot, with slaves holding torches and bearing gifts, all calling out Shalaam and traditional wedding greetings.

"They are here, My Lady," the steward said with a shocked look on his face as he met Avigail in the garden. "There must be hundreds!"

They streamed in, greeted by Avigail and Elias, and escorted to their places—gaily robed men and women, their gold jewelry sparkling in the lamplight. They all knew one another and laughed merrily as they looked forward to a feast.

Avigail graciously accepted the balls of frankincense that many of the guests had brought, and she lit the gum resin so that it burned in every room and filled the house with perfumed smoke designed to keep evil spirits away from the marriage ceremony.

When all were settled and ready, Leah came down, accompanied by her mother and Rakel, to the accompaniment of cymbals and incense, a solemn procession with overtones of excitement and joy. She wore a gown of many layers and colors, elaborately embroidered, with protective symbols painted in henna on her hands and face. Around her neck, many protective amulets representing Ugarit's gods, as well as good luck charms and a small bag of herbs guaranteed to repel demons known to be jealous of human love.

From a separate doorway, Caleb entered with Daveed and Elias. They came together before the canopy where two chairs had been draped and decorated as thrones. Elias raised his arms and called out, "Praise the gods of Canaan for they are in our presence tonight! Keep the names of Asherah and Baal and Dagon on your lips this night, that they bless and protect this union." He asked the couple to stand beneath the canopy. They recited vows, Elias tied their wrists together in a loose knot of soft hemp, declared them now to be married, while Daveed, seated nearby, recorded the moment on clay.

The guests cheered, Caleb and Leah took seats on the thrones, Elias gave the musicians the signal to begin while Avigail instructed the chief steward to start serving the feast.

Hannah, taking her place at the family table, smiled with pride and relief. Her daughter was no longer Bat Elias, but Isha Caleb. The gods willing, before a year was out, she would be called Em Yosia or Em Avram, and her status in life secured. (And perhaps, too, before much time has passed, the gods will give me a son for my beloved Elias). Sitting next to her mother, Tamar watched Leah beneath the canopy, as regal as a queen. Thinking of Baruch, the boy she lost because of Leah, thinking of the "frugal" wedding she must settle for, thinking of all the unfairness in the world, Tamar entertained her renewed vow to seduce Caleb.

Leah sat stiffly on her throne, burdened with much jewelry and a heavy headdress laden with coins—her father's wedding gift to them. She watched the celebration in numb detachment, having expected no one to come and now unable to grasp the numbers here, the cream of society, and the fact that she was married to the man sitting silently at her side, and who was still a stranger to her.

Caleb's own mind, on the other hand was sharp and attentive as he forced himself to smile and take in all the rich clothing, the jewels and gold and silver. He despised this family. They were soft and weak, and they were stupid. Everyone had heard talk of a double murder down by the docks, a rich man and his slave, not of Ugarit. From Damaska. Yet Elias and his vapid women had not made the connection. But Caleb was going to make the most of his life here. He scanned the laughing faces of his new in-laws and settled upon one which he suspected hid malicious thoughts. Sixteen-year-old Tamar with eyes that burned with black fire. That one he liked least of all, recognizing a heart that was as dark as his own.

Nobu kept his eye on the slaves serving wine. His god-voices had been loud all day, ever since his master threw away priceless pledge-notes on a girl he pitied! Pathetic Nobu, you are never going to get into the Brotherhood at this rate, you will never know the prestige and luxury of living within the walls of the House of God. You are doomed to be the slave of an ordinary scribe. He seized the first goblet of wine that passed within his sphere and gulped down the sweet drink until the voices faded away.

Among the celebrants were Hadar and her husband who, after much debate and thought, could not ultimately resist the prize of three pledge-notes from the royal house of Lagash. Hadar had decided that she would deal with Zira's anger when the time came, she had her husband to think of first, and now he had a greater advantage for opening his own trade agreement with merchants in Lagash eager to buy his purple dye.

The importer of African ivory was there, too, with his wife and daughters, along with all the other citizens who had been instructed by Jotham and Zira, directly or otherwise, not to come tonight. Collectively, Ugarit's upper crust decided that Jotham could not punish all of them for their attendance, and anyway, they now held precious pledge-notes from Lagash.

Also among the guests was the sallow-face, droop-shouldered agent who had spied for Jotham. He had so far not been able to find anything amiss about Caleb of Damaska, but he would continue his investigation, going as far away as Damaska if he had to.

And Daveed, although with a heavy heart, sent silent thanks to Shubat. He was glad the pledge-notes had worked and when he saw how many guests had arrived, was pleased he had made the sacrifice. He knew he could not make any more pledge notes, for too many would weaken the value of the others. And surely there was a limit to how many his father the king would honor.

Daveed must seek a sponsor in another way.

He watched Leah sitting on her bridal throne next to a smiling groom, and it tore him apart to think of her, in a little while, alone upstairs with Caleb. But Leah was forever beyond his reach. Daveed would carry his secret love for her in his heart as he devoted himself to serving the Brotherhood, guardians of the sacred and ancient library in the House of Gold.

Finally, the hour was late. The feast ended and the guests departed, stopping by the canopy to leave good wishes and gifts for the new couple. As Hannah and Rakel and Avigail escorted Leah to her new bridal chamber, Elias took Daveed to one side and, laying a hand on his shoulder, said, "I know what you did, Daveed, the sacrifice you made for my daughter. Those pledge-notes would have gained you a sponsor into the Brotherhood. I will never forget that. Now that I have a strong son-in-law in my house, and a scribe with a very sharp mind," Elias added with a smile, "Jotham will back away from his assault on us. Especially after he hears how many friends rallied to my side this night. Thanks to you. I owe you a great debt."

Upstairs in the bedchamber she would share with her new husband, Leah prepared herself while Caleb awaited her summons. She was not in love with him, but few women were on their wedding night. Love, she had been told, came later. And it would be as she had predicted: being married gave her advantages she did not have before. As Isha Caleb, I will be free to go out into the city and take Aunt Rakel among the purveyors of seeds and plants and find Moloch's Dream.

Bathed and perfumed, Leah dismissed the slave girls, asking them to send Caleb in, and then she slipped under the bed covers. She knew what to expect, Grandmother had explained it to her. And Leah had heard sounds of lovemaking coming from her parents' bedroom, Hannah calling, "Come to me my beloved Elias. Fill me with your strength."

And the love poem from Auntie Rakel's oak chest, which Daveed had read to her: "My love is like the cedar. He is hard and endures . . ."

But Caleb surprised her. He did not kiss her, or embrace or caress her. He wordlessly took her hand and placed it on his penis, curling her fingers around the shaft until it was hard. Then he rolled her over, pulled up her night dress and entered her from behind. She felt the maidenhead tear, and then pain as he thrust violently, over and over, until he climaxed. Caleb groaned. And then he pulled away and, rolling onto his other side, drifted off to sleep.

Leah lay blinking in the darkness. Caleb had not held her. He had not touched her to set her on fire. He had not acted out of passion but from cold animal lust. He had not even spoken her name. When her parents made love it was with sounds of passion and desire, wanting. Caleb had grunted. Like a beast. He had not even looked at her face.

She got up to clean herself. Blood from the torn hymen stained her inner thighs. She washed and dried herself at a basin, and changed her nightdress. Tomorrow she would burn the one she had worn tonight.

She listened to the night silence and tried not to think of Daveed, tried not to weep over lost love, lost chances and "what might have been." This was her reality now. Girlhood fantasies must be left in the past, along with the memory of a passionate rooftop kiss beneath a golden sun.

She was no longer a virgin, yet she felt no different. Her body might have undergone an alteration, but her heart remained the same. But tomorrow she would act like a contented wife. Tomorrow, people would address her as Isha Caleb. And soon, the gods willing, after a few tomorrows she would be with child and the memory of this night would fade.

CHAPTER SIX

Legend tells of an ancient race of people who lived on an island in the middle of the Great Sea. They were immortal, having learned the formula for eternal youth, and they practiced a special magic call al-chemi, through which they were able to transmute any ordinary substance into something of great price. The island was destroyed during a catastrophic earthquake, and its people perished. But a few managed to escape and make their way to the eastern shore of the Great Sea. Here they lived a short while before also going to the gods, but not before recording their wondrous secrets on clay tablets.

Those tablets, which contained the secret to living forever free of disease and worry, were said to be housed in the great library of Ugarit, whose guardians were the Brotherhood of Scribes.

Unfortunately, the secrets were written in a long-dead language and no one had ever broken the code.

These were Daveed's thoughts as he reverently approached the main portico of the complex of buildings that comprised the library, royal archive, and inner sanctum of the Brotherhood: the fabulous treasure within and the possibility of being of service to humankind by breaking those ancient codes and learning the secrets of the gods.

He had been to the House of Gold before, to watch and observe Ugarit's interesting practice of having its professional men sit in a great courtyard and receive ordinary citizens, a practice not found in cities to the east. He had also come once before to register his name on the roll of scribes, and to inform them of his intent to request membership one year hence.

He was here today on a more humble errand.

Unable to find a sponsor, Daveed had decided to go straight to the Brotherhood and throw himself on their mercy, lay his case before them, explain the special circumstances that were beyond his control, and request a waiver. Surely their hearts would be moved because they were, after all, a brotherhood.

"Master," Nobu fretted at his side. "What will become of me?"

As far away as Lagash and beyond, the Brotherhood at Ugarit was legendary for its austerity and strict rules of abstinence and moderation. Especially in the first year, the novitiate, when even celibacy was demanded. Daveed doubted he would be allowed to bring a personal slave. He turned to his old friend and companion, whose droopy-lidded eyes blinked slowly. Nobu was taller than Daveed, and he stood with his head thrust forward.

"Do not fear, old friend, I will find arrangements for you." Daveed smiled and laid a reassuring hand on Nobu's arm. "Besides, you know the brothers do not eat meat or drink wine, and that celibacy is strongly encouraged. You would not be happy among so much self-denial. I will see if you can stay on with Elias and his family in some household capacity." Daveed liked to think he was acting out of concern for his companion's welfare, but he knew that with Nobu in Elias's house, it would be a good excuse for Daveed to visit, once he was a resident here in the dormitory, a perfectly acceptable reason to pay a visit to the house of his former patron, to see his old friend Nobu, and perhaps ask after Leah, maybe run into her, make sure she was all right . . .

"Go home now, Nobu. This is something I must do on my own. I will probably return late as I expect to have much to talk about with my brothers here."

He watched Nobu walk away, slowly and in his turtle-manner, muttering to himself as he responded to god-voices, and Daveed knew he was going to miss him greatly.

But as he followed the colonnaded hall where men's voices rose to the marble ceiling, Daveed's thoughts shifted from Nobu, from the Brotherhood even, to Leah. It was best that she was married, he told himself, because the Brotherhood was going to be very demanding of his time and his heart. Even after the novitiate period, Daveed knew he would have little time for anything else.

Once again his heart expanded with love as he thought of her, pictured her in his mind . . . and recalled their kiss one month ago beneath a golden sun. He thanked the gods for granting them that one moment to sustain them for the rest of their lives.

But was it enough? he wondered now.

His thoughts darkened when he thought of Leah's new husband. Daveed found it odd that Caleb had yet to dictate a letter to his family in Damaska. Avigail had written, of course, informing her cousin that Caleb arrived safely and was now married to her granddaughter, a welcome addition to their family, with invitations to come and visit. But from Caleb himself, not a word (even though, strangely, Caleb had told Elias he had written to his family about the wedding and had received a reply about illness and financial woes. Perhaps he had used the services of a scribe here at the House of Gold).

He came to the entrance, a pair of tall wooden doors that swung away on hinges and now stood open. Cuneiform inscriptions in stone on either side identified this as the library and archives. Within, he saw a long dark corridor with torches in sconces along the walls. The floor was shiny. He shivered with pride as he stepped over the thresh-old. Ordinary citizens were not allowed inside this sacred precinct. And sacred it was, for here were contained the most ancient recorded words, written by the gods themselves at the beginning of time. Here was where he planned someday to honor Shubat in the highest calling.

A scribe appeared from a side doorway, dressed in the unique costume of the resident brothers: a tight-fitting shirt of soft brown wool above a white pleated-linen skirt that reached his ankles. He was bearded with long curly hair, and a gold circlet around his head to signify his status as an educated man.

Daveed introduced himself and explained the purpose of his visit. The man nodded, said, "Shalaam, brother, and blessings of Dagon. Come this way."

As they passed open doorways, Daveed glimpsed towering pillars with capitals carved and painted as flowers—majestic blossoms supporting a high marble ceiling. He saw scribes seated on stools, working in the glow of brass lamps, their hands moving swiftly with stylus and clay. Some would be students, Daveed knew, others would be about government work. The business of running a city fell to men who could read and write. To see these brother scribes going about their holy task made Daveed's heart expand with pride, and an eagerness to begin his own work—to enter the regimented life of a fraternity where self-sacrifice would be demanded of him, where his brothers came before himself, a life in which his faith would be constantly be put to the test.

Was there a way, he wondered in rising excitement, he could join now and still serve Elias?

At the end of the corridor, his escort passed Daveed to another scribe whose gold bands encircling upper and lower arms, the many gold rings on his hands, and a more elaborate circlet on his head signified his higher status. He said, "Shalaam, my brother," and introduced himself, but Daveed was so caught up in the excitement of the moment, the grandeur of the inner sanctum and the fact that he was so close to his destiny, that he did not at first realize what the man had said. He had called himself Yehuda. When Daveed inquired if he happened to be related to Jotham the shipbuilder, and the scribe said, "I am his nephew," Daveed was shocked.

He had heard that the nephew of Elias's enemy was a scribe, and now here he was, face to face with a member of the family that was ruining the family Daveed served. He was speechless.

Although he had never met Zira, he had heard Elias's loyal servants refer to her as a "donkey-faced hag." Daveed saw now the son's resemblance to the mother in the recessive chin and pronounced overbite. Yehuda was tall with deep-set eyes. Seeing the shadows under those eyes reminded Daveed that Leah had said that this man suffered from the falling sickness. Yet he had political ambitions so high, Daveed had heard, that he aspired to the very throne itself.

"What is your wish, my brother?" Yehuda asked, and Daveed noticed that his tone was nasal and deep.

"May I meet the Rab?"

"He is asleep right now."

Daveed frowned. "He is well, I hope? It is but noon . . ."

"He is old," Yehuda said, adding, "A new Rab will be appointed at the next rising of the White One," and Daveed caught something in his tone, or perhaps it was the way Yehuda adjusted his posture, that made him think: this man wants to be the Rab's successor.

"Noble Yehuda," he said, and felt an unexpected stab in his conscience—this man's uncle was trying to destroy Leah's family, and yet he was a brother scribe, a man whom Daveed must honor and respect. "I wish to become a member of this fraternity in eight months' time," Daveed said, careful now to avoid mention of Elias, skirting the topic of his current employment, "but I am without a sponsor as I am a stranger to Ugarit." Daveed had hoped that his pedigree, being a prince of the royal house of Lagash, would help get him into this fraternity. But now he must also be careful not to mention Lagash, for surely Yehuda would have heard that Elias's new apprentice scribe came from that city.

"There can be exceptions," Yehuda said as lights flickered in sconces around them, casting the scribe's narrow face in a procession of shadows. It was difficult for Daveed to read his expression. He waited for Yehuda to say something more, when he did not, Daveed said, "What sort of exceptions?"

"We have brothers in our membership who also did not have sponsors."

"Indeed?" Daveed's interest was piqued. And then he suspected what they did to get around the tradition of sponsorship: they would accept scribes who proved themselves in skill and speed, in ethics and honesty. There would be an exam, Daveed thought in excitement, knowing he would pass.

"Permit me to show you around," Yehuda said graciously, "and if at the end you are certain you wish to join us, I will tell you how it is done." He paused, glancing at Daveed's bare arm. "A question," he said. "The significance of the dagger? You are a warrior-scribe? We have no such caste here."

"I do not fight," Daveed said honestly. "The dagger is symbolic only."

They walked through the dormitory, a two-story building of private rooms, and from behind closed doors, Daveed heard music and feminine laughter. And he could swear he detected the aroma of roasted meats—pork and mutton. They passed a shrine where a god sat upon an altar, and Daveed noticed that the incense was cold, the purifying flame had died out. When they encountered a scribe whose pleated skirt was soiled, Daveed could hardly believe his eyes. It was unmistakably a wine stain.

They came to an archive with dusty shelves and tables littered with pens and ink, papyrus, styli, and clay. Daveed had the impression of disorder and disarray. The tablets were stacked haphazardly on the shelves—some broken! A scribe came in, so fat that he shuffled, and carelessly jammed a clay tablet onto a crowded shelf, not paying attention to where it went. There seemed to be no order to anything. Stacks of tablets stood in towers on the floor, as if carelessly left there. Daveed felt himself becoming incensed. This was criminal.

But the biggest crime involved the Brotherhood's famous emblem: a disc with flames shooting out all around its perimeter, like a fiery sun, and in the center, a human eye wide and staring. A symbol so ancient that its origin and meaning were obscured in the mists of time. Daveed wondered if it represented a solar deity, for that was how it appeared. But it was not revered, Daveed saw now. During his tour with Yehuda, Daveed had seen the symbol everywhere, on columns, on walls and doorposts, treated carelessly, he thought, for they were dusty and not in good repair, neglect that signified disrespect.

He was mortified. In Lagash, scribes were proud of their symbol and respectfully acknowledged it by a gesture or words of reverence whenever they encountered it. The symbol of a fraternity was like the nexus of a giant web, holding all the strands together. If that nexus was weak, the web would fall apart.

But it was more than that. Like the written word, a symbol—whether on clay or stone or painted on wood—possessed a power of its own. The mere creation of the symbol called its essence into being, bringing that symbol's power into a person's presence. But the solar eye of the Brotherhood was disrespected and neglected, as if the brothers saw it as nothing more than clay or stone or paint on wood.

Daveed was numb with shock. Where was the respect for their sacred calling?

When Yehuda said, "Have you any questions?" Daveed thought

of the neglected god they had passed earlier. "To which god do the brothers pray before they begin dictation?"

"To which ever they wish, or none at all. We do not hold to such strict rules here. The brothers are free to lead their lives as they wish. There is but one rule, when a scribe is paid for his services, he must give a portion of that fee to the Brotherhood."

"How is the day structured?"Yehuda arched a brow. "When are prayers?" Daveed said. "When is rising? What time do the brothers eat? When is Final Hour?"

"We are not like other houses who feel the need to treat their brothers like regimented soldiers. Each man lives as he wishes."

"Will I be permitted to see the sacred library once I am a member?"

"You have already seen it." Yehuda gestured to the room they had just left. Daveed felt as if a horse had kicked him. That dusty, disordered, disrespected pile of tablets and papyri was the sacred library? "But where," he began, his chest tightening, "would I find, for instance, the Book of Creation? I saw no labels.

"Yehuda shrugged. "I do not know. I have never looked for it."

"But who takes care of the library?"

"We all do, after a fashion." He gave Daveed a scrutinizing look. "Perhaps our fraternity is not what you are looking for. You seem to wish a more structured life."

"No no, by Shubat, I still wish to join. If I qualify."

"Qualify? What do you mean?"

"The exams I must surely take—"

Yehuda smiled. "There are no exams. The only requirement to join is a measure of gold."

"Gold? You do not wish to test my skills?"

Yehuda shrugged. "We are of varying talents and levels here. Some are more skillful than others. After you enter our house, we will put you where you can be of most use."

Daveed tried to keep from shouting as he said, "But how do you know I can even write?"

Yehuda said nothing but watched Daveed with deep-set eyes, and a chilling realization came to Daveed: that membership into the elite Brotherhood could be bought by men who had but the barest of skills or no skills at all!

He felt sick. Where was the honor, the pride? Where were the demanding standards that set this fraternity above all others? The symbol of the fiery disc, neglected and dishonored.

"Forgive me," he choked out. "I must be somewhere . . . I will think about this," and he stumbled back down the hallways and corridors filled with the aromas of rich food and lady's perfume, the sounds of flutes and laughter, passing men who were fat and smelled as if they had not bathed in weeks, trying to block the image of the neglected library from his mind—the dust and cobwebs, the broken tablets, the jumble of written records that might be the ancient Book of Prophecies or the property deed of a sheep farmer!

He staggered out into the blinding sunlight of the courtyard where doctors and lawyers and scribes plied their professions for gold, where ordinary citizens came with their needs and their wants, innocent men and women who believed these professional men to be honorable and governed by ethics—for were the lawyers and medical men any better than the scribes?—and he pushed his way through the crowd, his world coming down around him, his dream crumbling before his eyes, the pain of disappointing his god squeezing his heart.

He found the main road out of Ugarit and followed it, feeling darkness sweep into his soul for was there anything worse than disillusionment and the crushing of one's ideals. Blinded by tears, Daveed spoke a silent vow: after my apprenticeship with Elias is over, I will leave Ugarit and its corruption and take Nobu and Shubat to a city where I am not known. I will hang out my shingle and build a clientele of only the wealthy and powerful. I will become a rich man, and I will never again call another man "brother."

Leah wondered where Daveed went that morning, dressed in his finery. Nobu had come back a little while later, without his master, which was unusual. She tried not to think about him, tried to be a proper wife. But it was hard. If only Caleb would show passion, emotion, something. But he was indifferent to her. She might as well be a table or a chair.

She neared the garden gate. That morning, as Aunt Rakel had sipped her daily tonic, she had said, "Myrrh is the best way to keep evil spirits from infecting a wound. It is a sacred plant and so its gum resin makes a perfect plaster for healing." Leah wondered if she could grow a myrrh shrub. She would go into town to purchase seeds or cuttings in the marketplace.

They had found Moloch's Dream. Rakel had seen the plant and recognized it at once, although the merchant called it cannabis. Seeing that the curative plant was indeed available in Ugarit, Leah had wondered out loud if Zira might not have already given this medicine to her son. But Rakel had said, "Only my husband knew of its curative qualities in the case of the falling sickness. He found it by accident, and he never told anyone." To be sure, Leah had asked the plant merchant about the healing properties of the cannabis, and although he had recited a long list that included relief from the demons that cause pain, congestion, stiff joints, sleeplessness, he had not included the falling sickness. And so Leah believed she was indeed going to offer to Zira a cure she had no knowledge of.

She and Rakel had sown the young plant together and in the days since, Leah had carefully tended Moloch's Dream along with other plants she was nurturing in her private garden and from which she would make healing potions.

As she laid her hand on the old wooden gate, she curled her fingers around a medallion she had purchased at the temple of Asherah, hoping its power would give strength to her plants—a flat round stone, pale pink and engraved with the likeness of a tree, sacred symbol of Asherah.

Pushing on the gate, Leah stepped in and needed a moment to grasp what she was seeing. The garden was not as she had left it the day before—laid out with young green plants, new ivy, baby blossoms, tender grasses. At first she thought the wind must somehow have found its way within these walls, for every little plant and shoot had been pulled from its roots and were scattered everywhere. Moloch's Dream, snatched from the earth and shredded beyond saving. Her seedling! The "daughter" that was struggling to survive in the shadow of the dead "mother"—uprooted and lying against the far wall. No wind had done this. Leah saw human actions behind this. But who?

And then she saw an ivory flower lying among scattered stems and leaves. It was not a real flower, but Tamar's favorite comb that must have fallen out of her hair without her knowing it.

Tamar had been spiteful ever since Baruch went away to marry in another town because his father feared losing Jotham's ships for the export of his olives. Tamar rightfully blamed Leah for her broken heart—Leah herself accepted blame for the family's misfortune. But to do this?

Leah searched for Tamar downstairs, and then went upstairs. As she looked for her sister, Leah's initial anger turned to sadness as she realized how badly she had hurt Tamar. Now that Leah was in love with Daveed, she knew how Tamar had felt about Baruch.

Because of my disobedience, Tamar lost her chance with Baruch. I will make amends somehow. I will make it up to her . . .

Coming to her sister's bedchamber, Leah knocked on the door. When Tamar called out for her to enter, Leah stepped in. And froze.

Tamar and Caleb . . .

The room swam before her eyes. She felt as if the walls were falling in on her. Dimly, Leah heard Tamar's gloating laugh, through a haze she saw the cold hardness in Caleb's eyes. They did not move. They stayed just as they were, naked under a bed sheet with no pretense of dismay or modesty or shock at being caught.

Clutching her stomach, Leah turned and ran.

Coming down the road from Ugarit, Daveed was so preoccupied in his bitter thoughts and disillusionment that he did not at first see Leah burst through the outer gate and fly down the road.

He was already making plans to leave, even though it would not be for a few months. He would make inquiries about work in other towns, to find where the need for a scribe was greatest, but also where there was a large population of wealthy families. He would not go to a sheep or farm town, and certainly not to a village. But a thriving city like Damaska or Jericho, maybe even farther south, perhaps he might go all the way to Egypt where scribes were men of honor and lived by a code of ethics and morality!

He stopped when he saw Leah running toward him, her hair flying out behind. He called out and she ran to him, into him so that he caught her, he held her, and she sobbed in his arms.

"What is it? What happened?"

She sucked in air, gasped, struggled for breath. "Halla!" she cried. "Daveed, I cannot breathe! I cannot stop crying. Help me!"

He drew her away from the road and under the protection of an arbor that grew near the northern wall of the villa. Leah gulped for air, as if she were drowning. "I cannot—" Her throat made alarming sounds. Her chest heaved, yet no breath went to her lungs. Painful sobs broke from her throat and the veins stood out on her neck.

Daveed held her by the shoulders, as if to shake her. "Leah!"

Strange sounds came from deep in her chest. She opened her mouth. She couldn't breathe. He encircled her with his arms and squeezed tightly, feeling fragile ribs convulse for breath. "Breathe, Leah!"

She threw her head back. "I ca—"

Daveed bent his head and placed his mouth over hers, breathing into her lungs, blowing soft breaths into her mouth until her throat eased. She held onto him as he breathed for her, blowing in and then drawing the breath out of her until he felt her body start to relax and the strange sounds subsided.

He finally lifted his head and looked down at her. "Can you breathe?"

She looked into his eyes. Her fingers dug into the blue fabric of his cloak. "Yes," she whispered.

"What happened?"

"My garden . . . Tamar—" In halting words and broken phrases she told an astonishing story of hatred and destruction, adultery and betrayal.

When she was finished Daveed did not know what to say, he was so stunned. He didn't tell Leah about his own disillusionment that morning at the Brotherhood, as it seemed too much, and selfish. When she wept again in his arms, softly and without hysteria, and he felt her body quiver against his, Daveed's world changed yet again. All plans for another city vanished. He knew he would never leave Ugarit. He would never leave her.

Finally she drew back, her eyes tenderly swollen with tears. "What do we do about Caleb and Tamar?"

"Do not say anything yet to Elias or your grandmother. I must think about it. Your family reputation is already too frail to withstand another blow. I honor your father, I would not wish him harm. Perhaps I will speak with Caleb."

But Leah knew this was not Caleb's doing. She knew now that he was a loveless man, without passion or heat, and possibly without desire as well. She did not blame him, believing that some men were simply born that way. This was Tamar's doing. She had used Leah's husband against her. And Leah knew that Tamar would do it again.

Daveed," Elias said, "will you please dismiss your slave? What I am about to show you is not for his eyes."

Nobu didn't wait for his master's command. He dipped his turtle-head and said, "I must see to the repair of your robes," and made a discreet exit.

There were certain ironies to being the personal companion of a scribe. On the one hand, he was made privy to family matters that ordinary household slaves were not. On the other, because the scribe was taken into a family's most private confidence, his slave must perforce be dismissed.

Nobu did not trouble himself with this complex thinking as he left the wine shed and followed the dusty path back to the house. His god-voices had been plaguing him mightily since yesterday, when his master came home to inform him that he would not be entering the Brotherhood after all, and that he had no idea what they were going to do when his apprenticeship was up. Nobu thanked the gods that they lived in the house of a vintner, as the remedy for his voices was found here in plenty.

As Daveed followed his patron deeper into the storage shed, where fine vintages waited in wooden barrels to be poured into bottles and made ready for shipment, Daveed tried to pay attention to what Elias was saying. But he could think only of Leah. She had retired early the night before, complaining of a headache, so that she would not have to be in the company of her grandmother or sisters, who would certainly realize something was wrong. Daveed himself had stayed awake all night, pacing on the rooftop, angry, confused, trying to sort through the maelstrom of emotions that had gripped him. It had been a day of shocks—first, his disillusionment with the Brotherhood, and then to learn of Caleb's and Tamar's monstrous behavior. Daveed had told Leah he would think of what to do, but he had come up with nothing.

He had yet to see her this morning as the summons from Elias had come just after daybreak.

Wondering if he should tell Elias about his son-in-law's despicable behavior, Daveed walked among the wine kegs and listened to Elias's new plan to save his family and the wine business.

To facilitate business transactions, men of wealth such as Elias and Jotham made use of the Money Exchange adjacent to the House of Gold, where money lenders offered safe storage of a man's gold and silver, and where creditors and merchants could present collection notes and receive money in return. The bulk of a rich man's wealth, however, was always kept at home, where he could guard it and keep an eye on it.

"I have found a shipper who will take my wines down the coast and across the Cyprus," he said as he stopped before a large wine keg and took hold of it. "And four caravaneers who will carrying my wines north and east. But they require payment in advance instead of taking it from the profit at the other end. I am also going to pay off the last of my creditors so Jotham cannot pull any more of his stunts."

Elias shifted the keg to one side to reveal a wooden trap door in the floor. Removing a burning torch from a wall sconce, he bent to lift the trapdoor, and Daveed saw stairs descending to a cellar. "Follow me," Elias said, and down they went.

"As I have no more money with the bank, I must tap into my personal fortune. It will be a great expense, but such a sacrifice will stop the downward slide that Jotham sent me into. I have enough in this vault to stabilize my fortune and to rid us of Jotham's threat, and have enough left over to . . ." His voice died when they reached the bottom step and the torch illuminate a stone underground chamber.

That was completely empty.

Daveed looked around in confusion while Elias stood in frozen shock. The dusty floor was marked with distinctive rectangles where coffers had stood. Empty shelves lined the walls, and recessed niches were devoid of contents.

"Halla!" Elias whispered as he ventured further into the chamber. "Dagon protect us! What happened? I was in here but one month ago, and this vault was filled from floor to ceiling." His eyes grew wide as he scanned the emptiness in disbelief. Where were the polished stones of onyx, agate, carnelian, and turquoise? Where was the jewelry that had been in his family for generations, crafted from pearls, crystal, and coral? Silver vases from Babylon, plates made of the finest gold, a handsome malachite urn embedded with amber—priceless beyond measure!

A figurine from Sumer—a goat on its hind legs as it munched leaves from a tree, the entire piece made of solid gold and covered in polished lapis lazuli. A gold statue of Damuzi from Ur, his eyes made of rubies, his crown made of ivory. A bronze shield from a famous battle nearly a hundred years ago, a sword with gems encrusted on its hilt.

Elias's eyes stung with tears. It was a collection representing more than a century of generations contributing precious objects for the benefit of generations to come.

All gone.

"My lord," Daveed said, "who else knew about this secret chamber?" but he guessed the answer before Elias responded. The new son-in-law, Caleb. He would need to know, being the one who would take Elias's place as head of the family and the wine business.

Elias's voice was dead as he replied, "I brought Caleb here the other day. I swore him to secrecy. I told him that someday all this would belong to his sons and his grandsons."

"How could he have carried it all out? Surely such wealth must weigh a great deal."

Elias could not speak. But Daveed surmised that Caleb would have bribed a couple of slaves, who would have been only too happy to take some gold rings and run away where they would never be found. Daveed also suspected that wherever Caleb had taken the treasure, Elias and his family would most likely never see him again.

And then Daveed felt a chill go down his spine as the full impact of this moment hit him: the last of Elias's money was gone. The downward slide would continue.

The women were in the sunroom, at their mending. Hannah said, "I went into the Egyptian quarter today—"

Avigail made a sound of contempt.

Hannah took it in stride. She did not share her mother-in-law's hatred of Egyptians, and in fact found their wares in the marketplace attractive and useful, and such vendors as she spoke with seemed to be most agreeable. "And I heard a rumor that Queen Hatshepsut is ill. I wonder if this is true, and if so, what will happen if her stepson takes the throne."

"It is well known that Prince Regent Thutmose hungers to conquer the world." Avigail released an exasperated sigh as she pulled out a stitch and redid it. The mere thought of Egyptians made her lose control of her needle. It had been two generations since the first Thutmose marched into Canaan, seizing towns like Jericho, and setting up fortified garrisons under military officers, creating administrative posts for the running of the cities, making the local kings vassals of Pharaoh. But in the years since, Egypt had lost control of the northern towns, including Ugarit. Now, Egypt must be satisfied with annual tribute.

"Will there be war if Hatshepsut dies, Grandmother?"

But there was already a war going on. Avigail had seen the signs for years—the signs of change. Slowly, Egyptian fashions and customs, imported goods—even a god!—were infiltrating Canaanite society, and it frightened her. Everyone said it was the result of Hatshepsut's clever foreign policy. She used peaceful trade and commerce to make Egypt the richest nation on earth. Instead of building war chariots and making weapons, Queen Hatshepsut built merchant ships and manufactured exports to go to all the nations on earth, creating a demand for Egyptian goods that did not previously exist, making foreigners think they could not live without Egyptian glass, perfume, paper, turquoise.

Even the priestesses of Asherah were not immune. The women of the House of Elias had for generations provided the elegant vestments for the temple attendants of Asherah. But now they said they wished linen gowns, and linen came only from Egypt!

This is how we will be conquered, Avigail thought in fear. The weapons our conquerors will use are trinkets and fashion. Invasion by persuasion, conquering a people without their even knowing it!

Leah sat at her loom, deftly guiding the shuttle in and out of the warp threads, her companions unaware of her turbulent emotions. The sight of Tamar and Caleb in bed . . . Following Daveed's advice, she had told no one. Last night, she had lain awake in the dark, waiting for Caleb, but he never came. And where was Daveed this morning? She had thought she would see him, to hear what he had decided they must do, but he had been nowhere in the house.

Avigail wished Hannah had not brought up the subject of Egypt. It reminded her of her ancestral home in Jericho, where she was born. Her mother came from Ugarit, and that was how Avigail had inherited the bloodline of King Ozzediah. Her father's family had lived in the Jericho house for generations, and then on one fiery night, it was taken from them. Because of this Avigail vowed that never again would her home be taken from her. Not by the Egyptians and certainly not by Jotham and Zira.

Hannah said, "Is it true Egyptians cut off the foreskins of their infants? It is said that the Habiru hold to the same practice."

Avigail looked beseechingly at her daughter-in-law. "Hannah, dear, can we please change the subject? And where is Tamar? Her weaving goes neglected. Esther, go find your sister. She has been growing lazy of late."

"Yes, Grandmother," she said, and left.

"Really, Hannah, dear," Avigail began, "I do not know what has gotten into—"

"Caleb! Caleb man, where are you?"

The two women turned in the direction of Elias's booming call. "Halla, what troubles my husband?"

He stormed in, Daveed the scribe on his heels.

"Where is Caleb? Where is that scoundrel?"

Setting aside her embroidery, Avigail rose from her chair. "My son, invoke the gods! You look as if you have had a severe fright. Calm yourself. Why do you need to see Caleb? Why do you call him a scoundrel?"

"I was in the vault just now. The family treasure is gone! All of it! And only Caleb, besides myself, knew where it was hidden."

Hannah and Leah rose to their feet.

"Say a prayer, my son. Surely you do not think," Avigail began. "But he is your son-in-law. He would not dare steal from us." But even as she said this, a terrible feeling stole over her. Without another word, she hurried from the sunroom, Elias and the others staring after her, and a moment later they heard a cry.

"Mother! What is it?"

Avigail appeared in the doorway, shaken. "Pray for us, Elias! My gold and silver rings. My jewelry—it is all gone."

"Grandmother!" Esther said, coming back into the sunroom. "Tamar is not here. Her clothes are gone. Her jewelry. Her shoes, her combs. Grandmother, Tamar's room is empty!"

"I do not care about Tamar!" Elias shouted. "Where is Caleb?"

It was Leah who spoke, softly and calmly. "He will be gone, too, Father."

"What? What is that you say? Where is he?"

Daveed's eyes met Leah's. Then she said, "I found them yesterday . . . in bed together."

Elias staggered back and Daveed caught him. He helped his patron to a chair.

"My gold and silver rings were a legacy from your father," Avigail said in a strangled voice, her hands clasped so tightly together they were white. She trembled. "Asherah! Dagon! Baal! Help us! My son, your daughter and Leah's husband—" Her voice caught. "They stole from us and have run off together." She covered her face with her hands. "Blessed Asherah, what did we do to deserve this!"

"Daveed," Elias said grimly, "we will write letters at once. My mother will dictate one, and then I have several I must write."

"Me?" Avigail said.

"You will write to your cousin in Damaska and tell her that she sent us a thief and an adulterer! I demand compensation! Your cousin's family will make restitution of the money I have lost. They will come here in person and apologize to us in the public square! When word of this gets out—and it will for you cannot seal the lips of every slave and servant under this roof—we will be the laughing stock of all of Ugarit. And Jotham will have the biggest laugh of all!"

A week passed and the letters were well on their way, to Elias's friends who were still loyal to him, asking for help, to the Money Exchange, to lenders and creditors, but most of all to the cousin in Damaska. Avigail wrote a strong complaint and insisted upon financial restitution.

But as Daveed tramped over the rocky ground, he wondered if the adulterous pair had gone back to Caleb's home, and was in fact finding sanctuary there, in which case no restitution would come.

Or if were they far away, in a foreign town, laughing as they spent Elias's wealth.

Daveed's heart went out to Elias's family. They did not deserve such misfortune. Especially a man so honorable and honest as Elias.

If only he could help. But Daveed had yet to make friends or connections in Ugarit. And he had used up all his pledge-notes for the wedding feast.

But more than anything, his heart wept for Leah. She held her head high and insisted upon visiting the marketplace in the city, even though, as Elias had predicted, the news had spread like wild fire through the town. Gossips loved nothing more than seeing the rich and powerful pulled down. Daveed had followed her, to make sure she was all right, but Leah walked with two servants among the stalls and vendors and merchants, pausing to examine goods, even to exchange pleasantries with other folk, ignoring the exchanged looks, the smirks, the whispering. A deserted wife.

And his inner torment grew.

Therefore, he came out to this remote place in the countryside far from the city, so that he could more readily commune with his god and find answers. He did not know how the gods could even hear people's prayers when they were whispered in temples or household shrines, for there was so much noise and distraction. But here in the wilderness of Canaan, far from men, from walls and chariots, out here beneath the cleansing sun and pure air, among fragrant trees and shrubs and flowers, a man could find a direct path to his god and speak from his heart.

He had not brought Nobu with him, only Shubat, whom he now removed from the protective carrying case. Finding a large rock among the boulders that were scattered over this rocky landscape, he brushed it clean and set Shubat upon it, so that the god sat on his throne, his divine-wide eyes staring at Daveed.

He knelt and began to pray.

A sudden breeze came up, breaking his concentration so that Daveed opened his eyes. Something moved at the corner of his vision.

Looking down, he saw a serpent moving slowly through the grass. The creature was pink with dark brown patches forming a pattern along its body. The flat, triangular head was lifted off the ground as it moved forward. Daveed recognized it as being nonvenomous and so as it slithered toward him, he held his breath and watched. When the snake's nose bumped against a rock, Daveed expected it to go around. Yet the serpent remained still. When it proceeded to rub its face on the hard surface, Daveed watched in fascination. He realized after a moment that the serpent was about to shed its skin, and Daveed's sense of wonder grew.

Although encountering a snake was considered good luck, to witness a shedding was considered the greatest fortune as so few men experienced it, and so it meant that something wonderful was going to come to the observer. All of Ugarit still spoke of the lame beggar who, after witnessing the shedding of a snake's skin, stumbled upon a bag of gold rings that apparently had no owner.

The afternoon air grew warm and heavy as Daveed kept his eyes on the serpent. It was but inches from his sandaled foot, so that Daveed could see every perfection in the long scaly body, this miracle of nature, creation of the gods. The buzzing of flies and droning of bees filled the silence as the young scribe from Ugarit gave himself up to the purity of the wilderness, unable to move, scarcely breathing.

In awe he watched as the serpent rubbed its face repeatedly against the rock until milky skin came away from its eyes, revealing two shining brown corneas with narrow slits. The creature continued to rub the rock until it had succeeded in pushing away a cap of old skin to expose beautiful new skin underneath. A handsome snake to begin with, Daveed thought, it was now starting to reveal an even more breathtaking beast underneath.

The sun slipped toward the western horizon as Daveed lost himself in the wonder of this miracle. To actually witness the rebirth of an immortal creature! Shadows of trees and boulders shifted and grew long. The rolling green hills turned golden and then lavender. The snake toiled patiently and without rest, undulating in a hypnotic way as the outer skin rolled back, growing thicker, like a headband made of rolled cloth. The creature moved, and Daveed watched. The heat of the day left the countryside. Flowers began to close. Darkness filled the sun-pools. And the roll of dead skin grew thicker as it moved down the snake's body.

Daveed held his breath as the serpent pushed the last of its old life off the shining body of its new life, and then it slithered away, slowly, as if proud or in pain, or exhausted, until it disappeared under a hedge and Daveed was left alone with the remains of a creature that never died.

A long moment passed. Daveed felt as if he were caught between reality and the supernatural. How long he had stood there and watched the miracle, he could not guess. But rather than feeling stiff, or tired or hungry, he was filled with an unexpected exhilaration.

He felt as if the hand of Shubat had touched him.

He bent to pick up the sloughed skin—what a prize it would be!— and stopped. Serpents, because they were known to be immortal, were sacred. Their discarded skins were holy and must be left to disintegrate and return to the earth.

Turning to the statue on the rock, barely visible now in the deepening dusk, Daveed said, "I thank you, my precious Lord, for granting me this day of new hope. When I was at my lowest, you raised me up with a miracle." That a snake should shed its skin in front of a human, to make itself vulnerable to a sworn enemy—the creature did not slither away to do its business in secret, but chose to enter into the presence of a man who could have killed it!

It was a sign from Shubat.

And Daveed knew what it meant: Shubat had sent a reminder of the constant renewal of life, like winter to spring, the great and sacred cycle of life. And just as the earth died and must be reborn like the serpent, like a day dying into night and being born again into day, so must other things suffer corruption before receiving new life.

The Brotherhood.

This was his calling. To help the Brotherhood renew itself. Shubat was telling him that it was not enough that he be the Rab of the Brotherhood, to be the guardian of the sacred library, it was more. Daveed's destiny was to bring the fraternity back to righteousness. Back to purity and integrity. He knew this now. The fraternity must be born anew, as the serpent was.

* * *

S he was on the roof, looking at the lights of the city.

People feared the evil spirits of the night, and so after sundown, every household lit lamps. From the humblest shack to the royal palace, torches, candles, and lamps were lit to show any evil spirits that were passing by that this house was occupied and they were not to enter. Therefore, Ugarit twinkled and sparkled, as if the stars them-selves had fallen from the sky to decorate the city below.

Leah's heart was heavy with sadness—for her father, for her family. They had become the talk of the city. Esther cried every day. Avigail argued constantly with Elias. And Leah had been deserted by her husband.

Hearing a sound, she turned and saw Daveed standing in the starlight.

He came up to her, and she saw a strange new light shining in his eyes. In a soft voice he opened his heart and told her at last about his disillusionment and the shattering of his dream when he visited the Brotherhood. And then he told her about the serpent and the message from Shubat. "I was angry and confused when I left the Brotherhood. But Shubat has opened my eyes, for I see now that my brother scribes have lost their way. They need someone to guide them back to a life of respect and honor. I will find a way to meet with the Rab. I will discuss it with him."

He spoke with fire in his voice as he said, "And if talking to the Rab does not help, then I will enter the Brotherhood and fight to attain the title of Rab myself, for when I am the master of the Brotherhood I will lead my brother scribes back to the path of honesty, integrity, and honor."

He took her by the shoulders and said, "Leah, we were not free before now, I did not have the right to speak of my love for you. But I do love you, and when I am able, when my period of novitiate is over, I want you to be with me."

"You do not have that right, Daveed," she cried. "Nor do I, as much as I yearn to be with you. I am still married. Caleb is my husband, no matter where he is. And it is my duty to give my father a grandson, which I can only do with a husband. I must pray that Caleb returns."

Daveed's face darkened. "Would your father allow that man back into his house?"

"If Caleb is truly repentant, and if he promises to restore the money he stole, yes, for the sake of getting a grandson, for the sake of saving face and family reputation, my father would allow him back."

Daveed's fingers dug into her shoulders as he shuddered with desire. He wanted to kiss her, make love to her under the moon, but he would not dishonor the woman he loved. "Then I can only pray," he said grimly, "that Caleb does not return. For after seven years, under the law, if he has still not come back, you will then be free, Leah. And you will be free to marry whomever you wish. And I pray, my dearest Leah, that it is I."

CHAPTER SEVEN

Hannah stroked Elias's face as he slept.

They had just made love and as usual Hannah could not immediately fall asleep. Her husband always filled her with such a sense of love and well-being that she liked to prolong the moment.

Elias was handsome, tall, and broad-shouldered with a kind heart and an open mind. Everyone loved him. Even those too afraid of Jotham to do business with Elias, or to come to his house, to even acknowledge him in the street. What filled her heart so was the way her beloved took this tribulation in stride. "Do not worry, my dearest," he reassured her over and over, "Jotham cannot keep this up. The gods are with us. We will prevail."

Will we? she wondered now, wondering for the first time in her twenty-two years with Elias if he was going to be able to bring the family through this storm. It was a month now since Caleb and Tamar ran off, and they had not yet returned. No one knew where they were. The cousin in Damaska had not seen them. Hannah did not mind never seeing Caleb again, but she missed her daughter and prayed that Tamar was all right. In addition, with Caleb gone, the hope of Leah getting pregnant was also gone.

All because of the vindictive Jotham and Zira. How long could two people hold a grudge? Hannah had offered to apologize publicly to them, and they had turned her down. And offering Leah to him was no longer a solution, as Jotham had lost interest in her, saying he would not take another man's leavings, although, perversely, his vendetta against Elias continued.

And so, with Tamar gone and Leah in a place where she could not remarry, and with Hannah herself now entering that phase of life where she would begin to retain her moon-flow and therefore no longer be fertile, the House of Elias despaired of producing a male heir.

She got out of bed and, wrapping up in a woolen robe—the autumn night was chilly and damp—went to the inside balcony that opened upon the hospitality hall below, where this whole tribulation began—Zira's bad-luck words, Avigail's demand to know about Yehuda's falling sickness, Hannah's preterm labor, a baby born too soon. The house was silent but it twinkled, as at least one small oil lamp burned in every room.

Leah would eventually be allowed to remarry, Hannah knew, but she must wait seven years. It seemed an unreasonable law, but Hannah supposed it had its origins in a long-ago incident involving a husband who traveled to a distant land and, having fallen victim to circumstance, could not make his way home for years. When he did, he found that his wife had remarried. Seven years must have seemed reasonable to those distant lawmakers, deciding that a man, no matter how extreme his circumstances—whether in prison or captured by pirates—if he really wanted to get home he would make it in seven years.

Hannah sighed. Whatever, the law was the law. And with no other daughters to give her and Elias grandchildren, it was up to herself to see that male heirs were produced in this house.

Her thoughts went to a painful subject which she had been hoping to avoid. Men took slave girls for pleasure all the time. It was a practice as old as humankind. If offspring resulted, it was at the man's discretion whether or not to declare the child to be his, and to confer upon the child citizenship and full rights as a free-born person. Rarely was a female child accepted. And even in the case of a son, many factors entered into the decision.

Elias the vintner had never been faced with such a decision because he had never taken pleasure with a slave girl, or with any other woman. Wed to Hannah at age nineteen, Elias had eyes and heart only for her. He was besotted, as his mother Avigail would say. At first, it pleased her. Devotion to a partner was admirable—as long as it did not interfere with the health of the family. But this house needed sons, and Elias, Avigail believed, was being uncharacteristically selfish, and she had voiced this to Hannah. Known to all men as generous and fair-minded, Elias was, in this instance, being stingy and narrow-minded. Avigail had bluntly told her daughter-in-law that Elias planted his seed in his wife alone when he should be fertilizing other furrows. If a concubine bore a son to Elias, he could declare the child to be a citizen of Ugarit. Elias could bestow upon the son all the rights of a freeborn man, and declare him to be his heir. And this bloodline would no longer be in danger of dying out.

A bloodline, Avigail liked to point out, that descended through herself from King Ozzediah.

But Hannah knew that her husband would never take a concubine. And so it was up to her.

She could not bear the thought of her beloved embracing another woman. Hannah knew her heart would break and a new sorrow would be added to the sorrow of losing a baby. But it was necessary for the survival of the family. Males were needed. A female bloodline perished.

Vaguely, at the back of her mind, because she was unused to abstract thought, Hannah wondered if the tradition was backward. Shouldn't bloodlines be traced through women, since a mother always knew who her child was whereas the father could never be sure? She suspected that this was why some men waited before acknowledging the paternity of a child, until it was old enough to display family resemblance—his family.

She sighed. Fanciful thinking! The reality was, in Canaanite culture there must be sons, and there was only one way to achieve that. With the shocking departure of Tamar and Caleb—and Hannah doubted they would ever return—the family's chances for male children were almost nil (was there a man in all the world who could be persuaded or bribed to take poor Esther to wife?). And she knew Elias would not take the necessary steps. His love for her ran too deeply. Therefore, the distasteful and painful task rested upon Hannah.

She must find a concubine for her husband.

It was harvest time and the crushing shed was noisy with the sounds of clapping hands and stomping feet. The men held onto overhead poles to keep from slipping in the juicy sludge, their legs going up and down in time with the rhythm of the clappers—women and children who sat cross-legged among the crushing vats, knocking sticks together as they sang.

The outbuildings on the slope above the vineyard were a hub of industry as slaves brought baskets filled with grapes, emptying them into the wooden crushing tubs. In the main storage building—a mudbrick structure that was whitewashed each spring—Elias was counting the empty amphoras that were waiting to be filled. Daveed walked with him, recording the count.

Elias was worried about the new harvest. There was a system to the wine business: ripe grapes were emptied into crushing vats, the resulting juice went into the first fermentation barrels, and then the second fermentation barrels, until the final, mature wine went into empty wine-jars for shipment to local customers, or to caravans and boats for export. It was a time-tested and efficient system, but it required the constant moving of juice/wine from step to step, with the ready vintages leaving at the end of the process. But Elias was struggling to find customers for his wine, and so new wine had nowhere to go. Amphoras filled with recent vintages stood in the cellars, unpurchased. He had been forced to buy more amphoras (from Thalos the Minoan, paying up front in gold this time instead of their usual practice of credit—not an easy thing with his hidden fortune gone—stolen by his own daughter!) and if he did not find more customers, Elias would have a surplus of wine.

He thanked the gods that there was still one shipper who would take his wines down the coast and across the sea, a captain named Yagil, who was honest and who hated Jotham. The profits from those exports would help keep the family afloat.

As Daveed recorded the inventory of empty wine-jars, his thoughts were not upon empty amphoras and surplus wine. He was thinking of Leah.

He could not put from his mind the way she had sobbed on his chest, gulping for air, trembling in his embrace. Violence had gripped Daveed in that moment—the blinding desire to seek out Caleb and kill him. And now the brute was gone and Daveed knew that Ugarit's upper class whispered about Leah's abandonment, making it sound as if it were her doing, as if she were a flawed wife because happy husbands did not run away.

Daveed wanted to help her, help this family. Joining the Brotherhood was now more than a personal goal, it was a means of bringing power back to this house.

As Rab, I will declare Elias to be my friend, his family my family. And no man dare touch them.

With his renewed determination to join the Brotherhood, he had decided he would not pay a bribe to gain membership. He refused to start his career in that ancient and noble fraternity by dishonorable means. And so he had redoubled his efforts to find a sponsor.

The chief steward came into the shed then, to give his master a clay table that had just arrived. Elias passed it to Daveed, who read it and, frowning, said, "It is a notice from Captain Yagil informing you that he can no longer carry your goods and that you are to come to the docks and take back your amphoras."

Elias stared at his scribe. "Dagon is my witness, that cannot be! Yagil is known for keeping his word. And for his rivalry with Jotham. He promised me he would ship my wines!"

"It surprises me, too, sir, but there is no mistake. It is what is written here."

Elias tugged at his lower lip. "Are you certain of the seal? I know for a fact that Captain Yagil is in Sidon, collecting a shipment of barley beer. He will not return for weeks."

"I would need something for comparison. Have you any other contracts with the Captain?"

Elias shook his head. "I know Jotham is behind this," he growled. "No longer satisfied with buying up all my debts, he has resorted to forgery."

"We must have proof," Daveed said, "for that is a serious allega-
tion. You need a lawyer."

Elias waved a hand. "One lawyer leads to many, and I cannot
afford lawyers. Is there no other way?"

Daveed thought of the scribes in the Brotherhood. They would
certainly be able to compare the signature on this tablet with others
that Captain Yagil had stored in the royal archive, but he did not
trust their skill, nor their honor. The Rab, however, would be above
reproach, as he was known to hold himself to the highest standards of
his profession. Daveed had been trying to gain an audience with the
master of the Brotherhood but he was a very busy man, being second
in power only to the king. "I will ask the Rab to look at it," Daveed said
now to Elias. "You stay here, sir. You are needed at the vineyard. This
is your busiest time of the year. I will take care of this and return home
as soon as I have an answer."

Daveed had been back to the Brotherhood four times in the past
thirty days, to be told each time that the Rab was occupied. Each
time, told this by Yehuda, who spoke with significant pauses, allowing
Daveed to fill in the words. He knew the son of Zira was waiting to be
compensated for allowing him to meet with the Rab. In Lagash, the
Master of Scribes was accessible to all citizens, even though it might
take a while before the audience happened. But Daveed wasn't even
placed on the Rab's calendar. Not without a bribe!

On each of his visits, however, Daveed had made detailed note of
the inner chambers and corridors, had paid attention to the comings
and goings of scribes, had observed Yehuda's behavior as he walked
past certain doors—at one point the man had even stepped in front
of Daveed as if to block his way. Behind him, a plain and unassum-
ing door, as if to disguise the fact that something, or someone, very
important lay on the other side.

All registered scribes in Ugarit were allowed free access to the
library, and so Daveed strode with confidence and purpose, as if he
had business there, as he followed the main corridor. He smiled
and nodded at those he passed, keeping an eye out for Yehuda,
and when he arrived at the plain door, paused to look around. The
corridor was deserted. Except for men's voices coming from other
rooms, and the flickering of flames in brass lamps, there was noth-

ing of note. And so he put his hand to the bronze door latch, lifted it, and slipped inside.

The chamber was large yet surprisingly dim—in fact a solitary brass lamp hung from chains in the center of the ceiling. It illuminated a bed, carpet, chairs, and a table. Someone's living quarters. But if it were for a scribe, he would need more light! Daveed held his breath and listened, knowing he was trespassing, but suspecting he had entered a special room. Incense filled the air, and Daveed recognized it as rare and costly. So no ordinary man lived here.

"Is someone there?" came a voice from the darkness, startling Daveed. He looked around. The center of the room glowed softly from the light, but shadows hugged the outer edge, and beyond that was darkness. He could not see the walls. "Shalaam and the blessings of Dagon," he called softly. "Forgive the intrusion. Have I found the chambers of the Honored Rab?"

"Shalaam. Step closer, my son."

Following the direction of the voice, Daveed crossed through the circle of light and entered the darkness on the other side. "Forgive me, but I cannot see," he said.

"Nor can I, my son. Closer, please."

As Daveed's eyes adjusted to the dark, he gradually made out the figure of a seated man. His chair had arms and was raised on a dais, thronelike, his feet on a footstool. Daveed received the impression of wispy white hair and a long white beard. The man's robe was also white, and it glowed ghostlike in the dark. On the wall behind him a blazing disc gleamed of hammered gold, with flames shooting out around the perimeter, while a single human eye stared down from the center. The Brotherhood's sacred emblem.

"Are you the Rab?" Daveed asked.

"I am," said the seated figure, his voice reminding Daveed of dried leaves and dust.

Daveed searched for words but found himself unable to speak. He was standing before the Rab of Ugarit, a moment he had dreamed of for years. "Forgive the intrusion, Rabbi," he said, using the Canaanite term of address that meant "my master." "I have been attempting for some time to gain an audience with you. I bring greetings from my

Master in Lagash, and the blessings of Shubat." Daveed's heart raced. His palms were moist. What did one say to one's hero?

"Are you uncomfortable with the dark, my son? There are tapers and a flint stone, if you wish light. I am sightless and so light is wasted on me."

"The dark does not bother me, Rabbi, and my eyes grow used to it," Daveed said, and wondered if the Rab's blindness was the cause of the Brotherhood's decline. Perhaps the brothers perceived him as crippled, and a crippled leader loses the respect of his followers. If the brothers had lost respect for their Rab and no longer respected him, then they had lost respect for themselves and for their profession. Daveed trembled with emotion. He wanted to shout out his fury over such an outrage, wanted to march out of this dim chamber, take the brothers by their ears, and drag them in here to prostrate themselves before their exalted leader. How could they disrespect their Rab in this way? Dishonor their noble profession and their gods?

"Are you a scribe, my son?"

His awe had turned entirely to anger. Where was the honor in this fraternity? Why was this lofty leader left to sit alone in the dark? While the brothers indulge in music and women, meat and wine? His voice was tight as he said, "I am, Rabbi. I am registered on the roll of scribes here in Ugarit. I received my training in Lagash, where my father is king."

The Rab nodded, and Daveed saw a look of approval on the ancient features. "You bring a request?"

Daveed explained about the tablet which he suspected was a forgery. The Rab said, "Take it to one of your brothers. He can compare it to records that we have stored in the archive."

Daveed hesitated, debating whether to tell the Rab the truth about what was going on outside this cloistered chamber. He did not want to be seen as an informant on his own brothers. But finally he decided that the integrity of the Brotherhood was more important than what the Rab might think of him. And so he told the old man about the bribes, the lack of discipline, the loss of morals and ethics, the disarray of the library—Daveed's face damp with tears as he choked out each despicable word.

When he was done, the Rab thought for a long moment, and then he said, "I had worried that perhaps my blindness would be a problem. Now I realize that it is. My sight has always been perfect, and so I was able to serve in my office. The blindness is only recent, but clearly it has had a detrimental affect on this fraternity." The Rab paused. "I sense your anger, Daveed of Lagash. You traveled far to join us and you find the Brotherhood is not what you expected."

"I am disappointed, Honored Rabbi."

"Would you change things if you were Rab?"

The question caught him off guard, but Daveed had an instant reply. "I would, Rabbi, upon my oath to Shubat."

"Then you must know this: I was not always this way. My blindness crept slowly upon me. My predecessor ended up blind, as did the Rab before him. It is the price we pay for service to our high office. Each time we look at a tablet, read a letter, draft a contract, record an inventory—each time we create a word or read a sentence, a little of our sight is lost. No one knows why. Sight is sacred. It is like blood. If each day you opened a vein and drained a little out, the day would come when you had no more blood to give. It is this way with a scribe's eyesight. Are you willing to give up your sight for the honor of serving your profession?"

There was a time when Daveed would have readily said Yes. But he thought of Leah. How he loved to watch her when she didn't know it. That errant lock of hair, curlier than the rest of her hair, that refused to stay behind her left ear, as if it were Leah herself—not necessarily willful or disobedient, but with a strong character and free spirit. Bent over her mending, Leah would reach up and absently tuck the long tress back up under her veil only to have it tumble loose again. Yes, that was Leah, Daveed thought now, wishing to conform, to be dutiful, but possessing a questing soul. Searching, although she did not know this about herself.

If he were to go blind, he would miss that.

"You hesitate, my son."

"It is a difficult question, Rabbi."

The ancient head nodded. "Pray on it. Ask your god for guidance. And now, as to the tablet you wish to authenticate, go to the archive yourself, find a document signed by the same man, and compare. If that does not work, then go across the public courtyard and find yourself an honest lawyer."

Daveed smiled, wondering if the Rab were attempting humor, for everyone mistrusted lawyers. "I thank you for your time, Honored Rabbi. I pray that I am privileged to meet with you again. The blessings of Dagon and health for many years."

Now the old man did indeed laugh. A raspy sound, but a mirthful one. "Bless you, son, my days are numbered. And perhaps the man who comes after me will bring the Brotherhood back to honor and integrity."

Daveed stiffened, wondering if he dared be so bold. But had not the Rab himself already opened the subject? "Have you yet chosen a successor?"

"Then you do wish to become Rab someday?"

"As I said, Honored Rabbi, I am a prince of the royal house of Lagash. I trained for seventeen years in the great schools on the Euphrates. I can read and write in four languages, from Babylonian to Egyptian. I have mastered three forms of cuneiform writing and Egyptian hieroglyphs, both classical and hieratic. I am a follower of the ancient god Shubat, and have dedicated my life to his service. I cherish my profession and hold myself to the highest morals and standards. I ask, Honored Rabbi, that you give me a chance to prove myself. I would like to help bring the Brotherhood back to righteous ways. To this end, I will devote myself and my time in the singular pursuit of a sponsor into this membership, and I will gain entry, I give you my sacred oath."

"I have already chosen my successor," the Rab said. "Do you know a brother named Yehuda, the son of Zira and nephew of Jotham the shipbuilder? He is a worthy man to take my place. But I have recently heard something troubling about Yehuda, that he suffers from the falling sickness. If this is true, Yehuda cannot be Rab of the Brotherhood. But if this is only rumor, then the appointment must go to him, no matter how noble and educated you are, Daveed of Lagash, for he is a man of Ugarit."

"I know it only as rumor," Daveed said in disappointment. "I have never with my own eyes seen Yehuda suffer such a seizure."

The old man then waved crooked fingers and said, "Come closer, my son, I wish to tell you something that these walls cannot hear."

Daveed leaned forward, the Rab brought his face close and whispered something that made Daveed suck in his breath sharply and say, "Shubat!"

Hannah hated the slave market.

She had always let Elias purchase their household slaves, and when she could, she allowed them to eventually buy their freedom. Although for some it was the only way of life they had known, and although for some slavery was a punishment for a crime, for many it was the only way out of a desperate circumstance. Usually it was financial straits that drove a man to sell himself and his family into slavery, the money from the sale going to his creditors. Or fathers with surplus daughters selling the girls to relieve a financial burden. The reasons were myriad, and as Hannah walked among the groups of caged men, women and children—while the slave merchant barked in her ear the virtues of this one or that—she had no idea what she should look for in a concubine.

When she finally explained to the man exactly what she wanted a slave girl for, he brought her to a special pen where females of a more genteel upbringing were kept. When new slaves were brought to the market, young and nubile women with soft skin and pleasing looks were always set aside for special male customers.

"Have you any particular requirements?" he asked, greedily fingering the money pouch at his belt, anticipating doubling its weight.

Hannah gave this some thought. Finally she said, "The girl cannot be Egyptian."

He nodded. The prejudice was universal.

"And she cannot be Habiru," Hannah added, seeming to recall this as another of her mother-in-law's prejudices, although she did not know why.

He wrinkled his nose. "Habiru women never find their way to this special pen. Now here is one you might be interested in, my lady." They came to stand before a slender girl, seated by herself. She wore a plain homespun gown, with a dun-colored veil over her hair. She appeared to Hannah to be clean and in good health. "Her name is Saloma," the slave merchant said. "She is seventeen years old, unblemished from head to toe, a virgin. Her hands are soft for her family are shepherds and such people are known for their soft hands."

He went on to explain that the girl was being sold by her five brothers because their wives were jealous of her beauty. Hannah felt sorry for Saloma, to have such weak-spined brothers. She asked a few questions and learned that the girl came from a family that produced males.

She was perfect. Yet Hannah hesitated. When she first thought of bringing a concubine into the house, she had not considered the woman's looks, but now she found herself in a dilemma: the girl must be comely enough for Elias to want to bed her, yet the idea of bringing a comely girl into the house made Hannah suddenly jealous. For truth be told, Hannah herself was plain. Her parents had even despaired of finding her a husband when a handsome young wine merchant from Ugarit visited their town and fell in love with their daughter. Hannah had been secure in Elias's love since, but now, for the first time, she found herself thinking: What if Elias falls in love with her?

"I will take her," she said, and removed gold bracelets from her wrist that had been a wedding gift from Elias and which she had sworn never to remove. But these were all the money she had with which to purchase a second wife for her husband.

It is not known why," Aunt Rakel said as she and Leah worked in the garden, "but the leaves of the thyme plant, when crushed and mixed with fat and applied to a fresh wound, will keep the demons of infection away."

She had snipped several stems from the bush, separating them so that she could shave each sprig with a small knife, catching the leaves in a wooden bowl. Rakel's task filled the autumn air with a pleasant fragrance.

"Even more potent is the essential oil. We will distill these leaves, Rebekka, until we have oil of thyme, which is inhabited by a very powerful healing spirit."

Leah and her aunt were surrounded by the lush greenery Leah had re-planted in her garden with after Tamar's malicious destruction of it. Bartering with a few small jars of wine from her father's winery, Leah had purchased cuttings and saplings, young plants and mature ones, because seeds would take too long to germinate and she was eager to learn as much from Aunt Rakel as she could before her aunt's memory was gone forever.

But Leah had already learned about the thyme medicine—she had in fact applied the ointment to a wound when a slave accidentally cut herself in the kitchen, and the thyme worked its magic—and this morning more important questions shouted in her mind: What part of Moloch's Dream is used in a medicine? Do we use the leaves? The seeds? Roots? How are the parts prepared? How is the medicine administered? Is it taken in a drink? Is it eaten in food? But Leah dared not voice these silent thoughts to Rakel.

That morning, her grandmother had said, "I notice that Aunt Rakel is speaking of Jericho a great deal these days. Are you asking her questions about the past, Leah? Remember your promise. Asherah is our witness, Leah, you must honor your promise not to pester Aunt Rakel with questions about the past."

And so Leah's hands were tied. Surely there was another way to mine that precious lode of medicinal information! "Pardon me, Aunt Rakel," she said, rising from the marble bench. "I will be right back."

Leah went through the gate, and when it swung shut she stood by the wall and, placing her hand on the goddess medallion she wore on a thong around her neck, closed her eyes and whispered, "Forgive me, Asherah, for the deception, but we are in trouble and I must find a way into my aunt's mind."

She waited a moment longer, then returned to the garden. "Aunt Rakel?"

"Yes, dear?"

"A messenger has arrived from the temple of Moloch. He said the priests are in need of Moloch's Dream. Have we any to spare?"

Rakel looked up with a frown. "Moloch's Dream?" She turned to look at the young plant in the corner. "It is too immature. We must wait for spring. When the resin glands are turning a milky white and the small hairs have begun to turn orange, it is then time to harvest Moloch's Dream. And even then we must carefully harvest and dry the leaves. The priests burn them in a bowl, you know. That is how they commune with the gods. They inhale the smoke and visions come to them."

Leah smiled. "Thank you, Aunt Rakel. I will inform the messenger."

When Hannah returned with the concubine, she found Elias at the outbuildings, overseeing the placement of the amphoras he had sent the day before to the docks but which he had been forced to bring back. "I do not know what I am going to do, Hannah. I have nowhere to store these. I must keep them out of the sun or the entire vintage will be lost."

"Bring them into the house," she said. "We have empty rooms that are cool and receive no sun. We can store the jars there until you have settled the problem with Yagil, or perhaps find another shipper. Elias, I want to introduce you to someone. Come with me."

In the hospitality hall Hannah introduced the girl to Elias, who stood in shock as she said, "Her name is Saloma. She will take my place until she bears you a son."

"Hannah—"

She held up a hand. "Please, my husband, this is difficult for me. Do not make it harder. I know my duty to this family. So far, I have failed, and so it was up to me to find the solution. Saloma will be given a room down the hall from our bedchamber. She will be part of our family. We will treat her with respect. And pray that the gods favor us with a son."

She took Saloma to the house steward, giving him instructions, after which Hannah went into Tamar's empty room.

She was overcome with sadness. No son of her own. And of three daughters, only one who turned out truly well. We never know where life will lead, she thought as she sat on the bed stripped of its linens. When I started out with my Elias, I pictured a house full of lively healthy children. Now it is but one man and five women.

As she looked around at the bare walls, the hooks without clothes, the empty storage chest, the vacant niches meant for gods and lamps, she thought: How can three babies come from the same womb and be so different? Leah, a spiritual child. Esther, so deformed that she rarely left the house, yet with a disposition like sunshine. But Tamar—from the time she could walk and talk there was something calculated about her actions. Hannah did not know where the girl's greed came from. She wondered if it had happened during the pregnancy, had she herself experienced a greedy moment and unwittingly planted that seed in her unborn babe? It was said that whatever happens to the mother during such a time directly affects the infant. Look at Esther. Hannah blamed herself for the deformed lip that left the girl's teeth exposed. She had been shopping in the marketplace and had bumped into a man who had the same hideous cleft lip.

During her pregnancy with Leah, because it was her first, Hannah had stayed home, tended to her sewing, spending afternoons in the sunshine, napping. And so her eldest was an obedient daughter—except for that night a year and seven months ago. But even that could not be called a selfish act, for Leah had only left the hospitality hall out of concern for her mother!

But Tamar. Through her entire childhood and adolescence, grasping, scheming, selfish. Hannah loved her all the same and was in anguish worrying about her welfare. Stealing from her own family. Running off with that horrible man.

Oh, Tamar, my child, where are you . . .

It had been months since she lay in Baruch's arms, in his father's olive grove—an hour of bliss, of knowing the purest and sweetest love, before he said he would never see her again.

Tamar had thought the pain would never go away. But time had healed the wound—time, and her days with Caleb. From the moment he had first set foot in their house, she had sensed a darkness in him and that he had come to their home with ambitious plans, and it had intrigued her. The more she worked on her seduction of the fiancé from Damaska, the less Baruch occupied her mind until, the day Caleb succumbed to her charms, she realized that Baruch had been right: she did possess a special power over men.

When she and Caleb had sneaked into the wine cellar to help themselves to her father's hidden treasure, Tamar had smiled with glee, enjoying her sin, her revenge, relishing the thought of her father's horror when he found the vault empty. And then taking Grandmother's gold rings! Oh, the pleasure of gloating! Of knowing how upset they were all going to be. The delight had stayed with her while she and Caleb were on the road, walking southward in search of a caravan, purchasing donkeys along the way, sleeping on the wayside, making passionate, greedy love under the stars.

But she was growing tired of being with him. Now that she knew what a clever seductress she was, that she could have any man she set her eye upon, she wanted to go her own way. North, she thought, to the fabled city of Ebla. Or perhaps farther east, where there were rich men aplenty.

But she and Caleb were continuing south along the coastal road, toward Sidon and beyond, inland cities—Har-Megiddo, Jerusalem, Jericho—where she did not wish to go! That was why, when she awoke early that morning in the room they shared at a dockside inn, Tamar had slipped out without waking Caleb, and had gone to the caravanserai north of town, to find a merchant going north and then east. To a new life.

And she had found such a caravan! Traders from Jerusalem carrying Egyptian paper, linen, lapis lazuli—Jerusalem being the northern terminus of trade routes from Egypt, where goods were traded with northbound caravans. The caravans also carried news—rumors about Queen Hatshepsut's poor health. About the possibility of her stepson assuming the crown of Egypt. About young Thutmose having his eye on the conquest of Canaan.

Tamar cared nothing for politics. She giggled to herself as she hurried back to the dockside inn where Caleb still snored—he had a prodigious appetite for sleep, Tamar had discovered, especially when he drank too much wine the night before. And she had seen to it that his cup was never empty. During their flight from Ugarit, Caleb had sold her father's treasures to merchants who did not ask questions, converting the cumbersome goblets and plates and statues into more convenient gold and silver rings. She would take those rings and hurry back to the caravan and be on her way before Caleb even woke!

As she drew her cloak tighter about herself, for the autumn wind coming off the sea was cold, she glanced at the boats and ships in the small harbor—she did not even know the name of this fishing town—

and stopped when she saw a boat moving away from the dock. Laden with cargo, it sailed under the power of forty oars, twenty on each side, rising and falling to the rhythm of a drum. Tamar stared at a passenger at the rail, standing with feet apart as he watched the harbor town recede. He looked right at Tamar, and he neither smiled nor frowned nor acknowledged her in any way.

Surely the man only resembled Caleb, she thought as she searched the crowd for a dock agent. But no, those shoulders like giant hills, that thick torso . . .

"Sir," she said, running up to a man who was barking orders at dock workers unloading cargo. "Where is that ship bound?"

He followed her pointing finger and said, "The island of Minos."

"Minos! But that is across the Great Sea!"

When he saw the distress on her face, and then looked back and saw the man on the deck, the agent gave a shrug and turned away. Another one abandoned, he thought dispassionately. That was the way it was in harbor towns. Easy for a man to get away . . .

When she reached the top of the stairs, she saw the door standing open. The innkeeper was inside, sweeping the floor. He gave her a startled look. "Thought you'd gone with him. You can't have the room. A traveling merchant is taking it for the next month. You gotta leave."

Caleb had taken everything, even her clothes, leaving Tamar with nothing.

A black tide rose in her, starting in a cold pit deep inside herself, flooding her, chilling her bones and blood and finally her heart. How dare he leave me! she thought, forgetting her own plan for desertion. She curled her hands into fists. Betrayed by yet another man.

But it would not happen again. Tamar knew that. Baruch and Caleb might have won, but they were the last. She was learning quickly. The next time, she would be the victor, she would be the one to make the choices.

The immediate problem, however, was a lack of funds and a place to stay.

She returned to the wharf to watch Caleb's Minos-bound ship recede. She watched it until it was a small vessel on the water, and she thought: Good riddance. I am still the daughter of Elias the vintner, granddaughter of Avigail of Jericho who herself descends from Ugarit's beloved King Ozzediah. My mother is beyond childbearing, and Leah is without a husband, and no man will have Esther.

Tamar smiled as a new plan dawned in her dark mind, bringing light and clarity to her thoughts. A new plan that guaranteed security and money and status. Most of all, a plan that guaranteed survival.

She surveyed the busy harbor where men handled ropes and sails, carried cargo on their strong backs, laughed or argued or stumbled out of taverns. So many resembled Caleb in their size and strength and coloring. It would be so easy. When I return home with a swollen belly—Father's first grandchild—he will have no choice but to take me back. I will tearfully tell him how Caleb forced me to go with him, and forced himself on me and then abandoned me.

With a light step Tamar sauntered along the waterfront where taverns waited for ships to bring thirsty sailors. She would be choosy, select only men who could boast having many brothers or sons. I will demand payment and find an inn until my goal is reached.

The family will have no choice but to welcome me with open arms. And when I tire of them, I will begin my search for a life of riches and ease . . .

Nobu was so excited he forgot to drink his wine and so the god-voices were louder than ever. He did not care. He did not even listen or reply! A wondrous message had arrived for his master and he could not wait to deliver it.

As Nobu busied himself with Daveed's wardrobe, he thought ahead about dinner. Elias and his family treated their scribe so well that he ate at their table every evening, which meant Nobu ate well, too. What would it be tonight? he wondered as he slowly and methodically laid out Daveed's handsome dark blue tunic with the gold fringe, and a black cloak made of luxurious angora. These would do nicely. A prince needed to remind people that he was a prince.

And after today, Nobu thought with glee, all of Ugarit was going to be reminded.

Out on the main road, Daveed had to force himself to walk with decorum as he turned up the path toward the villa. His impulse was to run, he was so excited.

He wanted to see Leah, tell her the good news—what the Rab had whispered in his ear. But first he must report to Elias. After meeting with the Rab, Daveed had gone to the archive and searched for records of Captain Yagil's business dealings, hoping to compare signature seals. But the archives were in such disorder that he could not find any! Daveed would continue his search until authenticity was verified.

He went first to his room, where he would bathe and change clothes before meeting with his patron. He was greeted by a happy Nobu who fussed over him like a hen, Daveed thought, and wondered what had gotten into his slave. Too much wine from blocking out the voices? "Master! Invoke Shubat! Word arrived today from your kin, the wealthy gem dealer. He is back from Goshen and most eager to meet with you. Master, I believe you have found your sponsor into the Brotherhood!"

Good news, indeed, Daveed thought as he washed the dust of the day from his limbs and changed into fresh clothing. "I must speak with Elias," he said to Nobu. "I will see you at dinner."

But Daveed encountered Leah first. She was hurrying through the hospitality hall where they almost collided. "Daveed," she said. "I have wonderful news!"

"As do I!" Boldly taking her hand, not caring who saw, he led her to the stairs and together they climbed up to the roof where they stood alone and together in the vibrant rays of a golden autumn sunset, a cold breeze whipping around them as if trying to keep the pair close together. He took her by the shoulders, wishing he could kiss her, marveling at his power of resistance, for it took every ounce of his strength not to press his lips to hers. He looked into her eyes that glistened with a new joy. And he felt himself lifted in joy. He thought he could climb upon the golden rays of the sunset and dance on them. "What is your news?" he asked, wishing he could call her his love, or his dearest, but daring not, for she was still married and he would honor that status until the seven years were up.

She told him about her morning in the garden with Aunt Rakel. "She revealed to me the most marvelous thing! But you first, Daveed. What is your news? Tell me!" she said, caught up in the electricity of the moment, relishing the feel of the last light of the day on her body, watching how the sky behind Daveed glowed with yellow and orange and red hues, as if the sun itself were bowing down to this prince of Lagash.

"I met with the Rab, and as I was about to leave, he whispered something to me. Leah, the Rab himself will sponsor me into the Brotherhood! And I know I will be able to prove myself in his eyes, for he said that 'outside blood' is what the Brotherhood needs to be brought back to righteousness. Only Yehuda stands in my way, but if he does indeed suffer from the falling sickness, then the appointment to the post of Rab will be mine. Now tell me, what did your aunt say to you?"

Leah's smile fell and the dying day went cold. "She told me the cure for the falling sickness. Partly, anyway. It lies in the leaves of a plant called Moloch's Dream."

Daveed stared at her. He, too, felt the day go cold. Shadows slithered across the rooftop like evil spirits as Daveed's eyes locked with Leah's. "By Shubat," he whispered in disbelief. "Leah, the Rab said I could be his successor if it is proven that Yehuda has the falling sickness. But if you find the cure . . ."

"I must," she said, tears rising in her eyes. "It is the only way to save my family from certain ruin."

Daveed spun away and slammed his right fist into his left palm. "Yehuda cannot be allowed to take the post of Rab! He condones bribery! He turns a blind eye to lax behavior, the scribes ignoring the rules of their sacred society, committing sacrilege!"

"I am sorry—"

"Shubat is my witness, Yehuda will allow the corruption to run so deeply that the noble fraternity will decay from within, splinter, until men no longer wish to belong, and it will fade away! What then will become of Ugarit's men of reading and writing? Where will they be schooled? Who will teach them? The art of written communication might die altogether. Leah," he cried so that his words flew off the rooftop, "it is my sacred duty to watch Yehuda, and when I witness a seizure, I must report to the Rab, and the Rab will pass Yehuda over for the succession!"

With tears glistening on her cheeks, Leah said, "And I must find the cure for Yehuda's falling sickness so that Zira will spare my family. We cannot go on much longer. Oh Daveed, I cannot turn my back on my family."

"And I," he said grimly, "cannot abandon my brothers."

She collapsed weeping against his chest, her tears staining his tunic. "Daveed, what are we going to do?"

He put his arms around her, his own tears falling onto her veil. His throat closed. He could not speak. The gods were cruel. Daveed had no choice but to expose Yehuda's falling sickness, and Leah had no choice but to cure it.

CHAPTER EIGHT

The King suffers from The Demon That Crushes the Windpipe, Em Yehuda. They say he is having breathing problems. Spells of wheezing. They are getting worse to the point where he cannot breathe and his face turns bright red with the struggle for breath. He is surrounded by priests and physicians, and sacrifices are being offered up in all the city's temples. Citizens are praying for him."

Zira knew how the people of Ugarit felt about their monarch. King Shalaaman was a wise king, a great diplomat who had a talent for keeping peace and order and pleasing foreign powers. He kept the treasury full, taxes low, the people happy, and when he sat in judgment on capital cases, he judged fairly and few disputed his decisions. Shaalaman was not his real name. Born Yedayyah, he was so loved by the people that they gave him a name that meant "peaceful."

As the man finished his report—a spy paid to keep his ears open in the royal palace—Zira stared through the diaphanous hangings over the archway that led out to the balcony overlooking the sea. It was a cloudy spring day with the threat of rain, sounds of industry and prosperity rising from the harbor below. But Zira paid no attention to any of this as she chewed her lip deep in thought. Time was getting short. Yehuda must be appointed Rab before the king died.

Dismissing the man with a snap of her fingers—he had been well paid and needed no words of gratitude—she decided it was time to put her foot down.

Zira found her son in his private garden where he gave lessons to rich men's sons, boys who needed only a little reading and writing with no intention of becoming professional scribes. Time away from the pressures of working for the Brotherhood, Yehuda said. He liked taking his leisure with boys. The work wasn't hard. They didn't learn much, just enough to please their fathers. Yehuda said their laughter delighted him. He adored their youth, their innocence. Zira did not like to think of Yehuda, a grown man of thirty, with his students, none older than fifteen. He touched them too much, she thought, giving them encouraging pats on the shoulder, squeezing their arms. Sometimes he had them spend the night.

She put it from her mind. Scribes and their world were of no concern to her. More important issues troubled her heart. She had had ambitions to live in the royal palace for as long as she could remember, and now that ripe fruit was coming close to her grasp. She had broached this subject with him before, and he always dismissed her with a wave of his hand. As his mother—as Em Yehuda—she had to obey. But this time she was going to stand her ground.

"Send them away," she said, meaning the boys. Reluctantly, he did so, adding, "You have spoiled their lesson."

In what, she wondered? "The king's illness worsens. You cannot put this off any longer, my son. You must speak with the Rab about your appointment."

He rose from the bench, tall and angular, wearing a tight woolen brown shirt over a white pleated kilt. An elegant man, she thought, if a bit dour. "Mother, this is a very delicate situation, one that requires tact and diplomacy. It is not so easy as you think."

"Why are you so obstinate!"

"And when did you become such a harridan?"

She gasped. And the look of such astonishment on her face drove Yehuda into a guilt-ridden sulk. The throne was her idea. He was content with his pupils. Why was she so intent on being the Dowager Queen? Why did she have to be like that creature in Egypt, the evil Hatshepsut who no doubt ruled her unfortunate stepson the way Yehuda was ruled by his mother? What is it with mothers and sons, he wanted to shout. Why can you not leave us alone? I never even wanted to become a scribe! I had my friends, my chariot, my hunting bow, and my beloved Enoch whom you sent away—

"Aahh!" he cried suddenly.

Zira rushed to his side. "My son, what is it?" But she already knew. The eyes rolling back in his head, the strangled sounds, the dropping to the ground and the thrashing of his body like a fish flopping on a dock. The foaming mouth. The wet stain spreading on his pleated skirt. The bulging veins and purple skin.

"My son, my son!" she cried, throwing her body over his. Yehuda's head made sickening sounds as it banged on the marble paving stones. His muscles jerked and convulsed. Vomit seeped from his lips. And now another, more ignoble stain spreading down the white kilt . . .

His special companion came hurrying out with a pillow and wrist restraints. There was never anything anyone could do for the seizures, merely ride them out and keep Yehuda from hurting himself. Later, the companion would bathe him, change his clothes and put him to bed. Yehuda would sleep deeply through the rest of the day.

Zira drew back and sat on a marble bench to bury her face in her hands. "Asherah protect my son," she sobbed. Yet even in the horror and anguish of witnessing his affliction, her mind remained sharp and clear: if he did not speak soon with the Rab, she herself would seek an audience and make it clear that Yehuda was to receive the appointment in quick time or Zira would withdraw her funding of the Brotherhood which, over the years, had grown to a considerable sum.

But first a visit to the temple of El, Father of All, to make sacrifice and to beg the Great God to lift this abomination from her son.

Avigail eyed the remarkable peddler with suspicion. Traveling merchants coming to the gate of Elias's villa were commonplace, as the house lay on the main route leading to southern cities. She used to turn them away, thinking their wares too lowly for her family. But now she was not as choosy, and took time to inspect a peddler's offerings. Usually it was cheap cloth or inexpensive cheese. But this man, who stood in the damp chill of early spring in a ragged red and black striped robe, and a long unkempt beard, was trying to sell some very strange birds.

"They are called chickens, my lady," the man said in heavily accented Canaanite that made her think his home lay far from here. "They produce eggs on a daily basis and they cannot fly so you need not keep them caged."

"No bird lays eggs every day. It is a seasonal thing. Where do they come from?"

"The Indus Valley."

"I have never heard of it," she said, frowning at the fat brown creatures in the cage by his feet. They were rounder than normal birds, and made a curious buck buck sound.

"And they make for good eating, too. They are a tasty and juicy bird."

Avigail gave thought to birds that could continually produce eggs so that they would soon pay for themselves. But then she looked at the merchant again, looked past him and realized a family was traveling with him, for a woman and two children sat on a skinny donkey at the end of the path.

She realized they were Habiru, homeless wanderers who worshipped their god in a tent! And Avigail decided that no amount of eggs or plump birds on their dinner table was going to persuade her to do business with such people. She said, "Good day," and withdrew into the house.

Putting the itinerant Habiru from her mind, she hurried along the colonnaded hall, her thoughts scattering like grain on the wind. So much to do!

Ever since Caleb and Tamar had run off with Elias's hidden fortune, Avigail had had to find ways to keep the family in food and clothing. In the villa's laundry area next to the kitchen, she picked up a bundle of tattered and torn robes and gowns that would normally have been given to the poor but which now would be mended and worn again. Cutting expenses was Avigail's foremost thought.

Although she and the others made personal sacrifices without complaint, what Avigail regretted was having to dismiss their private guards. She had also had to sell the safe-house hidden in the hills, and had dug up the emergency gold buried there. All the security and safety she had carefully constructed over the years—since their flight from Jericho—gone.

But Avigail was made of tough fiber. Although born to privilege in one of Jericho's wealthiest families, her veins coursing with the blood of ancient royalty, she had been taught at an early age the value of honest work, and to be resourceful. All the women of this house—Hannah, Esther, Leah, even aged Rakel—worked at daily labors, whether it was weaving or mending, tending vegetable gardens, collecting milk from their goats. Elias had been forced to sell slaves, and to let paid servants go, so the family had to take up the slack. Thank the gods that Saloma, the concubine—who was six months pregnant with everyone praying for a son!—had surprised them all with a skill for spinning raw wool into fine strong threads. Even the cheapest wool Avigail could buy turned into quality yarn in Saloma's capable hands.

But there was one commodity for which Avigail did not spare expense. Every purveyor and vendor of amulets, magic spells, incense and oil who came to the gate found a ready buyer in the desperate and highly superstitious Avigail. Each of her girls now wore extra protective amulets to ward off bad luck, and prayers to Asherah and Baal were recited, morning and night, by every member of the family. Avigail saw to that.

As she neared the sunroom where she knew she would find Esther at her beadwork, Avigail wondered if it would be possible to sell some of Esther's necklaces. The girl had a talent for making colorful jewelry out of inexpensive beads, creating designs that delighted the eye. Perhaps the agent who had discreetly sold Avigail's household treasures might help her to sell Esther's beadwork—without anyone knowing where they came from, of course.

A small reflecting pool had been built long ago in the garden adjacent to the sunroom, and Avigail found Esther there, kneeling at the edge, bent over the water, looking into it. But there were no fish in there. What on earth was the girl looking at?

Avigail stopped short when she realized that Esther was looking at her own reflection. Esther, who could never be persuaded to look at herself in a mirror! She was doing something strange, Avigail thought as she watched her granddaughter.

"Dear child, what are you doing?"

When Esther came to her feet, Avigail was stunned. Esther was tall! And willowy. When had she grown? When had she entered young womanhood? Halla, Avigail thought, I have been so wrapped up in keeping this house going, in keeping my family together that I did not notice my youngest granddaughter was growing up.

And—to Avigail's further shock—growing beautiful.

For there was no other way to describe the young lady who came gracefully toward her. Esther had pinned her veil across her face, just the lower part, under the nose, concealing her mouth and chin. Her resemblance to Leah was strong, Avigail noted for the first time, but more than that, with the cleft lip hidden, Esther was actually a beauty!

"Auntie Rakel gave me the idea," Esther said as she unclipped the corner of her veil and drew it down. "She said that when she was a girl, the women of Jericho covered their faces when they went out of the house. I wanted to see how it looked."

"Yes," Avigail said slowly, the memory painful. "But . . . when did Rakel tell you this, dear?"

Esther shrugged. "Auntie Rakel talks about Jericho every day."

Avigail's smile turned to a frown. "What do you mean? I have not heard her speak of her life there. Not lately."

"She talks to Leah. In that little garden they work in every day. Where they make medicines."

Avigail stared at her granddaughter who, now that the veil was down, was deformed and ugly again. "Esther, what are you talking about?" But already Avigail had a suspicion.

"Leah is trying to learn the cure for the falling sickness so she and Auntie—"

Avigail dropped her bundle of mending and ran from the room, Esther staring in astonishment after her.

"We do not cure Moloch's Dream in the sun, as it reduces potency," Aunt Rakel was saying as she showed Leah how to cut the fan leaves off the tall stems, leaving only clusters of buds on the stem. "We slow-cure it by hanging the buds upside down in a dark, ventilated space over the course of a week or two. When the stem snaps, it is time to cut the buds off. We will then place the clusters in jars that are sealed tight. Every few hours, open the jar to release the moisture. Do this for a few days until the buds are dry and no more moisture gathers in the jar. Moloch's Dream will be ready for use."

Leah sat in the spring sunshine, trimming fan leaves to expose the precious buds that contained a powerful medicine. In just a few days, she thought in excitement, they would have the cure for the falling sickness and she would take it to Zira as a peace offering.

All she needed to know was in what quantities the dried buds were administered, and in what manner, because Aunt Rakel had warned her that too much of the medicine caused the soul to leave the body forever without the patient dying.

She loved coming here with Auntie Rakel every day, to work among the green bushes and leaves and grass, among the red and white and pink and yellow flowers, to listen to the droning of bees, to delight in the flash of butterfly wings, as she handled herbs and roots, making salves and ointments and teas that eased her family's physical ailments. But there was sadness in her heart this morning as she and Rakel harvested Moloch's Dream.

Daveed was leaving soon.

Although she had seen little of him in the months since they had stood in the rays of a golden sunset and discovered that their paths were at cross-purpose, and although he spent much of his time with his brother scribes, quietly making friends with men who believed as he did, that reform was necessary, Leah knew he was still here, officially living in this house and serving her father. A tenuous presence, but a presence all the same. Soon, this house would feel empty.

"Auntie Rakel," she said now, "how is Moloch's Dream given to a patient? Does one inhale it, as the priests of Jericho do? Or is it boiled into a tea?"

The elderly woman did not reply as she bent suddenly and plucked a feathery little plant from the soil, to examine its tiny pink flowers. "Bless my bones, this is cumin. Do you know, Rebekka, when cumin is boiled with goose fat and milk, it is an excellent remedy for an upset stomach. My Yacov suffers from stomach ailments. I think it is because I ate too many hot spices when I was pregnant with him."

"Auntie Rakel, who had the falling sickness in Jericho? How was Moloch's Dream given to him?"

The gate creaked open at that moment and Avigail stood there, staring in astonishment at the pair on the marble bench—the slender granddaughter in cream colored gown and veil, the elderly aunt, plump and shrunken, in dark gray. "Leah! What are you doing? Say a prayer! I told you not to torment poor Aunt Rakel with your questions."

Leah rose from the bench. "Grandmother, forgive me, I did not wish to distress you, but I—"

"Distress me! Leah, invoke the gods at once. You have defied me! And you kept it a secret to spare my feelings?" Outrage made her voice go shrill. "What in Asherah's name has gotten into you!"

"Rebekka," Aunt Rakel said, "Quickly say a prayer. How many times have I told you it is not ladylike to shout." Dropping the cumin, she looked around. "I must go find something. I believe it is in my bedchamber . . ."

"Rakel dear," Avigail said as she escorted the frail woman to the gate. "Why don't you go and lie down?"

After the aunt had gone, Avigail stepped closer to Leah and said, "See? You have agitated her. Tell me why you disobeyed my order that you were not to ask Rakel about?"

"Grandmother, look," Leah said, pointing to the tall, lush plant that grew against the wall, its green spiky leaves growing long and jagged, with dense clusters of buds in between. "We planted this months ago and now we are harvesting that part of it which contains medicine. It is called Moloch's Dream, and Auntie Rakel says it will cure the falling sickness. We can offer it to Zira in exchange for peace with Jotham."

Avigail set her lips in a grim line. "You should have come to me first."

Leah searched her grandmother's face, and saw new lines of worry, new shadows of fear. "Grandmother, why in the face of such strife will you not let me pursue the cure for the falling sickness?"

Avigail wrung her hands. She searched for words, for an explanation. But her reluctance—her fear—was something that could not be defined. It had to do with Rakel's past. With Jericho. She had no idea why Leah's trespass upon Rakel's past frightened her so. All she could think of was that Rakel knew secrets, and that some secrets were best left unspoken.

"Child, I just think that making her remember the past might be painful or distressful to her."

"I do not do this for myself, Grandmother. I do it to save our family. Oh Grandmother," Leah said suddenly, turning away, wringing her hands. "I wish I did not have to pursue this at all! I wish I was not aware of a cure for the falling sickness. Asherah forgive me but I want nothing to do with all of this!"

She turned an anguished face to her Grandmother, whose own look was one of puzzlement. "Then do not pursue it. Forget the cure—"

"Grandmother, did you know that Daveed is leaving soon? His apprenticeship here is almost over. He is joining the Brotherhood of Scribes."

Avigail blinked. Daveed? The scribe? What had he to do with this? "Yes, I knew that. But he has offered to come back whenever Elias needs him."

"But did you know that Daveed has sworn to keep Zira's son from succeeding to the post of Rab of the Brotherhood?"

Avigail stared at her favorite grandchild, a young woman of twenty now, known to all as Ish Caleb even though her husband was absent. Avigail knew of her granddaughter's pain of being abandoned, knew of the humiliation of being the object of gossip and pity because her husband ran off with her sister. And yet . . . Avigail sensed a new pain in the girl now, saw a new emotion on her face, as though a layer had been stripped away to expose a private agony not meant for the eyes of others. "What is it, Leah?" she said softly. "Tell me. Asherah is with us. What troubles you so?"

"Daveed has told me that the Brotherhood is in trouble. The Rab is blind and the brothers have fallen into immoral ways."

"Halla." Avigail whispered, tracing a protective sign in the air. "How can this be?" The Brotherhood symbolized the honor and integrity and stability of Ugarit itself. "Are you sure, Leah?"

"Daveed saw with his own eyes. The brothers demand bribes for their services, they dishonor the gods, they have become lax in their duties, in their morals. Daveed says it will get worse if Yehuda becomes the next Rab, and so Daveed is watching Yehuda for a sign of the falling sickness and when he sees it, he will report it to the Rab and Yehuda will not succeed him. Daveed will then start a plan for saving the Brotherhood."

Avigail took all this in, listened to the words, heard the passion with which they were spoken. And then she realized: her granddaughter was in love with the scribe. For why else would Leah be in such anguish about finding the cure for the falling sickness?

Avigail sank to the bench, suddenly weary. She had been so focused on keeping the family going that she had not seen the forbidden love blossom beneath her own roof.

"Grandmother," Leah said as she joined Avigail on the marble seat, "if I find a cure for Yehuda, the Brotherhood will be lost. If I do not find the cure, our family will be lost! What am I to do?"

Before Avigail could reply, Leah said, "Asherah is my witness, this is all my fault. I brought this calamity onto our family and now it is up to me to set things right. But to do so means I must betray Daveed. It breaks my heart to think of that, yet there is Father laboring in the wine sheds."

Avigail took Leah's hands and said, "First of all, there is no shame in honest labor. And this is not all your fault. Do you think you were alone in this house that night two years ago? I was here. Your father. Esther, Tamar, Rakel. So many things happened that night. Zira could have remembered her place and stayed silent. I could have ordered your mother to her room to lie down. I should not have been so direct in my inquiry about Yehuda's affliction. And your father could have apologized to Jotham. Asherah is our witness, Leah, we are all to blame, and now we must all work to fix it." She sighed. Like her granddaughter, Avigail herself now had a difficult choice to make: to keep the past buried because of nameless fears, or set aside her fears for the sake of her family. "And if that means," she said, "finding the falling sickness cure and offering it to Zira—"

"And what about Daveed?" Leah cried. "If we cure Yehuda, the Brotherhood will die!"

Avigail felt her shoulders sag beneath the weight of so many worries, the fate of this family, this house. "Invoke the gods, child. The Brotherhood is not your responsibility. And neither is Daveed. You love him. But your duty is not to him. You are still married to Caleb, and your priority is to this family. I am so sorry, dear child, that you have carried this burden alone. Find the cure for the falling sickness. Ask Rakel until she tells you, and then I will take it to Zira myself as a peace offering."

"Oh Grandmother, I am so confused!" Leah broke down and wept in Avigail's arms.

As she comforted her granddaughter, thinking how complex and unfair life could be, the enormity of the situation began to dawn on her: that, all this time, she had thought she had everything under control, whereas in fact she had no control at all!

The house steward entered the garden—a sour man who was enjoying his position in the House of Elias less and less each day. As more slaves were sold and servants let go, more work fell to him. "My Lady, a special visitor has come asking for an audience with you."

"Who is it?" Wondering: Jotham, with more attacks? Zira, to gloat? A nameless creditor from another town, tired of sending letters of collection?

"It is the young mistress, My Lady. The second daughter of the house, Tamar Bat Elias."

After Tamar and Caleb disappeared, Avigail told people that Elias had sent his son-in-law on a business trip, and that their middle daughter had gone to Jericho to marry a kinsman. It didn't matter that people didn't believe it. She was expected to save face.

But as she hurried through the house, a sudden turmoil of emotions—Tamar was back!—Avigail wondered what she was going to tell people now!

"Hello, Grandmother," Tamar said softly when Avigail came wordlessly into the hospitality hall. For the journey home, Tamar had carefully chosen subdued garments suited to her new modesty and humility—a dark brown dress that reached her ankles, loosely sashed below her bosom, a beige traveling cloak closed at the waist, and a tan veil that was devoid of ornamentation. Her only jewelry was a copper necklace and a bracelet made of twined hemp.

"Where is Caleb?" Avigail said without sentiment or ceremony.

"I ran away from him, Grandmother, as soon as I had a chance. He forced me to go with him." Tamar recited her speech as she had practiced it over the miles. Best not to tell them he had gone to Minos. Let them hope he might come back.

Avigail held up a hand. "I will not hear it for I do not believe you. You are not my granddaughter any more. This house is no longer your home. Go, and do not come back."

But instead of turning away, Tamar opened her traveling cloak, and when Avigail saw the swollen belly, she whispered, "Halla! Asherah be with us!"

Her first thought was: adulteress.

And then she thought: Elias's grandchild. And my first great-grandchild. Even though Saloma will give birth in three months, she might deliver a girl. But if Tamar's child is a boy . . .

Avigail trembled with a sudden glimmer of hope. Was this a sign from the gods? Did this signify that their bad luck was about to change? A grandson for Elias. Visitors coming by to congratulate, to bring gifts and blessings, with friendships being mended, former customers deciding that, with a change in his luck, Elias's wines might be good after all. So much joy and hope in this house that they begin to find their way back to life as it was before the night of disaster, two years ago.

Avigail clasped her hands so tightly together that pain shot through her fingers. Under other circumstances, back when the family was prosperous and enjoying good luck, she would not have had to make this decision. Tamar would be turned out of the house with no question. But circumstance had changed. Avigail now thought: The gods answer our prayers in most unexpected ways. "Very well," she said, "You may stay." I will tell people of a tragedy in which Tamar's young husband died. Doing his duty to the family, Caleb took the widowed Tamar, his wife's sister, under his protection, as his concubine. He got her with child, but then he was taken captive by sea pirates. Would people believe it?

It did not matter! Blessed Asherah, Avigail thought as her frail hopes blossomed into happiness. Tamar might be carrying a boy. The House of Elias will be saved!

"What is going on here!" Elias boomed as he strode into the hospitality hall, his handsome face flushed, his hands stained purple as proof of his need to toil as a common laborer. "The gods are my witness, she cannot stay under this roof. She brought shame upon our family! She is a whore!"

But Avigail fussed over him, her hands patting his broad chest. "Elias, my son, say a prayer. If the child is a boy he will be your grand-son. Think!"

He stood as unmoving and immutable as a statue, pondering this fact, caught between wanting a grandson and preserving honor. A man had his pride.

Hannah, having heard the news, came in, her veil fluttering, her eyes darting to Tamar, the naked desire on her face to embrace her daughter. "My love, Tamar is our flesh and blood. We created her."

"She has shamed us. She stole from me and slept with her sister's husband."

"But she has come back! The gods are with us. She is repentant, and she is with child. Elias, be practical. Tamar can be another pair of working hands."

"Another mouth to feed!"

"She does fine embroidery. We can sell her work, Elias. She can pay for her keep."

When Elias said nothing, Avigail said, "I will write at once to my cousin in Damaska. They will rejoice when they hear the news." And perhaps send gifts, she thought. Gold and silver for Caleb's first-born . . .

But Elias finally spoke, saying, "No! Caleb stole from us. He committed adultery with his wife's sister. He abandoned his wife. They would have known what an evil nature he had. They knowingly sent us a thief and a blackguard. When we sent letters about their kins-man's treachery, they denied any knowledge of it. They have forfeited any rights to this child. You will not write to them."

He squared his shoulders and lifted his chin in pride. "Wife," he said to Hannah in a stern tone she was unaccustomed to hearing, "tell our daughter that she may stay. But tell her never to speak to me or to linger in my presence. Arrange for her and the child to stay in sepa-rate quarters. I wish never to see her again."

He turned on his heels and stormed out while Tamar lifted her veil to hide her grin of victory.

Her name was Edrea and Jotham was in love with her. As he stroked the polished wood of the main mast, the sounds of the busy harbor faded away—the cries of gulls, the shouts of deck hands and stevedores, the sharp wind whistling in from the Great

Sea. It all vanished as Jotham had ears only for the sound of *Edrea's* ropes and sails and rigging.

Today was her birthday, the day of her launch. Jotham attended the christening of every one of his ships, he personally named each of them, and he loved them all. If Jotham ever caught a sea captain or sailor abusing one of this beauties, he had the man flogged within an inch of his life.

"It's unnatural," his sister carped. But what did Zira, or any woman, know about the personal relationship between a man and the boats he created? "It's why you do not have children," she said. And he had to admit she might be right. Jotham was never happier than when he was at his dockside shipyard, overseeing the laying of planks, the measuring of lines and sails, even the painting of good luck signs on the prow and stern. And he was careful to choose only names that would have a good influence on the ship's performance. Edrea was Canaanite for "powerful."

She will travel far, he thought in deep affection. She will sail to Minos and Mycenae, to the northern coast of Africa. My sweet beauty will carry oil and wine, ivory and grain. She will be welcomed in every port in the world, and when she is under full sail on the waves of the sea, she will bring tears to men's eyes.

The image filled Jotham with pride. This was what he lived for. Creating his beauties.

He stepped back from the main mast and looked up and down the new ship, at the shining decking, the perfect rows of oars, the furled sails made of woven flax. And felt . . .

He frowned. There it was again. The vague restlessness he had been feeling of late.

Squinting out over the sparkling water in the harbor, inhaling the fresh sea air, and feeling the blessings of a golden sun on his body, Jotham sensed the curious new hunger within himself. He did not know when it began, but it was growing. And now he felt as if ships weren't enough to satisfy him.

What was it he hungered for? He knew it wasn't lust for a woman. Now that Jotham was one of the richest men in Canaan, he could have any woman he wanted. And with them being so easily obtained—many mothers paraded their unmarried daughters before him—his romantic life had become jaded. Leah, the daughter of Elias, was the last girl he truly lusted after, and once she married a kinsman named Caleb, Jotham lost all interest in her—and in women in general, it seemed.

As he scratched his armpit, wondering if this was what boredom felt like, he saw one of his spies coming up the gangplank onto the new ship, a man wearing a leather kilt under a brown and black striped cloak. He was the same man Jotham had hired to gather information on Elias's kinsman, Caleb, who came to marry Leah. But when the fool ran off with the sister, Tamar, Jotham instructed his agent to drop the matter of Caleb and take on a more urgent and interesting assignment: spying on the mysterious Hittites in the north.

Jotham held up a hand to stop him. Like all men of the sea, Jotham was highly superstitious. No one was allowed on board until *Edrea* had been properly christened with the priests chanting spells over her, and the first sail filling with the breath of the gods themselves.

"Shalaam and blessings, my lord," the man called.

Jotham went down to meet him, eyeing the package the man carried. When he realized what it might be, Jotham's interest sharpened. "Shalaam and blessings, my friend, the gods are with us. Have you brought something for me?"

"I must show you this in private, my lord."

They stepped into the recessed doorway of a warehouse owned by Jotham. The agent looked up and down the waterfront to make sure no one was watching, and then he untied a string and peeled away the cloth wrapper.

Jotham's eyes bugged out. "Halla!" he whispered. "Invoke the gods, my friend! The rumors are true?"

"They are, my lord," the agent said in excitement. "It was at great risk to my life that I smuggled this out of Hatti, and at the expense of every copper ring I had to my name."

Jotham lifted the black-metal knife from the agent's hands, marveling at this solid proof of what could only be called a miracle.

There had been rumors in recent years about mysterious forges in the northern mountains where secret operations were producing weapons. Rumors were that they were made of iron. But everyone knew that iron was useless except as a heavy weight. And yet Jotham held in his hands a weapon that had been forged from iron ore! How was it possible?

"The secret, my lord, is the heat. In giant stone ovens, the iron ore is burned at such a phenomenal temperature that the metal separates from the ore. This changes the iron into liquid form that is then cast into molds and hammered into desired shapes, such as swords and daggers. Even tips for spears and arrows. It is stronger than copper and bronze. I have proof." Reaching to his belt, where a scabbard hung unseen beneath his cloak, he withdrew a bronze dagger.

"Strike me with the iron knife, my lord."

Jotham gave him a skeptical look. "Are you certain of this? My aim is good and my arm powerful."

"Strike me with it!"

Jotham raised his arm and brought the weapon down. His friend brought the bronze dagger up in a swift parry—and the bronze dagger split in two.

"Halla!" the shipbuilder cried, hefting the iron dagger up and down, feeling its weight and strength—its power. "May the gods be with us," he murmured.

And a new lust was born in Jotham's heart.

Tamar was indifferent to the child she carried. The unborn babe was but a means to an end, insurance for her survival. Once it was out of her, she would leave it with nannies, with her mother and grandmother, she did not care. Tamar's only thought of the future was how rich she was going to be. Now that she had a home and a name, she could work on her plan to find a man on whom she could work her charm—a man of wealth and means, and who would take her away to a fabulous life in an exotic land.

When the first pain struck, she welcomed it. Tamar hated how fat she had become, and clumsy, with swollen ankles and the need to urinate a hundred times a day! When the second pain struck, she informed Avigail who called the women of the family together to light incense, pray to the gods and assist with the birth.

She labored for fifteen hours, screaming, "Get it out of me!" And then it came—a healthy boy with robust lungs, and the instant he was placed at her breast, a violent change came over Tamar. She looked at the little red face, bloody and scrunched, saw the tiny quivering hands, heard the pathetic mewling, and an alien emotion flooded her entire being. Love. Maternal devotion. She cried as she held him to her breast and thought what a splendid little creature he was.

As Tamar recovered from her labor, holding the baby to her breast, she could not help gloating over her victory, could not help congratulating herself for being smart. And then she thought: this is true woman-power. For I have created life. And now they could never turn her out of the house. She had given them their precious grandson. Look how they smile, how quick they are to forgive me. Look at Grandmother hurrying off to tell all her friends, planning his naming feast, praising the gods for bringing this joy into their house.

It had been one month since she returned home and her father declared he never wanted to set eyes on her again, yet he came to her bedside every day now, to marvel at the life she suckled, the boy she had created. She saw pride in her father's eyes and she thought: I was not born a boy, but I have given you one. She knew her father had forgiven her and that, in time, she would be the honored daughter of the family. Perhaps the most honored woman, because not even her own mother had produced a living son.

My son . . .

She had not anticipated the maternal love, the intense bond she felt with this new person—made from her own blood. There were so many men in that nameless fishing town, she forgot their faces, how they smelled. They had nothing to do with the creation of this perfect child. He came from me. Only me.

I will name you Baruch, and from now on, for the rest of my life, I will never again be Bat Elias. I will have the honored name of Em Baruch . . .

Hannah came with food. Despite Mother Avigail's happiness to have a male child in the house at last, Hannah alone had completely forgiven Tamar. It was a mother's right, she thought, to forget her children's sins and shower them with love.

As she placed the tray beside the bed—a generous and expensive offering of blood sausage, pork chops, wine—she said, "Your grandmother and I are making arrangements for the baby's naming celebration. So much joy in the midst of so much worry! We have already heard from many friends. All will be coming to witness our happiness. And we have discussed the matter of the name. As it is the tradition in the Damaska branch of the family to name each firstborn son Uriel, we will honor that tradition."

"No, we will not," Tamar said quietly, looking at her baby, unable to tear her eyes from his perfection. "The child is mine. I created him. He sprang from my soul. I will choose his name."

"Nonsense," Hannah said as she reached for the baby. But Tamar shrank back. "No! He is mine. You will not name him. You will not raise him. You will not even touch him."

"I am his grandmother!"

"Father's concubine is pregnant. You can have Saloma's baby. You will not have mine."

Hearing the raised voices, Avigail came into the bedchamber. "Tamar, quickly say a prayer! You will do as we say. We must give him a name from Caleb's family."

Tamar tossed her hair. "He isn't Caleb's child."

Two blank faces stared at her. Tamar thrust out her lower lip as she plucked at the baby's swaddling blanket. How she hated her self-righteous grandmother and spineless mother. Giving themselves airs. Believing in their imagined importance. They were not going to take her son.

So she said again, "This child is not Caleb's," and delighted in the horror dawning on their faces. Emboldened, Tamar continued: "I did not run away from him, Caleb abandoned me. He went to Minos! I watched him sail away and he is never coming back. He left me before I was pregnant. I knew I could only come home on one condition, so I slept with many men. Sailors, farmers, travelers, blacksmiths. When I knew I was with child, I came home. So now he is mine alone. You cannot touch him."

The silence stretched. A wasp flew in from the garden and buzzed about, unable to find the way out. Avigail quietly left and returned with Elias. A look stood on his face that Hannah had never seen before, and it sent a cold wind through her heart. "Tamar," she said quickly, "take back what you said. Say the child is Caleb's. Say it three times and invoke the protection of the gods."

But before Tamar could realize what was happening, her father shouted, "You think that because you have a son I cannot turn you out?"

"Turn me out?" She tossed her head and tightened her hold on her baby. "What are you talking about?"

"You are a common whore and I will not have you raising my grandson."

"And would you deprive your only grandson of a mother?"

"He has a mother!" Elias boomed. "Her name is Leah!"

Hannah and Tamar stared at Elias in open-mouthed shock as he said, "You were Caleb's concubine, as Saloma is mine. And just as the child Saloma delivers will be Hannah's child, so is your son Leah's. Under the law, it is so."

As reality dawned on her, the awful truth of the mistake she had just made, Tamar said, "No! I am his mother!"

"You deprived Leah of a husband. You will not deprive her of being the mother to her husband's son."

"He is not Caleb's son! I slept with sailors. I slept with farmers, and boys and old men and—even with Egyptians!"

"By the gods, you she-devil!" Elias wrenched the baby from her arms and handed it to a pale-faced Avigail. Grabbing Tamar by her hair, he dragged her out of bed, across the room and out into the hall, while she kicked and screamed all the way. Hannah flew after them, crying, "No, my husband! Do not do this! Do not take my daughter away from me!" She pulled at his clothes and he pushed her so hard she fell backward onto the floor.

Dragging a screaming Tamar through the house, he flung open the front door to the warm summer night and threw her down the stone path. She landed on her hands and knees, looking up in shock.

"Get away from this house!" Elias shouted, tears of fury in his eyes. "You have shamed us enough. We will have no more of you!"

They were forced to listen to her pathetic cries through night, Tamar begging to be let back in, to see her baby, while they sat in somber silence. Elias stood his ground and told Leah she was now the baby's mother. He lit incense in every room until their eyes stung from the smoke. He prayed to Dagon and Baal, and invoked the name of every god he could think of. He summoned Daveed and dictated a legal document declaring his daughter, Tamar, dead. He dictated another, naming the child as Leah's. While Nobu rocked back and forth in the shadows, Daveed took down every grimly spoken word. And when he was done he sent a silent prayer to Shubat.

This was a bad-luck house. A doomed house. And he was helpless to save them.

In the morning, they heard no more sounds from the front garden, and when Leah went to look, Tamar was gone.

Although her father had declared that "the whore" was not to be allowed back into the house, that she was not to be given food or shelter, that her name was not to be spoken ever again, Leah went in search of Tamar and found her huddled in the olive grove that belonged to Baruch's father.

"Please tell Father to let me back in," Tamar begged. "Please tell him I am sorry." She was filthy, her long hair matted with leaves, tears streaking her face. "Asherah is my witness, I cannot bear to be away from my baby."

"I will come back tonight," Leah said gently. "I will bring food and clothing, and any copper rings I can find. But Father is in a rage. He will not let you see your son again."

That night, as the moon rose, maddened with grief and hunger and thirst, Tamar ran among the ghostly tree trunks, scratching her face on low hanging limbs. "Baruch, my love, are you here? Where are you? The baby is yours, Baruch. He is our son. All those men—" Her voice broke. "They meant nothing. As they lay on top of me doing their dirty business, I thought of you. The baby is our child. Born out of our love. Oh, Baruch, where are you?"

She looked up at the moon and saw Baruch's face. Her beloved. They had sworn eternal devotion. And then he went away. Her head throbbed. She felt her heart contract in pain. "I cannot bear this!" she cried to the impersonal stars.

Her chest heaving with sobs, she tugged at her nightdress, drawing it over her head, flinging it to the ground. Dropping to her knees, she clawed at the fabric, finding the seams, breaking her fingernails as she tore the stitches, separating the material where it had been sewn into a garment. She used her teeth to tear apart the delicately woven wool, shredding it, pulling threads apart, soaking the cloth with her saliva and tears as she sobbed and called out Baruch's name.

"I will never love another as I loved you," she cried, pulling at the cloth with all her strength until it came away in strips. The sound of ripping and tearing filled the warm night air. Tamar was oblivious of the soil beneath her knees, the pebbles and twigs cutting her. Moonlight washed over her naked skin as the nightdress was reduced to jagged strips. She shivered with anguish as she brought ends together, tying them in knots, dampening the delicate wool with her tears.

"Why did you leave me, Baruch? I gave you my heart. You took my heart. You killed me."

One by one, with her fingers turning raw, she knotted the strips until they formed a long tether. "Baruch! Baruch!" she called as she jumped to her feet and searched the overhead branches, as if she might find him among them. She flung the knotted strips over a sturdy limb and then madly searched the ground for a stepping stone. A small boulder lay nearby. She rolled it until it stood nearly under the branch, but not directly under. And then she tied the two dangling ends of the rope together, knotting them so that they formed a loop.

"The gods will bring us together someday," she wept as she stepped up onto the boulder and brought the loop over her head. "My Baruch. My beloved."

She closed her eyes and leaned forward, so that her weight was supported by the noose, and only her toes held her to the boulder. "Asherah be with me," she sobbed and she stepped off the rock. Her body swung away. She heard the tree limb crack and groan. The noose tightened around her neck. And then—

My baby!

No! I do not wish to die!

What have I done? Asherah!

Tamar clawed at her throat and swung her legs. Where was the rock?

Don't let me die! I want to live! I want my baby!

Her toes brushed the boulder. She kicked her feet, tried to gain purchase. She pulled at the noose, scratching her neck until it bled. She struggled for air as she dangled at the end of the rope. She could not breathe. Pain shot through her toes as she kicked for a foothold, but her feet were bloody, slippery.

Please . . . Asherah . . .I want to watch my son grow up . . . I did not mean for this . . . Help me . . . Someone help me . . .

* * *

Leah returned to the grove the next morning with food and drink, and found Tamar hanging from a tree, cold and dead. As she ran blindly back to the house for help, Leah was unaware that it was the same tree that had shielded two lovers one spring night when Baruch had taken Tamar's virginity.

When seven days of mourning were up, Avigail stood before the gathered family, the newborn in her arms, and said, "We will pray every day for Tamar and beg the gods to receive her soul and keep her safe. We will never again speak of the things she said the night before she died, for she was not in her right mind, she did not know what she was saying. This baby is Caleb's son. He is a son in the House of Elias. This precious baby is a sign from the gods that they have not abandoned us and that we must never give up hope. The gods in their wisdom took my granddaughter, but left a great-grandson in her place. In this way do they remind us of their justice and compassion. We will name him Baruch, as Tamar wished. And he will be the ever-lasting light in our house."

Leah was now forbidden to Daveed forever.

Because Elias declared the child to be Caleb's, and because a son could only be raised by kin, if Leah married again, it must be to a blood relative. She was now "Em" and beyond Daveed's reach.

"Go to the House of Gold, Daveed," she said. "There is no longer any need for you to stay here."

"Other than my love for you." He said this with sadness, for he knew that they were indeed about to go their separate ways, perhaps never to see each other again.

"I have a gift for you." He laid a hard clay tablet in her hand. "I searched in the archives for information on the falling sickness. I found this very old tablet. It is so old that no one can read the symbols. However, I was able to translate one word: valerian. I believe this is a recipe for a cure for the falling sickness. Perhaps if you mention valerian to your aunt, or show her the herb, it will spark the rest of her memory of the remedy."

"But the Brotherhood, Daveed. If I cure Yehuda . . ."

"Leah, if a man suffers from a terrible affliction and I know there might be a cure for it, but I withhold that cure, then I would be no better than my fallen brothers or Yehuda. I will not become Rab at the expense of another man's life. Pursue the cure, Leah, and save your family. If that means that I do not become the next Rab, then I shall find other means for bringing the Brotherhood back to righteousness. It is in Shubat's hands."

She lifted a necklace over her head and placed it over his, laying upon his chest the pink stone of Asherah, which the merchant at the temple had said was blessed with the goddess's power. "Asherah will protect you," Leah whispered, "for I fear you are facing darkness and dangers."

He took her face in his hands and said, "I believe, dearest Leah, that fate is not in our own hands, but in the hands of the gods. We can hope and dream, and do our best here on earth, and love each other as much as we can, but when it comes to guiding our own paths and fashioning our own destinies, we are without knowledge and tools. We must trust in our gods, in Asherah and Shubat, to bring us through this trial safely. Know, my dearest, that although we can never be together as husband and wife, I will always love you. And know, too, that if you should ever need me, Leah, you have but to call and I will come."

He kissed her, and he knew it was for the last time.

CHAPTER NINE

"The remedy for the falling sickness is taken as a cake," Aunt Rakel said as she stitched the frayed hem of one of Elias's cloaks. "Into a bowl of flaked almonds, dates, and dried figs, you crumble the cured buds of Moloch's Dream. Add butter and honey and mix well. Bake in an oven, and when cooled, cut the cake into squares. If ingested every day, morning and evening, the seizures will stop."

"But how much of Moloch's Dream do you put into the mixture, Aunt Rakel?" Leah asked. "You said that too little is ineffectual, too much is dangerous."

Rakel brought the garment close to her milky eyes and said as she studied her handiwork, "I will tell you a woman's secret, Rebekka, which we practiced in Jericho without our menfolk knowing. When you are worn out from childbearing and wish to have no more of it, and your husband insists you keep producing babies, you take a small snippet of sea sponge, tie it to a string, soak it in vinegar and place it high up next to your womb. Conception will not take place, and with the sponge being so soft, the husband will not be aware of it." She cut her sewing thread and added, "Half a lemon, with the fruit's meat scooped out, when placed like a cap against the womb will work just as well."

They were in the sunroom, working at their chores in the warmth

197

of a midsummer morning: Leah and Aunt Rakel, Esther, Hannah, and heavily pregnant Saloma. Their mood was somber as they sewed, embroidered, beaded, spun wool, or sat at a loom. Suicide was the worst bad luck that could befall a house. Since such a terrible incident invited evil spirits, Avigail had spent precious money for a priest to come through with purifying incense and special chants to chase away the bad luck.

And yet they felt joy as well. A son had been born at last in the House of Elias! Tamar's baby slept in a cradle among baskets filled with yarn and wool. Avigail had hired a wet nurse for the infant, but once Saloma gave birth, she would breastfeed this little one along with her own. Little Baruch was now the center of their universe. The women took turns holding him, walking with him. They delighted in his smile and tiny laugh. He was the promise of their future, their little flame of hope, and no matter what misfortune might come their way, Elias's women had only to look at Baruch and know that the gods were with them still.

Hannah worked quietly at her sewing. She missed her middle daughter, and knew that her grief would never end. Esther, too, was thinking of Tamar as she sorted colorful beads which she had obtained from an itinerant peddler who exchanged the clay beads for a bottle of wine. But Saloma had only known Tamar briefly, and so while she worked wonders spinning high-quality thread from flawed wool, thanked the gods for her good fortune. Rescued by Hannah from a life of slavery and hard work, she was about to give birth to a child whose father she had secretly fallen in love with. It did not matter that he called her Hannah when he climaxed, or that he stopped sleeping with her once she announced her pregnancy. She thought only of the smile that would come to his lips when she placed her newborn in his arms. And if it should be a girl, then Elias would return to her bed to try again for a son.

Leah and Aunt Rakel were the only two engaged in conversation—about old days in Jericho and an herbal garden that had produced remarkable medicinal cures. To everyone's amazement, Rakel's remedies worked. As Leah coaxed secrets from the elderly woman, and diligently committed them to memory, the women in Elias's house put the recipes to the test and found them to be reliable. Saloma's morning sickness, Hannah's monthly discomfort, and a winter fever that had swept through Ugarit—all eased by Rakel's herbal recipes.

Now they prayed that Leah could encourage their aunt to remember the precise measurements in the remedy for the falling sickness. The family's circumstance had become so desperate that Elias was selling the winery.

The others did not speak as flies buzzed in the humid air, bees found their way inside, and the occasional breeze came in from the garden, bringing floral fragrances.

Leah tried to think of a way to guide Rakel's thoughts, but there seemed to be no logic to her thinking. She often switched subjects, sometimes in midword. Leah felt the pressure of time. Despite being cheerful and talkative, Rakel seemed frailer these days. She had stopped drinking her morning tonic, was eating less, and had not touched wine in days. Her color was not good, Leah thought. Rakel was pale and her eyes had taken on a filmy look.

She thought of Daveed, at that moment preparing for the ceremony of the heliacal rising of the White One, at dawn tomorrow, at which time the old Rab would name his successor. The eyes of the city were upon the House of Gold, as everyone knew that the health of the Brotherhood reflected the health of Ugarit. Without men of writing and reading there could be no government, and without government there would be chaos. Everyone spoke of the old Rab, who had decided to retire and hand his job down to a younger man, and the citizens wondered who he was going to choose. The consensus leaned toward Yehuda, although several candidates were being considered. Ultimately, the decision was up to the gods, and so the old Rab was deep in prayer and meditation, awaiting their answer.

Blessed Asherah, Leah thought, please ask the gods to choose Daveed, for he will heal the ailing Brotherhood and bring it back to glory. If Yehuda is chosen, the Brotherhood will suffer, and it will be too late to do anything about it.

Aunt Rakel said, "The rule of thumb is: as much of the almond, fig, date mixture as you can cup in your hand—that is one measure. You mix four of those measures with Moloch's Dream. Then you have the remedy for the falling sickness."

Four startled faces turned to her. Leah froze. She had just sent a prayer to Asherah. Was this a response? The Great Goddess has unlocked Rakel's mind so that we can receive the cure. If I send it at once to Yehuda, Father will not have to sell the winery. But if I send the cure to Yehuda, Daveed will not be the next Rab and the Brotherhood will continue its corrupt ways.

Blessed Asherah, what should I do?

As Hannah and Esther and Saloma looked on, with Tamar's little Baruch stirring in his cradle, Leah set aside her sewing and, turning to Rakel, said, "Auntie Rakel, how many measures of Moloch's Dream do we mix in . . ."

As Avigail walked among the vines that carpeted the mountain slope behind the villa, she saw her son walking with a potential buyer for the vineyard. The man was frowning. He was the eighth person to come and look at the property. And he was shaking his head.

As she drew near, she heard the stranger say, "What about the house?"

"We are keeping the house," Elias said to the man from Ebla. "I am selling only the vineyards and winery."

"I am sorry, my friend, but why would I buy a property on which I cannot live? How would I guard my crops, keep thieves out, protect against trespassers? If you change your mind about the house, you can send word to me at the tavern called the Blue Heron, by the harbor."

As she watched the man go, Avigail saw the look of worry on her son's face. She saw how he squinted in the sun's glare at the white walls embracing the collection of buildings that made up his home. Elias's blood and sweat was in this soil, as was the blood and sweat of his fathers before him, going back eight generations. He had been born in that house, had enjoyed a full boyhood and youth there. He had brought Hannah into that house and his daughters were born there. And now his grandson, Baruch, had been born there.

When he saw his mother coming along the dusty path, Elias squared his shoulders and presented a confident air. "Mother! I'm glad you're here. There is something important I need to discuss with you. I'm afraid the man from Ebla has decided against buying the winery. But we are not defeated yet, Mother, nor will we be! I have come to an important decision. As you know, up to now I have resisted going to the royal treasury for a loan. But I will go to the bank at the House of Gold first thing tomorrow and obtain a line of credit."

She waited while Elias paused to brush a bee away from his face. He cleared his throat. "I am going to invest in a factory that friends and I are going to build on the outskirts of the city."

She narrowed her eyes. "What sort of factory?"

"One that will manufacture a new kind of weaponry."

"Halla!" Avigail pressed her hands to her bosom.

"Mother, the people of Ugarit cannot ignore the clouds that are gathering in the south. If Hatshepsut dies, her nephew will assume control and rumor is he wants to reclaim lands invaded by his grand-father. But a handful of farseeing men, myself included, know we must be prepared. The Hittites in the northern mountains have invented a process that turns lumps of iron ore into the strongest metal the world has ever seen. They are fashioning swords that will defeat those made of copper and bronze. We must follow suit. The world is changing, Mother. We cannot ignore it. If Egypt invades Canaan, we must be prepared."

Seeing her stricken look, Elias said more gently, "Mother, there are enough winemakers in the world. I wish to be part of the new age. If it is true what they are saying about the Hittites, that they are chang-ing the face of war, then we must be part of that revolution."

"I do not like this talk of war." The thunder of war chariots, men on horses, torches burning in the night as Canaanite blood runs into the sand . . .

"We will profit from it, Mother. You will see. With the loan I obtain from the bank, using the vineyard and winery as collateral, I will invest it in the factory. The swords and knives and shields it produces will be in demand everywhere. We will be rich, Mother."

Avigail wrung her hands. "Oh my son, this is not the way—"

"Papa! Grandmother!"

They turned to see Esther running toward them from the house, her hair streaming out behind her in the sunlight.

"Halla, child! What has gotten into you!"

"It is Auntie Rakel," the girl said breathlessly. "She has given Leah the cure for the falling sickness!"

They hurried to the house where Leah was saying, "Aunt Rakel, please talk more slowly. Is it four measures of the cake mixture to one measure of Moloch's Dream, or it is the other way around? You have changed it several times now."

The others in the room were watching with singular attention, their embroidery and spinning forgotten. They held a collective thought—Zira will reward us—with each holding a separate hope. Esther: we will have money to buy a husband for me. Saloma: my baby will be swaddled in the finest blankets in Ugarit. Hannah: we can buy a good husband for Esther. Avigail: we will not lose the winery after all, and my son will not build weapons of war!

Only Leah's private thought was not one of hope but of regret. Curing Yehuda meant Daveed would never be appointed Rab.

"What is the remedy?" Avigail said, rubbing her hands in anticipation of her visit with Zira. Shall I give her the formula up front, or demand something in return? What is the gracious way to handle it? Should I request that Jotham be present?

Leah looked up in frustration. "I believe she revealed it, Grandmother. But her mind is everywhere. When I try to clarify the recipe with her, she speaks of another! Now I can't be sure!"

Avigail pursed her lips and thought for a long moment. They were very close to their salvation. A level head was called for. Finally, she said, "Keep talking to her. We must not lose this opportunity. We will send for Daveed. He will record everything Rakel says."

"Grandmother, we cannot do that!" Leah said. "Daveed is preparing for the rising of the White One, when the new Rab will be named. He is praying and fasting and dedicating himself to his god. It would be wrong to call him away from that. Sacrilegious even. I will memorize what Aunt Rakel tells me. And I will remember the cure for the falling sickness."

Leah looked up from her place at Rakel's bedside. "Daveed! What are you doing here?"

"I was told you sent for me."

"I did no such thing. I know you are preparing for—" She stopped, then said, "That would be Grandmother. I told her we must not disturb you."

He came forward, his eyes on the woman in the bed. "What is the urgency?"

Leah described the morning's events, culminating in Rakel divulging the falling sickness cure along with other remedies so that Leah could not keep them all straight. "Grandmother said we should have you record them. But Auntie said she was tired and wanted to take a nap."

When Daveed saw how pale Rakel was, how shallow her breathing, and the vacant look in her eye, he said, "You should have summoned me sooner. I might be too late."

But he had brought his box and supplies, and quickly set about to preparing to take dictation. "Nobu came with me. He is waiting downstairs. I need to tell him to go back to the Brotherhood and await me there."

Nobu moaned softly as he leaned forward with cupped hands to catch water trickling from the fountain. He felt awful. And he was parched. He drank noisily then reached for more water.

"Fool, this is what you get for trying to silence us. We will not be muted by wine. We will speak our peace."

"Please leave me alone," he muttered as the morning sunlight in the garden stabbed his eyes. The hangovers were getting worse. He wished he could stop drinking wine, but he dared not for then the god-voices would fill his skull night and day.

"Are you all right?"

"I said leave me alone!" But he looked up suddenly and saw that it was a real person who had spoken. The youngest daughter, named Esther. "I invoke the gods, please forgive me. I thought I was talking to the demons in my head."

She came forward, her long dress and veils whispering against her legs. Nobu detected a fragrant perfume. He saw that she held her veil up to her deformed mouth. Despite his headache and upset stomach, it did not escape his notice that the girl had beautiful eyes. "Are you not well?" she asked. "Your coloring is strange."

Nobu was sitting on a marble bench, drenched in water that had run through his fingers. "It is but the result of too much wine last night. I pray to the gods that I could never take another sip, but I cannot!"

She sat next to him and he saw the concern in her eyes. "Why not?"

He explained about the god-voices that had plagued him since childhood. "Wine used to keep them quiet, but I find that of late I must drink more, which then makes me miserable the next day."

"But why do you fight your own thoughts?"

"Eh? My thoughts? No no. It is demons who yammer at me day and night. Or malicious gods, may Shubat protect me!"

"Poor Nobu, do you not know that it is your own thoughts you are hearing? I hear thoughts in my head, too. And there is nothing wrong with responding to them. I know plenty of people who talk to themselves. It is not a curse. I think it is a blessing, Nobu. Many people cannot understand their own thoughts. They have muddled minds. I would think that you have a very keen mind."

He blinked at her with his slow turtle-eyes. He noticed now that her forehead was finely formed and delicate, and her cheekbones exquisite. Wisps of black hair peeked out from under her pale orange veil and he was suddenly gripped with the desire to touch them.

"Why don't you abstain from wine for a few days and listen to your mind?" she said. "If you need to drink strong wine, then you can always take it up again. But how will you know if you do not try?"

"Do you mean listen to the voices instead of trying to shut them out?"

She nodded and he saw her eyes smile. He wished she would lower her veil. Now that he thought about it, the deformity was hardly noticeable.

"Pray for me, dear girl, I will try it."

She rose and said, "I will indeed pray for you. And now the message that I came to deliver. Your master will be detained here for a while. He wishes you to return to the Brotherhood."

As she spoke the words, Nobu looked up at the lovely creature and discovered something new about himself. He had once declared that he could not bear to stay in this house another day, now he did not want to leave.

Through the afternoon Leah gently encouraged Rakel to talk about her life in Jericho, guiding her back to the subject of the garden of healing herbs whenever she strayed to other topics. While the elderly woman spoke, Daveed's hand moved rapidly over his lumps of damp clay, capturing Rakel's wisdom and knowledge in symbols. She shared many formulas—from earache cures to binding a sprained ankle—but she could not be brought back to the subject of the falling sickness.

At sunset, Rakel dozed off and Leah lit the lamps and candles around the bedchamber. She smiled gratefully at Daveed. "You must return to the House of Gold now."

But he looked at Rakel, who seemed to have grown smaller in the space of one day. Her features were in repose, her skin had lost all pigment. And there were shadows around her eyes. He had seen this before, back in Lagash, when he had been summoned to a bedside to record dying words, to witness a last will and testament, to write one final letter. He wondered if Rakel was going to last through the night. "There is still time. I need only return before dawn."

"I will go fetch us some wine, and something for Aunt Rakel."

As she started to leave, Leah looked down at the clay tablets inscribed with Rakel's healing recipes, and as she stared at the incomprehensible lines and dots and triangles, she frowned. What was she supposed to do with these? Once they were sun-baked and stored safely away, how would she later be able to read them? How would she even know which was the elixir for stomach ulcers, which the salve for burns?

"Daveed," she said, "what do I do with these tablets? How do I know which is which?"

"You would find a scribe to read them for you." But as he said the words, he realized they were meaningless. Proud of the tablets on which he had captured Rakel's wisdom, Daveed had not thought it through. Without a scribe, the tablets were useless to Leah and her family. If illness struck this house, she would be at the mercy of a man perhaps waiting for a bribe. He pictured Yehuda, silent, waiting for gold to cross his palm.

For the first time in his life, the full extent of a scribe's power struck him. He had always thought of his profession as a service to others. But in truth, citizens were at the mercy of himself and his brothers. It was why strict rules of ethics and morals had been put into place, to keep scribes from preying upon the desperate.

"Can you teach me to read?" Leah asked suddenly.

The question surprised him. "I cannot teach you in one day what took me seventeen years to master. Writing is very complex. There are hundreds of symbols and each has many different meanings."

She laid her hand on his arm. "Go back to the House of Gold, Daveed. It will soon be time for the ritual with the Rab."

"I need to be here when your aunt wakes up. I will go up to the roof and meditate under the stars to prepare for my appearance before the Rab. Call me when Rakel wakens."

He kissed her—chastely, on the cheek—and hurried from the room.

When he reached the roof and delivered himself into the moon-light, inhaling the fragrance of summer blossoms, watching the lights of the city twinkle and sparkle in the warm, humid night, Daveed pondered the problem of the medicinal tablets he had inscribed for Leah, for in truth they were no help at all. Nor could he answer her simple questions. It reminded him of when he was a boy and he had asked an instructor why one symbol had so many different meanings.

The teacher had replied, "If we didn't then we would need thousands of symbols instead of hundreds, and no man can memorize so many."

Something flitted at the edge of Daveed's mind. Thousands instead of hundreds. Can those numbers be reduced? What if it were less than hundreds?

Strange new thoughts flooded Daveed's head. They confused him. He was unused to such analytical thinking, to reasoning out a problem. It was a scribe's duty to learn and then to repeat what he had learned. Working out something new was alien to Daveed's mind, yet he addressed it now, feeling a curious excitement invade his bones. He felt as if he had walked for miles and had come to a mysterious and challenging brink.

Fewer symbols . . .

What if a symbol stands for just one thing? he asked the night. What if it isn't a sound, and a syllable, and a word, and a verb, and a noun, and a concept? What if is just one thing?

With shaking hands, Daveed opened his scribe's box and withdrew a lump of damp clay. Unsure of what he was doing, knowing only that he was suddenly driven by a new impetus, he pressed the stylus to form two parallel wedges bisected by a third, with two triangles on the right edge. He stared at what he had just written. The symbol could stand for the sound of "O." It could also mean an "ox," since these wedges had evolved from an ancient pictogram that had looked like an ox. But it could also mean "might" and "strength." It could also mean "to pull" or "to carry." Finally it could also be part of a word that contained the syllable "ox." Daveed had forgotten how truly complicated writing was.

But if he were to choose . . .

He looked toward the east. The sky was turning pale. Dawn was perhaps an hour away. He must depart soon for the House of Gold.

Daveed refocused his thoughts on the complex problem before him. If he were to choose just one value for a symbol, which should it be? It made sense to choose the "meaning" symbol. The sign for an ox should just be for an ox. The one for a tree should be just that.

He frowned. There would be thousands upon thousands of symbols to memorize.

But if he were to choose just—

If a symbol stands for a sound, and those sounds could be laid together to form a word, how many symbols would we need?

Only as many as there are sounds.

His heart racing, Daveed picked up his stylus and chose a symbol that meant water, rain, cool, clean, or just "D". He pressed it into the clay. He then pressed in the symbol for "Ox" but using it now only as an "O." Finally, three wedges and a triangle that meant "Goat" or "graze" or "herd" but he used it only as a "G" and he saw that he had written the word "dog."

Daveed stared at his simple invention and trembled with presentiment. No other meanings. No need for context. A simple code of letters, and any man who had learned them could read this.

Daveed stared at the clay in astonishment. By Shubat, was it possible?

Taking up his stylus, his hand trembling now as he felt the universe move and shift around him, he pressed four symbols into the clay, each normally having several meanings but this time using only the sounds they represented—and he wrote the word "tree."

So simple, he thought, yet ingenious! Why had no one thought of it before?

The gods gave mankind writing and it was sacrilege to change what the gods had made.

A memory: Daveed toying with the symbols when he was eleven years old, making designs on clay, and the sudden sharp pain of the instructor's wand on his arm. The red welt rising. Daveed fighting back tears. The teacher's booming voice, "Words are sacred! You do not play with them for that is desecration!" Daveed never experimented with the cuneiform symbols again, but kept to the rigid code of what a scribe must do.

But the gods gave us the ability to think, he silently argued now, to reason and to solve problems. They gave us imaginations.

He thought of the moral decay of the Brotherhood because the scribes had gotten too powerful. They have a monopoly on reading and writing, Daveed thought. Even doctors and lawyers rely on them. Such power has corrupted them.

Lifting his face to the early morning wind, Daveed thought, Things must change.

He recalled certain men of Ugarit talking about smelting iron ore for the creation of deadlier weapons—stealing a secret process invented by the Hittites in the north. If the way men wage war can change, Daveed wondered now, cannot the way they communicate change as well? The Egyptians created a more efficient form of writing, the hieratic script. Is that why they are conquerors and we Canaanites are not? Our way of doing things is archaic and clumsy. Ugarit, like Lagash, is mired in customs and traditions that no longer work for the citizens. A more efficient form of writing, one that will allow more men to be able to read and write, could only improve the health of a government and its people. And scribes, losing their monopoly, would lose their power and ultimately their corruption.

Daveed observed the eastern sky. I will pray, he decided. I will lay the problem at Shubat's feet and do whatever my god commands.

He held his face into the cool wind blowing off the Great Sea, smelled the salty freshness, a fragrance that always made him think of hope and new beginnings. He closed his eyes and opened his heart to Shubat. He sensed unseen beings and spirits gather around him, as if the fading stars, when they vanished from the sky, came down to earth as guiding angels, messengers of the gods. Please, give me an answer, Daveed prayed. Reveal to me your cosmic wisdom.

And then . . . something else, a Greater Presence . . .

Daveed shuddered. His forehead broke out in a sweat. "Who are you?" Daveed silently asked, for he knew it was not Shubat. He felt the weight of the sky press down upon him, his body tingled as if the disappearing stars were pricking his skin. With his eyes still closed, Daveed opened his heart. "Speak to me, Lofty One . . ."

And suddenly he feared who, or what, it was.

Was it possible?

El was said to be the most ancient of all the gods—he was the Father—and he was worshipped far and wide from Canaan to Lagash and even in distant Babylon and Ur. It was even said that the nameless god of the wandering Habiru was El, for El was not a name, it was the Shemitic word for "god." And because the language of Lagash was similar to Canaanite, Daveed now addressed the ancient deity as El Shadday, which meant God Most High.

"I beseech you to bring your Elohim to the Brotherhood," Daveed whispered, elohim being the Shemitic word for the full concentration of El's many divine powers. Daveed knew that there was no greater force in the universe than the Elohim. He had never called upon them before, and it frightened him now to do so.

Sweat poured down his face. His body trembled with fear. It was said that the might of El could destroy mountains. El had caused the Great Flood of the earth that nearly erased all of mankind. No man spoke directly to so high and powerful a god, yet Daveed of Lagash dared to now.

And he sensed, rather than heard, a voice whispering: Mankind must read and write so that they will know Me. The written word will bring men to righteousness and follow My laws. . . . It is no longer right that words are sequestered in the hands of greedy, corrupt men. The Day of the Book is coming. My sons must be prepared . . .

"I do not understand, Magnificent One. What is the Day of the Book?"

He listened. There was no response.

Daveed opened his eyes and blinked in confusion. Were the gods ordering him to disobey? Had he imagined it?

Dawn was breaking on the horizon, a new sun about to bring a new day, a new year, and when he realized the sky was growing light, Daveed looked out over the city and realized he had time still to get to the House of Gold, bathe and dress, and make his audience before the

Rab. But he must leave now, this very minute, and run to the city with great speed.

And then he thought of Rakel, still sleeping, waking any moment, medicinal treasures spilling from her lips, so great a fountain of knowledge and wisdom that Leah would not be able to remember it all.

Turning his back on the pink dawn, turning deaf ears to the eruption of cheers and trumpets in the city—putting thoughts of celebrations and festivities and the name of the new Rab from his mind—Daveed was aware only that he was taking his first step of defiance since he had recited the Scribe's oath of obedience back in Lagash. He took two fresh lumps of clay and spent the next hour creating two new tablets. When he was done, he hurried back downstairs.

Leah was sitting by her aunt's bedside. "Daveed! You are still here! The Brotherhood—"

"Leah, it is not by accident that I went up to the roof and began to look at writing with a different eye. I believe I was led up there by a power even greater and more ancient than Shubat, perhaps El the Most High himself drew me up to be with him beneath the stars. Strange new ideas entered my head, such thoughts, Leah, as I had never experienced before! Look," he said, showing her a tablet that was still damp. "These are the thirty symbols of the thirty sounds we make when we speak. Leah, these are all we need! When you learn these, you will be able to read anything I write in this script."

"How—?"

He produced the other tablet. "This is one of your aunt's remedies. I rewrote it in my new code. Now look at this symbol," he said, pointing to a letter on the other tablet, which was long and narrow, and imprinted with a row of symbols. "This is the 'M' sound. Do you see this symbol on the tablet that I rewrote?"

She examined the prescription tablet. In the distance they heard the sounding of a great bronze gong. It signified the opening of the gates to the House of Gold. Daveed and Leah knew it also meant citizens were gathering to hear the name of the new Rab. She pointed to a symbol. "There," she whispered.

"Now this one," Daveed said, pointing to the code key, telling himself that the gong sound was simply a sound, nothing more, "is 'I.' Do you see it on the other tablet?"

She searched. "Here," she said, "it is right next to the M symbol."

He showed her two more, L and K, and asked her to find them.

"They follow the M and the I."

"Can you tell me what they say together?"

"No."

"Say them out loud, Leah. The four sounds. Say them with your voice and lips and tongue and you will have a word."

"M—" she began. She frowned. "I—I, no! It is impossible."

"Again," he said, pointing to the M, making her say the sound, and then to the I and to the L and then to the K."

"Mmmmm-i-lllll-k-k- Milk! Daveed! The word is Milk! It is, isn't it?" She looked from the code bar to the tablet and back, suddenly seeing the word spring from the four symbols.

"Milk is an ingredient in this remedy for a skin rash. Leah, this will be our secret code. Memorize these thirty symbols and their sounds, and you will be able to read anything I write for you. All of your aunt's medicinal formulas. You will not need a scribe to read them for you! Leah, we can start at once. As soon as your aunt is awake and up to talking. I will take dictation as you and she talk, and afterward I will transcribe my dictation in the new script."

Leah went to the bed and looked down at her peacefully sleeping aunt. Cheers from the city came in on the morning breeze. Daveed and Leah knew that the old Rab's successor had been named. "Auntie Rakel?" Leah said, touching the sleeping woman's shoulder.

When Rakel did not stir, Leah looked at her chest and saw with relief that it rose and fell with respirations. "Auntie Rakel?" she said more sternly. Now she shook her shoulder.

"Auntie Rakel? Auntie! Daveed, something is wrong. I cannot wake her."

CHAPTER TEN

Grandmother, why can I not marry whom I choose?" Leah asked as she looked down at two-month-old Baruch sleeping in her arms, his tiny eyelids fluttering in baby dreams. She said a silent prayer for Tamar, asking the gods to grant peace to her sister's soul.

"You are the mother of Caleb's son," Avigail said peevishly. "You are permitted only to marry a blood relation." She sat on a stool with a large wooden bowl in her lap, grinding lentils into flour. Few slaves worked in the kitchen now, and of those, none had the strength or vigor to grind beans.

"But why?" Leah asked. "Is it written in the Law? Is this rule inscribed in sacred books?"

"Because it has always been so," Avigail snapped. "Why are you being so willfully disobedient? A girl must never question her elders. Invoke the gods, child, that you should say such things!"

Avigail tried not to let her fear show. Was this another sign? The world was changing and it frightened her. She could not put from her mind a shocking sight she had seen that morning in the market-place. A man and a woman, browsing among spices, murmuring to one another, affectionately touching hands, addressing each other as husband and wife. The young newly wed couple, obviously in love, would normally have brought a smile to Avigail's lips. Except that the husband was Egyptian and his wife Canaanite. Avigail wasn't the only one who had stared in shock at the mixed-race couple. Had they no sense of decency? Was this the way the world was heading, with the breaking down of tradition and the old ways?

She thought about her son. Elias had obtained a loan from the bankers at the House of Gold and was going to pool it with money from other men to build a weapons factory. Weapons! Now the family had no money and they were deeply in debt. There would be no grape harvest in two months' time, and there were no buyers for the amphoras of wine sitting in the storage sheds. Where was Elias going to store the new wine that must be removed from the fermenting vats? He spoke of profits from the iron factory—but they had not yet laid a single stone of its foundation.

Avigail's troubled thoughts went to Saloma who was near her delivery time, which meant a new baby to take care of, along with Tamar's little orphan. And fourteen-year-old Esther, going into the city on the flimsiest pretexts to walk the streets with a veil over the lower part of her face, enjoying the attention of strangers. And poor Aunt Rakel, who had been sleeping in the "twilight slumber" for seven days, coming to the threshold of consciousness enough to take water, but no food, slipping back into the sleep that was not sleep.

And Hannah . . . Elias's wife had grown quieter in the weeks since they found Tamar's body in the olive grove. She could not be counted on to mend or weave or bake bread. She sat for long periods, staring into the distance.

So many to take care of!

And now rumors that the King of Ugarit was very ill, that special priests had been summoned, that scribes were at his side night and day to capture his final words. Secrecy surrounded the palace. The king's minsters would not tell the people what ailed him for fear someone might use the knowledge to work black magic against him.

"The ancestors gave us rules for a reason," she said to Leah. "What becomes of civilization if we choose to ignore—"

"Grandmother, Grandmother!" Esther said excitedly from the doorway. "Auntie Rakel is awake!"

* * *

Apriest-of-the-dying was sent for, as well as Daveed and his scribe's box. He had been at the House of Gold undergoing ritual preparations for entering the novitiate, and because he had told Leah to summon him the moment Rakel woke up, he had kept himself spiritually and physically pure.

Leah greeted him at the front door. "She woke suddenly and asked for her tonic. She thinks she is back in Jericho and waiting for her betrothed to visit. We must go."

But Daveed laid his hand on her arm and, glancing around at the deserted hall and corridors, whispered, "I have missed you."

"And I, you."

He took her hand and pressed something into it. When she saw the silver rings, she said, "No, Daveed, I cannot accept this."

"It is payment for a legal document I drew up. I have already paid a portion to the Brotherhood. I have no need of this."

Tears rose in her eyes. The silver would buy much needed bread and salt. "Thank you," she said, adding silently: I love you.

In Rakel's bedchamber Avigail lit the lamps and braziers, and had additional incense burners brought in, to blaze with so much perfumed smoke that it stung the eyes. Everyone gathered around the bed to listen to Rakel speak of the past. The only exception was Saloma, who sat on a chair in the corner, her feet swollen from pregnancy. She held little Baruch in her arms.

Leah watched Daveed as his hand flew over the clay tablet, rapidly pressing the stylus this way and that. He was dressed differently tonight. After the old Rab named Yehuda his successor, Daveed entered the Brotherhood as a novice, so that he no longer wore the one-sleeved tunics of Lagash, but the shirt of soft brown wool that hugged his chest and shoulders, and the white pleated kilt of Ugarit's scribes. He was still allowed to wear the symbolic dagger of Zh'kwan-eth on his left arm, and they had not made him cut his hair, so that the long black ringlets still fell over his shoulders, making him, Leah thought, the handsomest man in the city.

"My husband lost his sex drive," Rakel was saying as she sat up in bed, drinking her tonic of celery juice mixed with juniper berries, parsley and carrots, poppy seeds and cumin. She seemed unaware of the priest who was shaking a rattle and chanting softly, or the young scribe recording everything she said. Rakel smiled at Avigail and Leah, Esther and Hannah, calling them by different names, all from the past. "He was so bereft he told me he would not blame me if I sued for divorce. But I loved him and so I searched for a cure. A wise man in the marketplace told me of an aphrodisiac plant that grows only on the island of Minos in the middle of the Great Sea—a mint with purple flowers. It is called dittany. It was very costly and hard to find, but I did not give up. When I obtained the dittany, I brewed it as a tea and gave it to my beloved. Within days his manly vigor returned and he pleased me in bed forever afterward."

They had tried to ask her specific questions—the precise formula for the falling sickness remedy—but to no avail. Rakel spoke only of what she wished to speak of. As Avigail listened in fascination, she realized that her aunt's memories were astoundingly clear. Avigail had heard that this often happened when the soul was preparing to leave the body. The shackles of this life were falling away, revealing the past, like the layers of an onion.

The family remained standing through the vigil, praying, inhaling the heady incense, listening to marvelous tales from the past.

Near the midnight hour, when spirits walked the land and the people of Ugarit lit lamps and placed magic amulets on their doorposts, Rakel closed her eyes and drew in a deep, shuddering breath. "I remember when Avigail was born . . ." she whispered, and her voice took on a strange, timeless tone, as if it were already the voice of an ancestor. "Avigail's father, my brother, was married to a woman of Ugarit. She was said to have royal ancestors. A king of Ugarit, I believe . . ." Another breath, not as deep. "But she was barren . . . There was a Habiru slave in our house, her name was Sarah, and my brother set his eye upon her and took her to him."

Avigail frowned. This was a story she had not heard. Surely it was not true. Rakel's mind must be losing its hold on reality.

"When the Habiru slave told my brother that she was with child, the family moved to the mountains to escape the summer heat. I was married at the time. My husband and I went with them and we stayed there for six months. In the town of Jerusalem, high in the hills west of the Sea of Salt, the slave Sarah gave birth . . ."

Rakel's voice died and everyone at the bedside stood in silent waiting. Only Avigail began to realize the importance of what was being said, of what was coming. She felt the floor start to drop away from beneath her feet. No, she thought in fear. Do not say it.

After another labored breath, Rakel said, "When we returned to Jericho, Avigail's father told the world that his wife had given birth to the child. It was a girl and they named her Avigail. He sent Sarah away and told all of us that this was to be a secret. It could never be known that Avigail was not descended from King Ozzediah but had come from Habiru blood. And then Avigail married Yosep and went to live in Ugarit where she gave birth to Elias. He married Hannah and she gave him three daughters: Leah, Tamar, and Esther. I wonder what became of them."

Rakel's chest rose and fell in shallow breaths, and then the respirations came farther apart. While everyone stood in shocked silence, their faces cast in light and shadow from the many lamps burning, Rakel's last words hung in the smoky air as all eyes slowly shifted to Avigail, their honored matriarch, who herself stood with an astonished look on her face.

This was the nameless fear she had never been able to face. This was why she had not wanted Leah to probe Rakel's memories, and why she had always felt strangely uncomfortable around Habiru people—desert wanderers who lived in tents, calling no place home. The peddler at the gate, selling chickens that laid eggs every day. Avigail's inexplicable discomfort in his presence.

Had she overheard, as a child, the adults talking, Avigail grasping the significance of their words—that she was not the descendant of Ugarit's beloved King Ozzediah but was in fact the result of a union between her father and a Habiru slave? As the years passed, she would have forgotten the conversation, and its essence would have settled into her soul like an inborn fear, a prejudice she had never been able to explain.

The night they fled Jericho, sixteen-year-old Avigail saying, "The Habiru cannot build stone monuments for Pharaoh because they are an uncivilized people who know only how to erect goat's hair tents." Aunt Rakel's quick admonishment: "You must never speak disparagingly of a people you know nothing about."

Avigail pressed her hand to her stomach. Now she knew the

meaning behind her aunt's words that night, why Rakel would defend nomads who were unwelcome in every town. I was speaking ill of my own blood . . .

"It is done," the priest-of-the-dying declared solemnly, closing Rakel's vacant eyes. "Let us beg the gods to accept this woman's soul."

While Daveed recorded the moment and the family chanted with the priest, each trying to digest the astonishing revelation they had just heard, Avigail felt the world reel around her. The walls closed in, the smoke invaded her lungs and clogged her chest. Across the bed, Elias stared at his mother with a face so pale she thought he looked like a ghost.

Blessed Asherah, Avigail thought in shock. We are not descended from the kings of Ugarit. We are Habiru. Whose god is nameless and without form and whom they worship in a common tent.

My son, my son! she silently cried to Elias. Can you forgive me? I raised you to be proud of your royal bloodline. Instead, I am the daughter of a Habiru slave!

Avigail could not look at her granddaughters—Esther, who still hoped for a husband despite her deformity, but now whom no man would have; and Leah, who had just moments ago still had a chance for remarrying, but now no longer.

Avigail thought these things because she had seen the look on the priest's face. The astonishment. The distaste.

A secret that had been carefully kept for fifty-eight years, and now: This man will tell the world . . .

Despite Avigail's fears, the priest-of-the-dying could not tell the world as he was sworn to secrecy and forbidden to repeat anything he heard or witnessed at a deathbed. Fellow priests were not part of the rule, however, and so he was free to confide to them the shocking confession he had heard at the House of Elias. It took only one priest, wishing to curry Rab Yehuda's favor, to pass the titillating gossip to him, and Yehuda would certainly tell his mother the scandalous news of Avigail and Elias—and once Zira knew, everyone knew.

Therefore, when the citizens of Ugarit crowded into the great ceremonial hall for the installation of Yehuda as the new Rab of scribes, they were not so much there to celebrate his succession to the lofty, prestigious office as to see if Avigail and her son dared show their faces.

The ceremonial hall that stood adjacent to the House of Gold was vast, larger even than the royal palace itself, with towering pillars whose capitals were carved and painted as flowers—majestic blossoms support-ing a marble ceiling. It was necessary that the hall be large, as here all of Ugarit's important rituals, both religious and secular, took place, and as such rituals were open to the public, room was needed to accommodate the onlookers. Daveed stood with his brother scribes in a special section reserved for them, but the general populace poured in from all sides, and he had no idea where Leah and her family might be.

If they had even come. Were they too ashamed to appear in public? When Rakel had died, the girls of the family had broken down into bitter weeping, but Daveed wondered if it was as much for their departed aunt as over the terrible confession she had made. Habiru blood instead of royal. It shocked even Daveed, and it broke his heart to see how Leah tried to comfort her grandmother and sister. What this news boded for the family, he could only guess. The Habiru were generally despised and looked down on by Canaanites and Egyptians alike.

Could this be a final blow that destroyed the family forever?

As the colonnaded halls continued to fill with noisy, boisterous people, Daveed kept up his search for Leah.

Nobu stood behind him in respectful silence as he listened to his god-voices, wondering if they truly were, as Esther suggested, his own thoughts. This ceremony is not a good omen for Ugarit. We do not trust Zira's son. He demands bribes for his sacred services. He allows his brothers to lead immoral lives. He does nothing to restore rever-ence to the holy emblem of the Brotherhood—the flaming solar disc with the human eye. He allows forgeries to take place. Lies and deceit infest the fraternity. Now he will take his leisure with boys and allow the scribes to live as they please, with ordinary citizens at their mercy. Let us go back to Lagash where honor still means something.

"By Shubat," Daveed hissed. "Even here must you mutter so? Invoke the gods and hold your tongue."

Nobu hung his turtle-head and murmured, "May the gods have mercy on my wretched soul. I will keep silent, master."

The installation of a new Rab, the supreme master of all men who could read and write, was almost like a coronation, dignified and with much pomp and ceremony. It was an occasion to greet old friends, share news and gossip, and so the hall was filled with the thunder of a thousand excited voices as everyone talked about politics, what did this new young man mean for Ugarit, why was King Shalaaman not in attendance when no one could remember Shalaaman ever being absent for an important event.

Finally Daveed saw Elias and his mother take their places in the special section for Ugarit's aristocracy. He did not see Leah or her sister or mother, but he did see the looks the city's rich and powerful cast Elias's way—how they whispered behind their hands, some smiling with glee, some looking at him with disgust.

On everyone's lips, the word Habiru . . .

As the head of one of Ugarit's leading families—even though in impecunious circumstances—Elias had the right to stand in a section reserved near the throne. And Avigail, being his mother, also had that privilege. She had been tempted to stay at home because she knew that by now the whole city buzzed with the shocking news of her true bloodline, but she would not give the gossips the satisfaction. For the occasion, she brought out her finest gown and veils and held her head high, despite the fact that no gold and silver coins adorned her fore-head (while those of all the other ladies glittered with wealth) and she wore no jewelry. There was no shame, she told her son, in falling onto hard times. The shame would be in succumbing to such difficulties. One must always remember one's station in life. One must always save face.

They were now a house of double-mourning. A bare two months had passed since Tamar's shameful death. And Auntie Rakel had been laid to rest only six days ago. She had taken the cure for the falling sickness to her grave. It did not matter. Avigail doubted there was such a cure anyway, and now that Yehuda was being officially installed as the Rab of the Brotherhood, now that he was the high-est ranking scribe in the city, this placed him next in line for the throne. Falling sickness or no, Avigail knew that his mother's relent-less campaigning to gain the crown for Yehuda, the promises she had made, favors she had traded, meant that the unsmiling young man was going to be the next king.

And soon, too, if rumors were to be believed. For the first time in history, the King of Ugarit did not sit in attendance for the installation of the new Rab. King Shalaaman was nowhere to be seen, and everyone was whispering about his mysterious illness. Some even said he was on his deathbed and that it was only a matter of days before one of the city's most beloved kings went to the gods.

But Avigail forced her thoughts away from such gloom, and thought of her great-grandson, Baruch, who cried so lustily and ate so hungrily that she took it as a good omen for the future. One must think of sons, she reminded herself, her bosom swelling with love and happiness. And if Saloma were similarly blessed and there were two male children in the House of Elias, then trials and tribulations would pale next to them, for it was a sign that the gods were still with Elias and his family.

A blaring of trumpets silenced the crowd. All heads swiveled to the far end of the hall where two towering doors of polished cedar swung open. White-robed priests emerged, leading a procession as they carried censers that gave off pungent smoke. Acolytes followed, bearing the statues of Ugarit's patron gods on their shoulders. Next came musicians playing lyres, flutes, drums. Behind them, walking alone, barefoot, humble—Yehuda, striding toward the throne at the end of the ceremonial hall where the blind old Rab awaited him.

As Yehuda's family, Zira and Jotham enjoyed the singular prestige of standing at the foot of the Rab. They beamed with pride as the procession neared, the priests and acolytes and musicians taking their places in well-rehearsed precision. For the occasion, Zira had donned a stunning purple gown with a matching purple veil, so that people stared at her, having seen her only in black. She held her bony chin high, as if it took all her strength to stand beneath the weight of so many coins festooned around her head. Her arms gleamed with gold bracelets, and necklaces thick with sparkling gemstones covered her flat chest.

Yehuda took his place before the old Rab to recite oaths of honor and obedience that had been written so long ago no one knew who their authors were. And while his deep, sonorous voice rose up to the colorfully painted columns, Zira thought of the day when he would be reciting the vows of kingship . . .

When the swearing-in was over, the Rab came down the steps, assisted by aides who held his arms. The scribes were then called forward—the novices as well as the senior men—and together as a body they recited an oath of allegiance to the new Rab, promising to obey him and revere him for as long as they lived.

When it was finished, the crowd erupted in cheers and applause, shouting out the names of the gods to show how pleased they were with the divine choice of Rab. Men of reading and writing had a new, young leader. Ugarit continued to be strong. The gods once again smiled upon them.

D aveed was summoned to the chambers of the old Rab where they had first spoken, ten months prior. They were alone amid the shadows and the smoke, with the gold solar emblem barely visible above the old man's head. "You have disappointed me greatly, Daveed of Lagash," the aged scribe said. "You raised my hopes only to dash them. When you did not appear before me and I was forced to name Yehuda my successor, I realized that my fears had been realized: that there is no honor left in the world. The old ways are dying. You are proof of that. I leave the Brotherhood in a weaker state than I found it, and now there is no hope for salvation."

Tears filled Daveed's eyes as he dropped to his knees and said in a choked voice, "I had my reasons for not appearing before you, Honorable Rabbi, and they had nothing to do with you or the Brotherhood. My heart needed to answer another call. But I do not ask for forgiveness. I did dishonor you and my sacred profession, and for that I shall always be sorry, I can never redeem myself on that account. But I promise you this, Honored Rabbi, if my promise means anything to you any more, from this day forward I will serve and protect the Brotherhood. I will serve Yehuda as I have served you. I pledge myself to the salvation of this fraternity. Honored Rabi, I will bring my brothers back to righteousness."

"And what," came the labored voice, "if there is another need of the heart? What happens when you must answer 'another call' and break your vow?"

"It will never happen. I swear upon my family's honor, I swear upon this noble crest that I wear on my hand, I swear upon my love for my profession and for the written word, I swear—" Daveed choked out with tears, "upon my reverence for you, Honored Rabbi, and most of all I swear upon my love for my personal god, the ancient Shubat, that I will never again break a promise to the Brotherhood."

The Rab closed his eyes and said wearily, "Then you have given me hope once again, Daveed of Lagash, for I fear that under the guidance of Yehuda our fraternity will die. I go to the gods in peace, my son, because I believe you . . ."

The banker's name was Izaak, and he did not like what Jotham was forcing him to do.

As they weighed gold rings on a balancing scale in the privacy of Izaak's office at the House of Gold—the hour was late, the clerks had gone home—he rued the day he had gone to Jotham to ask a favor, promising to do anything in return. Now payback was at hand. In the form of dishonorable dealings.

Banking transactions were confidential, the records kept under lock and key. Izaak had taken an oath never to betray the trust of a client, and now he had no choice. The client was Elias the vintner, and the confidential information he was revealing was the loan Elias had taken out on his villa and winery for the purpose of investing in a new iron smelting factory. How Jotham found out about the loan, Izaak did not know, but when the shipbuilder had presented himself at his door just an hour ago, bearing a chest filled with gold and silver rings, Izaak had cursed his own weakness, the hour of his birth, and even the gods themselves.

"There!" Jotham said in satisfaction when the scales achieved even balance. His gold rings equaled the gold ingots Izaak used for counting money. "That is the exact amount Elias owes the bank. With interest." He held out his hand.

Izaak felt sick. The walls of his office were lined with shelves containing clay tablets. Here were the records of financial dealings, loans and payments, trade agreements, deeds to property that was being held as collateral. And the tablet that contained the details of Elias's bank loan. Jotham had just paid that loan and now he wanted the tablet. It was not an illegal transaction, just unethical and dishonorable. And Izaak could lose his lucrative position in the bank if this were ever found out, so he would never speak of it. And Jotham knew this.

With great reluctance he handed the tablet over—both sides covered in cuneiform writing that outlined the details of Elias's contract with the bank, and a signed promise to pay back the full loan upon demand. Izaak knew of Elias's financial strife—knew it better than any man—and therefore knew what a blow this was going to be. The final one, most likely.

He knew that in addition to the feud between Jotham and Elias, and the cause of it—a daughter!—Izaak knew also that, in addition, Jotham was driven at this late hour on a hot summer night by a lust that could not be slaked by any woman. He wanted controlling interest in the new iron ore smelting plant a consortium of businessmen was going to build. By buying up Elias's interest in it, Jotham now held the majority of shares. He also was breaking his enemy, once and for all.

Watching Jotham leave, with the precious tablet clutched in his greedy hand, Izaak the banker, thinking this was the worst night of his life, turned to the statue of Dagon in a wall niche, set flame to a fresh ball of incense, and began silently to pray.

Jotham arrived at Elias's house, demanding to be seen. Without ceremony he held out a clay tablet, saying, "This is a collection note I had drawn up. You see my signature there, and that of my nephew, Rab Yehuda, who wrote this note. It says that I am the owner of the bank note you signed when you borrowed five weights of gold from the money lenders. That bank note is safely in my possession, and I will give it to you when you hand over this money. The villa and winery, which you gave to the bank for collateral, will of course revert to you. If you do not pay me this amount at once, however, this house and your winery become my property, and I will put your family out onto the street."

Elias, speechless, stared at the tablet. Although he could not read, he did recognize signet seals, and he could read numbers. And he had no reason to doubt Jotham. So he did not send for Daveed. But there was no money left in the house, nothing left to sell, he could not even sell the winery as, technically, it belonged to Jotham.

"I will need a day," Elias said, the breath trapped in his chest. He felt a strange new pain there, and remembered that his grandfather had died after a demon had taken roost in his heart and squeezed it dry.

"A day?" Jotham said. "Very well, I will return tomorrow at this time." If Elias did not have the money, Jotham would sell the property. Either way, he would have enough money to buy the ruling shares in the iron factory.

Elias watched him go, a fat self-satisfied vulture of a man, and as he heard women's voices drift through the house—his mother telling her girls to get on with their chores, tasks normally carried out by slaves and servants but now the job of Hannah and Leah, Esther and Saloma—Elias came to the dreaded realization that there was only way to pay the debt so that his family could continue to live under this roof.

He must sell himself into slavery.

The night was hot, perfumed, with late summer blossoms nodding on heavy stalks. Leah's father had gone into the city on urgent business and had yet to return, while the women were in Saloma's bedchamber, sitting vigil. Her delivery time was near. Tamar's baby, Baruch, was with his wet nurse.

Leah and Daveed were on the roof, seeking relief from the humid heat. Downstairs, Avigail and Hannah sat with Saloma as she prayed to Asherah for the safe delivery of her child. Daveed had left Nobu at the dormitory to sharpen his various pens and styli, and to prepare clay for tomorrow's assignments.

Daveed had come to be with Leah to be supportive during her family's time of trouble, but mostly to offer friendship and love. Yet he could not help voicing his own troubles. "If Yehuda becomes King, then the corruption will spread from the Brotherhood to other areas of government. He must be prevented from ascending the throne."

"Daveed, people do not know of Yehuda's moral decay. They have heard rumors of his falling sickness, but that is all. Zira has done a good job of making people think Yehuda is a pillar of morality and honor. You and I know differently, but we are the only ones! You must let people know. If the rich and powerful men of Ugarit know the truth about Yehuda, they will not vote him king."

Daveed shook his head. "I cannot tell anyone, Leah, for once they learn about the corruption within the Brotherhood, men will lose faith in us. And then not even I could bring the fraternity back from that brink. I made a solemn vow to the old Rab that I would do everything within my power to help the Brotherhood."

"But if you say nothing, Yehuda will be crowned king and the Brotherhood will sink into further decay!"

Daveed went to the edge of the roof, where a low wall came to waist level. He bent, placing his hands on mudbrick that still held the day's heat. "There must be another way."

Leah went to his side. "Is it so certain the king is going to die?"

"They are saying he will not live to see the dawn. May the gods protect him."

"What ails him? He was so healthy and robust not long ago."

"I heard that it is The Demon That Crushes the Windpipe."

Leah stared at him. She frowned, searching her memory. Then she said, "Daveed, did Aunt Rakel not give us the remedy for that?"

"I do not recall."

"In Jericho the disease is called Burning Lung. But it is the very same."

He looked at her. Because of the hot night, she had forgone wearing a veil. Her hair was pinned up off her neck with combs. "Are you sure?"

"Describe the king's illness."

"They say the demon attacks when the day is cold and damp, and when it rains. But also when the King is angry or anxious. At these times the demon invades his body and closes his throat. The king cannot draw in air. He wheezes. There is pain in his chest. The attacks were once infrequent, with long spells of good health in between, but now the inability to draw air into his lungs comes more frequently. The priests and magicians say that the demon grows strong and will soon kill him."

Leah looked out over the sparkling city and thought back of her days in the garden, at Rakel's side. "My aunt told me once that when she was a girl, she had a cousin who suffered from such spells, and so the family went to the Sea of Salt where miraculous healings are legendary. Her cousin's suffering abated while they were there, and came back when they returned to Jericho. The Egyptians say that the evil spirits that fill lungs with congestion, that make joints painful and swollen, and that close the windpipe are spirits that yearn for sunlight and dry air. This is why on cloudy, rainy days some people feel pain and stiffness in their hands, the lungs labor, and windpipes squeeze—the demons are searching for a warm place and air that is not filled with smoke."

"And the anger, the anxiousness?"

"That is when the king is least vigilant in protecting himself from harmful spirits. He forgets to pray and invoke the gods, and the demons fly in. I am sure of it!"

Leah turned and ran from the roof, Daveed following. Downstairs, in her bedchamber, she picked up a small ebony chest where she once kept jewelry and precious items. Lifting the lid, she brought out the tablets Daveed had written in his special script the day they had kept vigil at Rakel's side. "I thank the gods Grandmother sent for you to record my aunt's words. I could not have remembered this formula among so many. Here it is!"

As Daveed read his own writing, Leah said, "It is an Egyptian cure. Rakel said that before the first Thutmose invaded Canaan and let his agents steal the family home, they numbered Egyptians among their friends. Auntie said her mother learned this cure from an Egyptian physician. I am sure it will work!"

Daveed thought this over. "The problem is how to get to the King. Shalaaman is surrounded by physicians and priests, ministers and courtiers, not to mention palace guards and soldiers. They have wrapped his illness up in such secrecy that the palace itself will be impregnable. Leah, we might possibly hold in our hands the fate of Ugarit itself. But how do we get inside the palace?"

As soon as the slave master saw who his late-night visitor was, he knew the nature of their business. Everyone spoke of the dire straits Elias the vintner had fallen into. And in the past weeks, Elias had brought slaves to be sold. The man wondered if Elias had any slaves left to sell. Perhaps this time it was the concubine?

"Shalaam, my friend and brother," he said, rising from his desk where he had been counting money. "The blessings of Dagon."

"Shalaam and the blessings of the gods. I have come to do business with you."

"I am your servant," the slave master said with a bow. "Who do you wish me to sell?"

"Myself."

The man's eyes flew open, and then they flooded with greed, for Elias would fetch a handsome price. He was virile, robust, and he knew about grapes and wine. "What price are you asking?"

Elias handed him Jotham's collection note, and the slave master, who knew how to read, pursed his lips over the gold-weight Elias needed. "It can be done," he said. "It is a high price, but you are worth it. I warn you in advance, my friend and brother, that a local man will not purchase you. But I have some wealthy out-of-town buyers looking for special slaves. I believe we can get this gold-weight for you."

"I will return at noon tomorrow," Elias said, for that was when the weekly public slave auction was held.

To assassinate a king was the worst crime a man could commit. If caught, the execution was long and excruciating: the victim's hands and feet were chopped off, then his genitals, and finally, he was skinned like a rabbit while still alive.

As much as Rab Yehuda wished Shalaaman would die, he dreaded the execution more. And so he waited anxiously in a chamber off the throne room to be called to record Shalaaman's final words. Yehuda had been sequestered in there for days, trying not to pray for Shalaaman's hasty demise. Yehuda feared the gods as much as he did executions. But his patience was wearing thin. It was nearly dawn, the king's physicians and magicians had been at their rituals all night. Why couldn't Shalaaman just die?

Rab Yehuda's predawn musings on life and death, crowns and kings were interrupted by a servant who came in to say that visitors had arrived insisting upon being seen. They had been there for hours and claimed to have a cure for the king. "A scribe named Daveed and a young woman saying she has an Egyptian cure," the servant added with a sneer.

"An Egyptian cure, you say?" Yehuda rubbed his receding chin, his deep-set eyes looking inward. An Egyptian cure . . . His lips curved in a smile. "Bring them in."

"Shalaam and blessings of the gods, Honored Rabbi," Daveed said when he and Leah were escorted into Yehuda's presence.

"You claim to have a cure for the king's ailment?" Yehuda asked in a concerned tone.

As Daveed explained about the condition that people in Jericho called Burning Lung, and that he and Leah and brought a proven Egyptian remedy, Yehuda could scarcely believe his good luck. Moments ago, wishing the king would die, and now these two arriving with a plan that was certain to kill Shalaaman, for everyone knew that Egyptian medicine did not work in Canaan. Yehuda tried not to smile as he thought: Let these two be the assassins . . .

Because Daveed was a prince of Lagash and Leah the daughter of a noble family, they were granted admittance into the royal bedchamber where so many censers burned, and braziers gave off pungent smoke, that Daveed and Leah themselves could barely breathe.

Here, they were met by an astonishing sight.

The treatment for a closed windpipe was typical of all medical treatments. Priests and physicians disguised themselves as something frightening to the demons that caused diseases. In this case, since it was believed that the Demon That Crushes the Windpipe was afraid of lions, two priests dressed as lions ran toward the king, growling viciously; when they reached the royal bed, they clawed the air savagely and then retreated to turn around and repeat the attack.

Leah stared in amazement. The men wore enormous lion skins, with heads, paws, and tails intact. The lions' heads were fitted over their own heads, and brought low over their faces, with enormous black manes flaring out. The priests' arms fit snugly into the lions' front legs like sleeves, while the hind legs and paws dragged along the floor. They gave an impressive performance, rushing, attacking, growling, but they had little effect in scaring the demon from the king's chest. His Majesty struggled desperately for breath. And when Leah saw that his lips were turning blue, she said to Daveed, "We must move him to the sunlight now."

Yehuda conferred with the royal physicians and magicians who looked at Daveed and Leah with suspicion. When Daveed thought

Shalaaman might expire while the debate went on, Yehuda finally barked orders and slaves carried the king to the rooftop where a beautiful garden had turned mudbrick and stone to a green paradise. The priests and magicians prayed and chanted and continued to wave magic amulets and wands while Leah stayed at the king's side, to watch his face for signs of distress or improvement. She spoke to him soothingly in a soft voice, reassuring him that he was going to be all right, to ease his panic. And after a while, beneath the warm sun and above the haze of the city, with fresh breezes blowing over Shalaaman's body, while Leah calmed him with her voice, the coughing and wheezing began to subside.

To everyone's amazement, the coughing stopped altogether and the king was able to draw deep breaths. The more he inhaled, the quieter his chest grew until there was no more wheezing, which meant the evil spirits had flown out.

The king opened his eyes and the first face he saw was Leah's. Shalaaman smiled. He was cured.

My son, my son!" Avigail cried when they arrived at the busy slave market. "Please do not do this!"

"Invoke the gods and do not worry, Mother. I will go for a good price, for I am strong and healthy, and I have business acumen as well as my skills as a vintner. I will not be a slave under a whip. I will be . . ." He searched for words that would comfort her. "As Daveed was with us."

"He wasn't a slave!"

"He was an indentured servant. It is almost the same thing. Trust me, Mother, vintners throughout Canaan, and as far south as Jerusalem, even to Lagash in the east—all know me and my reputation. Grape growers and winemakers will compete to purchase me. The money will go straight to Jotham, but you will get to keep the property. Sell the vineyard if you can, but keep the house."

Avigail had told Hannah to stay at home, where Saloma awaited the birth of her child. But Hannah would not be parted from her husband, and so Saloma was in the watchful care of Esther and Leah.

Hannah had always hated the slave market, and she wondered now, as they entered the compound where an excited and noisy crowd waited for the auction to begin, if she had lived all her life with a premonition of this terrible day. She could not stop crying as her husband disappeared behind the slave block—a platform where the slaves would brought out for inspection.

Avigail spotted Jotham in the crowd. She knew he was there to receive the money from Elias's sale.

The slave master came out. A burly man with a hairy chest, wearing a leather kilt and carrying the symbolic whip of his profession. He invoked the gods to watch over today's proceedings, and then announced in a booming voice the opening of the auction. As the slaves were brought out one by one, the crowd entered into a vigorous and lively competition of bidding—on men with broad backs, purchased for hard work in fields, on construction, at the docks; on women for kitchen work and other menial tasks; on children for labor at small tasks or in places too small for adults. As the morning wore on, the crowd grew boisterous with anticipation, as they knew that the more interesting and expensive offerings came toward the end.

"Now here is something special," the slave master announced as Elias was brought out.

Avigail covered her face and cried, "Asherah be with us!"

Her son stood on the platform stripped down to his loincloth, shackles binding his wrists. But he stood proudly, his head held high. The crowd grew uncharacteristically hushed. A man of wealth and power was putting himself up for sale. And then the murmuring began, the looks of confusion. A few left the crowd, to run back through the streets. Jotham stood in the shadows at the sidelines, making sure he was not cheated of a single copper ring.

The slave master began to extoll the virtues of the man who stood before them. The bidding started.

Nobu hurried into Daveed's cell and said, "It is time, master. The auction will begin. We must not be late."

Daveed finished his prayer to Shubat, traced a sign of reverence in the air, and rose to his feet. With so many worries on his mind, Daveed did not notice his slave's sudden concern for the welfare of Elias and his family. He did not know that Nobu had fallen in love.

"I am ready," he said. Daveed had no idea how his presence at the slave auction was going to help Elias. All he knew was that he could not let his honored patron stand on the slave block without the presence of at least one friend. And if by chance someone were able to step forward and rescue Elias from such a calamity, Daveed wanted to be on hand to offer advice, or to read letters, contracts—anything to help the man who had been his patron for more than a year. But mostly, to be there for Leah. It would tear her apart, Daveed knew, to see her father sold and taken away in chains.

As he and Nobu hurried down the corridor, they saw Rab Yehuda at the end, standing with two scribes, giving them orders. When Daveed drew near, Yehuda's deep-set eyes shifted from the others to him. "Where are you going, Daveed?" he asked.

"I have personal business, Honored Rabbi."

"And I have work for you," Yehuda said. "At the apricot orchards belonging to a grower named Xylus. He has several letters to dictate, and two legal documents to be drawn up."

"But Honored Rabbi, Xylus's farm is miles to the south of here. It will take me the better part of the morning to reach it, and then with so much to be written . . ." Daveed bowed his head. "I will leave at once, Honored Rabbi." He and Nobu would stop by the slave auction before they left town.

Yehuda added, "You will be staying the night."

Nobu started to protest, but a look from Daveed silenced him.

Rab Yehuda started to turn away, but then stopped and addressed Daveed again.

"Leave at once," he said. "Do not attend to any other errands in the city. Xylus awaits you." Daveed clenched his teeth as he bowed his head and said, "Yes, Honored Rabbi. The gods be with you."

Halla!" cried Saloma as she clutched her abdomen. Leah and Esther were instantly at her side, murmuring words of reassurance, bringing wine to her lips, and praying out loud as they anxiously waited for the baby to come.

The crowd at the slave auction grew as word spread through the city that Elias the vintner had put himself up for sale.

Men came to see it with their own eyes, some to express pity, some to gloat. Friends conferred among themselves—how much money could they scrape together to purchase him? But what would they do with him? He was bankrupt, how would he pay them back?

"How much will you pay for this fine slave?" the slave master called out.

"Ten-weight of silver!" shouted a buyer from Sidon.

"That is robbery!" shouted the slave master, but he was pleased. "Who is smarter than that?"

"Twenty-weight of silver!" called out a man in robes that identified him as coming from faraway Jerusalem.

"The gods are watching," the slave master cautioned. "Be fair, my friends. Be honest!"

"One-weight of gold!" cried a man whose fringed robes and cone-shaped hat identified him as Babylonian.

Jotham grinned. Soon, the iron factory would be under his control.

Saloma squatted on the birthing stool, calling out the names of the gods with each contraction, her face bathed in perspiration. Leah knelt before her, hands outstretched, ready to catch the baby, while Esther grasped Saloma's wrists to steady her. "Asherah is with us," she said. "Call upon her, Saloma."

The bidders elbowed and jostled for space, the courtyard at the slave auction was getting so crowded. Besides the bidders, onlookers were making lively wagers among themselves as they bet on who would win the auction for Elias the vintner.

"Two-weight of gold!"

"Three-weight!"

"My friends, the gods are smiling! Do we have four-weight?"

Say a prayer, Saloma, it is almost here!"

"Push, Saloma!"

"Asherah be with us!

* * *

S old!" shouted the slave master, pointing to the Babylonian. "For five-weight of gold. The gods are pleased."

A sherah!" cried Leah as the infant slipped into her waiting hands. "It is a boy! The blessings of the gods upon you, Saloma. You have given our father a son!"

Z ira paced in and out of lamplight, wondering where Yehuda was. A warm evening embraced the city of Ugarit, its lights reflected brightly in the waters of the harbor. Music rose to the stars, and the aromas of many dinners, many gardens, many perfumed lovers filled the night. But Zira was in no mood to enjoy it as she anxiously awaited her son's return.

When Yehuda entered the room, she ran to him. "What news?"

"The king has been cured."

"Are you sure?"

"The cure that Daveed the scribe and one of Elias's daughters brought to the palace has worked. The king's choking spell abated, and in the time since has not returned."

Her voice grew shrill as she said, "Why in the name of Dagon and Baal did you let them near the king?"

Yehuda pressed his lips together. His plan had backfired. He was so certain that Egyptian remedies were worthless. But he did not tell his mother. "I protested, but the priests and royal physicians insisted the two be allowed to try their magic. And it worked."

She eyed her son. "How well is the king?"

"Shalaaman has made a remarkable recovery."

"By Dagon!" she shouted as she shot to her feet. How on earth had this happened? She had been so certain the king would die before the next full moon that she had boasted to her friends they would next be visiting her at the palace.

Now she would be a laughingstock.

She stopped and said, "One of Elias's daughters?" It could only be Leah. The girl who had insulted them!

A cold wind swept through Zira's heart at that moment, driving away the warm, perfumed evening, bringing fresh coldness to her already cold heart.

They will be sorry for this . . .

"There is a tablet," she said to her son, "a loan contract your uncle purchased from the bank. Are you familiar with it?"

"I am." Yehuda was the one who had told Jotham of its existence.

"My brother has already presented a collection note to Elias's family. I wish to draw up another."

Yehuda arched an eyebrow.

"Do not ask questions," Zira snapped. "Fetch me that document. And bring your scribe's box. Avigail Em Elias is going to learn the true extent of Zira Em Yehuda's power."

A vigail was at the household shrine the next morning, lighting precious incense to Asherah in gratitude for giving the family another son, when the tablet arrived. She thought it might be hopeful news that Elias's purchase by the Babylonian had failed, that perhaps his friends had scraped together the money to rescue him. She hoped it was anything except what it turned out to be. "It is a collection note," Daveed said when he arrived after her urgent summons. He and Nobu had just returned from Xylus's apricot farm in the south.

"How is that possible? Elias paid all our debts. The money from his sale was handed over to Jotham by the slave master. It must be a mistake."

Daveed studied the tablet. "There is no mistake. This collection note is for the money from the loan Elias took out of the bank. But . . ." He looked at Avigail. "May I see your son's copy of the agreement?"

Avigail retrieved it from Elias's private office and Daveed inspected the original document comparing it with the collection note that had just come from Jotham. They details were exactly the same.

Except for one.

"Here," Daveed said, pointing to a cuneiform symbol on Elias's copy of the loan agreement, "is the amount of gold Elias withdrew from the House of Gold. It is listed in weight. This collection note, which represents the bank's copy of the loan agreement, contains all the same details with the exception of the gold weight, which is written as ten times the amount."

"Ten times! What does it mean?"

"It means, Em Elias, that Jotham is attempting to cheat you again."

"By Dagon, we shall not pay it!"

Daveed pursed his lips as he studied the two tablets. Leah kept silent as she watched him worry over the problem, Esther at her side, wringing her hands, thinking that with the birth of her baby brother the day before, this should be a house of rejoicing.

Finally Daveed said, "It is not so simple, I am afraid. Em Elias, you would need to take your case to the courts, and it would be your word against Yehuda's, as he is the man who drew up this note. Here is his seal. And Rab Yehuda is now a very powerful man. You do not have the money for the lawyers you would need, and a case like this could go on for years."

"But you can tell them! The judges will believe you, Daveed."

He shook his head. "Mine is a small voice compared to Yehuda's. They will not listen to me."

"But the judges have only to compare the original loan document with this collection note."

"And Yehuda will have no trouble destroying the bank's copy of the loan document."

"We have Elias's copy of the agreement. And the banker will testify."

Daveed shook his head. "I doubt he will, Em Elias. It was unethical of him to sell your son's bank loan to Jotham. To save himself, the banker will not speak on Elias's behalf. Honored Avigail," Daveed said gently, "your son is now a slave. His word carries no meaning in a court of law. There is no way you can fight this."

"Why is Jotham doing this?" she cried.

Daveed held his tongue to spare her further pain. He suspected that it was not Jotham at all but his sister who was bent on this new vendetta, and he knew it was because he and Leah had saved the king's life. It was being said that Shalaaman might be on the throne for another thirty years, he was so healthy. And with that, all of Zira's plans and ambitions for her son were dashed.

"Will you—" She pressed tears from her eyes. "Daveed, will you tell my son the news? I have not the heart . . ."

They went together to the slave market, Avigail and Hannah,

Leah and Daveed. Not wishing to leave Esther and Saloma alone and unprotected, Daveed ordered Nobu to stay at the house—a task he eagerly embraced.

Hannah had brought Saloma's baby, while Avigail carried Baruch, and they went to the slave cages where Elias was waiting to be claimed by his new master, a grape grower from Babylon.

Because of his noble status, and because the slave master did not wish to offend the gods, Elias was kept separately from the others in a holding cage by himself. The floor was covered in fresh straw and there was room for him to pace. He was clothed again, and the shackles removed.

When Elias saw the newborn, he broke down sobbing. "My son, at last," he said. "Name him Aaron." Elias reached through the bars of the cage and rested his large hand on the tiny soft head, whispering a prayer. He did the same for Baruch. And then he laid his hand on Hannah's cheek, which was damp with tears. "I love you, wife," he said. "You are no longer Isha Elias but from now on bear the respected title of Em Aaron. You bring honor to our house."

"My love," Hannah said tearfully. "It pains me to place bad news on top of good, but you must hear what Daveed has to say."

After listening to Daveed's grim news, he said, "Then I have lost my house, my properties?"

"All of it, my lord. All to Jotham."

"By the gods, how did this happen? I have been tricked." He grasped the wooden bars of his cell and cried, "This is unfair! Bring the slave master! We must correct this injustice."

The man came and said apologetically, "I understand your distress, my friend, but there is nothing I can do, as the gods witness. You and I had a legal agreement, Elias. And the Babylonian purchased you in good faith. I cannot return his money and break our contract. This is a matter between you and Jotham."

Elias turned to Daveed in desperation. "Daveed, you must get my house back for my family. Take Yehuda to court. Promise me!"

The Babylonian arrived moments later. It was time to leave. Daveed promised to watch over the women—Avigail, Hannah, Esther, Leah, the concubine, and the babies—although, as a novice scribe, he had no idea how.

Elias then entrusted Daveed with the safekeeping of his signet ring that bore the engraving of a man sitting beneath a grape bower, his arms up lifted in prayer. "I will keep it safe, Honored Master," Daveed said with great sadness.

Elias embraced his mother and then his wife, kissing each. "Although I sold myself into slavery, I pray it is not forever. I will buy my freedom and return someday. I promise."

With two-day-old Aaron in her arms, Avigail said, "Although I am filled with sadness at losing my son, I am also filled with joy to hold my grandson in my arms. Can a woman's life be fuller? I am a woman to be envied. Do not despair, my beloved son. Baruch and Aaron are proof that the gods are with us. Proof that there is yet hope for our family. These sons give me strength and courage, and I pray that if you have moments of despair, think of these babies—angels from the gods as a message that we should never give up hope."

They wept as they watched Elias go, shackles on his ankles and wrists, yet walking with the proud bearing for which he had always been known.

The women were gathered—Avigail and Hannah, Leah and Esther and Saloma with the two babies—to await Jotham's arrival. They had no idea what he planned to do now that he owned the property. Daveed was not there, as he had been called to the house of a baker who needed a will drawn up. But he had assured them he would come as soon as he could.

To Avigail's surprise, it was not Jotham but Zira who appeared on their threshold. She did not smile or greet Elias's women with respect, she simply walked past them as if they were not there. She went through the rooms of the villa, looking into everything, their storage chests, boxes, rummaging through clothes hanging on hooks, picking up things to examine them. Zira sniffed empty perfume bottles and kicked worn sandals aside.

Avigail was mortified.

When they were back in the hospitality hall, Zira lifted her long narrow nose and said, "You will move out of the bedchambers and clean them, make them ready for new people."

Avigail blinked in confusion. "New people?"

"Tenants. We are renting this house."

Avigail said, "By Asherah, why are you doing this to us?"

"My brother needs the money. He is investing in an iron factory. He nearly bankrupted himself buying Elias's notes."

"And my son paid every bit back, down to the last copper, though we could ill afford it!"

"Can he pay this?" Zira produced the falsified collection note from the folds of her dress. The one for ten times the gold-weight of the bank loan.

"You know he can't. My son—" Avigail could not bring herself to say it. Elias, taken away in chains . . .

"Then the house is legally mine. I myself will not be living here, however. I will rent out the property. I might already have a tenant. You will be his servants."

"Servants!" Avigail cried. She tipped her chin. "We are not servants."

"You are Habiru. That is all you are good for. Unless you would rather leave right now, all of you," Zira added pointedly, looking from Avigail to Leah, to Hannah, Esther, and Saloma carrying the two babies. "You can leave right now with just the clothes on your backs and take your chances in the streets of Ugarit."

Avigail closed her eyes. Jericho, the war chariots, running from their house in the middle of the night. Her mother, cut down like wheat. The long, mournful trek northward.

No. I will not go through that again. I will not put my granddaughters and the babies through that ordeal. We cannot leave this house. It is ours. And with the help of the gods, I will find a way to get it back.

D aveed arrived at the villa to find Leah helping her grandmother and the others to move their belongings into the now deserted slave quarters, where Zira had said they must live.

She ran to him and he drew her into his arms, into a warm kiss. His eyes glistened as he looked down at her, placed his hand against her hair. "I have sent an urgent letter to my brother in Lagash. I asked him for money. I do not know if he will send any, or how much, but when it arrives, it is yours, Leah, all of it. And anything I earn as a scribe, I will give to you."

As a novice in the Brotherhood, the thankless and unwanted

assignments went to Daveed. But when a year was up, he would be a fully vested scribe with all rights and privileges. He would find clients and build up a private practice. And then he would ask Leah to marry him.

"But money from my brother might not be necessary." Daveed smiled. "Leah, I have a wonderful surprise for you. We have been summoned to appear before the King! My darling, I believe he is going to reward us for saving his life."

Leah turned to Avigail and said, "Do not give up hope, Grandmother. King Shalaaman is known for his compassion and kindness. If he asks me how I wish to be rewarded, I will ask that he restore our home to us. He is a wise man, Grandmother. He will see that his life is worth far more than a simple house! Say a prayer!"

They stood before the king in a private audience chamber where Shalaaman was flanked by priests and physicians, and several of his wives. He was dressed in simple white robes and a modest gold circlet on his head. Leah thought that, although his coloring had improved, he still appeared weak from his ordeal.

"On behalf of the gods of Ugarit," King Shalaaman said in a weary voice. "I thank you for saving the life of your sovereign. The gods wish to reward you. State your desires."

Daveed spoke first. "Your Majesty, I ask only to be allowed to enter the Brotherhood as a full member, forgoing the year of novitiate."

The king conferred with his advisors, one of whom was a scowling Yehuda, and then said, "I will grant you a shortened novitiate, Daveed of Lagash. For coming to the aid of your king, you will be required to serve only six months, after which you will be granted full membership."

When the king turned to Leah, she said, "Honored Sovereign, I ask that my house be restored to my family," her heart racing as she felt Yehuda's shadowed eyes on her.

Shalaaman again conferred with his advisors and then he turned a magnanimous smile to Leah. "When I was choking to death, when I felt the life being squeezed out of me, I heard a soothing voice, speaking calmly, coaxing the demon out. You are a demon-charmer, Leah

Em Baruch, and the gods have sent you to protect Ugarit's monarch. Therefore, for saving our life, Leah Em Baruch, it is our pleasure to grant you an even greater reward than a mere house—the chance to serve your monarch. Beginning today, this hour, you will take up residence in the royal palace, to be at your sovereign's side always. The gods have spoken."

She stared at him in shock. She looked at his generous smile, his expectant manner. Her eyes went from Shalaaman to each of the powerful men flanking the throne. She caught the faint smile on Yehuda's lips. Leah knew that when the king spoke, his word was final. She had never spoken up to authority, and had no idea how to do so now. "Thank you, Your Majesty. The gods have made you a wise and generous man."

Shalaaman snapped his fingers and an important looking servant stepped forward. "This man will take you to your new quarters. And when you are settled, you will return to this hall and dine with the royal family."

Daveed and Leah were escorted down the long corridor to a small room off the royal bedchamber, where they realized Leah would be held as a kind of prisoner, pampered, and taken care of—but a prisoner all the same.

"The king believes it was your presence that cured him," Daveed said in dismay. "When the demon left his chest, Shalaaman saw you standing next to him. He believes that you are one of those rare people who, by their mere presence, have the ability to keep evil spirits away."

"But I will be a prisoner here! How can I take care of my family? How will I get my home back?"

"As a novice, I must live in the dormitory at the Brotherhood, but I will check on your family each day and make sure of their fair treatment. When I can, I will take them money. And it is only for six months."

"Daveed, you must get the house back for them. Do not let Zira take our home."

"I love you, Leah, with all my being, and I will do everything within my power to—"

"You already have the power!" she cried. "Use it! You know Zira has no right to our home, that the collection note is false. Denounce Yehuda and I will get my home back."

"By Shubat, Leah, by all the gods, do not ask me to do that. I made a promise to my Rabbi on his deathbed to protect the Brotherhood. Denouncing Yehuda would destroy the Brotherhood."

"Daveed!" she sobbed. "You can save us!"

He took her by the arms. "Leah, I swore an oath. I cannot break it. All a man has is his honor. If I lose that, I lose my soul."

"What about your oath to me? To protect us?"

"Yehuda is my Rabbi," Daveed said in a strangled voice. "I cannot expose his secrets. But I will protect you, Leah. I will find a way. I will send money to your family. I will go there when I can and check on them."

"It is not enough! Daveed, the King will listen to you. You can save my family and my home."

"Leah," he cried, "I cannot break my promise."

"By Asherah," she whispered, "did my father sell himself into slavery for nothing?"

His hands fell away from her arms. "This is who I am, Leah, what I was born to do. My allegiance is to my profession and to my god."

"I thought you loved me."

"I do, and with all my heart. Zira will not keep the house, I promise you."

"So many promises, Daveed! You cannot keep them all. My father is gone. We have lost our house. And now I no longer have you!"

"Do not say that, Leah. I cannot breathe without you! I will find a way."

She stepped back. "No, you will not. The Brotherhood will always come first. If you abandon us now, Daveed, I will never forgive you. And I shall always hate you."

Daveed looked at her in horror. And suddenly he felt his world crumble around him. Shadows closed in. All warmth left his body. He saw himself in the center of a black maelstrom, and he saw no way of escape. "Leah," he whispered, barely able to breath. "Leah, do not say that you hate me . . ."

Royal guards arrived at that moment to inform her that His Majesty wished her in his presence. They stepped forward, but Daveed took her by the arms. "Take back your words, Leah!" he said. "Quickly say a prayer and recant your words of hatred, for you kill my soul if you allow them to stay."

"Come on!" barked the guards as they each took hold of Daveed and Leah and pulled them apart. As one dragged Leah back to the throne room, Daveed tried to follow, but a guard barred his way with a spear. Leah looked back and saw the anguish on Daveed's face as they both realized their world had changed forever. Their dreams were dashed. The gods had abandoned them.

Zira arrived at the villa with a lawyer who informed Avigail that his client had found a tenant for the villa.

Zira swept past Avigail and paused to look at the carving in the stone doorpost, Elias's seal showing a man seated beneath a grape arbor. "I will cover that with my brother's seal, to identify this house as his," Zira said. "You will get the rooms ready for the new tenant."

She went inside, the lawyer on her heels. Avigail followed Zira through rooms and down corridors until they arrived at Elias's private office. In horror, Avigail watched as Zira opened storage boxes and searched the crowded shelves. When she came upon a stash of clay tablets, Avigail said, "You cannot touch those! They are my son's private documents!"

Handing the tablets to the lawyer, who examined them, Zira said, "They are my property now." When the lawyer handed one to her, saying, "This is the one," Zira dropped the tablet to the floor and ground it beneath her foot.

Avigail stared at the dust in stupefied silence. It was not necessary to ask which document Zira had just destroyed. Avigail knew it was Elias's copy of the bank loan agreement.

"I will fight you," she said in a deadly tone. It was no longer for herself or the girls, but for her grandson. This property was Aaron's birthright.

"Fight me and I will sell you all into slavery," Zira said archly. "I have the legal right, so do not think I would not do it. Get ready for the new tenant. He is Egyptian."

Zira smiled as Avigail clutched her stomach. "Egyptian?" she whispered.

"Your new master has come from the Valley of the Nile. And you will obey him or be out on the street and never be allowed to set foot in this house again."

PART TWO

CHAPTER ELEVEN

They were awakened by the thunder of war chariots and galloping horses. Wrapping themselves in warm cloaks against the cold morning, Avigail and her family ran to the end of the path to see soldiers racing along the main road toward the city. Their leather breastplates over coarse green tunics, and familiar two-horse chariots identified them as Canaanite warriors. They were coming from the south.

"What has happened?" Avigail called out.

A rider reined in his horse and shouted, "Megiddo has fallen!"

By his copper helmet, Avigail identified him as a captain. Two bows and a quiver of arrows were strapped to his back. He rode up to the end of the lane and said, "Pharaoh has taken the city and now his great army marches northward! There has been much slaughter and pillaging, madam. Take my advice, if Pharaoh comes this far," he said, squinting toward the south as if he could already see the pennants and war chariots of the Egyptian forces, "move your family inside the safety of the city walls. This house and its vineyards will be their first target."

He glanced past Avigail to the three woman and two small boys huddled in fear. "Pharaoh is rounding up all fugitives and taking them captive. Anyone without a home, anyone caught in the open. He has thrown an invisible net over the land and is bringing in people as if they were fish in the sea. It is said that the desert wanderers, the Habiru, have been hardest hit and are now prisoners of Thutmose."

Avigail swallowed in fear. It was Jericho all over again.

"It is said that Pharaoh needs people to build a new city. He is grabbing up everyone he can, even women, to be taken back to Egypt. The gods be with you, and remember the safety of the city." He gave her a salute and galloped off.

Avigail looked up at the gray, gloomy sky. The spring morning was damp with the threat of rain, reminding her of another fateful rainy day—seven years ago when their misfortune began.

As she turned her face to the wind blowing in from the Great Sea, she felt her small family gather around her like ducklings—Hannah, Esther, Saloma, and the two boys, four years old, born two months apart, Baruch and Aaron. Drawing the little ones to her, Avigail looked toward the northeast where black plumes of smoke clogged the sky, sending a foul stench over the city: Jotham's iron-smelting factory where weapons were being forged. Finally she looked toward Ugarit with its massive protective walls and thought: War is coming.

And she and her family were alone and unprotected.

The Egyptian tenant who had rented the villa and winery these past four years was gone. When news reached Ugarit, three months prior, that Queen Hatshepsut had died and her nephew, the third Thutmose, was now Pharaoh of Egypt, the kings of Kadesh and Megiddo, seeing this as an opportunity to rid Canaan of Egypt's influence, formed an alliance with other rulers and launched a revolt. When Egyptians in Ugarit heard this, they packed up and left, fearing for their lives.

And now, Megiddo had fallen. There was nothing to stop Pharaoh's march north and there was no doubt that Thutmose would come because Ugarit was the gateway to the north and east, a hub of the world's most vital trade routes, and a major harbor for all sea lanes. Any man intent upon conquering the world, as Thutmose was rumored to be, must control Ugarit. And everyone was saying that Thutmose would take the city at any cost.

Avigail shivered. How was she going to protect her family?

The villa stood empty. At least the Egyptian vintner and his family had been a presence. And they had not been tyrants, as Avigail had feared. At first, it had made her ill to see Egyptians moving into her home. She had lost sleep, had lost weight. But over the weeks and months, as she accepted that, for her family's sake, for the sake of survival, she must tolerate the foreigners' presence, her sickness and fear subsided into a numb tolerance.

She hated to admit it but the Egyptian had increased the grape vines and revitalized the wine business, and although he had treated her and her family with indifference, not learning their names, barely aware of their existence, he also had not mistreated them. Avigail and the women and boys ate well and were allowed to make their own clothes using the villa's resources—sheep's wool and goat hair.

But now they were alone, a small family of females who were not strong.

Hannah—silent these days. Ever since the baby died, that fateful night seven years ago, her words had grown scarcer. Tamar's suicide in the olive grove had stolen yet more words from Hannah's throat, and it seemed to Avigail that the last of her daughter-in-law's words went when Elias was taken away in chains. That was just over four years ago. They had not heard from him since. They did not know where he was, if he was alive even. But they prayed daily that the gods bring him back. Little Aaron, a smart boy with his father's engaging ways, was no solace for Hannah because even though she was legally his mother—Hannah was now Em Aaron—he had come from Saloma's body.

Saloma herself, however, was healthy and tried to bring cheer to her companions. She took care not only of Aaron but also of Tamar's orphan, Baruch, because even though he did have a mother, Leah had gone into the palace more than four years ago and they had not seen her since. And Esther, nineteen years old, did her best to remind her family that the gods were with them still.

Feeling the boys' arms around her thighs, hugging her for reassurance, Avigail patted their heads and said, "There is nothing to fear, my angels." And as she spoke these words, and felt their fleecy locks beneath her hands, she sent a silent prayer of thanks to Asherah. In these dark times, Baruch and Aaron were two beacons of shining light. Whenever Avigail felt despair, she had only to listen for their laughter as they ran through the house, and her heart was lifted. She blessed Tamar for returning home when she was pregnant, bringing Baruch into their lives. And she blessed Hannah, her courageous daughter-in-law, for taking the matter of a concubine into her own hands. It was not an easy thing for a wife to do. But she had selflessly set her own feelings aside for the sake of the family, and now two strapping boys were on their way to manhood.

Avigail filled her days and nights with dreams for these sons of the House of Elias. They would not both be vintners, she decided. Perhaps bright little Aaron would be a lawyer.

Oh Elias, my son, if only you were here to watch these angels grow up, experience the joy of teaching them to walk, to play games with them, to make them laugh! Where are you, my son? Will you come back to us? Are you being treated well? She looked up at the dark, rain-threatening sky and wondered what the sky was like over Babylon. Was her son working in a vineyard beneath a sunny sky? Were the gods of Babylon being kind to him? Avigail would not give up hope of seeing him again. Elias had said that he would work to buy back his freedom and come home.

Elias was not the only one she hoped to see again. Avigail prayed daily that Leah return to them.

She was traveling with King Shalaaman and his Court on a tour designed to build alliances and create pacts and treaties with rulers to the north and east. Shalaaman's advisers had suggested that he fortify Ugarit with friends should young Thutmose decide to overthrow his aunt and reclaim the lands conquered by his grandfather forty years ago. Shalaaman had packed up his court—a massive convoy comprised of his wife the Queen, his concubines, many princes and princesses, ministers and courtiers, physicians, priests, seers, scribes, musicians, cooks, and entertainers—and embarked upon a city by city tour of goodwill and friendship. In his innermost circle was Leah, whom Shalaaman believed kept the Demon That Chokes the Windpipe at bay. Without her, it was said, he would succumb to the demon and die.

And so Leah's family had not seen her in more than four years, but they did hear from her through letters, sent from towns and cities with exotic sounding names. When such tablets arrived, Avigail would send for Daveed. He was not always available. Sometimes they had to wait for days until he was released from his many duties at the Brotherhood, but when he came it was always a time for rejoicing. Avigail would make Daveed welcome in the kitchen, giving him wine and honey cakes stolen from their Egyptian master, and they would sit at Daveed's feet as he read greetings and news from their sister. Avigail missed her granddaughter and feared she might never see her again. It is all my fault, Avigail thought as she recalled that rainy night, seven years ago, when Hannah went into premature labor. How differently things would be now, Avigail thought in melancholy, if I had not spoken up to Zira the way I did.

She sighed. It did no good to dwell on the past. Besides, if it was true that Megiddo had fallen, then King Shalaaman would have no choice but to cut his alliance tour short and return to Ugarit. Which meant Leah would be coming home.

She started to turn back inside and then stopped, her eyes fixed southward. She thought: Megiddo has fallen. And its full import struck her. What if Ugarit fell? Will we become Egyptian? Will we forget who we are? Will we forget the names of our ancestors and the traditions they laid down for us long ago so that we could live honorable and fulfilling lives, and be righteous in the eyes of the gods? Learn a lesson from Jericho! A Canaanite city overrun by the first Thutmose who established a garrison there filled with Egyptian soldiers, with agents taking over Canaanite homes and businesses. How many people in Jericho still know their origins, their identity, for I have heard that Canaanites in Jericho wear Egyptian linen, the men shave their beards and use cosmetics. The women cook ducks and geese in the Egyptian fashion, instead of pork and kid. Egyptian gods inhabit the temples—even the Egyptian custom of circumcision has been adopted by Canaanites. If Egypt conquers Ugarit, our people will vanish and it will be as if we never were.

But those who fled Jericho that fateful night long ago, still remembered who they were. And that was why Avigail reminded her girls on a daily basis: "I am Elias's mother, you are Elias's wife, you are Elias's daughter, these boys are a son and grandson of Elias. This is Elias's house and this is who we are." To Baruch and Aaron she said, "Your grandfather is Elias, and you are the son of Elias. We are Canaanites descended from Shem the son of Noah. We worship Asherah and Baal. Never forget."

As she turned to go inside the empty villa, wondering who Zira was going to rent it to next, Avigail saw, coming down the road from the city, a group of slaves bearing upon their shoulders a litter curtained in rich purple and gold fabric. She recognized it as belonging to the house of Jotham.

Z ira silently cursed the cold spring weather as she sat on soft cushions beneath a warm bear skin. She wore lamb's wool slippers and thick woolen mittens. Aches and pains plagued her joints. Hot stones, fresh from an oven, had been placed inside the litter before she left her villa by the sea, but they did little good to dispel the cold that had invaded her bones.

Zira was feeling the passage of time. The years were beginning to fly by faster than before, reminding her that she was fifty-five years old and still not living in the royal palace of Ugarit.

But she had not given up her determination to see Yehuda on Ugarit's throne. After Elias's meddling daughter cured Shalaaman of the choking sickness, Zira began campaigning more than ever among the powerful families who would know what to do when they saw which way the wind was blowing. She reminded her friends at every opportunity that Shalaaman was an absent king who ruled Ugarit from hundreds of miles away. "He leaves us alone and unprotected. My Yehuda would never do that. He knows where his loyalty and duty lie. And as Rab of the scribes, my Yehuda is privy to all royal correspondence and documents. He knows how government is run, he understands diplomacy. Should Shalaaman succumb to the Demon That Crushes the Windpipe, my son would be able to step into his shoes and no one would notice the transition. What other man in Ugarit can say that of himself?" Her friends agreed, but Shalaaman was in good health, they said. Since the girl who kept such demons away had joined his inner circle, the king had not suffered a single attack. And that was more than four years ago!

Zira thought of little else. The problem of Shalaaman occupied her mind night and day. Overthrowing the king by revolution was not an option, not with Egypt rattling swords in the south. And assassination was out of the question—every man in Ugarit feared the gods. And so, Zira decided, other measures must be taken.

She had a plan.

The slaves brought the litter to a halt and lowered it to the ground.

Zira emerged through the purple drapes and onto a cushioned step, held in place by two kneeling slaves. It made her taller than Avigail, so that she looked down on the mother of Elias.

"The villa stands empty," she said, ignoring proper etiquette in order to point out Avigail's lowly status: slaves did not receive greetings of peace and blessings, nor were they addressed by the respectful titles. "Now that Megiddo has fallen to Egypt, no one will want to rent this property, or live here. Everyone wants to live within the city walls. Therefore, I can no longer afford to continue to feed and clothe you and your family."

Avigail lifted her chin in pride. "It was the Egyptian who fed and clothed us."

Zira looked around. "Where is this Egyptian that he would attest to your claim before a panel of judges? I see only four lazy women with two bratty boys freeloading at my expense." She paused, relishing the moment. "I am putting you all on the slave market."

The three women standing behind Avigail drew in sharp gasps. "You cannot sell us!" Avigail cried in outrage. "We are freeborn women."

Zira smiled. This was her clever plan. Before the king left Ugarit, four years prior, Zira placed a spy in his inner circle, and he sent reports on a regular basis via letters, informing her of the king's health. He also told her that every single day the demon-charmer, Leah, asked the King to be allowed to go home. And every day, Shalaaman refused. With Megiddo in Egypt's hands, Shalaaman would have to cut his tour short and return to Ugarit—bringing with him the girl Leah. All Zira had to do was lure Leah away from the king, rendering him vulnerable to the demon of the choking sickness. In short time, he would cough and wheeze and die from lack of air. And Yehuda would take his place.

"You are part of the chattel that came with the property. Do not forget the ten-weight of gold you owe my brother. Can you pay it? Now?"

"You know we cannot!"

"Then I claim recompense by way of the slave market." Zira had already arranged with the slave master to have them sent to another town for sale. Once Leah heard of this she would find a way to escape the king's clutches and go in search of her family. And then it was only a matter of time before the king began choking again "My lawyers will be by tomorrow to inspect the house and close it up."

As she watched Zira ride away on the shoulders of slaves, Avigail turned to Esther and said, "Go quickly to the House of Gold. Ask for Daveed. Tell him to come at once on a matter of extreme urgency!"

Nobu thought that if his heart grew any heavier, it would fall out of his chest. He had never known such pain, such misery. He had not known that being in love could make a man so wretched.

He might as well be in love with the moon. In his fifty years on this earth, Nobu the royal slave had enjoyed the sexual talents of whores, tavern wenches, dancing girls, temple prostitutes, and lonely house-wives. And while he had given them totally of his physical attention, his own artful skills at lovemaking, leaving every one of them smiling and satisfied, never had he given his heart.

Until now.

When did it happen? he wondered as he prepared his master's bath. When did he stop thinking of Esther as deformed and freakish, and suddenly see her as beautiful?

Nobu laid out the combs and sharp knives for his master's haircut, the shampoo and curling oil, and tried to think back over the past six years since his arrival with Daveed at the house of Elias the Vintner.

"At first you paid the youngest daughter no heed. She was thirteen years old, skinny and quiet, with a cleft lip that left her teeth hideously exposed. And then all that confusing time with Daveed trying to get into the Brotherhood, losing his sponsor, giving away his precious pledge-notes to bribe people to attend Leah's wedding. You stood by helplessly as you witnessed how your master fell in love with a girl forever forbidden to him, and attached to a family that was spiral-ing downward into certain ruin. The Prince of Lagash! The middle daughter running away with Leah's husband, to return pregnant, and then to hang herself. A cursed house if ever there was one. Daveed choosing to stay and help Leah with her dying aunt while the ceremony of the rising of naming the next Rab came and went. Finally, to learn the shocking truth of the family's bloodline . . ."

Nobu poured boiling water into the bronze washing bowl, and scented it with jasmine, his master's favorite fragrance.

Through all that, Nobu you slow-thinking turtle, Esther was

there, in the background, a quiet girl hiding her face with a veil. You gave her no thought. You never even saw her. Until when? What? It happened during the past four years, each time Daveed was summoned by Avigail and the two of you went running to that house of tragedy—occupied by Egyptians! Love blossoming each time. Or did it all begin the day she came upon you by yourself at the fountain with a hangover, as you waited for Daveed, and she heard you muttering to yourself and when you explained, she had said what a wonderful thing it must be to hear one's own thoughts with such clarity?

Nobu paused to listen for his master's footfall in the outer corridor. There was a commotion going on beyond the thick walls where the Brotherhood lived, out in the city. News of some kind.

She called the voices my own thoughts. Was it possible? Nobu had never realized it before, but every time the voices sounded in his head was when he had stopped thinking. Was it really himself he was listening to rather than mischievous gods bent on tormenting him?

He abstained from wine and other strong drink, as Esther had suggested, and listened to his voices. And Nobu discovered an astonishing thing. The voices were speaking wisely and logically. They advised him well, and observed the world, commented on everything around him. He realized in amazement and pride that if they were indeed his own thoughts, then he was a very clever fellow, if not a downright brilliant one. From that moment, Nobu's life changed in two dramatic ways: he no longer tasted wine, and therefore felt in excellent health. And he had fallen in love.

In the days since Elias was taken away in slave chains, Nobu had seen the man's mother, wife, concubine, and daughter living in the slave quarters of their own home, serving Egyptians. Avigail would send for Daveed, and he and Nobu would be greeted so eagerly and with such warmth it brought tears to his heart. Avigail and Hannah, Esther and Saloma, even the two little boys, greeted himself and Daveed like soldiers returning from battle, treating them like heroes. Nobu had never felt like a hero before.

Each time, while Daveed read a letter or wrote one at Avigail's dictation, you looked for Esther, tried not to hold her eyes too long, tried not to let your feelings show. When she let her veil slip, you no longer saw a deformed mouth but one that looked as if it were always smiling. Her eyes were beyond alluring. And she had grown tall. She filled your thoughts. She lifted your soul. She occupied your dreams. You want to save her from the world. But she will never love you as you love her. She will always be beyond your reach.

The noise outside the walls grew. People in the streets shouting. Scribes now running down the hallways. Something had happened . . .

Invoke the gods, Brother Daveed, the corruption is worse than we feared!"

They were meeting in secret—four young scribes with courage in their hearts but worry in their eyes—Brothers Daveed, Efram, Eli, and Yosep. Friends whom Daveed had carefully sought out and cultivated, young men who believed in honor and the restoration of the integrity of the Brotherhood.

"Blessed Shubat, help us," Daveed said. "What have you found, Brother Efram?"

Efram shed his woolen cloak and moved closer to the brazier that burned against the cold spring day. Holding out his hands, rubbing them, he said in a low voice, "I have spoken with certain men and they tell me that Yehuda has personal information about Judge Uriah."

Daveed's face darkened. Judge Uriah was Shalaaman's brother-in-law, and the highest legal authority in the land during the king's absence. "What sort of personal information?"

"It is said that Uriah engaged in a dalliance with the unmarried daughter of a prominent family here in Ugarit, getting her with child. The family was outraged, and when the girl named him as the father, Uriah became desperate. He could not afford to have his wife learn of the bastard, as the money and bloodline are hers, not his. He paid the family a sum of money, and then falsified a marriage contract between the girl and a man who does not exist, saving her honor and legitimizing the child. Rab Yehuda found out somehow and holds this information over Uriah's head. Daveed, Yehuda visits the archives daily, he reads all correspondence and legal documents."

"That is his right, as Rab."

"But he uses the information against people. His power is growing. Soon, no one will be able to stop him, not even the king."

Brother Eli spoke up. "You have heard what they are whispering about Yehuda and his stance on Shalaaman's diplomatic mission?"

Daveed nodded. It was being said that Yehuda believed Ugarit should attack the northern cities and make them vassals instead of allies. To fight a war on two fronts was folly. But Yehuda was blinded by power—a power that was growing.

"We must find a way to stop him," Brother Yosep said. He was the youngest of the four, still in the novitiate, with eyes that blazed with idealism and passion. It was Yosep who had brought Efram and Eli into Daveed's secret circle.

Daveed looked at the water clock in the corner—a large urn filled with water that dripped slowly all day, the descending water level marked off in hours—and said, "Attend to your duties now, my brothers. We will meet again tonight after prayers."

When he was alone, Daveed looked up and down the corridor. He needed to bathe before praying to Shubat. He had a full day of writing ahead of him. Where was Nobu with the bath water?

Daveed had been told the night before that he would be going to the house of a silversmith to record the man's last will and testament. In the afternoon, there were two property titles to write up, and a contract between pig farmers who could not agree on the line between their properties. Hardly the holy work he had expected to be doing here in the Brotherhood, but he did not mind. Words were words, letters were letters, and all were sacred. Besides, living at the Brotherhood and filling mundane assignments allowed him to quietly pursue his passion: his new script.

It also allowed him time to visit the house of Elias where he read letters from Leah . . .

Daveed still felt the sharp pain of her final words to him, spoken more than four years ago when she went into the palace expecting a reward only to find herself a prisoner of King Shalaaman. Her last words to him: I shall hate you . . .

They had not spoken since, although Daveed had glimpsed her in the first months after her father was taken away in slave chains. At a moon-ritual in the grand ceremonial hall, and again during a procession celebrating the king's day of conception. Both times Leah had been at the monarch's side.

Daveed had written letters to her, placed in the safekeeping of men who rode out to whichever city the king was visiting, carrying foreign correspondence to him and government matters that required his attention. Leah would make use of the royal scribe's services, Daveed was certain, to hear what he had written to her, and she in turn would dictate to the scribe a letter of her own. But no replies had come from Leah—not in more than four years, and it pained him that she was still angry with him.

As he had promised, he did what he could to help her family, taking them money, checking on them, letting the Egyptian vintner know that they had a friend at the House of Gold. But the Egyptian seemed a decent master, being more concerned with his grapes than with the plight of his servants. The money, however, was small as Yehuda assigned Daveed to menial tasks, sending him on mundane errands, not even allowing him to teach. The request for money that Daveed sent to his brother had come to naught. He had written back that their father's counselors and military advisors said that Lagash must build up its defenses in the event that Hatshepsut should die and her nephew launch an invasion of Canaan. Money in the royal treasury, Daveed's brother had said, was going into weapons, chariots, horses, and to increasing the size of the army.

If only King Shalaaman felt the same, for then he would stay in Ugarit and build up the army and defenses instead of traveling far and wide to forge alliances. With the king here in Ugarit, Daveed and his like-minded brothers could take their petition to Shalaaman and lay their cause before him—a plea to reform the Brotherhood.

And if Shalaaman were still here, Leah would still be here.

As Daveed checked his scribe's box to make sure it was well stocked with damp clay and papyrus, pens and inks, brushes and styli, he told himself that if he and Efram and Eli and Yosep were unsuccessful in invoking the king's aid, then he would use another tack, one which even his co-conspirators did not know about.

Daveed was going to teach the king his new script.

King Shalaaman was known for being open minded, and for being interested in novel ideas. Daveed was certain that if he could demonstrate his code of just thirty symbols to His Majesty, Shalaaman would be struck by a thirst to learn to read and write.

Daveed had tried to teach the new way of writing to his brother

scribes, but they were fractured into different cliques, not the cohe-
sive fraternity the outside world saw. Few grasped the value in his set
of thirty symbols, and many feared Yehuda who had vocally forbidden
any experimentation with other styles of writing. Daveed knew that
before he could persuade his brothers to accept the code, he needed
to unite them into a single credo, bring them back to feeling like a
true band of brothers. But how?

He would not give up hope that his new script would be an instrument for reform. He remembered the snake shedding its skin, and his
epiphany that old ways must continually be sloughed off in order for a
living thing to continue: the body of the Brotherhood is like the body
of the serpent. If we do not slough off the old ways, like the snakeskin,
then they will strangle us and we will die. And so we must slough off
the old archaic writing system in order to survive. After all, did not
our enemy the Egyptians streamline their own hieroglyphics with the
hieratic script? The scribes of Canaan can do no less!

Daveed saw now that the day Avigail sent for him to record Rakel's
memories, on the eve of naming the next Rab, had been a test from the
gods, for now he had something wonderful to offer the Brotherhood,
and in fact scribes and men everywhere. He had faced the east that
night and faced a decision. He could have left the roof and gone to
the House of Gold where he would have been chosen as the new Rab.
He would have brought the brothers back to the old ways. But because
he chose to help Leah instead, he had created a new way of writing.
Thus do the gods work their wonders.

Perhaps not the gods, he thought, but one god. It was El who spoke
to me . . . El Shadday, God Most High.

Nobu came flying into the cell, startling Daveed. "Master! Have
you heard? Megiddo has fallen! They say the king of Kadesh climbed
over a wall and escaped Thutmose's soldiers and he is now a fugitive."

"Megiddo! Then Egypt is at war with Canaan." Daveed had heard of
the coalition of rulers, led by the king of Kadesh, staging a revolt against
Egypt. All of Ugarit, Daveed included, had been certain they would be
victorious, for their combined armies were said to be great. Their defeat
could only mean that Pharaoh's army was even greater. "This means King
Shalaaman will be forced to return to Ugarit." This is the chance we have
been waiting for. Our chance to act against Yehuda . . .

"Master," a whey-faced Nobu said, "Lady Avigail has sent for us. She says it is extremely urgent."

That is it?" Yehuda asked the scribe. "That is everything?"

"Word for word, Rabbi," Brother Yosep said as he awaited a favorable sign from the Rab. Yosep was so eager to curry his master's favor that the slightest hint of a smile would have been like a gift of gold.

"Who are the other conspirators?"

"Besides Daveed, there is Brother Efram and Brother Eli."

"And you are sure they have no suspicion that you are a spy?"

"None, Rabbi, I swear upon the gods. They foolishly believe I am one of them and that I agree with their treasonous talk."

Yehuda digested this information and nodded. "You have done well, Brother."

"What should I do now, Rabbi?"

"Continue to meet with the traitors. Do not let on that you are reporting to me. You will be rewarded for this, Brother Yosep."

As he watched his cowardly spy slip out of the chamber, Yehuda decided it was time to act. Reaching for his cloak and hurrying out, he thought: Daveed is getting too confident. He is making too many friends. Yehuda now knew of twelve brothers who sided with Daveed on the issue of reforming the Brotherhood. They planned to petition the king as a group, and Yehuda was not certain even he had the power to fight them.

On top of that, Daveed intended to demonstrate his new writing system to Shalaaman—a man known for his love of what is new. Daveed had had little success in bringing the other scribes to his way of thinking. A script of thirty symbols that would enable any man, from a shepherd to the king himself, to read and write. Scribes would not longer be necessary.

Shalaaman must not be allowed to see Daveed's new folly.

As a cold rain blew in off the harbor, Yehuda wrapped his leather cloak tightly about himself and plunged into the night. His destination was not far. He leaned into the wind as he followed the lane down to the docks where boats and vessels bobbed on the churning water, glowing lanterns swayed, and torches sputtered. He squinted through the downpour for a sign above a door, indicating which was the Gods' Blessings tavern.

Daveed had to be gotten out of the way. But not even Yehuda would step over the line and commit murder. The idea had come to him when he had heard a report on one of Thutmose's clever military strategies, the kidnapping of important people, such as the sons of monarchs. Already, it was being said, Thutmose's spies had ridden to Sidon and Tyre and Kadesh to capture the sons of those kings, knowing that while Thutmose held them, their fathers would not resist the Egyptian forces.

Yehuda had witnessed the passionate quarrel between Daveed and Leah the day the king had been cured and, he had seen how, on a few occasions afterward, they had looked at each other with hunger and yearning. But it was their correspondence that Yehuda had intercepted that told him the true story, letters from Daveed to Leah, and her replies, filled with apologies and forgiveness and declarations of love. Yehuda had read them and then crushed them beneath his heel because why should they be rewarded for saving the king's life and robbing himself of the throne? But now, by a strange irony, the solution to his problem lay within those very letters.

The owner of the Gods' Blessings tavern was a jolly, rotund man named Kaptah, whom one would never take for an Egyptian spy. But Yehuda had known about him for some time, intercepting all correspondence before sending it on—dispatches from Pharaoh Thutmose, Kaptah's reports back on the state of Ugarit's military strength and intelligence.

Yehuda came in with the wind and forced the tavern door closed as he shook off the rain. A few heads turned his way, and then returned to indifference as the smoke-filled establishment was the haunt of weary sailors and jaded whores.

The room was furnished with stools and low tables, braziers and lamps, a counter displaying jugs of beer and wine, plates of cheese and olives, a basket of stale bread. Kaptah was wiping down the counter as he greeted the stranger effusively. "Shalaam, and the blessings of the gods, my friend and brother! Stay, warm yourself, and enjoy the finest wine this side of the Euphrates River!"

"You are Kaptah?" Yehuda said, keeping his cloak about himself, the hood still covering his head.

"I am! And how may this humble servant of the gods make your evening brighter? A woman perhaps?"

Yehuda held up a hand. "I know you received orders to kidnap a prince."

The fat hands ceased their labor. Kaptah blinked. "I beg your pardon?"

Yehuda said nothing while Kaptah studied the mournful long face of the stranger. There was something chilling about the eyes that did not blink, and the prominent teeth that seemed like those of a beast.

Kaptah sniffed in indignation. "You read privileged correspondence?"

"I read everything."

Kaptah shrugged and continued to wipe the counter.

"Your indifference does not work on me," Yehuda said. "I do not care what crimes you are plotting. Kidnap all the princes you want, the King himself if you dare, it does not concern me. I came to you to inform you of a certain individual in the King's personal entourage, a young woman whom he keeps with him at all times. If you do me the favor of kidnapping her during your harvesting of the king's sons, I will not have you arrested and executed for being an enemy spy."

The tavern owner dipped the cloth in water and continued to clean while digesting what the stranger had said, determining how he should respond. Finally he said, "A princess?"

"A witch. She prevents illness by her mere presence. His Majesty cannot empty his bowels without the girl nearby. He is terrified that if she were to leave or be taken from him, the Devil That Crushes the Windpipe will return and kill him. She is the most valuable hostage your Pharaoh could wish for, more valuable than Shalaaman's own sons. Her name is Leah and I will point her out to you. I assume you have men in position?"

Kaptah pursed his lips and glanced around.

"Do not waste my time, man. I assume your abductors are in place, ready to strike?"

"They are."

"What is your plan?"

Kaptah studied the long mournful face with deep-set eyes and prominent front teeth. He didn't like the stranger's looks but, suspecting he was a person of high rank and power, decided that cooperation would be the best tack. "You know that at the beginning of Shalaaman's alliance tour, he took another wife—the princess of a royal house. A year later, she gave birth to twins. Not only would Shalaaman hate to lose them, but the princess's father as well, the king of a powerful city. With but one blow, Thutmose cripples two enemies."

"A wise move. Even wiser is to strike twice at the same moment. When is it to happen?"

"At the midnight hour of the first night the king spends at the palace. He and his entourage will not be well organized, having just arrived. And having traveled, they will all sleep the sleep of journeyers. My men will slip into the princelings' nursery and take them and their nursemaids. We will be far from Ugarit by the time the deed is discovered."

Yehuda dug deep into a leather bag on his belt and pulled out a gold ring. "When your men take the twins, have another man take the girl Leah. My informants tell me that she sleeps in an alcove off the royal bedchamber. At the midnight hour, have another of your men take her, silently. But listen, she is to be well cared for until she reaches Pharaoh. No harm must come to her or her value is lost. Do you agree to this?"

The man grinned. "The gods smile on us, my friend!" He clapped a mug of beer on the table. "Join me."

But the Rab with the long mournful face said nothing as he threw down the gold ring and walked out.

When Daveed and Nobu arrived, Avigail brought them to the fire in the kitchen, to warm themselves against the cold and rainy night. She had little to offer them, but offered it all the same, bread and cheese and salt fish that was to be the family's supper for a week. Daveed thanked her and declined, instead pressing copper rings into her hand that she accepted graciously with tears in her eyes.

She then told him of their dire situation. While his master listened, Nobu kept his eye on Esther, the light of his heart, and thought how pale she was. She stood in the shadows of the kitchen, like a ghost, holding her veil to her face. He wished he could take her into his arms and comfort her. But it was not his place, and he did not want to frighten her. She seemed so timid, and she would certainly have no awareness of his tender feelings for her.

And now—Zira's new plan to further torture this family by selling them into slavery!—Nobu could barely keep himself from bellowing outrage.

But Daveed was saying in a comforting tone, "Do not worry, dear lady, Zira might have the legal right to sell you into slavery, but we also have the legal right to fight it. In the past few years at the Brotherhood, I have made friends with honest lawyers. I will go to them. I can block Zira's actions and stall until I can take your case before the court of judges."

"Asherah's blessings on you, dear Daveed," Avigail said, embracing him. "And blessings upon the gods for having brought you to this house six years ago. We will pray for your success."

They called her the demon-charmer, and nothing Leah said or did could persuade anyone otherwise. When she tried to tell the king that it was the sunlight and warmth that coaxed the choking demon from his body, Shalaaman merely waved his hands, saying, "I myself heard your voice as you charmed the demon and drew it from my chest. You cannot go home, Leah. Your reward is to stay with your sovereign."

And so she had no choice but to escape.

It was midnight and the king slept. Leah did not plan to stay away permanently, for that would only bring punishment upon her loved ones. She planned to be back before dawn, before Shalaaman awoke. It was dangerous, but she had to see her family.

And there was the need to find a safe place for her tablets.

During her journeys with King Shalaaman, Leah had found idle time on her hands, and so she had painstakingly taught herself Daveed's new script. Once she was proficient in pressing stylus to clay, she recorded eighteen medicinal cures, along with their magic spells, on tablets that she had then baked to a hardness and added to her personal belongings.

But now she worried for their safety, as she slept in an alcove and anyone passing by could steal her precious possessions. The tablets would be safe in her father's house, she knew, and so she would take them with her.

As she dressed in the shadows while the king slept, Leah's heart raced with excitement and anticipation of seeing them all again—Grandmother and Mother, Esther and the little boys. She had even missed Saloma.

But most of all, Daveed . . . No letters, no responses to her own letters to him. Had he received them even? She so regretted her words of anger the day she had cured the king's choking sickness. The pain on Daveed's face when she had said, "I will hate you forever." She had relived that terrible moment many times during her sojourn among other lands, wishing she could go back and change everything. She had carried Daveed in her heart night and day, prayed for him, dreamed of his dark eyes, his strong arms, his passionate kiss. And now she was back in Ugarit.

Soon, my love, soon . . .

Finally she secured her most prized possessions in protective soft cloths in her bag, objects that had traveled on her person from one foreign city to another, because they connected her to home and loved ones: the tablet with the valerian recipe that Daveed had given to her, the love poem found among Aunt Rakel's things, the gold fertility amulet that was supposed to have brought her luck seven years ago.

She closed her eyes and said a prayer of thanks to Asherah. She had so missed Ugarit and her family. She had thought about them every day, written letters as often as she could, and prayed for them. Now she was back, in the city of her birth, and her home lay just a few miles to the south. Please, she asked of Asherah, persuade the King to let me go.

They had traveled to many towns and cities in Mitanni in the north and east, even as far as Carchemish on the northern tributaries of the Euphrates. Shalaaman had returned with peace treaties, alliances, pacts, and trade agreements, all recorded on hundreds of clay tablets, all now being sent to the archive at the Brotherhood where they would be safely preserved. Shalaaman, being wise, had foreseen conflict with Egypt and had created a strong alliance. He had even married a princess who gave him two sons—an even stronger tie with another kingdom. They had heard that Thutmose had conquered Megiddo. There was little doubt he would push northward. Shalaaman with his alliance would be ready. But just in case, the king had sent word ahead, when they were three days out of Ugarit, that the city was to begin fortification measures, the army was to be called out in full force, and every able-bodied man was to be conscripted as a temporary soldier in the defense of the city.

In the morning, work would begin on the city walls, food and water and other supplies would be brought inside in case of a siege. Fear was in the air, but excitement as well. Leah worried about her family in their villa that lay in the path of anyone arriving on the road from the south. Her reason for sneaking out tonight was not only because she needed to see them again—she had missed them so terribly!—but also to coax them to come into the city and find lodgings until the Egyptian threat had passed.

Leah tiptoed from her alcove off the royal bedchamber and moved silently along secret corridors, pausing now and then to listen to the silent palace and to make sure no one was aware of her escape. She would run the six miles to the villa, an easy effort as her heart would make her feet fly. She would embrace the members of her family, hide the eighteen tablets in a safe place, and then tomorrow, she would find a way to get a message to Daveed. She needed to ask him why he never wrote to her, why he never answered her letters.

She did not see the shadows step from a closed doorway, did not hear their stealthy movements. It was not until a large hand went over her mouth that she realized too late that she was not alone in the corridor. She tried to scream, but the hand held her mouth too tightly, and a strong arm clamped around her waist, knocking the breath out of her. Leah kicked as her abductor lifted her off the floor. She saw the other man, tried to lash out at him with her foot.

She saw the fist. Saw it come down. Felt a sickening blow, and then blackness swallowed her.

At dawn the entire population of the House of Gold and the Royal Palace was awakened with the hue and cry of a kidnapping.

The king was in an uproar, and when news reached Daveed, when he heard the identities of those taken captive—Leah and two prince-lings—he knew at once it was the work of the Egyptians.

But surely it had been too easy. The timing was too perfect. The targets too accessible with no mistakes, no one even knowing the horrendous crime had taken place until empty beds were found by slaves.

Then he knew who was really behind it.

"Where is she?" he shouted as he flew into Yehuda's chambers, the same room where he had met with the old Rab. "Where did they take her?"

Yehuda did not look up from his breakfast of honey-porridge, bread, and goat's milk. "What makes you think I know?"

Daveed slammed his fist on the table, making dishes rattle. "You know everything that goes on in this city! Where is she?"

Yehuda calmly sipped the milk and then dabbed a cloth to his lips. He raised his long face to Daveed and said, "They took her south, to Pharaoh's encampment on a plateau called Har-Megiddo. But," he added quickly, "I do not advise you go after her. The king has declared that every able-bodied man in Ugarit more than the age of twelve is to join the army. No man may leave the city, starting this very moment. Anyone leaving will be executed as a deserter."

Daveed turned on his heel and stormed out. With a smile, knowing his advice would go unheeded, having known all along that Daveed would go after Leah, Yehuda returned to his breakfast.

They purchased swift mares and two pack animals at the horse market outside the city walls.

"Master," Nobu protested. "If we leave, the king will come after us and have our heads for desertion. Or if he does not, then we can never return to Ugarit. Think what you are doing!"

Daveed said nothing as he hastily loaded their packs onto a horse and, stripping his arms and brow of gold and gems, and removing his carnelian signet ring, hid the jewelry in a sack containing bread, nuts, and salt fish.

Nobu tried another tack, "I confess, Master, that I have given my heart to the sister, Esther. If you and I go south, we leave them without a protector!"

"Then stay!" Daveed shouted. "I am going after Leah!" Removing his fine angora cloak and tucking it into the blanket that would serve as his bedroll, Daveed donned a coarse brown cloak, purchased in the market-place to give him the look of a man of lesser means. Then he mounted.

Nobu eyed his own horse. The last time he had ridden such a beast was six years prior, when they had journeyed from Lagash to Ugarit. With great reluctance, he hoisted himself up. At the hour of his birth Nobu was consecrated to the royal house of Lagash and had served them loyally since—he could do no different now. Silently sending a prayer to every god he could think of, including those who might not have names, entreating them to protect Esther and her family, Nobu took up the reins and prayed that he did not break his neck before they could return to Ugarit.

Yehuda watched as three scribes made a thorough inspection of Daveed's quarters, systematically smashing every single tablet they found written in his new script.

"That is it, Rabbi," they said amid the rubble. "We have searched. There are no other tablets. The heretic's writing no longer exists."

Yehuda smiled. Daveed would die trying to rescue Leah, and his precious new code would perish with him.

Avigail stood at the end of the path to watch the main road. A cold, biting wind whipped through her cloak, and the first freezing raindrops fell. She was watching Daveed and Nobu ride south, away from the city.

They had stopped by to inform her that they were going after Leah. Daveed had then given Avigail a gold bracelet, saying, "I wish I could give you more, dear lady, but I might need to pay Leah's ransom." He had remounted his horse and said, "Pray for us. We will return."

To her surprise, the turtlenecked Nobu with his familiar barber's kit slung over his back, had blurted, "Tell Esther not to worry!" They had then goaded their horses into a fast gallop and disappeared down the southern road.

Now Avigail stood watching the road become swallowed by the night. What if they did not find Leah? What if she never came home? It was just herself now, with Hannah and Esther, Saloma and the two boys—alone and defenseless, facing the slave block.

CHAPTER TWELVE

I am not one of the nursemaids," Leah protested again. "I do not belong here. Please let me go."

But the Egyptian soldier said nothing as he passed cups of water and bowls of porridge and honey to the passengers in the covered wagon. Accepting the food and handing it to her companions, Leah saw in the morning light a ragtag band of women and children come down the dusty road and approach the soldier. They were becoming more numerous, refugees fleeing the advance of Pharaoh's army. Leah felt sorry for them. Victims of war, they had lost their men and their homes and had no where to go. When one of the women begged for food, another guard attacked her with his whip, driving them off.

The guards closed the door on the back of the covered wagon, sealing Leah and the frightened nursemaids in semidarkness to worry about their fates.

They had been traveling for ten days—a tedious journey spent in the swaying, jolting wagon that never stopped except to allow the women to find places along the road to relieve themselves. Their flight from the palace, after their terrifying kidnapping, had been swift, as the wagons and contingent of guards raced down the southern road to be well away from Ugarit by dawn. The women knew that by the time their absence was discovered, King Shalaaman's soldiers would never be able to catch up. And once they passed through the mountains in the south, several routes opened up. Those in pursuit would not know which one the abductors had taken.

"Where are they taking us?" one of the nursemaids asked as the porridge lay neglected in her lap. Shadows smudged her eyes, and she had lost weight. One of the others, who fed one of the babies from her own bowl, said, "We will know when we arrive. But they will not kill us. They need us to take care of the princes. If these babies die, Pharaoh will have no hostages to hold against our king. The gods are with us."

The first lowered her head and grumbled, "Egyptians eat babies. Everyone knows that."

Leah reached over and patted the girl's hand. "Iris is right. You will be treated well by the Egyptians. Pray to Asherah and harbor no fear."

Even as she spoke these words, Leah herself felt fear. Although she protested to the guards that they had made a mistake, she knew why she had been abducted. She was valuable to the king and no doubt Pharaoh would hold her hostage so that Egypt could occupy Ugarit with little resistance.

She was constantly on the lookout for a chance to escape, and had already tried three times, each time to be swiftly caught and brought back. She did not know how she would find her way back to Ugarit, but she had to try. If she became a prisoner of Pharaoh Thutmose, she might never see her family or Daveed again. But the guards kept a close eye on her, and when they let her out of the covered wagon to answer nature's call, they tied a rope to her ankle and the other end to the wagon.

When would they get to where they were going? She lifted the leather flap that covered the wagon's small window and saw that they no longer traveled through woodland or hills but had entered a flat plain. And then she felt the vehicle slow down. Now she heard voices—other sounds, too, as the wagon stopped and the rear door opened.

Leah and the nursemaids stepped down to see an amazing sight.

The plateau between two mountain ranges was covered as far as she could see with a vast, noisy, confusing, and overwhelming encampment of tents, men, animals. Soldiers everywhere. And smoke so thick the light of the noon sun barely pierced it. Her wagon had come to a halt amid horse corrals where hundreds of mares and stallions were confined. Nearby, camels beyond counting were tethered, and, behind them, rows of chariots ready for war. Egyptian troops, charioteers, and animal handlers milled about with such cacophonous industry that Esther wanted to clap her hands over her ears.

Her blood went chill. The rumors were true: the Egyptian army was the largest the world had ever seen.

As Leah watched the nursemaids being taken away from the other wagon—with the two princelings in their arms—a guard strode up, an officer, Leah judged, by his bronze breastplate and helmet. He said something to her in Egyptian and turned away down a path between tents and campfires. Leah assumed she was supposed to follow.

She looked around in amazement. The plateau near the city of Megiddo was a stunning sea of tents and huts, lean-tos and makeshift shelters, each with a campfire that sent smoke up to the sky. On the thick hazy air she heard laughter and shouts, cries and weeping, music, the braying of animals, the clanging of metal as blacksmiths forged weapons. She saw workers crafting bows and arrows, butchers slaughtering animals, women balancing jugs of water on their heads. It was like a small city, Leah thought. Laundry was laid out to dry on shrubs and boulders. Aromas filled the air as thousands of dinners were being prepared. She saw men marching, riders training horses, chariots undergoing repairs. A military city, she thought. But then she saw beyond, on the other side of a creek, another encampment, larger than this one, spreading away to the foothills of the mountains, and there she saw children and old men, and women stirring pots over cookfires. The captives, she thought, having heard of Thutmose's roundup of refugees and desert dwellers, anyone without a home. She had heard they were intended for Egypt, to work there on Pharaoh's new monuments.

The officer brought her to a tent that was larger than the rest, and constructed of stunning blue fabric. It was surrounded by heavily armed guards.

The officer indicated that she was to wait, and then he barked an order at her and held out his hand.

"I do not understand your language," Leah said.

He reached over and tugged at the strap of her carrying bag, which was still slung over one shoulder and across her breast. Leah thought briefly of protesting, but knew the man would be able to take it easily, and so she removed the bag that contained clay tablets and the gold fertility amulet, and handed it to him.

After he went inside, Leah surveyed her surroundings, wondering if she could run from this place.

The tent she had been brought to was grander than the rest, with space around it and heavily guarded by sentries in special armor. To what high ranking person did this tent belong? "Blessed Asherah," she whispered. "Protect me."

D aveed and Nobu had ridden night and day for ten days, stopping only for brief sleep, gobbled food, and to rest the horses. The closer they had come to Har-Megiddo, the more refugees they had encountered. Passing through a land called Galilee, they had seen entire families fleeing before Pharaoh's army, carrying all their worldly goods. Then Daveed and Nobu crossed a river and had seen the smoke of a thousand campfires, and now they sat on a small hill that looked out over a plateau and from here they saw a shocking sight. Megiddo—cosmopolitan, ancient, famous and rich—ablaze with a hundred fires, Egyptian soldiers coming through the city gates with plunder. Through the smoky haze, Daveed saw the unceasing rape of the noble Megiddo as the boisterous soldiers came away with such prizes as fine horses, statues made of gold, and women slung over their shoulders like sacks of grain.

"Master," Nobu said. "This is not good. All the trade routes of the world meet at this place. And now it is in the hands of Egypt!"

Daveed said nothing. He was thinking that Ugarit, being itself the hub of major trade routes, was like this conquered town, except that Ugarit also overlooked a world-class shipping harbor. How much more desirable was that northern city? Pharaoh Thutmose was not going to stop here.

Nobu was thinking the same thing, his fears growing. He was worried sick about Esther back in Ugarit. He had thought of nothing else since embarking for Megiddo. Was she all right or had Zira sold her into slavery? When we get back I will go straight to Esther, and if she is not there I will search for her—to the ends of the earth if I must.

They rode down the hill to the western perimeter of the massive encampment where men tended sheep and goats in pens. Daveed and Nobu dismounted and donned fine robes and jewelry, with Daveed restoring his royal signet ring to his finger. "We must find Leah," he said, wondering where in all this chaos and mass of humanity they could even begin to search. "She cannot be far. She would have arrived yesterday or this morning."

Leading their horses through the encampment, they saw people from different cultures, heard many tongues, saw unfamiliar costumes—testament to Pharaoh's far-reaching net.

"We must find the king's main camp," Nobu said, looking this way and that in rising dismay. How did Pharaoh intend to control so incohesive and disorganized a mob? How will we find Leah? It might take us days, weeks! While poor Esther is suffering the calumny of being sold into slavery . . .

"Up there," Daveed said, pointing across a creek. "That must be the military camp. These are Pharaoh's captives."

Leading their horses across the muddy creek, Daveed said, "There is an officer," and he pointed to a soldier giving instructions to the sentries. He wore copper chain mail and carried a baton fitted with a horse's tail. Clearly a man of rank.

For ten days Daveed and Nobu had debated how they were going to rescue Leah. At first, they had thought it would be simple: find out where she was being kept, sneak in under the cover of night, grab her, and ride off. It had been a short-lived fantasy. The more fugitives they encountered, the more they had heard about the size of Pharaoh's army, the more Daveed had realized he and Nobu had left Ugarit with naïve notions.

Another plan was called for.

"You there!" he called to the man in the tongue of the Nile Valley. "Captain! I wish a word."

The officer eyed the two strangers with suspicion, and then, seeing their horses—which only wealthy men could afford—taking in their fine clothes, the gold and jewels, and most of all the straight back with which the youngest carried himself, the tone of authority and confidence in his voice, decided they were worthy of his attention.

"I wish to speak with your superior on a matter of urgent international diplomacy."

The captain, unlettered and unschooled, trained only to drill soldiers in warfare, had no idea what Daveed had said.

So Daveed held out his hand to show the man his signet ring. "This is the seal of the royal family of Lagash. I am a prince of that city and I wish to be taken to your king, the great and revered Pharaoh Thutmose."

This the captain understood. He stared at the strangers for a moment, and then he roared with laughter. "Two simpletons from Lagash," he bellowed, "think their arses are better than anyone else's!" He thumped his chain-mailed chest and said, "I am the supreme commander of the king's royal sentries, and even I cannot gain an audience with the Sacred and Eternal Thutmose, son of the gods, the glory of the sun!" He spat on the ground and ran his hand across his mouth. "You will have an audience with the bars of a cage, and in the morning I will turn you over to my men for target practice."

He signaled to two burly soldiers, who came up with spears. As Nobu shouted his indignation, Daveed stood his ground. "You have some recently arrived hostages, do you not, Captain? From Ugarit? I have been sent by the king of that city to negotiate an agreement with your Pharaoh, regarding those hostages."

The captain's grin faded as he narrowed his eyes at the stranger. A nobleman without a doubt, and a man of wealth. Educated, too, as he spoke perfect Egyptian.

"You would do well to heed me," Daveed added.

"Master," Nobu said nervously. "You do not have the authority to speak for King Shalaaman. He would have our heads for this."

"Be quiet," Daveed said, although he was certain the Captain did not understand Canaanite. Daveed knew it was a dangerous gamble. Should his deception be discovered, it would be execution for them both. But if the ploy worked, and he was able to return safely Leah to Ugarit, Shalaaman would not be angry but would in fact reward them.

"I must confer with my superior," the captain finally said.

274

* * *

Leah did not know how much time had passed since the royal guard had brought her to this impressive blue tent. The sun had set behind the mountains. Torches flared with light throughout the camp. She thought of trying to run away, but there were too many troops, all of them armed, some of them on horseback. She would not get far.

A man finally emerged from the tent. His long white linen robes, black wig, and green cosmetic around his eyes reminded her of the Egyptian physician she had spoken to at the House of Gold six years ago. He looked impressive with his tall walking stick made of ebony and gold, and the lapis lazuli collar around his neck. And then he surprised her by calling out in perfect Canaanite, "Ask mercy of the gods and humble yourself before he who guards His Majesty's blood and wind, who preserves His Majesty's bowels, who protects His Majesty's digestion and composure. Show humility before the Most High Physician of Egypt, His Majesty's right hand—the Honorable Reshef. Ask mercy of the gods!"

A second man emerged, tall and lean, wearing the same black wig and long white linen robes. His eyes were rimmed with blue cosmetic, his thick lips had been rouged red. His most prominent feature was his nose, which was large and boney and beaklike.

When he confronted her, he did a strange thing. The Chief Physician quickly raised his hand before his face, palm out, and he whispered words in Egyptian. Then, lowering his hand, the asked in Egyptian, "You are the demon-charmer?" with the staff-carrying steward translating in Canaanite for Leah.

"They call me that, my Lord, but I am not a demon-charmer," she replied, realizing that one of the Egyptian scouts her abductors had met and conferred with on the highway must have ridden back to this camp to inform Physician Reshef of their valuable hostage. "I cured King Shalaaman using a remedy that comes from Jericho. I am of no value to you, my Lord."

He dismissed this. "Whether or not you repel demons is not the point. The fact that your king believes you keep him alive is what is valuable to my Pharaoh. You will be our prisoner until such time as peace is negotiated with Ugarit."

"When will that be?"

"It is not for me to say. It could be months, it could be years. Or perhaps this will all end in war and you will never return to your city. It is up to your king." He snapped his fingers and a guard appeared holding Leah's carrying bag, which he handed to Reshef.

Reaching inside, the Chief Physician brought out the tablets. "What are these?" he asked through the staff-bearing interpreter.

"One is a poem, my Lord. The second is a remedy for curing the Demon That Chokes the Windpipe. And the third is a medicinal recipe that calls for valerian. But it is written in an ancient tongue and I have not been able to translate the rest."

"Are you a healer?"

"No, my Lord, women are not permitted to practice medicine in Ugarit."

Painted eyebrows arched over eyes rimmed with blue cosmetic. "Then your people are indeed backward, as I have always heard. In Egypt, many physicians are women, and some teach at the House of Life. There are other tablets in here. Tell me about them."

Although Reshef could read and write, it was only in his own language and in hieroglyphs. Nonetheless, he had seen enough correspondence from foreign countries to recognize the ancient Sumerian of the valerian tablet. But the eighteen tablets that lay in the bag were written in symbols unfamiliar to him. "What language is this?"

"Ugaritic," she replied. When she saw his frown, she added, "It is in a new script."

Dark eyes beneath thick black brows gave her a piercing look. "A secret script?"

Her heart jumped. His tone was chilling, and she suddenly remembered she was a prisoner of in a military camp.

Before she could reply, they were interrupted by a messenger who spoke urgently with Reshef. He gave an order to the man, who ran off, and then spoke to the interpreter who said to Leah, "We are informed that a representative of your King Shalaaman has come to negotiate your release."

As Leah followed the physician and the staff-bearer to a waiting carrying chair, she marveled at Shalaaman's swift dispatching of someone to get her back, and she wondered who it was.

THE SERPENT AND THE STAFF

Reshef rode in the carrying chair while Leah walked alongside with the staff-bearing interpreter. Up ahead, Megiddo blazed with fires that turned the night sky scarlet. Although Leah could not see the dead littering the nearby fields, she smelled the decaying corpses and she wondered if families were not permitted to bury their fallen loved ones.

She passed country houses that had been gutted by fire, smoke enshrouding the silent ruins. That is my father's house, Leah thought, picturing her family home after Pharaoh invaded. Where did the inhabitants of that house go? She shuddered to think of it.

As they passed through the city walls and down streets strewn with rubble and bodies that had yet to be cleaned up, sounds of wailing and urgent praying coming from darkened dwellings, Leah wondered whom Shalaaman had sent to negotiate for her release, and if he would be successful. Would Pharaoh Thutmose demand Ugarit's total surrender before he would return Shalaaman's demon-charmer? And would Shalaaman agree to such extreme terms? What if he put the safety of Ugarit first, deciding to challenge Egypt rather than capitulate? Would Leah be Thutmose's prisoner forever?

Blessed Asherah, do not let him execute me to set an example!

At the foot of the palace steps, where the smashed statues of Megiddo's gods and royalty lay scattered as testament to Egypt's conquest over them, the slaves lowered Reshef's carrying chair. From here he walked, mounting the stairs to massive cedar doors inlaid with ivory and bronze. They stood open, with Egyptian soldiers standing guard. Where was the king of Megiddo, Leah wondered as Reshef led her to a plain wooden door which a guard snapped open at their approach. Had he taken flight after the king of Kadesh supposedly climbed over the north wall and fled for his life? No doubt any princes left behind were now the prisoners of Pharaoh.

They followed cold stony corridors illuminated by wall sconces, and as they descended stairs and walked past closed doors behind which men screamed and cried and pleaded to be let out, Leah realized they had come to the city's prison. Her skin crawled with foreboding. Surely diplomatic negotiations were conducted in the throne room, not in dungeons.

They entered a large subterranean chamber where the walls were damp with moss. Leah saw chains and shackles, instruments of torture. Poor wretches crouched in cages too small for them, barely alive, begging for water. Captives lying on the floor, unconscious and moaning—some had no hands, some no feet, their arms and legs ending in stumps covered in a black substance.

Egyptian soldiers came to attention when they saw Reshef. Leah looked around in terror. Where was Shalaaman's ambassador? Why had she been brought to this terrible place?

And then a man stepped into a circle of light. Leah blinked. He was tall with broad shoulders, his one-sleeved tunic leaving his left arm bare, a rich blue cloak hanging down to his calves. When she saw the long black hair and closely cropped black beard, she cried, "Daveed!" and ran to him.

He took her into his arms and kissed her. "Leah, my Leah, thank Shubat you are all right."

"What is this?" Reshef demanded in Egyptian, so that the interpreter had to repeat the question in Canaanite.

"The hostage you hold is my wife," Daveed replied in Canaanite with the staff-bearer translating. Leah wondered why Daveed would speak Canaanite when he could speak Reshef's language. And then she realized there would be an advantage to Daveed keeping that skill a secret.

"You claim to be a prince of Lagash and a representative of King Shalaaman of Ugarit. Are these things true?"

"They are." Daveed held out his hand to show Reshef the carnelian ring with the winged angels engraved in the stone. "My wife, Leah, is descended from Ozzediah, a beloved king of Ugarit." Unused to speaking a lie, Daveed watched the physician's face, to see if he had been convincing.

But Reshef said, "And you are a scribe?" He pointed to Daveed's scribe's box where a quaking Nobu stood gray-faced between two guards.

"I am."

"Then you are privy to your sovereign's military plans, which you will now impart to us."

Two guards seized Daveed by the arms and brought him to a bloody chopping block. Leah watched in horror as they pinned his right hand down on the block, while Chief Physician Reshef took a stand next to a pot containing molten pitch, the black substance, Leah realized now, that coated the amputated limbs of the other wretched prisoners.

"We know about the factory where iron ore is being smelted for its metal. How many weapons have thus far been forged?"

Reshef put his questions through the aide with the tall ebony staff, who then passed them to Daveed in Canaanite. The guards held Daveed by his arms as they pinned his right hand to the bloody chopping block. A third guard held an axe ready to come down and strike through the wrist.

"Please do not do this," Leah begged. "He does not know anything."

The interpreter did not bother translating her entreaties for Reshef, who continued his questions: "Who are the kings with whom Shalaaman has signed pacts? What are their terms of war? Does the alliance plan to launch an attack against Egyptian forces?"

He paused and studied Daveed's face. After a moment, Reshef held out one of Leah's clay tablets. "What is this secret code? To whom was this message brought? Your wife was carrying it. Is there a Canaanite spy among Pharaoh's advisors?"

"My Lord," Leah said. "It is not a secret code. I can demonstrate."

The Chief Physician waved a hand. "I care not for the ways others write, for the Egyptian way is the only way, as our sacred hieroglyphs are called 'the gods speak.'" He turned to Daveed, who stood stiff and silent. "Tell me Shalaaman's military plans."

As Leah watched in helplessness, trying to think of something to say, to save Daveed from torture, she was suddenly overwhelmed by a feeling of being watched. The back of her neck crawled. She slowly turned and peered into the dark shadows of the dungeon. Something was there. Lurking. Watching. Evil.

Her eyes delved the darkness until they discerned a shape. A grotesque little man stood there, sharp beady eyes glinting with keen interest. She was not sure he was human. It brought back a memory of when she was a child and visiting the marketplace. A crowd had gathered around a spectacle. A foreign vessel in the harbor had brought a shipment of rare and exotic beasts from Africa. A long-necked creature called a giraffe, a pair of lions, a horse with black and white stripes, and a squat, misshapen being that walked upright and was covered head to foot in hair. The trader had called it a chimpanzee.

She turned away but her back prickled with fear. She watched Reshef, heard his questions, saw how stoically Daveed stood in silence. But Leah could not stop thinking about the misshapen creature in the shadows, she could not help a second glance over her shoulder. She searched the shadows, but the grotesque thing was gone.

"What is the strength of King Shalaaman's army?" Reshef pressed again.

When Daveed still did not speak, the Chief Physician signaled to the soldier with the axe, who tightened his grip. To Daveed Reshef said, "I will ask you once more. If you do not answer, you will lose your hand."

"I will never betray a confidence," Daveed finally said, "for I took an oath upon my personal god when I became a scribe in Lagash. I would give my life before betraying that oath."

"Very well," Reshef said and nodded to the axe-wielding guard. "We shall see how well you live as a one-handed scribe."

"Wait!" Leah cried. "I can tell you what you want to know, my Lord."

"No, Leah!"

"Daveed, I swore no oath."

"Leah, do not sacrifice your city and your people in order to save me!"

Reshef gave the signal and as the axe came down, Leah flew at the soldier, seizing his arm. Another soldier leapt forward, hitting Leah in the shoulder blade with the butt of his spear, to send her sprawling on the slimy, foul-smelling floor.

"My lord," Daveed said, "I beg you to let her go. I am a more valuable hostage. My father is the King of Lagash. Pharaoh does not need this woman. He can have me instead. And I will stay willingly, in exchange for this woman's freedom. You need not fear that I will try to escape."

But Leah came to her feet and said, "I will tell you want you want to know! I was at King Shalaaman's side for four years!"

When Reshef hesitated, and then fixed a dangerous eye on Leah, Daveed quickly said, "Do not believe it, my lord. She is just a woman. Egyptians are known for giving their women too much power. You even allow them to inherit property, to run businesses, to read, and to write even. You permitted your last queen, recently gone to the gods, to call herself King. The men of Canaan are not so lax. King Shalaaman would never have spoken of important matters in front of this woman."

Suspicious eyes slid back to Daveed. "I suspect there is an untruth here. Speak the truth now, prince of Lagash, and I will spare your hand. Tell me Shalaaman's military plans."

A fine sweat broke on Daveed's forehead. The color drained from his face. "I cannot," he said.

"Very well," Reshef said, "may the gods have mercy on you." He gave the signal and the axe came down. Daveed braced himself and Leah screamed. But the blade stopped at his wrist. As Daveed and Leah watched in bewilderment, another man stepped forward from the shadows, dressed in white robes with a leopard skin over his shoulders. He held a long white egret feather, which he dipped in red ink. He then traced a red line on Daveed's wrist, incanting a spell as he did so.

"This is the Feather of Truth," Reshef called out in a sonorous voice. "With it we sever the hand of falsehoods. We cut away the hand of lies. We amputate the hand of untruths. Behold, the Great God Thutmose takes away your hand! Behold, the Great God Thutmose restores your hand!"

The two guards released Daveed and his knees gave way. Leah ran to him and held him up, sobbing, as he leaned on the chopping block to catch his breath. Nobu cried, "Thank Shubat!" and burst into tears.

Reshef wrinkled his huge nose and said, "It is well known that Canaanites do not bathe. It would be an abomination to bring such foul creatures before my king."

"We've been riding for ten days," Nobu wailed. "You ride a horse for that long and see if you smell like a rose."

"Nobu!" Daveed said in a weak voice.

But Reshef was unconcerned. He gestured to the guards, saying, "Prepare them for His Majesty," and the three were taken away.

In a daze, Leah allowed herself to be taken along the dank corridors, Daveed and Nobu walking behind with an escort. When they reached the top of the stairs, and looked through another doorway, she saw that they were in the palace, in a well-lit hall flanked with columns. Courtiers and slaves were hurrying to and fro, soldiers and guards murmuring among themselves, and she remembered that the city of Megiddo was now the military headquarters of a conquering king.

Her escort stopped before a doorway inlaid with gold designs, and the two doors swung open when the entrance guards banged their fists upon them. Leah was delivered into the care of women who seemed to have been expecting her, drawing her inside as the doors closed. She knew where she was. The perfumed air, the sound of women's voices, the gold columns and marble chairs and reclining sofas, the linen hangings, children's laughter—she was in the harem.

It was very crowded. She wondered where all these girls and women slept, how they managed all to be fed, and as her head cleared and her dungeon terror faded, she saw now that many girls were weeping, others frowning, some giving orders, there was even a heated argument next to a fountain that spewed a fragrant mist. The women were of all ages and races, some slender, some plump, dressed in myriad costumes and headdresses. Leah realized, as she was taken to a sunken bath and stripped of her traveling clothes, that many of these must be captives of Pharaoh, while others were the wives and concubines and children of the king of Megiddo.

She could only imagine the chaos of such a situation, the anger and bitterness and jealousies. Leah knew of the hierarchies that existed in harems, that there was a long established order within these cloistered walls, and that newcomers, with their own rankings of status and pecking order, would disrupt a structured world.

Leah closed out the noise, shut her eyes to the feminine chaos and allowed herself to be bathed and perfumed and oiled and dressed in a fine linen dress with an Egyptian collar and gold bracelets. She did not know to whom these belonged, she did not care. She wanted only to be with Daveed again, and to find a way to escape from this nightmare.

When she was ready, the eunuchs who guarded the main door—two overweight Canaanites with big stomachs and fatty breasts, as perfumed as the women they guarded—opened the doors and Reshef met Leah on the other side. Daveed and Nobu stood with the Chief Physician, their hair freshly done, their bodies smelling of sweet soap, and wearing the heavy, embroidered robes of Megiddo Canaanites. She anxiously searched Daveed's face. "Are you all right?"

But it was Nobu who answered. "They tried to dress my master's hair but everyone knows Egyptians shave their heads and wear wigs! Their barbers know only how to scrape jaws and scalps smooth. I would not let any of them touch my master."

"Nobu," Daveed said with a sigh, "your loose tongue is going to cause us to lose our heads. Keep your silence when we are taken before Pharaoh."

Leah knew, from being part of Shalaaman's court, and from the many throne rooms she had visited in the past four years, that only royalty and nobility could stand before a king as honored guests. And so it was through Daveed's royal blood and Leah's famous ancestor Ozzediah that they were allowed this audience. But what if the truth of her own lineage were to be discovered—that she was not descended from Ozzediah at all but was in fact Habiru? Our necks will be on the chopping block, and this time there will be no symbolic red line drawn in paint.

Like the harem—like the entire palace and city, Leah imagined—the throne room was a chaotic scene, with toady delegates from nearby towns and provinces jostling for attention, eager to bow down to the conqueror. Important-looking courtiers running back and forth bearing scrolls and clay tablets. Generals debating among themselves. Prisoners of war, naked and kneeling with their hands tied behind them and bound to their ankles.

Daveed and Leah also saw the new statues of gods that had replaced the gods of Megiddo, standing on pedestals with incense burning at their feet—gods with the heads of jackals and cats and beetles; a hippopotamus that walked upright; a bare-breasted woman with cowhorns sprouting from her head; falcons, hawks, and vultures; baboons and crocodiles. The three visitors from Ugarit knew that this was merely to be the first of many cities that would fall to a man who had his eye on Babylon itself. And the gateway to that fabled city in the east was Ugarit. Thutmose might sit now upon the throne of Megiddo, but the throne of Ugarit controlled a harbor that received ships from a thousand ports, Ugarit stood at the terminus of highways that stretched as far as Mitanni and Hatti and to the gulf where the mighty Euphrates spilled her waters.

It is only a matter of time, Daveed and Leah thought in cold fear, and these strange gods of Egypt will replace Dagon, Baal, and Asherah.

Megiddo's royal throne stood upon a marble dais that was reached by a gold and marble stairway. The throne was carved from ebony and decorated in so much gold that it was almost blinding in the torchlight. Finely dressed men—wearing the ubiquitous white linen gowns and black Egyptian wigs—flanked the throne, as did military men in shining bronze helmets and breastplates. On the wall behind the throne were colorful scenes of former kings of Megiddo engaged in lively combat and conquest. And upon the throne of Megiddo itself, wearing the double crown of Upper and Lower Egypt, the symbolic flail and crook in his crossed hands, sat Pharaoh Thutmose, successor to the infamous Hatshepsut. His arms and ankles were laden with gold, the collar about his neck was heavy with gold and precious gems. His robes were of the finest linen and draped his squat form almost elegantly. Behind him, slaves stood holding magnificent ostrich feather fans.

Leah stared at the king in shock, for he was the grotesque creature who had observed Daveed's interrogation in the dungeon. The sight of him astounded her because the most powerful man in the world was very short. His head, she knew, would barely reach her shoulders. He was also the ugliest man she had ever seen. Leah would go so far as to call him repulsive. Pharaoh Thutmose's forehead was so low and flat as to be nearly nonexistent, with a heavy brow ridge and deeply set eyes. His nose was short and looked as if it had been smashed, and his jaw was disproportionately large for his skull. She wondered briefly if he was human even, and then the large mouth moved and the king spoke.

"Bring the representatives from Ugarit forward." And Leah witnessed again the curious gesture as Thutmose raised his hand before his face, palm outward, while he whispered words that were not translated into Canaanite.

A courtier with a tall staff bellowed in a loud voice, "Bow down to the Lord of the Two Lands, He Who Commands the Sun and the Wind, Sovereign of All the World, King of the Sky and Earth, Radiant in Splendor."

"Eyes downward," Reshef hissed to his three charges. "It is forbidden to look upon the face of the Living God of Egypt."

Pharaoh Thutmose spoke in Egyptian and the interpreter addressed Daveed in Canaanite: "The Feather of Truth has found you worthy, Prince Daveed of Lagash and Ugarit."

Leah thought Pharaoh's voice surprisingly deep for one so young—everyone knew that Pharaoh Thutmose was barely twenty-two years old. "You have proven your integrity to us, Prince Daveed of Lagash and Ugarit. We are satisfied that you would truly give your life before betraying your oath of confidentiality. Therefore, we will call you friend and listen to what you have to say on behalf of your king. If your terms are amenable, we will have letters drawn up, and we will select elite representatives to accompany you and the hostage back to Ugarit. I look forward to forging a peaceful alliance with King Shalaaman."

"Your Majesty," Daveed said in Canaanite, while the interpreter spoke in Egyptian. "My sovereign greatly looks forward to engaging in dialogue with Egypt's mighty king. He is certain an amicable agreement can be arrived at. But King Shalaaman is in great need of his demon-charmer and would be most grateful if Your Majesty, who is known for great compassion and beneficence, would allow this woman to be restored to King Shalaaman's presence."

The deep-set eyes beneath the thick bony brow stayed on Daveed's face like two evil pin pricks of dark light, Leah thought. She did not trust Egypt's ugly king. She did not trust Physician Reshef. She did not trust anyone in this court. She wanted only to leave, with Daveed and Nobu, as quickly as possible.

"The request is a reasonable one," Thutmose said. "We must pray over it and ask the gods for guidance."

He paused. Gesturing to the dagger strapped to Daveed's bare arm, Pharaoh said, "What is the significance of this weapon?"

"It is a symbol of days in the past, Your Majesty," Daveed said, keeping to the truth as much as he could.

"You are not a fighter?"

"I do not fight, Your Majesty."

Thutmose flicked his wrist and Reshef, with two guards, stepped forward to flank the three from Ugarit.

Pharaoh then said to the interpreter, "You need not translate what I am about to say."

The man nodded and held his tongue while Thutmose addressed Chief Physician Reshef.

When Pharaoh was finished speaking, Reshef bowed low, and then instructed Daveed and Leah and Nobu to bow low and retreat from the throne room. In the outer hall, he told them through the interpreter that they could choose wherever they wished for accommodations. "There are many rooms. Find what you can. We are still very disorganized, still settling in. Once His Majesty appoints his minister here, and a loyal staff, the palace will be better organized and run smoothly in the Egyptian fashion. I cannot spare guards for you tonight. But the palace is sealed. For the safety of everyone inside, there is no coming and going at night. Maybe the gods keep you safe."

When Reshef and his staff-bearing companion left, Leah turned to Daveed. "What did Pharaoh say that was not translated for us?"

"He said that we are not leave the palace. That we will remain prisoners until Thutmose has destroyed Ugarit and made a slave of its king." He tapped the stiletto on his arm. "That is why I did not tell him the whole truth of my weapon. In case it is needed."

"You were right, master," Nobu said as they hurried through the maze of corridors and hallways that created a warren of the palace of Megiddo. "Keeping your knowledge of their language from the Egyptians was a clever thing. But how long can you keep it up? Sooner or later they will realize that you understand what they are saying among themselves, and we will surely lose our heads then!"

"I expect us to be long gone from Megiddo before that happens, my friend. Invoke the compassion and aid of the gods."

"I do not trust the Egyptians," Nobu grumbled.

"Nor do I. Make no mistake, we are prisoners of war."

They found empty rooms, and chambers crowded with people. And as Reshef had warned, every entrance to the outside was locked and heavily guarded. But Daveed would not give up. They had to escape.

When they reached the top of a long flight of marble stairs, Daveed pushed on the door and the trio found themselves on the palace roof, beneath the moon and the stars. Here, a lush garden grew, with shrubs, small trees, flowers, and a trickling fountain. Daveed went straight to the edge where a waist-high wall enclosed the garden and from where he could look down and see the camped guards surrounding the palace.

He came back to Leah and Nobu. "It is no use. We are trapped here for now."

"I will find a way out, master," Nobu said, striking his chest. No one was more eager to return to Ugarit than he.

Nobu hastened down the stairs so that Daveed and Leah were alone together for the first time since they had last seen each other, at the palace of Ugarit, and she had told him she would hate him forever.

She had thought about him every day since, and dreamed of him every night. Her heart had leapt at the sight of him just an hour ago, and she had thought he was going to die. Daveed was her love, her passion, but now, as she looked at him across the intimate space, she felt awkward and at a loss for words.

"I was so afraid I would never find you," Daveed said. "Nobu and I rode night and day. When I heard you had been kidnapped—"

"Daveed, you heard King Shalaaman's edict, did you not? That all able-bodied men were to join the army and that any who fled the city would be executed for desertion? It is dangerous for you to go back. Shalaaman could have you executed before you could even explain." She took a step toward him. "If we are allowed to leave at all. Especially if Reshef finds out you lied to him. Not once but three times."

Daveed tenderly laid his hand on her cheek. "I did not lie, for that is my sworn oath. When I told him you are my wife, Leah, I spoke the truth, for in my heart, you are my wife. And when I said you are descended from Ugarit's legendary King Ozzediah, it is true. In name, you are his descendant. Anyone in Jericho will tell Reshef that. And," he smiled, "while King Shalaaman did not specifically send me here to negotiate for your release, I like to think he would have. And when we return, I know he will reward me. But Leah, why did you never answer my letters? I waited for four years."

"Halla! I never received them! Did you receive mine? I wrote so many."

He shook his head. "I suspect Yehuda intercepted them as part of his scheme to weaken me. By Shubat, I missed you."

She saw starlight reflected in his dark eyes. "Daveed, I am so sorry for the words I spoke that last day."

He stood immobilized against the stars, unable to take his eyes off her hair, which hung long and unbound. He had rarely seen Leah without a head covering. "They offered me an Egyptian wig," she said when she saw how he stared. "I asked for a veil, but my dressers were Egyptian and they do not wear veils."

Daveed was overcome with the sight of her this way. It gave her the look of a free spirit, a daughter of nature, pure and unhampered by fashion or tradition, or the rules of men so possessive of their women that they keep them covered up.

Taking a step closer, Daveed bent his head and pressed his lips to hers. When he lifted his head, he murmured, "'My love's breasts are like two moons. They delight me. They are filled with honey. I await my lover beneath the tamarisk tree. I await her kisses and her embrace. She holds me all night long. And then she empties me. Her leaving is the coldest of dawns. I know only sorrow until she brings joy to me again.'"

She laughed softly. "I almost showed Physician Reshef how to read that poem." She laid her head on his chest and heard the steady reassuring thumping of his heart. "I wish I were your wife, my love. I wish we were free to marry. But under the law, I am still Caleb's wife."

Daveed drove his fingers through her hair, lifting her face to his. "You are my wife. You have been the wife of my heart almost from the first moment I saw you, and no laws of men or ancient traditions will keep me from you." He bent his head and kissed her again, for a long tender moment, and then the kiss grew urgent. With reluctance he drew his head back and said, "The world is changing, Leah. I know that now, for we are witnessing the greatest force on earth. No army is greater than that of Pharaoh. He will march to Ugarit, and then on to Babylon, and that will mark the end of the old ways."

"I love you," she whispered, tears rolling from her eyes. And as Daveed bent to kiss her again, they heard footfall and heavy breathing, and the doorway to the stairs flew open.

"You were right, master!" Nobu blurted as he came onto the roof. "This palace is sealed tighter than that blasted Chief Physician's anus!"

Daveed stepped away from Leah, his look turning dark. "In the morning, when they open the palace, there will be much coming and going of visitors, military scouts, generals, diplomats all wishing Pharaoh's ear. They cannot possibly watch every small door and window. We will find a way out then."

Nobu had brought food. Bread and olives, fig cakes, almonds, cheese. "I will retreat down the stairs, master, and stand watch." But he yawned and he knew ten days of riding and today's shocks would make him sleep.

When they were alone again, Daveed offered Leah something to eat. But she shook her head. She had not eaten since that morning, on the road to Megiddo, but she was not hungry—although another appetite began to sharpen as the horrors of the dungeon and the threat from palace guards retreated from the enchanted rooftop garden.

They stood in the warm spring night under a full moon, inhaling the perfumed air and feeling the gentle breeze on their faces. An easterly wind carried the smoke of many fires away from the city. For this moment, they could forget they were caught in the middle of a war.

Daveed took Leah by the arms and said, "You complete me. Without you, I am half a man."

Daveed stepped away and removed his tunic so that he stood in only his kilt. Leah saw, lying on his bare chest, the medallion she had given him, bearing the symbol of Asherah's sacred tree. She smiled. "The goddess has indeed protected you. I shall recite prayers of thanks every day for the rest of my life."

She saw the stiletto dagger in the moonlight, still strapped to his upper arm. She knew he would not remove it, as the elite caste of warrior-scribes swore sacred oaths never to do so.

He drew her to him again, and Leah molded her body to his, closed every space that stood between them so that she felt every inch of his warmth and vitality. Daveed pulled her so tightly to him that she almost could not breathe, and his mouth pressed so hard on hers that her head was bent back. She had never felt so alive. Had never known such desire. She curled her arms around his neck and held tightly to him, vowing never to let him go. No matter what happened after tonight, what treachery Pharaoh had in store, or what dangers lay ahead, Daveed was hers, and she was his. Two hearts joined, never to be separated again.

The king's private rooftop garden offered relief from the sun in the form of a wooden gazebo, where Daveed now led Leah, to spread his cloak on the floor and take her into his embrace away from prying eyes.

She wept with joy. He sighed in ecstasy. When Daveed drifted off to sleep, Leah stayed awake, marveling at the intense passion of their union. They lay on their sides, with Daveed at her back, his right arm under her, outstretched so that she placed her hand in his curled fingers. His left arm was draped over her and as she listened to his rhythmic breathing, felt his warm breath on her neck and cheek, she knew that this was the one moment in her life for which she had been born, and which would stay with her always.

Daveed, her sweet protector, the light of her heart, keeper of her soul.

When Leah awoke she found that it was still night, and Daveed was lifted up on one elbow, gazing down at her. He drew a stray lock of hair from her face and smiled. He then grew serious. "I will find a way to get us back to Ugarit. Yehuda's corruption grows. But now that Shalaaman has returned, I can go to him and expose the corruption."

"And he will appoint you Rab."

"Only if you agree to be a Rab's wife." He kissed her softly. "We would not have to live at the Brotherhood, but have a fine house of our own. We will need plenty of room for all the children we will have. And you will be my eyes, dearest Leah."

She gave him a puzzled look. "Your eyes?"

"It is the sacrifice the man makes for service to his profession. The old Rab was blind, and so were his predecessors. He said that all Rabs lose their sight, so it has been for generations."

"Halla, that is an unfair price to pay," Leah said, wondering why the gods of writing would deny their servants the gift of reading.

"Forgive me, Leah, I should have exposed Yehuda four years ago. But I was blind in my loyalty to the fraternity. I see now that I was wrong. By protecting Yehuda's reputation, I thought I was protecting my brothers. Instead, I have only done them more harm. And your family as well. By my inaction I did them a great injustice, Leah, and I vow to make it right."

"We will get our house back," she said, marveling at the feel of him, his nearness. "Once you prove that the collection note Zira holds—"

"I am not speaking of the house," he said. Daveed sat all the way up and looked down at her. "Do you not know? Leah, what was the latest news you had of your family?"

She searched her memory. "We were in Haran, just before news of Megiddo came. I received a letter from my Grandmother saying they were well and that their Egyptian master was a fair-minded man."

"By Shubat!" Daveed shot to his feet. "I thought you knew."

She looked up at him, a muscular god glowing in the moonlight. "Knew what?"

"The Egyptian tenant has left Ugarit and Zira is going to sell the villa. Leah, she is putting your family on the slave block."

"Halla!" she hissed and sprang to her feet. "Quickly invoke the gods on their behalf." Grandmother and Mother, Esther and Hannah, little Baruch and Aaron . . . Slavery! "We must go at once!"

"I will find a way, if I must pay bribes or make promises for King Shalaaman that he cannot keep. Even if we have to escape under the cover of night, Leah, we will find a way back to Ugarit."

They dressed quickly, noting that the eastern sky was turning pale, which meant the palace would be waking up. As Daveed fixed the leather belt around his waist and retrieved his blue cloak, the door to the stairs shot open and Nobu came flying out.

"Master, Pharaoh is looking for you!" Four soldiers stood behind Nobu, with spears and shields. "King Thutmose is demanding that you join him. This military escort is to take you to him at once."

Daveed frowned. "Join him for what?"

"Master, I have heard that Thutmose is leaving at once with five divisions of infantry and chariots for a mountain called Karmel. They say it is an invasion. Oh, master, you are being ordered into battle!"

CHAPTER THIRTEEN

There it was, at the end of the tree-lined lane. A private villa called Hathor's Pleasure Garden. Avigail could not read, but there was no mistaking the images painted on the white walls and gate: graphic depictions of male and female genitalia.

Hathor's Pleasure Garden was a whorehouse.

Avigail had traded Daveed's gold bracelet for more practical rings of copper, silver, and gold, and had been able, through a clerk at the High Court, to extend her petition for time to challenge Zira's claim on her family as property. But the grace period was up and no more extensions were possible. Today was the day Zira was coming with the slave master to take them away.

Avigail had prayed that Daveed would have returned by now. Or Elias. She had made appeals to male friends, all of whom had offered regrets. Avigail and her family were all alone with no male protector. Zira had backed them into a corner. Avigail was now desperate and would resort to anything to save the family and their home.

She had tried for days to find a lawyer who would take her case, going each morning to the great court of the House of Gold, asking one man to another, only to be turned down. She could not afford their services, nor had she any possibility of winning. But two lawyers took pity on her and told her of a man named Faris who might be able to help as he was known to have the keenest legal mind in all of Canaan. She went to his residence where the house steward had told her she could find Faris at Hathor's Pleasure Garden in the north quarter of the city.

And now she stood at the threshold, struggling for control. Her strong sense of pride and decency made her want to turn around and go home. She had come here to break her own personal rules of ladylike conduct. Paying a call on a strange man without the protection of a male escort, without a companion of any kind. And then to cross the threshold of an Egyptian establishment! Not all Egyptians had fled Ugarit. A woman named Nefer-Merit had stayed. Her name and her house were notorious as far south as Tyre and as far north as Carchamesh. Finally, and perhaps worst of all, Avigail had never in all her life set foot inside a bordello.

She had also been told that the man she had come to see was a disreputable fellow who had been banned from the fraternity of lawyers for accepting bribes and spitting on a judge. In another life, Avigail would have had nothing to do with Faris, nor would she have reached for the rope and rung the gate bell, as she did now, setting aside her self-respect for the sake of her family.

Her heart raced as she prayed no passersby would recognize her. Avigail had one decent gown and veil to her name. Made from finely spun wool, thanks to Saloma's clever ways with a spindle, and dyed with the juice of crushed red berries that grew wild in the foothills behind the villa. Avigail had painstakingly woven the fabric and sewn the garments against the day of Elias's return, for it would be a special occasion and she wanted to greet her son properly dressed in his honor.

But that day might never come, and today was the day she must take crucial, unpleasant steps to save her family. And so she wore her new clothes with pride, albeit without coins on her forehead or bracelets on her wrists. She stood before the gate of the infamous bordello with a racing heart, praying to Asherah for courage. She also prayed that the stranger of whom she was about to ask a favor did not notice that she was barefoot.

An Egyptian steward, dressed in a pleated linen skirt, sandals and leather collar, opened the gate. His eyes were rimmed with blue cosmetic and his lips painted red. His black wig came to his bare shoulders. When Avigail stated her business, he stepped aside and closed the gate behind her.

Avigail could hardly believe her eyes. The plain, high walls of Nefer-Merit's house concealed a breathtaking paradise. She had heard that Egyptian gardens were the most beautiful in the world, but she had never believed such reports, having always held to her own prejudice in thinking that Egyptians were a dirty, immoral race. Although the Egyptian vintner and his wife had surprised Avigail with their penchant for etiquette and cleanliness, she had thought they were the exception of their race, rather than the rule. But now, standing amid this lush and spacious—and eye-pleasing—garden, she wondered if there were a side to Egyptians that she had never known.

The formal pool was large and rectangular, filled with clear water in which colorful fish flashed about, with lily pads floating on the surface, and majestic stalks of reeds and papyrus decorating the edges. Leafy trees had been spaced so that patches of golden sunlight lay between pools of dappled shade. Fruit, luscious and ripe, hung from branches, and flower petals littered the ground. Red and blue birds with magnificent tails perched tamely among the leaves. The air was filled with the fragrance of incense and perfume, and with the strains of musical instruments playing sweet melodies.

But the most astounding feature was the people—men lounging on chaises while being waited on by beautiful women. She was shocked when she realized not all the women were serving food and wine. A great deal of caressing and kissing was going on. She blushed fiercely when she espied one naked man in the shade of a tamarisk tree being pleasured by four young females.

She quickly looked away and wondered how she was going to find, in this garden of debauchery, a man named Faris. Although many of the customers were naked or half-clothed, she spotted one who was fully clothed, an enormous man reclining on a chaise in the shade of a sycamore, eating with both hands. From a description she had received at the House of Gold, she surmised this was the man she sought, for the two lawyers had also called him a dissolute libertine with a laugh that could shake the snows of Mount Lebanon.

Two young ladies, wearing nothing more than bracelets and necklaces, and long black Egyptian wigs, had their arms snaked around his corpulent body, stroking his groin and thighs, and purring like cats. They gave Avigail an amused look when she approached and asked if she could have a word with him.

Faris took a large bite from a greasy mutton chop and eyed her up and down. Faris had unusually thick and long eyelashes, making him look almost feminine, except that his hairline was receding and a shadow covered his jaw. He seemed not to mind the interruption. Nor did he seem surprised to find this woman, who clearly did not belong here, addressing him. She wondered if he always conducted his business in this place. "Who sent you?"

Trying to ignore nearby drunken laughter and the sounds of love-making, she said, "Two lawyers who conduct business in the courtyard at the House of Gold."

He smiled. "I am no stranger to lawyers, or the courts. The judges know me well, too!" He guffawed and bits of food flew from his mouth. "Tell me your problem."

Avigail explained her situation and when she spoke the names of Jotham and Zira, he barked out a dry laugh. "Those two! A slippery pair of serpents. So they are about to sell you and your family into slavery."

"Can you help me?"

Faris shook his head and a crumb of honey cake fell from his chin onto his chest. "Invoke the gods, dear lady, for no amount of legal advice can save you. You cannot win against Zira. She and her brother are too powerful. Jotham owns the iron factory and holds a monopoly on shipping. And Zira is the mother of Rab Yehuda, slated for the throne when King Shalaaman falls. The hag and her brother own the judges, too. The senior judge, Uriah, will definitely vote against you as Yehuda holds some damning information on him. You will not receive a fair or impartial hearing. The judges will have made their decision against you before you even set foot in their court. The gods forgive me, I am sorry."

Despite his lack of manners and sybaritic ways, Avigail sensed he was genuinely sorry. And despite the fact that he was fatter even than Jotham, and was known for whiling away his days in a brothel, Faris gave the impression of having a good heart, for he had listened to her tale with interest, had given it singular consideration, and had looked her in the eye when he spoke to her. But mostly, Avigail liked his laugh.

"I must save my family and my house," she said.

Faris pursed his lips, examined the remaining meat on his mutton bone, consulted the sky and the sun and the overhead leaves of the sycamore, and then said, "There is something I can do, but I require payment. I cannot live the way I do without money."

When Avigail brought out a small bag that jingled, and reached inside, he said, "All of it."

"But I need to buy bread for my family."

"All of it, or leave."

She emptied the purse on the table littered with scraps of meat, bread crumbs, fish spines and pomegranate skins. Faris's keen eyes made a quick calculation of their worth. "Is this all you have?"

"I told you, I cannot now even afford a loaf of bread."

"It is nowhere near my usual fee. I charge much more than this, and men gladly pay it, for I am the smartest and cleverest lawyer west of Babylon." He paused to smile at one of his attendants, to stroke her cheek and kiss her tenderly on the lips. He returned to Avigail. "What else can you offer me?"

Avigail thought for a moment, then she straightened her back and said, "Praise the gods, there is indeed something I can give you, my lord, and it is something no one else in the world can."

He gave her a dubious look. "What would that be?"

"The chance to defeat Zira and Jotham in a court of law."

Faris's feminine eyes settled on Avigail and studied her from beneath long black lashes. Finally, he threw back his head and laughed, and it was so heartfelt and booming that Avigail imagined the snows of Mount Lebanon cascading down its slopes.

"As the gods are my witness, we have an agreement!" he said, then he reached out and scooped up the rings with his chubby hand and slipped them within the folds of his voluminous robe. "There are three things you must do, dear lady. Listen carefully as you must follow my instructions to the letter and in the order I tell you. Do not deviate or you will fail."

As she listened, Avigail's mouth ran dry. When he was finished, she said, "Pray for me, my lord, I cannot do those things. Will you speak for me in court? I will find a way to pay you."

297

"I have been banned from Ugarit's court of law. The mercy of the gods upon you, Avigail Em Elias, you must do this on your own."

"Blessed Asherah, I cannot!"

"Then take your family out of Ugarit and go into hiding. There is nothing more I can do for you."

But Avigail would not be dissuaded. Her eldest granddaughter had been abducted and her son had sold himself into slavery. She was not going to lose the family remaining to her, nor was she going to lose her home.

"The blessings of Dagon," Avigail said and turned to go. But Faris said, "Wait," and, picking up a crusty loaf of bread studded with green and black olives and glistening with oil, handed it to her saying, "I will pray for you."

As Avigail awaited the arrival of Zira and the slave traders, she wrestled with her conscience. She did not want to do what Faris had advised. It went against everything she believed in. But as she stood at the end of the lane, watching the pedestrians and wagons and horses pass by on the main road, she embraced little Aaron, holding him tight. And when she saw Baruch standing apart, she gestured to the boy to come to her and she wrapped her arm around him. For these little ones, she thought as she held them close, she must fight Zira as Faris had advised. To secure the birthright of these boys, she must set aside her conscience and her personal values.

Avigail kept her eye on the city gate.

Ugarit was in a panic, tension filled the air. Rumors were rampant, so that no one knew what was really happening. Canaanite troops drilled with weapons on the fields outside the city, where military tents had been erected, and chariots were lined up, with warhorses in makeshift corals. Preparing for war. Avigail had heard that the rich families were stocking private yachts with supplies and slaves, some were even already living aboard in the harbor, ready to flee should the Egyptian forces approach Ugarit. The slave trade was booming as the wealthy bought manpower for protection and to help them escape.

Avigail knew that if Zira was successful in getting her and her family to the slave market, they would all be bought, and most likely be separated, to be taken to different cities.

We will never see each other again, Avigail thought as she finally sighted the familiar purple-curtained litter on the shoulders of slaves. I will not let that happen.

Jotham's sister alighted from the conveyance, followed by a man in long fringed robes with a cone-shaped hat on his head. Zira had brought her lawyer along, no doubt to show the world, Avigail thought bitterly, that her theft of Elias's property and persecution of his family was all legal, that she was not being unfair or underhanded. She had also brought four large men from the slave market, coiled whips in their hands.

"Where are the others?" Zira asked without ceremony.

"They are inside. Zira, why can we not stay and serve the next tenant?"

"There will be no next tenant."

"Then you do indeed plan to sell the property?" Avigail had hoped Zira would change her mind.

"King Shalaaman has been suffering from choking attacks of late. Not serious episodes, but as we all know, once the choking demon invades the chest, it grows stronger until it kills its host. It is only a matter of time before the king goes to the gods, and when that happens, the military generals will appoint my Yehuda in his place." She held out her arms. "My son believes this villa will be a perfect command post from which to oversee his defense of Ugarit from Egyptian invasion."

Avigail's eyes widened in horror. "He would make this a military garrison?" She imagined the soldiers, the rough troops, horses tramping through. "Please, do not do this. I beg of you."

Zira snapped her fingers and the slavers came forward with shackles and chains.

"By Asherah," Avigail blurted. "I cannot help it that my granddaughter cured King Shalaaman of the choking disease."

Zira narrowed her eyes. "My son was meant to ascend the throne four years ago. But now King Shalaaman is possessed by the demon again and this time your meddling daughter is not here to interfere with what the gods have ordained!"

Avigail stiffened her spine and squared her shoulders. "Stop this action now, Em Yehuda, and leave us in peace. Believe me, it is in your interest as well as my own that we end this conflict between us. If you persist, then I will have no choice but to fight you."

Zira laughed. "Fight me? You have no male protectors, no friends, no home, and you are penniless. I know you have come to the end of the grace period you petitioned for. There is nothing left. With what do you intend to fight me?" She shared a smug smile with her lawyer.

Avigail lifted her chin. "My status as a citizen of Ugarit. I have learned that, by law, I do not need petitions or fees or even lawyers. It is my right to challenge your claim on my property in a court of law, before the high judges."

"Really, this is beneath you, Avigail. It is a stall tactic that will not work."

"I do not want to stall. By all means, call the judges at once. You are rich and powerful enough to take your case before them without delay. I wish this to be over with just a much as you do."

Zira narrowed her eyes. "You have no case. You cannot possibly win. Why continue to waste time?"

"I know my rights."

"I am sure you do. I hear you have spent days in the great court at the House of Gold talking with lawyers, like a common citizen. It is beneath you, Avigail." Zira sighed. "Very well. It is after all but a short distance from the court house to the slave market. I advise you bring your entire family with you, as it will make the transition to the slave block swift and without delay."

CHAPTER FOURTEEN

The leader of the elephant caravan has agreed to carry you and your two companions to Ugarit."

"Halla! That is good news," Leah said. "The blessings of the gods on you, Paki. And is there any news yet of Pharaoh Thutmose and his campaign to Karmel?" Twenty days had passed since she and Daveed had made love on the palace roof, twenty long and anxious days since he had kissed her good-bye, saying he was going into battle. "I've seen scouts riding in from the northwest. What have you heard?"

Paki the eunuch said, "Nothing yet, dear lady, but as long as there is no bad news, then it is good news, is it not?"

Leah had discovered a fact of palace life in every city in the world: the most reliable source of information, news, gossip, and rumor was the harem eunuchs. Paki was from Africa, and the first of his race Leah had ever set eyes on. She had not known a man's skin could be so black. Paki was tall with a large belly. He wore a colorful turban and long white skirt that was anchored at his waist by a wide leather belt. He wore no shirt or tunic, but a peculiar shawl made of white wool that draped his hefty shoulders and was knotted at the front over fatty, feminine breasts.

Paki did not remember the name of his people or the land where he was born. Egyptian traders in rare animals, ivory, and slaves had abducted him when he was a boy, far up the Nile, and brought him by ship and by land to a place called Beersheba. There Paki and other boys like him had been castrated and turned into half-men destined to serve in harems throughout the world. He did not curse his life nor his fate. He cursed only Egyptians.

He especially hated the Egyptian women who had joined Megiddo's royal harem—the wives and concubines of Pharaoh Thutmose. Arrogant women who simply moved in and took over, bringing their own eunuchs, disrupting a hierarchy that had been established long ago. Paki once had power; now he was an underling, and so he was eager to play a part in disrupting Thutmose's plans, if only to assist one of his hostages in escaping. "The caravan is due to depart at the Midsummer Festival."

Like all wise military leaders, Thutmose ensured the continued safe passage of trade caravans through his conquered territory, regard-less of national affiliation. After all, he was invading this land in order to enrich his own coffers. If trade were hampered, then there would be no flow of goods and money. Caravans were considered neutral parties, to be left unmolested by his troops. In this way Leah knew she and Daveed would get away. But would he be back in time? She yearned to go home, find her family, release them from slavery, and bring them all together again in the villa by the vineyards. But what if Daveed did not return in time? She would not leave without him.

When they had said good-bye on the palace rooftop, twenty days prior, he had removed his carnelian signet ring and pressed it into her hand, saying, "For as long as you hold this ring, I will always come back to you." She clasped it now in her hand as she went to the window that looked out over the city walls.

The harem was housed in a high tower, secluded and protected from the world, and from where the women within were afforded a generous view of that unreachable world. Fields of tree stumps surrounded Megiddo, the local forests having been razed to provide firewood for so many campfires. Beyond the tree stumps lay a marsh-land where a mountain creek branched out into little streams on their way to the main river. In the foothills, backdropped by green and fertile mountains, the two massive camps had been laid out—one for the soldiers, one for the captives.

Leah could see from a window in this tower, the sprawling military camp. She marveled that local Canaanite women, having lost their menfolk and their homes, had gone to live on the fringe of that settlement of soldiers, joining with their conquerors in a way that Leah supposed was as timeless as war itself. The women went as cooks and laundresses and bedmates, serving their masters in order to survive. Just as much the victims of war as the soldiers whose heads were bashed in by Pharaoh's bloodthirsty troops. They had banded together for survival.

But Leah had banded with no one, as she did not intend to stay. While she slept and ate in the harem, she kept herself apart from the others. There was intense rivalry between with wives and concubines of the imprisoned king of Megiddo and the wives of Pharaoh, who could be ruthless in their tactics. Paki had explained to her the Egyptian practice of forming an image of an enemy and mutilating or "injuring" it in some way to reduce that person's power. Leah had seen for herself how jealousy among Thutmose's wives had spawned a lively and lucrative (for the eunuchs who smuggled in the wax dolls and long pins) practice of black magic. Leah did not want to get caught in the middle of so passionate a conflict and so she had made neither friends nor enemies among the women.

The ladies of this high tower spent long hours braiding each other's hair, sitting in front of mirrors painting their faces, or spreading a sugar paste over their bodies to remove every single hair. Their baths were long and languorous and had to do more with leisure than cleanliness. They played a board game with sticks and dice, called Hounds and Jackals, which was not unlike Ugarit's popular Fifty-Five Holes. They listened to music and ate delicacies and drank wine and amused themselves with their babies and children and waited for Pharaoh to come in the evening and choose one of them for his bed.

Caged birds, Leah thought. Pampered and forgotten. While out there, across the charred fields and marshland, hungry captives struggled for survival in crude tents. Less than a mile apart, yet it might as well be a thousand. Leah had never really pondered the inequities of life before now, and how different lives can be merely based on the accident of birth. Babies born within this tower would know a life of luxury and ease, while a baby born out there might be lucky to thrive at all.

While the wives of the Megiddo king were Canaanite and practiced customs and traditions familiar to Leah, the Egyptian women were foreign and in many ways baffling. Their manner of speech was rapid with much interrupting, raising of voices, and gesturing. They had the curious habit that she had seen before, of suddenly lifting the right hand, palm out, in front of their faces, like a shield. And then an oath of some kind was uttered. Paki had some knowledge of the Egyptian language and explained that the dwellers of the Nile Valley governed their lives by magic spells. "They utter them with extreme frequency, as if to weave an invisible cloak of protection around themselves. The hand raised before the face wards off evil spirits. Their favorite oath seems to be 'I know you—I know your name.' I believe they intend the spell to win the favor of any spirits lurking nearby, good or evil. Egyptians believe that spirits like to know that they are recognized, and this pleases them. In the case of demons, they are less likely to cause harm to someone who knows who they are."

Paki wrinkled his black nose and said, "Egyptians are a superstitious lot, whereas you Canaanites are religious. There is a difference you know."

From the window Leah could see military scouts riding into the camp, jumping from their horses to run into the blue pavilion. She had watched divisions march out under banners with commanders at their head to quell small rebellions that were breaking out in the region. Rumors flew of the swift and terrible punishment of Pharaoh's troops. Insurgents were either slain on the spot, or dragged back to be added to Pharaoh's growing population of monument-builders.

If he reaches Ugarit, the same will happen there. Across the charred fields, she could see women gathered at the creek, dipping clothes into the water to pound them clean with stones. They would be Canaanite or Habiru, Leah thought, wondering at their hard lives, wondering about the life of bondage that awaited them in Egypt. She thought of the Habiru concubine Rakel had spoken of on her death bed, a woman named Sarah who was Avigail's real mother. After Avigail was born, Sarah had been sent back to her people. Did she go on to have other children? Were descendants of that Habiru woman in that wretched captives' camp? The women in rags, starving, are they my cousins?

"Say a prayer," Paki murmured. "Here comes the Egyptian dog."

She turned away. Such poor creatures were not her concern. She must focus on getting herself and Daveed away from Megiddo and back to Ugarit—to her mother and grandmother, to Esther and Saloma and the two boys. And a new determination. The more she saw families torn apart, the more she knew she must reunite her own. And that meant searching for her father in Babylon and finding a way to purchase his freedom. We are the House of Elias the Canaanite. We are meant to be together.

As Pharaoh's Chief Royal Physician, Reshef had free access to the harem, which he had visited every day since Leah had taken residence here. He came to check on the health of the wives and concubines and children that belonged to Thutmose, and also to interrogate Leah on the nature of the eighteen tablets.

The Royal Egyptian scribes had been able to decipher the valerian tablet and the love poem, but not the rest, which included the cure for the Choking Demon which Daveed had inscribed four years ago. Though they tried, they could not crack the new script. And so Reshef came every day to ask Leah to translate the tablets for him.

He insisted it was merely idle curiosity on his part as everyone knew that Egyptian medicine was superior to all others. But Leah would not tell him what he wanted to know. When she had told Reshef of her search for a cure for the falling sickness, and how she had conferred with healers in the towns and cities of the Euphrates River, he asked her to share that knowledge with him. She told him a few recipes, but when she saw that the arrangement was not reciprocal, that Reshef had no intention of divulging Egyptian medical information to her, she began to claim forgetfulness. Like Daveed's secret that he could speak Egyptian so that his captors would speak freely in front of him, Leah decided that her own secrets—medicinal formulas collected during her four years of journeying with King Shalaaman—might be of value down the line.

The Chief Physician approached with such a silent step that Leah wondered if he practiced tiptoeing so that he could eavesdrop on people. He raised his arm as he approached, hand in front of his face, palm out, speaking words that Paki translated as "I am protected from harm." Then he said, "You said that when you visited the King of Harran, you learned of a rare herb that grew on an island in the Euphrates."

While Paki translated for her, Leah looked at the Eye of Horus that lay on Reshef's chest, and she was reminded of something Paki had told her: "Egyptians believe that, long ago, the evil god Set clawed Horus's eyes out, blinding him. Thoth, the Healer, was sent for and he restored Horus's sight. Since then, Thoth the Healer and Horus the Healed are among their most revered and powerful gods. Men wear the Eye to let evil demons know that they are under the protection of the Healed One."

Leah thought the Eye of Horus a beautiful symbol. Made of gold and a stunning shade of blue lapis lazuli, the eye had a flat lower lid and an arching upper lid, the gracefully curving eyebrow following the line of the upper lid, while a tear cascaded from the eye's inner corner to sweep up in an elegant curl. A reminder of the preciousness of sight.

A sight, Leah remembered now, that was going to be denied to Daveed in later years, for he had said that all Rabs of the Brotherhood lose their sight as a sacrifice they made in the service of their brothers.

And so, with Paki translating, she now said, "I do not recall the herb, my lord. But perhaps my memory will improve if I might ask about a blindness remedy I have heard of. It is well known that Egypt is unsurpassed in the treatment of eye diseases and—"

Reshef sniffed sharply through his large, bony nose and said, "What is the rare herb you found on an island in the Euphrates?"

Leah was wondering how far she could challenge the arrogant physician, when a messenger came in and conferred urgently with Reshef.

Without a word, the Chief Physician turned and left with the messenger.

"Paki, what happened?"

"This is most unusual," the eunuch said. "Reshef has been summoned by His Majesty."

Leah's eyes widened. "His Majesty? Are you sure?"

"My fluency in Egyptian is flawless. The messenger said, 'His Majesty commands your presence at once.'"

"But there has been no news of Thutmose returning to the city!"

"None at all, dear lady."

"What does it mean?"

"I would venture to say that, for secret reasons known only to Thutmose himself, he never left the city."

Leah ran to the window and looked out. Presently, below, she saw Reshef and the messenger hurry through the city gates and down the road toward the military camp. When they arrived at the blue pavilion, both slipped inside.

Leah blinked in confusion. If Pharaoh Thutmose was in that large tent—if he was still here in Megiddo—then where was Daveed?

She had not taken her eyes off the blue pavilion since early afternoon, when she had seen Reshef hurry inside. Now it was night and she was certain he was still there. He had been urgently summoned by His Majesty. Why? Was the king ill? Had Thutmose been injured in battle and rushed back to Megiddo?

Blessed Asherah, do not let Daveed be lying dead on a foreign battlefield . . .

Giving up her post by the window, she went in search of Paki and when she found him, whispered, "I need a cloak. I must go out."

"You are not allowed to," he said.

"I must know what has happened to my husband and his slave."

"I will go with you, dear lady, and in this way you can leave the palace." Had the king of Megiddo ordered Leah's house arrest, Paki would not have let her set foot outside the harem. But as the order had come from the despised Egyptian king, Paki was only to happy to disobey.

Choosing a plain cloak among the many fine garments in the harem, so that she would not draw attention to herself, Leah followed the eunuch through the maze of hallways until they came to a side door. A few copper coins to the soldier standing watch and the pair were in the dark streets and hurrying toward the blue pavilion.

The massive tent glowed against the stars with torches and lamps, and Leah saw shapes moving inside, the shadows of people walking about. Reshef's assistant physicians, she thought. Thutmose would be no different from Shalaaman or any other ruler she had met: if he was ill or injured, a large staff of doctors, priests and magicians would be working to save him.

They reached the pavilion and slipped between two sentry guards to search for a way in. When Leah's hand brushed the blue cloth wall, she discovered it was a heavy linen, and it reminded her of a meeting her father had conducted with a businessman years ago. The importer had been hoping to get Elias interested in investing in the linen trade. "The Egyptians currently hold a monopoly on linen," the man had said to Elias, "an industry second only to beer in importance to their national economy. They are so expert at the manufacture of linen that they are capable of producing a textile so thin as to be transparent, or so thick that they use it for the sails on their ships."

"I fear there is no way inside," Paki whispered, deciding he had made a mistake in coming with her. To be an annoying gnat buzzing around Pharaoh's face was one thing, but to be found trespassing on his hallowed ground, snooping, was another!

"Invoke the gods, Paki," she whispered as she felt up and down the linen walls for a break in a seam. "Lest your words bring bad luck upon us. Up ahead, I think."

They rounded the corner to find Chief Physician Reshef blocking their way, a grim expression on his face.

Guards seized the intruders and when Reshef growled something in Egyptian, Paki said, "The Chief Physician says it is death for anyone to enter His Majesty's private tent."

"Ask him if His Majesty is in there," and she pointed to the tent.

Paki asked and Reshef's eyes flickered. "Yes."

"Ask him about Daveed."

When Paki translated, Reshef shook his head. "Your husband is not in there," Paki said. "The Chief Physician does not know where he is."

She tried to break free and bolt for the doorway. "Fool!" Reshef hissed when the guard caught her. He said something in Egyptian and Paki's knees knocked together as he said, "The Chief Physician says our necks will be on the chopping block if we dare to enter. Please dear lady, I beg of you. Let us humble ourselves and tell him we are sorry to cause offense, and ask him to let us return to the harem."

But Leah said to Paki, "Thank you for all your help, my friend. I pray that the gods bless you in abundance. Now please ask Physician Reshef to grant me an audience with His Majesty and to allow you to return to your duties in the harem. Please tell him that I forced you to come with me."

The eunuch did as told. Reshef spoke and Paki translated: "He says the blame is not mine for I am only a slave obeying the whim of a foolish woman. I am free to go. But he said that he is only granting you this audience because His Majesty is interested in the clay tablets written in your secret code. Since you would not answer the Chief Physician's questions, perhaps you will answer His Majesty's. But you must never speak of what you see inside this tent tonight."

"Tell him I swear a solemn oath upon my gods."

Paki translated and Reshef replied in a derisive tone.

"What did he say?"

"The Egyptian dog says that all the world knows Canaanites are a superstitious people and do not respect their gods the way Egyptians do. By the sacred spirits of my people in Africa, I swear this is a backward world."

Reshef snapped an order and the pair were escorted into the splendid blue pavilion where, at once, they were met by a pleasant sweet fragrance and the welcoming glow of many torches and lamps.

There were few people inside—all men, of varying military rank. They stood in the center, in what appeared to be a circle, looking at the floor and talking all at once. Leah tried to make out, in the flickering torchlight, the object of their attention. She realized it was an enormous map, and the generals were using long sticks to move figures around on it.

She had seen this before—in the palace at Haran, north of the Euphrates. This was a war room, where military strategy was worked out, the movements of troops and chariots, the location of towns and key positions. Tiny soldiers lined up in divisions, along with horses and chariots. Set up here and there were isolated figures, taller than the rest, wearing crowns, to indicate the kings of foreign cities. Each was pierced with an arrow, and it made Leah think of the wax dolls which Thutmose's jealous wives had stuck pins into, to weaken a rival's power.

And then she saw—

She gasped, and quickly covered her mouth.

A person sat on a high throne, giving orders to the generals, receiving reports from the scouts that hurried in and out, pointing to places on the map. Leah did not understand what was being said, as it was in Egyptian, but she knew who the person was.

It was not Pharaoh Thutmose.

Leah could not move. She was hypnotized. Although declared dead, the woman on the high throne, dispensing orders to officers, could be none other than Hatshepsut herself.

Leah could not believe her eyes, and wondered if this was in fact someone else. The woman was not regally attired, but wore a white linen sheath with a plain white shawl knotted at the breast, a black wig cut straight at the shoulders, a gold headband with a cobra on the brow.

And then a memory came rushing back. The rainy night, seven years ago, before Zira spoke her poisonous words, sending Hannah into premature labor, setting off a chain of events that had led to this remarkable moment. Jotham and Leah's father talking about the female Pharaoh of Egypt, Jotham saying, "I hear she insists upon being addressed as 'His' Majesty."

She stared open-mouthed at the face beneath the straight-cut bangs of the wig. There was some resemblance to Thutmose, in the mannish jaw and deep-set eyes, but where the nephew was ugly, the aunt was majestic.

Leah guessed the queen was about fifty, and although robust of body, there were lines and shadows of fatigue and a strain on her health, and Leah realized the reason behind Reshef's endless interrogations and demands to know what was inscribed on the eighteen tablets.

But there was no mistaking the power this woman wielded over every man in this pavilion. Leah had never known a woman could wield so much power. In the royal palace of Carchemish, when King Shalaaman brought gifts and greeting before the king, Leah had watched the queen at his side, a stiff silent woman who sat like a statue while her husband received their distinguished visitors. In the northern city of Haran, where Avram, the father of the Shemites, grazed his cattle on the plains, the local queen had not even been in atten-

dance in the throne room where a hundred splendidly robed courtiers stood among magnificent columns overlaid in gold, malachite,
and turquoise. In the venerated city of Mari, the queen stayed in
the harem with her attendants while her husband entertained King
Shalaaman and his traveling court. Only in the desert town of Palmyra
did Leah see a queen on her own, but she had been surrounded by
male advisors, all of whom told her what to do.

Hatshepsut was a marvel unto herself. Leah felt her charisma, as if
it were an actual physical energy emanating from her person. Leah saw
how it affected these men, powerful in their own right. Their queen
rose from her throne and every man in the tent bowed low and raised
his right arms in salute. She took a step forward, and men in helmets
and breastplates, in priestly robes and leopard skins, fell back a step.

Where did such power come from? Was Hatshepsut truly the
result of sexual intercourse between her earthly mother and the god
Amon-Ra, as she claimed? The world was full of stories about the gods
taking physical form in order to have relations with mortals, but Leah
wondered if they were true.

Or did this woman simply possess a personality so strong, a self-
confidence so unshakable that no one dared question her authority?

Leah heard Reshef say something in Egyptian and the queen
replied—in a deep, throaty voice that resonated throughout the
massive tent causing Leah to tremble. She wondered if the queen had
given the order for her execution.

Leah did not want to die. She could not allow it to happen. Her
family needed her. She had not meant to stumble into the presence of
the supreme ruler of the world—for surely it was Hatshepsut who was
giving the orders, not Thutmose.

I must speak up, Leah thought. I can tell her that I meant no
disrespect. I will throw myself upon her mercy.

But fear silenced Leah's tongue.

If I had spoken up to King Shalaaman the morning I cured him
and he made me his prisoner, I might have been allowed to go home,
I might have prevented Zira from selling my family into slavery. But I
held my tongue and calamity befell my family.

And now, they needed her more than ever.

Shaking with fear, Leah thought: Hatshepsut's power comes from within, from her soul. Her power is her very essence. A power that comes from her gods . . .

Asherah! Leah called silently. Grant me the same power. For if one mortal woman can be a channel for divine force, cannot another also be? Give me strength, blessed Asherah. Be with me now, Mother of All. Hear the plea of your devoted daughter. I must speak up in my defense but I am afraid.

And then Leah realized that Hatshepsut was looking directly at her. She could not tear her gaze away from the piercing, deep-set eyes rimmed with black kohl, unblinking, like the eyes of a hawk, formidable, as if the great queen could see through Leah's skin and flesh and bone, right into her very soul.

She wants me to speak. She is giving me the power to speak.

Taking in a deep, steadying breath, Leah said, "O Radiant One, daughter of Amon-Ra, daughter of the sun, wearer of the crowns of Egypt . . ." She had no idea what she was supposed to say, but she had witnessed enough meetings between King Shalaaman and other monarchs to know that ostentatious praise was expected.

At first, no one translated. After a collective gasp of shock, the gathered men stood in frozen silence, waiting for the queen's reaction. Not even Reshef spoke or moved, nor the guards that stood on either side of the brazen intruder.

"Your radiance blinds me," Leah said. "Your glory blinds the world, O great and magnificent daughter of the gods. I did not mean to disrespect your sublime presence. I came to pay homage to the living god of Egypt."

When Hatshepsut said nothing, but kept those unblinking eyes on her, Leah realized in shock that the queen understood every word she was saying.

With growing confidence, Leah said, "I am no commoner, Your Majesty. I am no ordinary woman. My great-grandfather was married to a daughter of the great King Ozzediah. And I am the wife of a prince of the royal house of Lagash." She bowed low at the waist and said, "Nevertheless, I humble myself before your magnificent and glorious majesty."

She waited, bent at the waist, her eyes on the rich carpet beneath her feet. The military men and priests and magicians and advisors draped in sacred leopard skins held their tongues in the incense-filled air. Leah felt eyes on her. She caught the flickering of torch-light at the corner of her eye. The breath was trapped in her throat as she expected the order of execution at any moment, and then she heard the throaty voice say in Canaanite, "I know you, I know your name."

Puzzled, Leah looked up and saw that Hatshepsut was holding a hand to her own face, palm out. She repeated the words in Canaanite, and then she said, "Au-à rekh kua-ten. Rekh kua ren-ten," which Leah assumed was the Egyptian translation.

"I come with gifts, Oh Radiant One," Leah said, inspired with new confidence.

"My Aunt Rakel lived to be eighty-seven years old, and the day she went to the gods she was still in perfect health. She attributed her long life to a daily tonic which she drank every morning. I know the secret formula for that drink."

While she waited for a response, Leah wondered why Hatshepsut would stage her own death. And then she thought: although the Queen called herself King, and wore men's clothing and a false beard before the Egyptian people, her hubris must end there. Monarchs the world over were always depicted on their monuments as conquering heroes, and Egyptian kings were no different. Hatshepsut must have suspected that her people would not accept the image of a woman wielding a mace and bashing the heads of enemies. To go into battle, she must be hidden. She had waited until her nephew was ready.

"Wise and mighty daughter of Amon-Ra, whose radiance blinds this humble servant from Canaan, I fear that if your stepson leads an invading army toward Ugarit, my king will destroy anything of value, to prevent it from falling into enemy hands. And this includes our famous library. The hundreds of medicinal recipes that have been collected and recorded there will be turned to dust."

Emboldened, Leah said, "Remember Radiant One, that Ugarit is an international seaport and so our physicians have spoken with people from all over the world, collecting their medical secrets. Men from the far north, with hair the color of wheat and eyes the color of lapis lazuli, came with their strange recipes and reported cures. Our physicians prize these above all, Your Majesty, for never have they seen healthier or more robust people."

Hatshepsut spoke a command and the two guards seized Leah by the arms and held her while Reshef spoke. Paki translated in a tremulous voice, "He said, your foolishness has cost you your life. For daring to looking upon the sacred radiance of His Majesty, for daring to speak to the great King Hatshepsut, Leah the Canaanite must die."

His companions knew him as Gozer, but that was his sixth name in as many years. He had gone by Dathan and Yafet and others, and he had passed himself off as a brick mason, a baker, a camel trainer, a sailor, a wool dyer. Tonight, at the campfire where men from various roads and walks of life were gathered for protection and the sharing of food, he was Aram the silversmith. As his fellow travelers spoke of news and war and politics, Aram wondered where he would go next. Ugarit came to mind, where he had been known as Caleb and where he still had a wife and family who lived in a villa next to a vineyard.

He was in need of money and a place to hide. Would it be prudent to go back? What had Tamar told the family, for surely she had returned home after he had sailed for Minos?

He shivered inside his cloak and looked up at the stars. This mountainous land was godforsaken. The locals called it Jerusalem, which meant "the dwelling place of Shalem," an ancient Canaanite god. But Caleb saw no gods in these hills, just a collection of wooden buildings, stone huts, squat tents, sheep and goat corrals, and, down the road, a crude garrison housing the soldiers of the local Chieftain, a churlish man named Haddad. Crouched at the foot of the fortress's walls were travelers at their campfires, eating, laughing, shouting, snoring, counting on Chief Haddad's protection in these perilous times.

Caleb sat with five men whose names and occupations were of no concern. He would not stay here long. He kept his mouth shut and his ears open as he watched for an opportunity. He had to keep moving.

The island of Minos had been a pleasant spell until the Blue Devils had found him. He broke into the house of three sisters, tying them up and making them squeal one by one until he silenced them and the

Blue Devils went away. But he did not sufficiently cover his tracks and was caught at the harbor. The local prince had Caleb tortured to the brink of death. It was months before he was able to escape and stow away on a ship . . .

He glowered into the campfire at the memory. Three girls living alone in a cottage on the edge of an olive grove. How was he to know they were sacred bull dancers dedicated to a god that lived in an underground labyrinth? The whole island had gone up in arms against him.

"With Megiddo beneath his heels," one of his companions was saying, "and all lands north, east, and west of Megiddo under Egypt's power, Pharaoh will turn his sights southward, no doubt on his return to Egypt, and we lie directly in his path."

Megiddo lay 150 miles to the north. Pharaohs' army had marched northward along the coast, bypassing the insignificant settlement of Jerusalem with an aim to catch the richer prize. Travelers from the north reported that Pharaoh had taken several divisions on a trek to Karmel, north of Megiddo, and so for now the region occupied by Jerusalem and smaller towns and villages, ruled by splintered chieftains and warlords, was safe. But that was not to say they would stay safe for long.

The travelers fell silent, ruminating over their fates. Hearing the clop-clop of hooves and the creaking of wheels, they looked up to see a man leading an ass-drawn wagon along the bumpy track. "Greetings!" he called out in three languages. "I come to gladden your livers! Only the finest Egyptian beer. Wine from Jericho! Which will it be?"

They saw the barrels in the wagon, wineskins hanging from the sides. Caleb's companions happily produced copper rings, and the man rolled a barrel out of his wagon, to stand it on end next to the campfire. As the merchant pried open the lid, Caleb debated the wise use of his last copper ring. He could not sit here without drinking, and yet he needed to keep the men talking, to determine what he was going to do next, and with whom.

Giving the vendor his copper ring, Caleb cheerfully received the long reed which the man handed out to each of the thirsty travelers. As the beer merchant took his donkey and wagon to the next group, Caleb and his companions dipped their long hollow straws into the barrel and proceeded to suck heartily.

Soon, they were very loquacious. And Caleb listened.

One of them dragged a sleeve across his mouth and, jerking his thumb toward the garrison, said, "The word is, Chief Haddad is so afraid of Pharaoh Thutmose that he is arranging to send his youngest daughter to Megiddo as a willing hostage, a gesture to assure Pharaoh of his loyalty and as proof that he will not resist should Egypt wish to turn Jerusalem into a vassal."

Another man grumbled, "All the Canaanite warlords are afraid of Pharaoh. No one expected Megiddo to fall, and now they worry about their own miserable necks."

The first man took a long draw on the beer, smacked his lips and said, "They say Thutmose treats his hostages well. They live in the palace and receive the same food and luxuries as members of the royal family. A prince of Jabneel and his wife are so-called guests. They were abducted from their palace and it is said they have no desire to be returned to their home! Princelings of Ugarit were taken, and they live in the harem at Megiddo with their nursemaids, unharmed and well fed."

At the sound of "Ugarit," Caleb's ears pricked up.

"King Shalaaman is furious, I hear," a third man said, "for they abducted a woman as well, who is said to be his personal demon-charmer. The daughter of a wealthy vintner who cured Shalaaman of an illness."

Caleb ran this around in his mind. A vintner's daughter . . .

Was it possible? During his brief time in the house of Elias, Caleb had known of Leah's healing garden, the old lady's knowledge of medicinal remedies. And now Shalaaman is cured by such a girl? It seemed unlikely it could be any other vintner's daughter.

Caleb took a hearty sip of beer, wiped residue from his beard and said, "Friend, I lived awhile in Ugarit. Do you know the woman's name? The demon-charmer?"

The man shrugged. "Who cares what any woman's name is? But if she is indeed a demon-charmer, then Thutmose will keep her near him and she will live well."

During his journey eastward from the coast, Caleb had heard many stories regarding the conquest of Megiddo and Pharaoh's occupation of that ancient city. It was said he had moved his own Egyptian wives into the harem there. Most likely, Shalaaman's princelings and the demon-charmer were being kept there as well.

A life of luxury and ease, Caleb thought, hidden away in a woman's world where no one would think to search for him. A life that would provide him with victims when the Blue Devils struck. A harem filled with women and children, guarded by soft, fat eunuchs.

"I heard this afternoon," the fourth man said, "that Chief Haddad is having trouble recruiting trustworthy men to escort his daughter to Megiddo. He fears they will abandon the caravan as soon as they are away from Jerusalem. Men who have no appetite for combat and who fear the Egyptians."

Muttering that he needed to urinate, Caleb rose on unsteady feet and stole away from the campfire. When he neared the heavily guarded wooden gates, he straightened his back and walked with a sober stride, for he had taken little of the strong brew. Announcing to the guards that Aram the silversmith had urgent business with their chief, he was taken into the compound where soldiers grumbled over fires and eyed the intruder with suspicion.

Chief Haddad's headquarters was the only brick building within the wooden fortress, being one story tall with a stairway leading up to the roof. Inside the dimly lit interior, Haddad sat at a table, squinting over a map, while two men in kilts and leather breastplates tried to make sense of the features drawn upon it.

"Dagon take the man who brought me this map!" Haddad barked. "It is useless!"

He looked up. A piggy-faced man with purplish lips, the supreme chieftain of the region's warlords did not impress Caleb. "Shalaam and blessings of the gods," Caleb boomed.

"Who are you?"

"I am the answer to your prayers, Noble Haddad. I hear you wish to send your daughter to Megiddo but cannot find honest men who will take her. You see before you the most honest man in the world." He smote his chest. "Ask anyone from here to Babylon. They will sing the praises of Aram the silversmith. As it happens, I am traveling to Megiddo on important business. I would be honored to escort your lovely daughter and see that she is delivered into Pharaoh's hands unscathed."

When he saw Haddad's suspicious look, Caleb said with his most winsome smile, "Of course, I expect to be paid well for my efforts, but I swear by Shem who guards this place that you will not be sorry."

He almost laughed at the workings of luck and fate. Moments ago, a fugitive on the run. Now, on his way to luxury and reclaiming Leah as his wife.

M aster, will you fight?" Nobu asked, pointing to Daveed's arm dagger. It did not matter that his Egyptian charioteer overheard, for the man did not speak Canaanite.

"If I am not pushed to it," Daveed replied, "I will not fight. I do not trust Pharaoh. I fear he will keep me in his circle if he were to learn of my combat skills. He might even press me to train his men in the techniques of Zh'wan-eth. For the sake of our freedom—if we are ever to return home, I must keep my martial art a secret." Nonetheless, whenever he could, Daveed stole away from the camp to practice his combat exercises. He did not wish to fight, but he wanted to be ready should he need to defend himself and Nobu.

They were following the foothills of a mountain range called Karmel, which in both Habiru and Canaanite meant "fruitful land." Daveed sensed the Great Sea up ahead, as he knew that was their destination. The air blew cool and crisp, and the occasional lost seagull strayed across the blue sky. Why Pharaoh would bring him to this remote garrison, Daveed could only speculate.

It had been twenty days since he said good-bye to Leah on the palace roof, after a night of lovemaking. He carried her in his heart day and night, her name never far from his lips, wishing to be back at her side, wishing never to leave her again. As Leah filled his thoughts with the memory of her softness in his arms, how freely she gave of her body, the sweet kisses and soft moans that drove him to ecstasy, Leah also filled Daveed with a new inspiration. Although he had always dreamed of belonging to the Brotherhood of Ugarit, and although that dream had expanded to a desire to be appointed Rab, such dreams had been for himself or for the sake of his brother scribes. But now, as he rode in the chariot beneath a crisp blue sky at the head of a thousand troops, Daveed realized that all his goals were now for Leah. He wanted to be appointed Rab for her, to make her proud to see her husband as one of the important men of Ugarit, to give her great stature among the women of Canaan.

He could not wait to get back to Megiddo and take Leah home to begin their life together. He did not want to be part of this insane military campaign. Daveed rode with the supply column, alongside ox-drawn sleds bearing grain and beer and oil and onions. Pharaoh had explained that a garrison had been built on the cliffs overlooking the sea, an isolated outpost difficult for enemies to reach, but also not self-sufficient and so this column was vital. Accompanying the supplies were five divisions of infantry and two of chariot. More than a thousand troops heavily armed and restless for a fight.

Daveed and Nobu rode side by side in separate chariots, vehicles drawn by four horses and designed to hold two men: the charioteer and a bowman. Nobu held on tightly and cursed every rock and rodent hole that jolted his vehicle. Daveed's scribe's kit was slung over Nobu's back, as well as his own barber kit. When they camped at night, the Egyptians mocked the two men from Ugarit as Nobu dressed his master's hair and beard. And Nobu silently cursed them for being uncivilized with their shaven heads and false wigs.

The bulk of the Egyptian army was infantry, and Daveed had learned that they were raised by press gangs that roamed the Nile River valley, forcing men into military service. The principal infantry weapons were the javelin and the short sword, and officers carried a baton to distinguish them from the ranks. For protection, many wore close-fitting helmets and mailed tunics made from fiber matting. Each man carried a shield of ox hide over a wooden frame, square at the bottom and rounded at the top. Although Thutmose's infantrymen were mostly Egyptian, his archers were Nubian, armed with composite bows made of laminated layers of bone and wood. They marched in lines identified by strips of colored cloth held aloft on forked staffs at the head of the ranks—blue, red, orange, yellow, white, and black. Daveed was now afforded a better view of Egypt's might, as every evening in camp he watched foot soldiers being drilled, charioteers, cavalrymen. As commanders shouted orders, the men engaged in contests with swords, scimitars, axes, and clubs. He saw Egyptian soldiers practicing on men who wore green kilts and leather collars—

the uniform of the Canaanite army. These were prisoners or deserters from a recent battle who had been brought along to be forced to fight or to be used for practice, and they fell beneath daggers, bows, slings. As they trained for combat, the Egyptian soldiers wore nothing except a penis-sheath and a string around their waist.

Every evening, Daveed listened to the impossible boasts of Thutmose and his generals. Now that Pharaoh knew that Daveed would give up life before he gave up a secret, nothing was held back from the new scribe. He became privy to the military secrets of Ugarit's enemy, as well as observing the foreign customs of Egypt. He learned also that, as in the cities on the Euphrates, Egypt conducted international correspondence and agreements on clay using the universal cuneiform writing system developed long ago in Babylon. Why they should do this, Daveed did not know, although he surmised it had something to with the fact that paper burned while hardened clay lasted forever, thus a testimony to the speed with which rulers forgot their treaties and promises.

Along the way they had launched raids on villages and settlements, taking food and cattle and wagons, and rounding up the able-bodied menfolk. As always happened in times of war, women followed, bringing children with them, along with washtubs, cooking pots, portable looms. When the Egyptian army made camp at night, the followers made their own, and soon a symbiosis was formed in which the women exchanged services for food and protection. Daveed knew that romances would even bloom, or perhaps just relationships of mutual convenience, so that soldiers would marry and bring their wives back to Egypt with them. Thus had warfare, through the centuries, ensured the spread of populations, traditions, and faiths.

But so far this column had seen only lackluster skirmishes with no great spoils to reward the troops, and as the trek stretched on in days, Daveed saw the soldiers grow sullen, and they grumbled.

Although Daveed was a prince and had learned to hunt and ride and drive a chariot, and although he had been trained in the martial art of Zh'kwan-eth, he was unfamiliar with warfare and had never witnessed a battle. But even so, he knew enough that Pharaoh's soldiers were becoming dispirited. They were not here voluntarily, and, after days of marching, they were turning into an army of disgruntled malcontents, constantly complaining. The foot soldiers trudged with slumped shoulders and weapons held every which way, marching out of tempo so that they were more like a line of shuffling prisoners than proud military men. How had this mob of men, lacking in enthusiasm and zeal, managed to defeat the Canaanite army at Megiddo? And how did Pharaoh Thutmose expect them to fight the Habiru who were known to be fierce and proud and bloodthirsty? Daveed imagined that at the first sound of the trumpet, this lot would drop their weapons and flee into the hills.

By Shubat, he wondered for the first time since leaving Megiddo, are we going to survive the battle?

Daveed was roused from his musings when, out of the silence, up ahead, a trumpet blew and the march came to an abrupt halt. He saw riders coming around a hill, scouts whom Pharaoh had sent ahead, and he saw a hurried exchange between the scouts and Thutmose. Orders were given and the troops were mustered into straight lines, their officers striding among them with whips, bringing the recalcitrant troops to attention. Daveed exchanged a nervous glance with Nobu, who stood next to his charioteer like a statue made of white marble. He had gone pale with fear, and Daveed saw how his old friend trembled.

Pharaoh Thutmose stood in his electrum-plated chariot, drawn by four plumed horses, and held his arms aloft until the valley fell silent, despite the army amassed there. The lone cry of a hawk, high above, was the only sound to be heard.

"Soldiers of Egypt!" the king of Egypt shouted, and Daveed was astounded at the timbre and power of his voice. For one so short, Thutmose's voice carried on the wind like a great trumpet, so that even the cavalry at the rear of the column could hear him.

"This day I lead you into battle, for my scouts report that the Habiru are encamped beyond the hills. Their numbers are like the grains of sand in the desert, like the stars in the firmament. Their numbers are greater than ours, so that each of you must fight ten men. But the Habiru are nothing compared to the warriors of the Land of Kem! They are like children and old women compared to the fighting men of Amon-Ra, the greatest god in the world!

"Today I lead you into glory! Today your names will be known to the gods and they will hail you as the greatest fighting force in the world. If you die today, you will cross over to the Western Land with Anubis himself leading the way. Your hearts will be placed on the Scales of Truth and you will be judged worthy of an afterlife you cannot even imagine!"

The troops turned to one another, grinning and nodding.

"If you die today, you will be lifted up into the rays of the sun. You will ride in Ra's solar boat for eternity, drinking sweet wine and enjoying the embrace of beautiful virgins. This will be your reward for defeating Egypt's foe today."

The troops murmured eagerly among themselves.

"But if you do not die today," the king cried, "if you fight valiantly and make this plain run with Habiru blood, you will enjoy a triumphant entry into Egypt on the day that we return. Your mothers and wives will scream with pride and delight until they have no voices left. Women will throw themselves at you, for you will be heroes of a great conquest. They will want to lie down with you. They will be eager to take your seed between their legs, for you are the bravest of all men! Each of you will be rewarded with his own farm, jars of honey, and fields of wheat. And you will never have to toil again!"

The soldiers erupted in cheers and slammed their swords and daggers on their shields to fill the valley with a deafening roar. Even Daveed felt his heart expand with sudden zeal, felt the power of Pharaoh's voice and words invigorate his weary bones. He looked at Nobu whose face was now radiant with joy, as if he too could not wait to slay the Habiru foe and earn his own farm on the Nile.

Thutmose gave a signal and the men at the head of each column raced with their forked standards draped with colored ribbons to an ox-drawn sled. From beneath a protective cover, they drew out new staffs—tall and straight and polished. Atop each was a gold insignia. They ran back to the heads of their ranks and held the golden standards aloft.

Daveed knew that these effigies were carried on tall poles so that they could be seen above the dust of battle, and he saw that each staff bore the effigy of the god protecting that regiment. The golden shapes of falcons, crocodiles, and hawks were designed not only to keep the troops organized into their respective companies, but also to inspire them with courage and bravery.

The gold shone so brightly in the noon sun that rays shot out in brilliant flairs, blinding the men. They cried out, covered their eyes, and fell to their knees. From behind the protection of his own hand, Daveed saw how skillfully the bearers turned the poles this way and that, slightly, deftly, catching the sunlight, sending bright flashes here and there, to each division. It was an impressive display. And the effect was total.

But Daveed noticed in curiosity that not all the effigies were of gods, some were abstract symbols that he himself could not identify. And yet these men, who could neither read nor write, knew at once the meaning of the images so that on Pharaoh's command, the once-dispirited men shot to their feet and, rallying behind each golden standard, jumped up and down, shouted, creating a great, zealous noise, so that by the time the trumpet sounded again, the war chariots in the front suddenly sprang forward, bowmen with arrows ready, the cavalry charged at a gallop, and the foot soldiers took off at a great run, eager now to engage the fierce foe that awaited them around the next hill.

But suddenly the enemy was upon them in a surprise attack, swarming down from the hills, appearing from behind boulders and trees, emerging from ravines on the backs of galloping camels. Shrieking, waving swords, volleying arrows, metallic swords, and daggers flashing in the sun. Daveed and Nobu held on as their charioteers raced headlong toward the bloodthirsty horde. But they saw that troops they had once suspected would run at the first sight of the foe now plunged headlong with weapons held high, inhuman shrieks tearing from their throats.

The Habiru were famous for their skill with the sling—launching rocks and stones with such accuracy that it was said they could put out a man's eye as they raced past him in a chariot. Daveed thought that there was no more chilling sound than a rock whistling past his ear, so close that he felt the wind of its passage.

"Master!" Nobu wailed from his chariot.

"Pray to the gods!" Daveed shouted back as his own chariot hit a large stone. Daveed held on as the vehicle flew into the air to jolt back down with such force he felt his teeth rattle. His driver seemed fearless, handling the reins with large hands and arms that bulged with muscles. The horses, too, were fearless as they rushed headlong toward the enemy while arrows and stones and spears flew past their heads. Daveed clung to the chariot with every ounce of his strength as he recited the names of all the gods he could think of, even calling upon those gods whose names he did not know.

His bowels swam with fear. He heard a high-pitched wail and recognized it as Nobu's cry. Daveed looked across and saw, through the clouds of dust, his friend crouched in the chariot so that only his head showed.

But Pharaoh's soldiers did not weaken. If the bearer of a gold standard fell, another was quick to take his place, raising the golden god or symbol aloft to keep the troops inspired, to keep the fire burning in their blood. They charged among the Habiru with a ferocity that startled Daveed. Where had this fervor come from? Surely it was not just Pharaoh's lively speech?

No, he thought as his body snapped from side to side with each swift veering of his chariot. It is something else . . .

As Daveed thought he was about to meet certain death—he prayed to Shubat and whispered good-bye to Leah—the drivers suddenly turned off and raced up a slope from where Thutmose and his generals were observing the fray.

Daveed was both fascinated and repulsed by the mayhem below, as men went at each other with clubs and axes, bashing and slicing this way and that until the afternoon air was filled with the screams of the wounded and dying. Horses and camels fell as their legs were cut from under them. The stench of blood soon filled the air. The noise was deafening and so much dust was kicked up that Daveed wondered how anyone could make sense of the battle. But Thutmose and his senior officers seemed unperturbed as they watched in silence.

The Habiru fought fiercely but were soon overwhelmed by Pharaoh's enthusiastic forces. The battle died down when there were more men strewn on the ground than standing, and Daveed saw, when the dust settled, that it was mostly Habiru who were dead. Before the fight was even over, while men continued hand-to-hand combat on the perimeters, Egyptian troops were ravaging the bodies of the enemy, looking for plunder, cheering when a bronze bracelet was claimed, or a copper brooch that had fastened a cloak. Mostly, they collected weapons and danced and cheered among the slain Habiru until Pharaoh himself stood up and called for silence and made another pretty speech about valor and rewards and the blessings of the gods.

After the battle Daveed and Nobu watched in horror as five Habiru captives were tied together, their long hair pulled up into a collective knot. With one stroke of his sword, Thutmose severed their necks so that when the torsos fell, he held triumphantly aloft five heads bleeding from the neck. One of the generals explained to Daveed that this maneuver, known to Pharaohs down through the ages, was called "gathering flax."

While noncombatant military personnel began at once to erect a camp beside the battlefield, Habiru survivors were rounded up and tied together in makeshift corrals. From what Daveed had heard of Thutmose's plans for erecting monuments to himself up and down the Nile Valley, he was going to need every able-bodied man he could lay hand to. Daveed felt sorry for the captives. Instead of dying the honorable warrior's death—on a battlefield after a valiant fight—they were destined to perish in a distant land, carving stone out of foreign quarries, perhaps reduced to hobbling around with the waterskin to quench the thirst of stronger workers.

Daveed wondered if the invisible god of the Habiru was powerful enough to reach that far. If he had no form, no name, how was he going to hear the prayers of his people in far-off Egypt?

The sun dipped behind the western hills. As shadows stretched across the plain of carnage, animals were captured and brought in, campfires were lit, tents were erected, and soon the troops got busy with a celebration of the day's victory. As the night filled with the laughter and singing of drunken soldiers, loud boasts and curse-filled arguments, Daveed produced lumps of damp clay and recorded everything he had seen, not only the battle itself but also the aftermath when the Egyptians had gone through the slain enemy and cut off their hands and feet, to bring them before Pharaoh as trophies, and to ensure that the spirits of the dead could not walk the land and wreak vengeance upon their victors.

Cooks brought food and drink around, handing Daveed and his

slave mugs of watered beer and bread filled with beef and onions. As Nobu stared into the flames of their campfire, he drank the weak Egyptian beer and listened to the voice in his head. There was a time when he would have stupefied himself with wine to silence the voice. But now, because of Esther, he stayed sober and listened. It was in this way that he learned what he must do.

"Master," he said, interrupting Daveed's writing, "I nearly died today and never is a man's mind as clear or his vision as acute as when he faces his own mortality. Master, I am sick at heart. I am in that most miserable of states that can befall a man. I am in love. And I need to be in the shadow of that dear soul who lights up my heart. I need to be near her."

Daveed watched his old friend in mild surprise. He knew of Nobu's nighttime escapades with women in the streets and taverns. It was a subject they never discussed. But love? "Who is the lucky woman?"

Nobu hung his head and Daveed saw the flames of the camp-fire glow on a patch of bald pate, making him think of the irony of an expert barber losing his hair. "I spoke of her to you when we left Ugarit, but you did not listen. It is the sister of the one you love, Master. The one named Esther. Oh, just to speak her name makes my heart swell." He lifted woebegone eyes. "She needs my protection, Master! She will be sold into slavery if I do not return at once to Ugarit and intervene. Master, I will take the family to Lagash. I have friends there who will help us."

Nobu knew something else now, too—that the voices were not a curse but a gift, nor were they god-voices but his own—a gift given to him the hour of his birth so that years hence they would speak inside his head thoughts he was not aware he had, reminding him of some-thing he had not known he had forgotten—that Esther needed him.

Daveed laid a hand on Nobu's shoulder, faithful companion of so many years. "I understand your agony, you old rogue, but it would be folly for you to ride back to Ugarit on your own. We are in a war-torn land. Lawless men thrive in such a climate, and they prey upon the unprotected. You would not survive. But take heart. I promise you this: when we return to Ugarit, I will make of you a freed man. I will draw up a document of manumission, releasing you from slavery. And as a freed man you will have the right to declare your heart to the girl."

Nobu's eyes filled with so much naked gratitude that Daveed felt sorry for him. Nobu was considerably older than Esther and, after all, a slave, even though freed. But as Daveed had never thought he himself would lose his heart so utterly and eternally to a woman, he sympathized with Nobu and silently wished him well.

Daveed resumed recording the battle on clay, and while he worked, something crept to the edge of his mind. Something important. It was the same elusive thought that had come to him on the battlefield. He had not been able to grasp it then, nor could he grasp it now. He felt like a man walking through a forest, knowing he was being stalked by something unseen, yet, when he turned his head, nothing was there.

It seemed to have something to do with the troops' astonishing fervor after Pharaoh's speech. No . . . beyond that. When the soldiers reacted to the appearance of their golden standards—the symbols and effigies of the gods. That was the moment that had infused their blood with fire.

Looking upon a symbol they recognized, that held meaning and power for them, uniting them . . .

The Brotherhood came to Daveed's mind, and the sad neglected state of the Solar Eye. The brothers should react to the emblem of their fraternity the way Pharaoh's once-grumbling troops had reacted to their beloved golden standards. Yet they did not.

And suddenly it came to him, the elusive thought that stalked the edges of his mind: he had gotten it backwards. He had thought the Solar Emblem of the Brotherhood had fallen into disrepair because of the indolence of the brothers. But it was the other way around! The brothers had fallen from the path of righteousness because the Solar Eye had lost its power.

Daveed nearly cried out. All this time he had thought that the Brotherhood simply needed a stronger leadership, that the fraternity had grown weak because the previous Rab was old and blind. But now, after seeing how unenthusiastic and disgruntled soldiers were transformed into valiant warriors at the mere sight of a symbol, he realized that this too was what the Brotherhood needed.

A new symbol to unite them.

As he shook his head in wonder at the workings of the human

mind—or was it Shubat at work in his mind?—Daveed made another astonishing discovery. While he had wandered inside his head, thinking of symbols and men, his hands had taken on minds of their own, for there on the damp clay, newly imprinted with his stylus, was a symbol he had recently found in a corner of Ugarit's ancient archive. He had not known the identity of the symbol, but suspected what it might be. He had intended to look further after he returned from Megiddo, but what amazed him now was that his strong-willed hands, working on their own, had carved into the clay that ancient and forgotten symbol, an engraving of graceful curves and circles and lines instead of the regimented triangles and dots that comprised standard cuneiform.

He stared at the ancient symbol from the archive at the House of Gold and he knew what he must do with it. Shubat had shown him, through warfare and Egyptian military, what he must do to truly save the Brotherhood. And he knew also that nothing must get in the way of his returning to Ugarit and achieving his new goal.

D aveed awoke the next morning to find Nobu gone, his bedroll no longer on the ground. His travel pack and barber kit were also gone. And Daveed suspected that if he were to check their horses, which they had brought with them from Megiddo, Nobu's would not be at its tether.

"Shubat protect you and keep you safe, old friend," he whispered. "I pray that you make it home."

The bodies of the Egyptian dead were loaded onto sleds and the column resumed its march. Daveed glanced back in the morning sunlight to see hundreds of corpses strewn across the plain, vultures pecking out eyes and making good feasts of chest cavities. He suspected that once the Egyptians were well away, the women and children, who had stayed in hiding, would come out and bury their menfolk.

What is the name of this place? he wondered as the column began to enter a mountain pass that climbed to the sky. Will that battle be remembered even? And what of the heroic warriors who were now food for birds and flies, what were their names?

I will write about what I saw, and truthfully. I will record everything I see and hear for future generations.

But when the march came to a halt at the top of a mountain, as the pass widened and a magnificent ocean vista opened before them—a glistening blue sea stretching away to the distant horizon—Daveed gasped and his jaw dropped when he saw exactly what it was he was going to write about. Because the chilling sight that lay before him far eclipsed an insignificant battle on a nameless plain.

And he knew now, with a feeling of foreboding and a terrible chill, why Pharaoh Thutmose had brought him, Prince Daveed of Lagash and Ugarit, to this mountaintop called Karmel.

"Shubat," Daveed whispered as he stepped down from the chariot to walk to the edge of the cliff.

Daveed knew that the rich people of Ugarit were not worried about an invasion. Before he and Nobu left on their mission to rescue Leah, he had heard that wealthy men were loading supplies and gold onto private vessels in Ugarit's harbor. Should Egypt attack, they would have plenty of advanced warning from the scouts along the southern road, giving them enough time to evacuate the doomed city and sail away to safety.

But Daveed saw now as he was filled with dread that there was no safety for the people of Ugarit, rich or otherwise. King Shalaaman, he knew, was like all other kings of northern Canaan—he did not fear an Egyptian invasion from the sea. Egypt rarely sailed far from its own river, and such vessels as crept up the coast of Canaan were small trade vessels, designed for peaceful commerce.

But what filled the natural harbor below the cliffs of Mount Karmel could in no way be mistaken for merchant ships. While Canaan built defensive walls facing the highway, Egypt had been quietly building an armada.

Daveed shuddered in premonition: there were too many ships to count, they were large and well-manned with gigantic sails the likes of which sailors on the Great Sea had never seen. And no ships of Ugarit could stand up to these.

"As you see with your own eyes, Prince of Lagash, no country in the world can claim such a flotilla as this," Thutmose boasted. "Not even the sea peoples of Minos and Mycenae can make such a claim. See how the rowers are protected? Their arrows are tipped with pitch, which will be set on fire so that while we are able to volley fire, my sailors cannot be touched by Ugarit arrows."

Daveed knew what the result would be. First, all the vessels in Ugarit's harbor would be set ablaze. Then, flaming arrows would be aimed at the wooden buildings crowding the docks. Fires raging through the city, unstoppable in the summer heat driven by prevailing onshore winds. Ugarit would launch defensive ships, but Daveed knew from the number of oars, the special shielding, the additional rigging, and oversized rudder designed to be managed by four men, that the Egyptian ships would be swift and undefeatable by any Canaanite vessel. The battle would be won before any true fight could take place, guaranteeing total victory for Egypt, and total annihilation for Ugarit.

He thought of the iron weapons Jotham's factory was producing and he realized that the way men waged war was changing. He suspected that should full-scale conflict break out between Egypt and the cities of Canaan, the map of the world, and its people, would be changed forever.

Now he knew why Thutmose had brought him along on this campaign. To show him Egypt's true might. "I promise you, Great One," he said, "that when I return to Ugarit, I will report exactly what I have seen. I will tell King Shalaaman of Egypt's might, for it is clear to me now why you brought me along."

Thutmose laughed. "Is that what you thought? Prince Daveed, I want you to inform your king and your father in Lagash of what you have seen of Egyptian might, but you are to write to them, not tell them in person. You can never leave, for now you are my most valuable hostage and I will keep you with me until I march all the way into Babylon."

CHAPTER FIFTEEN

Today was the day of the midsummer festival, and Avigail had succeeded at last, after much effort and calling in favors, in obtaining a court appearance. She was to present her case before the judges in ten days, at which time they would decide in either her or Zira's favor.

But the problem now, Avigail thought as she neared her home on the southern road, was what to do about the family. The court clerk, reviewing her case, had instructed her to bring the whole family with her on the court date. He did not say why, but Avigail knew: it was in case Zira won, they would all be quickly seized by the court's guards and taken away to the slave market. In this way, no plaintiff was given the opportunity of absconding should he or she lose.

To Avigail's surprise, although Zira had accused her of attempting to stall and stave off their inevitable sale into slavery, it was Zira who had dragged her feet these past days, ever since Avigail had demanded her right to speak before the High Court. Avigail suspected it was because of rumors of King Shalaaman's ill health. No doubt Zira was hoping he would die before she had to face Avigail before the judges, for then Yehuda would be elected king, and he would have the legal right to overturn any ruling the judges might make.

But now Zira had no choice: they would face each other in court in ten days. At which time, the fate of Avigail and her family would be in the hands of the gods.

Or corrupt judges, she thought as she neared the gate of her villa, recalling what the discredited lawyer Faris had told her in Hathor's Pleasure Garden—that Yehuda knew secret, scandalous information about the court's senior judge, Uriah. But she would cross that bridge, as the saying went, when she came to it. In the meantime, she must make arrangements for her family. Especially Baruch and Aaron, four years old with their lives and bright futures ahead of them. No slavery for them!

"Shalaam and the blessings of the gods, dear lady!"

Avigail paused at the gate and stared at the stranger coming up the road, his smile as sunny as the noon day. She did not at first recognize him, as he had lost weight and his skin was bronzed. But she would know that slow gait anywhere, that head thrust forward like a turtle's.

"Nobu!" she cried, her eyes darting past him, to the traffic on the road, searching for another familiar face.

"Alas, dear lady," he said when he reached her, "Daveed and Leah are not with me. But be assured, your granddaughter is safe in the palace at Megiddo, and being well taken care of." As he spoke, Nobu conducted his own eager search behind Avigail, looking for and finding the object of his delight. Esther stood beneath a vine bower, the two boys on either side, watching shyly.

"Come inside," Avigail said, disappointed that Leah was not with him, yet heartened to see a familiar face. There was a time when the mumbling Nobu had annoyed her. Now she saw a dear friend.

She took him into the kitchen, where Hannah and Saloma were boiling leeks and onions for their dinner. They received Nobu with joy and the two little boys, now over their shyness, tugged at the visitor's cloak with a million questions. While Nobu wished the women would silence the two little rascals, he said nothing, because he knew Baruch and Aaron were the only joy in their lives.

He had brought food, and although he saw how hungrily Avigail eyed the cheese, bread, and salt fish, she said, "The youngest eat first. I will have what is left."

She portioned it out to Aaron and Baruch, whom she admonished not to gobble, and then to Esther, who softly thanked Nobu for his generous gift. There was not much left for Saloma and Hannah, but they each gave of theirs to Avigail so that all ate.

"The gods be thanked," Avigail said as she savored the tasty bread and olive oil on her tongue, "and now tell us news, Nobu. We have been so worried."

Certain that the grandmother could hear the thunderous pounding of his joy-filled heart—his precious Esther had not yet been sold into slavery!—he explained how the gods had favored him in his journey from southern Canaan by leading him to a caravan that was sorely in need of a skilled barber. "In this way I paid for my safe passage to Ugarit, and in this way, too, will I secure passage to Lagash for I have come to take you all to my beautiful city in the east where I have friends who will give us shelter and a safe place to hide. Quickly pack your possessions. I will find a caravan going in that direction. And once we are settled, I will get word to Daveed who will surely join us there. Leah, too, if Pharaoh is generous." Nobu said nothing more on this matter, as he did not wish to alarm Avigail or Leah's sister, but while in Megiddo Nobu had heard that other princes were being held hostage there and that although they lived a life of privilege, they were nonetheless prisoners of Egypt, destined never to see their homes or families again.

Avigail took a bite of sharp cheese and chewed on it as she chewed on what Nobu had just offered. "It is tempting," she said. "But we would be runaway slaves. Criminals. We would be fugitives for the rest of our lives, calling no place home. The gods did not give me the gift of these two boys only to throw it away for fear of slavery. And I would not dishonor my son's name this way, for I know Elias will return someday. And remember, Nobu, that Elias did not run from his responsibilities. He accepted his fate with his head held high and not a man in Ugarit can call him dishonorable."

She ate an olive while the others waited in silence. Then she said, "But I do worry for these boys' safety and well being, and so I thank you for your offer. This is what we will do. I was instructed to bring my family to the High Court to witness my appearance before the judges. Stand with them, Nobu, and listen for the judges' decision. If they decide in favor of Zira, leave Ugarit at once, taking Esther and the boys with you."

"But I would take all of you, dear lady."

She shook her head. "Asherah be praised for bringing you to us, dear Nobu. But you will travel more swiftly with Esther and the boys. Hannah and Saloma and I would slow you down. And we would be conspicuous, for Zira will send out the hue and cry, and all the towns east of here will have an eye out for one man traveling with four women and two little boys. Take Esther and the boys to Lagash, and find a way to send word to Daveed and Leah. I pray that this does not come to pass, but if it should be so, protect my granddaughter and my precious Aaron and Baruch, for they are the future of my bloodline. And I will pray, dear Nobu, that in time, by the compassionate will of the gods, my family will all be reunited one day, and in our own home."

CHAPTER SIXTEEN

How dare that Canaanite dog ignore me!"
The courtiers and priests and magicians and scribes and military officers stood in silence as their king flew into a rage upon receiving news that there was still no reply from Ugarit.

Thutmose strode about the interior of the blue pavilion, a short man with an explosive temper, pacing back and forth with an energy that frightened those in his presence. Some even wondered if the sheer force of his anger might set fire to the linen walls and tent posts, the furniture and carpets, even the very clothes on their backs! He was after all Pharaoh, son of Amon-Ra, a direct descendant of the sun.

He turned to Chief Physician Reshef. "Which of the hostages is most important to Shalaaman?"

Reshef measured his words before speaking. He was not finished with the Canaanite girl. Although she had finally translated the eighteen tablets written in a secret script, there was still much contained within her head that she stubbornly refused to impart—cures and spells and ancient wisdom she had gleaned from cities on the Euphrates. "The two princelings, Your Radiance. Twin sons born to a princess whom Shalaaman married in order to forge an alliance with a king. These mean more to Shalaaman than the Canaanite girl he believes to be a demon-charmer."

Thutmose absently scratched his arm as he gave this thought. As he was not in his throne room, nor tending to matters of government, nor receiving foreign dignitaries, Egypt's conquering king wore only a plain white pleated kilt under a gold belt, his torso bare except for a wide gold collar inlaid with precious gems.

He wore no crown, simply a gold headband with the sacred cobra on his forehead. But no one was deceived by the modest dress. The kilt and belt and headband belonged to the most powerful man on earth. Thutmose held the life of every living creature in his hands. With a word, he could kill every man in this tent. With a gesture, he could raze Megiddo to the ground.

"Then I will send him the head of the demon-charmer," he said at last.

Reshef gave him a startled look. That had not been his intent. He had thought Thutmose would choose one of the twins to be an example. Not the girl!

She was to be his gift to the woman of his heart.

Reshef not only worshipped and adored and admired Queen Hatshepsut, he was in love with her. It went beyond the physical. He would not even dare to imagine them together as lovers, for that would be blasphemy. She was his goddess and it pained him when she visited her tomb and mortuary temple, the Mansion of A Million Years, to check on the workmen's progress because it was a reminder to him of her mortality, a reminder that the day would come when the light of his heart would no longer walk this earth.

He wanted to give Hatshepsut a gift that no other man—or god— could give her. Immortality.

The Canaanite girl had boasted of arcane knowledge that she had gleaned from the magicians, healers, scribes, and priests of distant cities. Although Egyptian medicine and physicians were far superior to any other in the world, Reshef harbored a small hope that an ancient god in a foreign land had given the secret of eternal life to a mortal. Everyone knew that when the gods walked the land, they were immortal. Human ancestors, too, were said to have been giants who lived for hundreds of years. Somewhere on this vast earth, beneath an alien sun, perhaps in a long-forgotten cave, or buried beneath an ancient, nameless mountain, that secret lay hidden, waiting to be rediscovered.

Reshef wanted that secret for the love of his heart. He wanted Hatshepsut never to die. Not just for his sake, but also for the sake of Egypt. It was Hatshepsut's brilliant strategy that had launched this invasion of Canaan. When she decided it was time for Egypt to conquer the world, her nephew and co-regent, Thutmose, had simply wanted to launch an invasion. But the supremely wise and canny Hatshepsut had thought it better if the Canaanites "brought it upon themselves." The great queen was known for her peaceful, and highly profitable, expeditions to the land of Punt. She did not want to be known as an aggressor. And so she decided she must "die." As she had predicted, once news of her death reached Canaan, the cities rose in rebellion. And now the conquest of the world had begun.

Soon, Egypt would rule every land, and grow to be the richest, most powerful force on earth. Reshef desired to see Hatshepsut on that glorious throne for generations to come.

"Bring the demon-charmer to me," Thutmose barked. "And bring me an ax." Reshef cursed silently. There was nothing he could do. Once Pharaoh spoke, there was no countering it. The Canaanite girl's secrets were about to die with her.

"And bring also the Canaanite scribe, Daveed," Thutmose added, "that he can write the letter that will accompany the demon-charmer's head to Ugarit."

The Habiru were gone.

Yesterday was the day of the midsummer festival, but there were no celebrations in Megiddo. Pharaoh had made a triumphant entry into the city, while the many hundreds of new captives were added to the prison camp. By sunset the great march to Egypt had begun.

It was strange now, Leah thought, to look out from the harem tower and see in the smoky morning light only the military camp, alive with music and campfires and the shouts and laughter of soldiers back from battle, happy to be alive. Of the other camp, only crude shelters and smoldering fires remained. Under Egypt's remarkable skill for organization and efficiency, the entire population of Habiru captives had uprooted itself, folded its tents, rounded up its animals, and trekked up

337

through the mountain pass that would take them to the trade route for Egypt—a mass of men, women, children, goats and sheep, camels and donkeys, Egyptian cavalrymen, charioteers, and foot soldiers.

Leah wondered how many would survive the journey. How many would arrive at a place called Goshen, where they would toil under Pharaoh's whip to build a city to the glory of Amon-Ra.

Now Leah awaited news of Daveed. She had not seen him in the procession through the city, but several of Thutmose's generals had separated themselves from the column when they reached the blue pavilion. Leah had seen men dismount their horses or step down from chariots, to attend to whatever business awaited them in the military camp. She prayed that Daveed was among them.

"Lady Merit?" a young serving girl said as she came up with a goblet of sweet wine.

Leah shook her head. She was in no mood for wine. She wanted only to see Daveed.

"Does the Lady Merit request anything?"

As Hatshepsut had decreed, Leah the Canaanite was indeed put to death. It was a symbolic beheading, with many declarations of removing the impudent eyes of a trespassing Canaanite, severing the wind of the blasphemous foreigner, silencing the tongue of the enemy spy. An egret feather, dipped in red ink, traced a line around Leah's neck, where the axe would have gone, and the magicians declared her head to be restored, and that she had been reborn into Egyptian life. She was even given a new name: Merit.

In this way Leah learned the Egyptian belief in the power of the spoken word. Now she understood the symbolic severing of Daveed's hand in the dungeon. Reshef and the priests had truly believed that by announcing out loud that they were amputating his hand, that the amputation had in fact taken place. It was a strange concept to Leah, but it was only one of many strange things she had learned about her captors.

Sending the serving girl away, Leah looked around the harem, at the women engaged in dressing hair and experimenting with cosmetics, lounging on couches, swimming in the sunken baths. Pampered ladies. Their every whim granted—except for freedom. But few wanted to leave, Leah had learned, for where could life be better than this? Pharaoh's wives and concubines and children were indulged and spoiled, and had every luxury at their fingertips, including a staff of lady doctors who saw to it that these women knew no pain or suffering.

The feminine healers fascinated Leah. They wore long white linen gowns and black wigs, and upon their breasts, the Eye of Horus, which itself was said to possess great power. They trained at the House of Life for ten years, and were so fastidious in their cleanliness that they bathed and changed their clothes four times a day in elaborate rituals.

Leah had made their acquaintance to learn from them as much as she could. And she had learned that, in many ways Egyptian medicine was the same as Canaanite. They created medicinal formulas from herbal recipes, but each recipe needed an accompanying incantation. Like Canaanite physicians, Egyptian healers knew that medicine only cured the symptoms, whereas magic spells and chants, spoken by magicians and priests, cured the cause. The Egyptians, however, added a third element in their healing practices. After the patient recovered, he or she was given a protective amulet to prevent the illness from coming back.

When she saw Paki the African eunuch enter the harem, she ran to him. "Paki, is there any word of Daveed? Have you heard if the scribe from Lagash returned with the king?"

Paki's black face turned ashen and his eyes darted from side to side. When Leah saw perspiration appear on his brow, glistening beneath the edge of his colorful turban, she grew alarmed. "What is it?"

"You have been summoned to the blue pavilion. We must go at once, dear lady. They are saying that Pharaoh is very angry with your king. They are saying that he is furious that King Shalaaman has not replied to any of his demands. They are saying that Thutmose is going to hold a demonstration that will surely catch the attention of Ugarit's defiant king."

"What sort of demonstration?" Leah said, although she feared she already knew. For the past twenty days, she had reluctantly translated her eighteen tablets for Chief Physician Reshef, stretching each one out, pretending not to be able to read her own script, feigning forgetfulness, hoping to prolong her time in the royal harem until Daveed's return. Reshef never let her forget that she was a hostage of Egypt, a pawn in a deadly game, and that she continued to stay alive at the pleasure of His Majesty Hatshepsut. But Leah could not drag her feet forever. She translated the last of her tablets two days ago, and now she knew her life was no longer in Hatshepsut's hands, but in those of her powerful nephew.

When Paki told her she was to be decapitated, she said, "Perhaps it will be symbolic."

But he shook his big head. "I fear that this time, dear lady, there will be no egret feather and red ink."

"We shall see," she said, and she picked up her veil. "The gods are with us."

Guards waiting outside the harem took Leah to the blue pavilion, where Paki was left outside, to wait and worry.

She had last been inside this tent twenty days prior to stand before Queen Hatshepsut, and now it was crowded and filled with the smoke of so many censors and torches it stung her eyes. The two guards, one on each arm, brought her before the throne and forced her to her knees. Seated before her was the grotesque little man who planned to rule the world. She trembled as he rose and came down the steps toward her. When he drew near, Leah detected a faintly sweet odor coming from his body. It reminded her of death.

Thutmose lifted his hand before his face, palm out, and recited a spell. Leah knew that this was a popular spell: "Au-à rekh kua-ten. Rekh kua ren-ten." Which meant, "I know you—I know your name." Where Canaanites spoke words to summon the power of the gods, Egyptians believed that spoken words themselves created power. "Ankh-à en maat," meant, "I live in truth." "Au khu-nuà," was, "I am protected."

She knew that Thutmose chose the "knowing" spell in case her power to charm other demons came from a demon within herself. By declaring that he knew its identity, Thutmose had nullified that demon's power over him. She knew this because the familiar staff-bearing interpreter stood behind the king and translated the Egyptian words into Canaanite. Thutmose said, "Demon-charmer of Canaan, know that your power does not work here. The gods of Egypt are stronger than those of Canaan. My radiant power is stronger than any on earth. I am protected from your bad luck and evil power. Why has your king refused to acknowledge my correspondence to him?"

"I do not know, Your Radiance," she said, keeping her eyes on the floor as she knelt. "Perhaps he is ill. Without me, King Shalaaman will fall victim to the Demon That Chokes the Throat."

"Your king has insulted My Radiance. Even from a deathbed, he must reply to the son of Amon-Ra. I have received no reply. Therefore, I will demonstrate my power and the seriousness of my intent. I will make a gift to him of your head and see how well he fares with the choking demon then." Thutmose looked around. "Where is the Canaanite scribe? Where is Prince Daveed of Lagash?"

"I am here, Radiance," a familiar voice called through the smoke and Leah's heart jumped with joy. Daveed! "It was necessary for me to purify myself before entering into your radiant presence," Daveed said.

With her gaze still on the floor, Leah felt Daveed draw near, and then she detected the familiar fragrance of his soap, the oil for his hair. Out of the corner of her eye, she saw his sandaled feet and it took all her will power to remain kneeling.

Daveed addressed Thutmose through the staff-bearing translator. "Your Radiance, if I may speak before recording the words you wish to send to the King of Ugarit. I have been in my tent writing down everything I saw and heard and experienced on Your Radiance's magnificent march to Karmel. I have sung your praises, I have inscribed words that will make the military leaders of Ugarit quake with fear. I spoke of Pharaoh's limitless power, his courage and bravery, and how the miserable Habiru immediately gave up the fight when they were blinded by your radiance, which is brighter than the sun's. I am but a humble scribe, Your Majesty, although it is true that I am a prince, and I shall send those same true praises of Egypt's might to my own father, the King of Lagash. But I wish to ask a favor of Your Magnificent Radiance."

Thutmose gave Daveed a long look and seemed almost amused. "You are very brave, Prince of Lagash. But since you are so accurately describing my brilliant campaign in Karmel, I will listen to your request."

"The life of this woman, My Lord."

The gathered company gasped and exchanged looks.

"Why would you care?" Thutmose asked sharply.

"She is my wife, Your Radiance. And it would pain me to lose her."

"Wives are easily replaced," Thutmose said with a dismissive gesture of his hands. "Prepare the clay for my letter to Shalaaman."

"My Lord," Daveed said, and the courtiers murmured at his reckless bravado. "I have something of value to offer in return for this woman's life."

"There is nothing you could possibly have that I want, or that I cannot seize when and where I wish."

"What I offer is hidden, and only I know where."

"Speak, and make it the truth or the gods strike you dead."

"Our archive holds many treasures, Your Radiance. Legend tells of a young king named Ozzediah who ascended the throne of Ugarit during a time when the cities of northern Canaan were perpetually at war with one another and there was no peace in the land, no commerce or trade, with towns and villages laid to waste. Ozzediah was a man of vision and great faith, and in his twentieth year he led an expedition into the mountains in the far north, to go in search of the ark that carried a man named Noah and his family during the Flood. Ozzediah found the ark and brought back twelve pieces of wood from it, presenting each of the pieces to twelve kings in northern Canaan. The wood was so sacred, and reminded the people that El would never again bring a great flood to mankind, that the kings declared peace among themselves. But the slivers of cypress wood, still coated with pitch, are also said to contain so much magic that each grants eternal life to whoever touches it."

"Eternal life already awaits me," Thutmose said, raising his hand before his face, palm out, adding, "I am protected."

"There is a translucent blue stone of very ancient origin. It is said to have come from the stars, and whoever holds the stone, and looks into its heart, can see his or her future."

"My seers tell me the future. They tell me that Egypt will know greatness for the next thousand-thousand years."

"In Ugarit's great archive there is an ancient dagger fashioned from an unknown metal, which, when suspended on a string, always points to the north."

Thutmose made an impatient sound.

"Perhaps Your Radiance would be amused by a round crystal that came from a mysterious land beyond the Indus Valley that makes very small objects appear large, and when held up to the sun, lights fires."

"Prepare your clay, scribe," Thutmose snapped. "It is time to inform your king that he has tried my patience. I have shown him lenience and he has responded with offense. Your king will be brought down. He will kneel before me. All of Ugarit will be laid to waste."

"My Lord," Daveed said. "We hold the ancient Sumerian Tablet of Destinies, stolen from that land centuries ago. Surely you have heard of the tablet's great powers."

Before Pharaoh could silence him, a strange sound suddenly filled the smoky air and all heads turned. It was the rattle of the sacred sistrum, an instrument carried by the priestesses of Isis to announce the goddess's presence. Leah brought her head up and saw, behind the throne, the linen drapes stir as if in a breeze. The gathered company fell silent. She sensed the collective awe of these powerful men. The sistrum sang again, the drapes parted, and a figure emerged from the darkness into the golden torchlight.

Many in the tent fell to their knees. Leah saw that only those men of the highest rank remained standing, although they bowed low and turned their eyes to the floor. She looked up at Daveed and saw the stunned look on his face. His eyes were wide, his mouth hung open. And she realized he had not known that Queen Hatshepsut was still alive.

Like her nephew, the queen was modestly attired in an ankle-length dress that came below her bosom, and was held up by two wide straps that covered her breasts. Her black wig was squared off at the shoulders and bangs, the headband plain gold with the familiar cobra on the forehead.

Her voice was low and as smoky as the air in the tent when she spoke. "We wish to hear more," she commanded in Canaanite.

Daveed could not at first speak. He could only stare at the woman who was a legend, and whom he had thought dead. Struggling for composure, Daveed cleared his throat and said, "Your Eternal Radiance, great daughter of the Sun, know that we in Ugarit possess dried roots from the original Tree of Life, and a vial of blood from the first man, Adam."

When she did not seemed impressed, Daveed added, "I found a scarab beetle, Your Majesty, which was given to the King of Ugarit as a gift from your own revered ancestress, Queen Tetisheri. The scarab is still alive."

Hatshepsut held her hand to her face, palm out, and whispered a spell. Then she narrowed her eyes. "Why do you tell us of these secret treasures?"

"They are yours in exchange for the life of this Canaanite woman who kneels humbly before you."

"Why would your king part with these treasures?"

"He knows nothing of them, Your Majesty. I am ashamed to say that when I entered the Brotherhood of Scribes, I found their sacred archive in deplorable disarray. I have spent the past four years organizing and setting it right. In my labor I came across long-forgotten treasure. To guard against them being forgotten again, or lost or destroyed, I secured them in a safe place. King Shalaaman has been absent from Ugarit these past four years and he only recently returned. I did not yet have a chance to inform him of my discoveries. But I make them available to you, Your Majesty, if you spare this woman's life."

"How do we know you speak the truth?" she said.

Daveed tapped an amulet that hung on his chest. "This Feather of Truth was given to me when I passed a test under the scrutiny of Chief Physician Reshef. It forbids me ever to speak untruths. I am also bound by personal sacred oaths to forever speak only the truth."

Hatshepsut opened her mouth to reply, but was stopped by a sudden cry. Everyone in the tent froze—the guards, officers, courtiers, Pharaoh Thutmose himself, all watching the queen for a sign. She shifted her eyes to Reshef, he exited at once, disappearing behind the drape through which His Majesty had made an entrance.

Everyone stayed silent, listening. Another cry from beyond the linen wall, quickly followed by another. Leah saw a ripple of pain cross Hatshepsut's face, and now she saw a furrow between the painted brows, and a haunted look in her eyes. Someone was sick. Someone close to the queen.

"Radiance," Leah said, eliciting gasps from those around her.

Hatshepsut shifted her heavily painted eyes to Leah and rested there, impassive and unreadable.

Leah's heart raced as she said, "Perhaps I can help. As you know, in my travels in the Land of the Two Rivers, I witnessed many cures. I do not mean to offend the gods of Egypt, or to impugn the reputation of your physicians, but sometimes another pair of eyes sees things that others have not."

The moment stretched, until finally Hatshepsut turned and walked out, but not without first sending a subtle signal to two guards who immediately stood on either side of Leah, bringing her to her feet, to escort her behind their monarch. Daveed followed and no one stopped him.

A smaller room was hidden behind the throne, constructed of the same heavy blue linen, the air filled with smoke and sweet incense. Leah could not at first see anything as the chamber stood in complete darkness, but soon her eyes adjusted, and she saw the ghostly shape of Hatshepsut's white dress. Then she saw men in physician's robes. Finally, she made out the shape of a bed. Wondering why no lamps burned, she stepped forward, and turned her head to listen.

Someone lay upon the bed, moaning in pain.

Daylight found its way through breaks in the tent and under the walls where they were pegged into the ground. It was enough for Leah, when her eyes fully adjusted to the lack of light, to see a youth lying on the bed. He wore only a white loincloth, and his head was shorn except for a long lock of black hair over his right temple. A handsome youth, she thought, and she wondered: The queen's young lover?

But when she saw Hatshepsut's attitude as she bent over the boy, the softness of her profile, the worry, Leah reassessed her thinking: Not a lover, a son. And she remembered hearing a rumor once, about Egypt's unmarried queen giving birth to a love child.

"What ails the boy?" Leah asked, and Reshef said, "A demon has taken possession of his head. It drones so deafeningly that it causes the prince great pain."

"How did the demon enter his head?" Leah asked, stepping closer.

"Through his ear," Reshef said. "Sometimes it sleeps and the boy feels some relief. But then the demon awakens and the buzzing is worse than the pain."

"Radiance," Leah said to the queen, "I witnessed the exorcism of just such a demon in the city of Haran. I can attempt to do so now. But I will need light. A candle or a lamp."

But Reshef said, "Your Majesty, light will only drive the demon deeper into the boy's skull. And then it might never come out. This is why we must keep the prince in darkness."

Leah spoke up, saying, "I am not as wise or experienced in medicine as your own physicians, Your Radiance, but in Ugarit we are afflicted with more ailments than the people of the Land of Kem are. I have heard that the Choking Demon does not afflict Egyptians. This is because your land is dry and warm and full of sunlight. In the north, on the shore of the Great Sea, Ugarit knows cold and damp seasons, and so demons seek warmth in men's chests, robbing them of breath until they die."

"But demons prefer darkness," Physician Reshef countered. "Everyone knows this, for that is where evil spirits are born, in the cold and the dark."

"We in Ugarit believe this, too, but also that demons are attracted to light. They leave their cold, dark world and seek heat and sun." When she saw she still had not convinced him, Leah said, "I have learned a great deal from the physicians of Canaan because, as everyone knows, there are more evil spirits in Canaan than in Egypt."

Reshef inclined his noble head. "This is true."

"I believe I can draw the demon out of this young man's skull."

The Chief Physician and bedside attendants turned to the queen, who nodded.

While a candle was being sent for, Daveed said quietly to Leah, "If you succeed in this, Hatshepsut will keep you here, as Shalaaman did."

"The boy suffers, and it is a simple cure. Perhaps His Majesty will be different and allow us to go home."

"Cure the boy," Daveed whispered, "and I will find a way to get us home."

When the lighted candle was brought, Leah saw the skeptical look on Daveed's face and she thought: He is right. Hatshepsut will be like all other monarchs, greedily keeping what is not theirs.

"The boy's arms must be restrained. Turn him on his side, opposite from the side through which the demon entered."

Leah stepped up to the bed and brought the candle, that smelled powerfully of beeswax, to the side of the youth's head, and she held it there while everyone watched in anxious silence. The boy moaned and winced and cried out. And then suddenly, he went still. His moans subsided. He drew in a deep breath. "The demon is gone," he whispered.

Leah drew back and marveled at a truth she had just learned, because she had witnessed something that no one else in the room had—what she herself had not seen when the Euphrates man was exorcized of the Darkness Demon: as she held the candle to the boy's ear, Leah had seen an insect fly out, a small black fly. She realized it must have flown into the ear and gotten trapped, creating a frightful buzzing sound in the poor boy's head. But the light of the candle had shown the confused creature the way out. And now it was free, buzzing in the air.

But no one heard it as everyone began talking at once, rushing to the bedside, praising the gods, thanking them for this miraculous cure.

I will ask to be allowed to go home, Leah thought as she anticipated the reward to come.

They returned to the outer chamber, leaving the queen to fawn over the youth, and when she emerged from behind the linen hanging, Hatshepsut said, "It is true, Leah of Canaan, that you are charmed. What is the source of your power?"

Before Leah could reply, His Majesty held up a hand and said, "Never mind. Were you to tell me, it might rob you of that power. What comes from the gods is theirs alone, even though I am the daughter of Amon-Ra, the greatest god of all. We will reward you, and your benevolent spirits, for your healing here today. What is your wish?"

"To return to Ugarit, Radiance. As soon as possible. With my companion, Daveed of Lagash."

Pharaoh Thutmose, who apparently had no interest in his aunt's lovechild, was standing on the enormous war map on the floor and had been in a murmured discussion with his generals. He now spoke up: "I have other plans for the girl. She is to be used as a warning to King Shalaaman."

Hatshepsut held her eyes on her nephew for a long moment, while everyone waited. The pair, who had once been woman-king and co-regent, but who were now Pharaoh and Queen, locked eyes. And then Hatshepsut turned to Leah and said, "My physician told me of a series of clay tablets you translated for him. He said they are written in a script unknown to my scribes. Is this true?"

Taken aback by the sudden change of subject—the queen had not even responded to her request to be allowed to go home—Leah stumbled over her words. "It is a script invented by Daveed of Lagash, Your Radiance." She looked at Daveed as she said this, and she saw similar puzzlement in his eyes.

Hatshepsut turned to Daveed. "You spoke of treasures in your archive. You spoke of ancient spells and formulas and books. In what script are they recorded?"

"Your Majesty?"

"How are they written? In the incomprehensible and cumbersome scribbling of Canaan?"

"I believe so . . . and other scripts. Ancient ones."

"And your own secret code?"

"Not yet, Your Majesty, but I hope someday to translate the precious writings into a simpler script, much as the far superior form of writing in Egypt evolved from complex hieroglyphics into the clever hieratic code you use today."

His Majesty said, "This is true. The Egyptian way of writing, of doing anything, is far superior to the way things are done in the rest of the world. But as sovereign of the greatest nation on earth, it behooves us nonetheless to make ourself aware of what lesser states are doing. Perhaps someday letters and documents and treaties will be recorded in this new writing, though it be inferior. We shall keep you here, so that you can translate these things for us."

"Keep me here!" he blurted.

"Not you," Hatshepsut in a dismissive tone. "The girl Merit who used to be Leah, for we trust her and she must be in the royal presence. It is not fitting that a strange man, a foreigner, no matter how high born, linger in our radiant presence."

Halla! Leah thought. Now I shall be a prisoner of yet another selfish monarch! I must go home. My family needs me. They are being sold into slavery!

"May I speak?" Leah said. "Perhaps His Majesty would not wish to rely on my fallible and faulty powers of reading and writing. Perhaps the Radiant One herself would prefer to read letters and documents written in the new script."

A gasp went through the audience, followed by a deadly silence. Men exchanged looks. Had the girl just challenged the mightiest ruler in the world?

Hatshepsut's voice was crisp as she said, "Are you implying that you could teach me to read the script?"

Leah sensed all eyes on her. "No, Your Radiance, for I am not worthy to walk upon the dust beneath your feet. What I meant to say in my clumsy manner is that no man on earth can teach Her Radiance anything, as surely the daughter of the great god Amon-Ra already knows all things. It is simply that this code has been temporarily forgotten by Her Radiance, since the Divine Majesty must think of so many things in a day, more things than there are stars in the heavens. It would be my humble honor to refresh the Divine Majesty's memory of this code, that is all. And once it returns, the Divine One will no longer have need of so inconsequential a person as myself to translate but will possess a unique skill known only to two other people in the world—Daveed and I."

Silence followed, and then Hatshepsut said, "Shalaaman does not know the new code?"

"No, Your Splendor. No man on earth. No woman, either. O Supreme One, this new code is surely going to sweep across the world, for its simplicity and clarity, and the kings and princes of Canaan would quake at the thought of Your Divine Radiance already knowing it, and reading their letters herself. They would say to themselves, truly Egypt is great, truly the great god Amon-Ra is great that his earthly daughter should read a secret code that we have only just learned."

The Queen's heavily painted eyes met Leah's.

Leah pressed on, while her heart raced. "The kings and princes of Canaan and Mitanni and Babylon and even as far north as Hatti would declare Your Majesty the most clever and superior of all the world's rulers, for Your Majesty would be the only one not in need of relying on a translator. Does Your Radiance not already astound with her fluency in foreign tongues? How much more awesome that Your Radiance reads foreign scripts as well? Is this not the mark of a truly universal monarch?"

Leah felt the back of her neck crawl as Hatshepsut stared back with unreadable features. Even Thutmose awaited his aunt's response.

Another moment of majestic pondering, and then the Queen said, "Very well. You will help me to remember that which I already know, for it is as you say, the daughter of the great god Amon-Ra is indeed all-knowing."

She snapped an order in Egyptian and slaves immediately vanished, to return a moment later with a small box inlaid with ivory. They took it to Physician Reshef, who opened it and brought out a stunning Eye of Horus, wrought of shining gold and lapis lazuli so blue it rivaled the sky. The Eye was suspended at the end of a gold chain, and when Reshef handed it to His Majesty, Hatshepsut fastened the chain under her hair so that the Eye of Horus rested on her bosom, catching the torch light. "Words are power," she said. "The sacred Eye will protect us should you inadvertently write something harmful. We will begin." Hatshepsut turned and strode back to her throne.

Leah stared at the sovereign. "Now?"

Hatshepsut sat upon her regal chair, hands resting on ebony arms carved into panther's heads. "There is only now. Bring clay and stylus. Sit here, by our royal feet. Demonstrate to the daughter of Amon-Ra the new script of Canaan. Show me words and I will recognize them."

Leah glanced at Daveed who immediately opened his scribe's box, and as he handed her a lump of moist clay and a triangular reed, she heard Pharaoh Thutmose spit out words in Egyptian that, by their tone, sounded like an expletive. As he and his generals returned to their study of the map, addressing matters of strategy and conquest, Leah gave Daveed a questioning look and then approached the throne.

The courtiers and military officers, however, kept their attention upon their monarch, no doubt ready to praise her when she "remembered" the code, while Physician Reshef took a stance behind the throne.

When Leah sat on the edge of the throne's dais, Daveed joined her, dropping down on one knee to murmur, "I will help you. Perhaps we can make this go swiftly."

But before Leah could bring out the tablet that contained the thirty symbols, to teach the Queen the code, Hatshepsut said, "Write the word for 'god.'"

Leah did so, pressing the stylus into the clay, holding it up for Hatshepsut to see. A slave stepped forward with a torch so that when the queen leaned forward and looked at the tablet, the flame cast light on it.

"Yes," she said. "That is the word. I recognize it. Write the word for 'father,'" she said.

Leah did so, and lifted the tablet.

Hatshepsut nodded. "The memory is coming back. Write the word for 'eternity.'"

As Leah pressed the stylus into the clay, forming wedges and triangles, her alarm grew. Was Hatshepsut was going to have her write down every single word that existed? It was no way to learn a new script! Daveed and I will be prisoners here for the rest of our lives!

"If I may humbly suggest, Radiance," Leah ventured cautiously. "It is a code of just thirty symbols. Once the thirty are learned—I mean, remembered—there is no limit to what Your Radiance can read."

"Write the word for 'power,'" His Majesty snapped, and Leah pressed the stylus into clay.

"Write the word for 'surrender.'"

Asherah save me! The extreme vanity and egotism of Egypt's queen rivaled that of King Shalaaman. And a host of other rules whom Leah had stood before—vainglorious despots who used human beings as objects for their personal profits and gains. Of course, it was this extreme vanity that made them feared and powerful rulers. But . . .

Leah pressed more symbols into the clay and thought: Extreme vanity . . .

And she wondered if perhaps the very traits that gave Hatshepsut her strength were also her weakness.

When the queen asked for another word, Leah quickly incised the clay with the thirty symbols of Daveed's code, and when she lifted it up, and Hatshepsut said, "I remember this," Leah replied, "The gods are surely rejoicing, Your Radiance, for what you have remembered is the entire code itself! Now that your memory of this script has returned, there is no limit to His Majesty's power to read."

The queen fell silent, and Leah was certain everyone could hear the pounding of her own heart as she wondered if she had stepped over a line. Keeping her head humbly bowed, she studied the gold sandals that protected the royal feet, gold straps encrusted with pearls and gems. She sensed Daveed behind her, frozen, while the queen towered above her like a seated statue.

The moment was broken when a guard came into the tent, striding up to Thutmose, to bow low and announce the arrival of a delegation from the district of Jerusalem. "They have brought a gift for Pharaoh from Chief Haddad."

Thutmose glanced at the map on the floor and, finding the symbol for the stronghold of Canaanite warlords in the south, he gave a curt nod and took a seat on his throne. Guards at the pavilion's entrance drew aside the linen hangings and the foreign delegation of eight men and one veiled girl came in.

Leah stared in astonishment at the man who walked at the head of the group. Surely it was not Caleb!

While his companions were detained, the large man in a brown tunic beneath a black cloak was brought before the royal pair and told to bow low. He did so, with great formality and subservience, but Leah saw how his eyes shifted from Hatshepsut to Thutmose and back to Hatshepsut. And then when he saw Leah, seated at the Queen's feet, the glint of recognition in his eyes, she knew it was indeed the husband who had deserted her.

Leah felt her face burn hot with fear. How was it that this evil man could be in this place at this time? Surely it was a coincidence! Blessed Asherah, let Caleb's sudden appearance have nothing to do with me. Do not let him claim me as his wife. Do not let him tear me away from my beloved Daveed . . .

Through the court interpreter, Caleb announced the purpose of his mission: to bring peaceful tidings to the Radiant Splendor of Egypt from his humble patron, Chief Haddad of Jerusalem. After reciting a list of ostentatious praises of the royal pair, and pointing to the girl who was now Their Majesties' hostage, and reiterating that Chief Haddad prayed the Great Ones of Egypt would consider him a friend—when it was apparent Caleb had delivered his message and had nothing more to say —Thutmose made a gesture of dismissal and the two guards stepped up to escort Caleb out. But he said, "If I may be granted further words, Your Majesty." He pointed to Leah. "This woman is my wife. I have come to claim her."

Thutmose frowned. Turning to Daveed he said, "You told us she was your wife. One man with two wives is natural, but one woman with two husbands is an abomination. Which of you tells the truth?"

"I am the truthful one, for I recited marriage vows with this woman in the city of Ugarit, and that man," Caleb said, gesturing to Daveed who had stepped away from the thrones, "witnessed it."

"Is this true?" Pharaoh asked sharply.

"It is true, Your Majesty, but this man deserted—"

Thutmose held up a silencing hand. "Why do you tell us this?" he said to Caleb. "This woman is our hostage. Why do you claim her? Surely you know you cannot take her away, and you must return to your chief in Jerusalem."

"I need not return to Jerusalem, Your Majesty. The men who came with me can return and give Chief Haddad your message. I wish to be with my wife."

Hatshepsut spoke. "You are willing to be our hostage?"

"If that is what it takes to be with my beloved wife," Caleb said, noting that Leah looked well fed and taken care of, in fine linen clothes. What the travelers had said in Jerusalem was true. Hostages of Pharaoh were well treated.

"Besides," Caleb added, "I will see to it that she does not try to escape. That man," he said, pointing again to Daveed, "would return her to King Shalaaman and turn Ugarit and its forces against Your Majesties. I will see that this woman stays here, as your hostage, thereby putting Shalaaman at your mercy."

"Your Majesty," Leah said, rising to her feet. "I do not wish to be with this man. Daveed of Lagash is my chosen husband."

While Pharaoh pondered this, Caleb said, "I am willing to fight for my rights." He drew himself up to show his beefy, brawny strength. Everyone saw that he towered over Daveed.

When Daveed said suddenly, "I accept the challenge," the gathered military men chuckled.

"No!" Leah cried. "You cannot do this." Her heart raced. Has Daveed kept his fighting skills up? Has he put himself through the Zh'kwan-eth exercises? He still wears the dagger, but it has truly become symbolic. "This man from Jerusalem is not my husband, Your Majesty. He deserted me—"

Thutmose silenced her. "It will be a fight to the death," he decreed in a commanding voice. He looked at Daveed, adding, "No weapons."

"Your Majesty, as a warrior-scribe I swore an oath never to—"

"Daveed of Lagash," Thutmose said, skewering him with piercing eyes, "when My Majesty asked you about the weapon on your arm, you said it was symbolic only. You will now remove your symbols. And your clothes, both of you."

They stripped down to loincloths and Daveed surrendered his daggers. In this almost-naked state, the differences between the two men were striking. Caleb was large with bulky arms and a barrel chest. The many scars attested to the brawls and fights he had engaged in over the years, whereas Daveed had the smooth skin of a man who spent his days over papyrus and clay. Brawny Caleb looked a giant compared to Daveed who was smaller and wiry.

Leah chewed her lip in fear. Perhaps Daveed will be faster on his feet, she thought, and quicker to deliver a blow. But if Caleb was able to land a well-aimed punch—those fists looked like clubs!

In the flickering torchlight of the royal pavilion, the two faced each other like wrestlers, a sport known to both Egyptians and Canaanites. Half-crouched, arms flexed, hands open, they began circling.

Leah felt her heart rise to her throat as she watched Daveed—outmatched by the larger Caleb—and prayed he did not get killed. When Caleb threw the first punch, catching Daveed off guard to send him reeling backwards, Leah pressed her hands to her mouth.

The only sound inside the tent was the scuffling noise of bare feet on the woven rug as they circled again, watching each other, Daveed's face set in grim seriousness, Caleb grinning with confidence. He struck out again, but this time Daveed dodged the punch, and in a quick move, bent low and sent his fist into Caleb's belly. Now the strikes flew, as they punched and jabbed, dancing on their feet, bobbing and weaving, Daveed landing blows, Caleb landing blows, and both managing to evade the hit that would send them sprawling.

While the military men in the crowd admired Daveed's quick reflexes, how fast he was on his feet, his ability to bend low, sweep under Caleb's enormous arms, and deliver punches to his opponent, Caleb had the greater size and strength. And all fighting men in the crowd knew that Caleb had only to wear the smaller Daveed down, keep him moving, dodging, swinging until his energy drained away. Sweat dripped into both men's eyes. Daveed tried to kick Caleb's feet from under him but succeeded in only making him jump back. A powerful right fist flew at him that Daveed sidestepped by a hair.

Leah gasped. The blow to his temple would have surely sent him down, possibly killing him. Thutmose's generals watched with keen interest, thinking the scribe's defense was excellent. The challenger's offense, however, was superior.

Daveed kept his elbows tight against his rib cage as he ducked and maneuvered around Caleb, evading the heavy punches that came flying without pause, sending sharp jabs into Caleb's ribs and abdomen. When Daveed dashed in and sent a powerful uppercut to Caleb's jaw, drawing blood, Caleb stopped grinning. He countered with a blow to the side of Daveed's head, lacerating his scalp so that blood dripped onto his shoulder.

Thutmose leaned forward on his throne, arms on his knees, as he kept his eyes on Daveed.

Caleb lunged, jabbing Daveed in the neck. Daveed staggered back. He dragged his hand across his eyes. Both men were sweating profusely now. Caleb's grin returned as he saw Daveed sway and shake his head. Another punch sent Daveed to the floor. He landed on all fours and everyone watched with held breath as Caleb brought his right foot back to deliver a mighty kick. But Daveed quickly caught the foot and, jerking it upwards, sent Caleb flying onto his back. But he was back on his feet in an instant, while Daveed took seconds longer to regain his stance. He swayed. He blinked.

To Leah's dismay, and the disappointment of many of the onlookers, including Pharaoh Thutmose who had taken a liking to the prince from Lagash, it was apparent that Caleb was going to win. But as Caleb stepped in to deliver the final, lethal blow, to everyone's surprise Daveed suddenly darted away, twirled, sprinted to one of Hatshepsut's scribes, and before anyone could realize what he was doing, snatched the reed pen from the scribe's hand, spun around and flung the pen like a dart, driving it into Caleb's neck.

He screamed, cupped his throat and staggered back while the two monarchs and the courtiers, the generals and slaves and Leah stared in shock, wondering what had just happened, as it had happened so quickly.

Drenched in sweat and panting for breath, Daveed brought himself before the Queen and her nephew and said, "Leah is my wife."

Thutmose smiled at Daveed, a look of admiration on his face. "Never have I seen such fighting! Such agility! And your accuracy with the pen is astounding. I will make you an officer in my army. You will train my men—"

"You are free to go, both of you."

All eyes turned to Hatshepsut.

Fury rose in her nephew's face. "I will keep Daveed, and I will send the girl's head to Shalaaman as a sign of my intentions."

Hatshepsut rose from her throne, a slow, deliberate gesture, and remained standing on the dais so that she loomed over her nephew. As the two locked eyes, Leah suddenly understood something about this royal pair: Hatshepsut assumed the throne of Egypt when her nephew was only two years old. Now that he had risen to the throne in his legal succession of his father, Hatshepsut must relinquish her former power. But it was not an easy thing to give up. And Thutmose, as everyone could see, grew in power each day. Giving him this warrior-scribe, Leah realized, and letting him train troops, perhaps his own personal bodyguards, was something that Hatshepsut, in this power struggle, was not prepared to do.

Leah realized that, despite their love for Egypt and their united vision to see her rule the world, the royal egos came first.

"You are free to go," the Queen said again. And Thutmose said nothing.

Daveed bowed. "Your Radiance's generosity is beyond even that of the gods."

As they stepped back, Hatshepsut gave an order to her guards. "Finish him off," she said, meaning Caleb, who lay moaning and bleeding on the floor.

"Your Majesty," Daveed said, "it is not a fatal wound. I purposely—"

But Daveed was ignored and the guard thrust his sword through Caleb's belly. As the body was dragged out, Leah watched, and thought of the days she had spent with this man, the nights in his bed. Then she thought of the man at her side, Daveed, her true husband. As he put his clothes back on, the blood congealing on his scalp so that it no longer bled, Leah remembered something.

"Your Majesty, if I may . . ."

The queen waited. Leah felt all eyes on her and wondered if she was about to step too far. But she must. "If I may ask a favor, Your Radiance. It is well known that Egyptian physicians have mastered the treatment of eye diseases and blindness. I wish to know only one remedy, Your Radiance. For the 'reading blindness.' If I may humbly ask."

"My Chief Physician, Reshef, will see that you have it. In exchange you will give him the thirty-symbol key to the new code so that he may learn it and relieve me of the tiresome task of having to read it myself." Hatshepsut turned to Daveed. "Prince of Lagash, as soon as you reach Ugarit, you will see to it that the rare treasures you spoke of are secured and then you will arrange for their immediate and safe transport to my palace in Thebes. I will be departing at sunrise to return to Egypt, where I will see to the commencement of the building of a new city to the glory and exaltation of my divine father, Amon-Ra. I will expect the treasures to arrive in my kingdom in the shortest time possible."

Daveed bowed low and said, "It shall be done, Your Radiance."

Pharaoh Thutmose spoke for the first time. "The Prince of Lagash may leave, but the Canaanite woman cannot go. She is a hostage."

"We have the two princelings," Hatshepsut said. "And I gave my word. This woman may leave."

Thutmose voiced his displeasure and Hatshepsut said, "Megiddo lies in ruins, nephew, its people vanquished, their spirit broken. This is not profitable for Egypt. Strong allies make Egypt strong. We will send representatives to Shalaaman and offer him trade and tribute agreements. We will send priests who will carry our gods to Ugarit. We will send ministers and people who will settle there. And to protect them, we will send a small force of soldiers. But we will go to Ugarit in friendship."

She turned and walked out, her courtiers and priests and magicians and scribes hurrying after her.

Pharaoh turned a scowl to Daveed and said, "I will send you home with letters of peace and greetings. And I will send you with an armed escort, that you might return to Ugarit unmolested."

Daveed bowed low and said, "His Radiance is generous beyond measure. May good luck and beneficent spirits fill all the days of his life."

Thutmose dismissed him and then turned to his senior general to confer quietly. At the pavilion's entrance, Daveed stood aside to allow Leah to pass first, and as he did, looked back at the Pharaoh and his senior officer. Their voices carried, and Daveed listened. Then he followed Leah out of the tent.

"Daveed," she began, but he pulled her into his arms and kissed her. "I have so much tell you," he said.

"Daveed, you're hurt." She touched the blood on his scalp. "Let me see to this wound."

"Leah, listen to me."

"You must be hurt elsewhere—"

"Leah, I am all right. My wounds are minor. They can wait. Listen, these past forty days I have seen much and learned much."

In front of the guards and sentries outside the pavilion, in the midst of military men and messengers coming and going, and a very relieved African eunuch named Paki, Daveed took Leah's face in his hands, and said with passion, "Everything I have witnessed and experienced makes me realize that I should have exposed Yehuda for his corruption long ago. I was a fool for thinking I was protecting the Brotherhood by keeping his immoral ways a secret. Had I exposed him when you asked, I would have saved both your family and the Brotherhood. But I was blinded by misguided loyalty and idealism. But I see now, my dearest Leah, that life is brief and that while we enjoy our short time on this earth, we must work to the greater good. I promise you now, upon all that I hold sacred, that when we return to Ugarit I will expose Yehuda for what he is, I will reveal the corruption in the Brotherhood and I will vow to King Shalaaman to bring my fraternity back to righteousness."

"We are going home," she whispered, tears glistening in her eyes.

"But there is more, and I can barely put my new vision into words. Leah, I tremble with excitement to tell you the news, for I received a message from Shubat on the evening following a bloody battle with the Habiru." He told her of the lethargic soldiers who grumbled and had no zeal for battle, and how they came to life at the appearance of their golden standards. How they were transformed before his eyes. How unified they suddenly were. Forgetting themselves and their own necks for the sake of glory and honor. "It came to me, Leah, that the

Brotherhood is weak because the Solar Eye has lost its power. This is how I will save the Brotherhood—by replacing the Solar Eye."

She felt Daveed's energy flow from his fingertips into her own flesh, so that she too trembled. "With what?"

"When I was searching the archives and finding the treasures I spoke of, I came across the oldest part of the archive. I believe it was built a thousand years ago. And there I found an ancient, obscure symbol. When I saw it, I realized I had seen it before, when my father took me to visit the ruins of Sumer, the oldest city on earth. There, on a wall that is old beyond counting, I saw the same symbol: snakes coiling up a rod with outspread wings. My father said it was the symbol sacred to Ningishzida, Sumerian god of medicine. He was also Lord of the Good Tree, which symbolizes knowledge. This was the first symbol the gods gave to mankind, for it embodies three divine elements: wisdom, eternal life, and the promise that the gods speak to us. I believe, Leah, that this is the same symbol I once told you about, which the gods gave to mankind but was lost, a symbol of writing and knowledge, a reminder that the gods are always sending us messages, that we are to write these down for future generations. I believe Shubat has guided me all this time—to the archive, to the wall in Sumer, to the plain of Karmel where he made his wishes known to me. Leah, never has my vision been more clear, my purpose more defined! For this is how I will save the Brotherhood, Leah, I know this now. By replacing the powerless Solar Eye with the more-powerful and ancient tree with serpents and wings."

His grip tightened on her arm and he moved her away from the hearing of others. In a low voice he said, "But first we must save Ugarit and your family. And we must travel with extreme haste. Did you see Pharaoh confer with his general just now? They did not keep their voices low and so I heard what he said. It was an order for the general to ride swiftly to the coast and give Admiral Hayna orders to set sail for Ugarit. Leah, Thutmose has ordered the admiral and the Egyptian fleet to set fire to the city, to destroy Ugarit and its citizens entirely. And I fear that with southerly winds at the back of their sails, Pharaoh's warships will arrive before we, on our horses, can."

CHAPTER SEVENTEEN

Gathering Hannah and Esther and Saloma, and Aaron and Baruch, telling them to stay close to Nobu while they were in the city, Avigail led her family down the road and through the city gates, from where they made their way to the building of the High Court. Guards at the imposing entrance told Avigail to go down a narrow alley and knock on a green door, and so she embraced each of the women and boys and said, "The gods bless you, Nobu, for coming home to us. Remember your promise to take care of Esther and the boys. Now go inside, and you will shortly see me stand before the judges."

She went down the alley and knocked on the door. An irritated clerk, mumbling about the day's busy schedule, admitted her and showed her into a room where a variety of people were crowded onto benches, or pacing to and fro. They were mostly men, and all were accompanied by lawyers. Avigail stayed to the side, wringing her hands and praying that she would remember every word the dishonored Faris had spoken to her, and that she would not, in her nervousness, forget the order in which she was to say them.

Finally she was called into the great Hall of Law, which in typical Ugarit fashion was a grand chamber, with high ceilings and columns and a marble floor that shone. Avigail was brought to stand before a dais that supported three thrones, upon which sat the men whom she knew to be judges.

Their tall headdresses, decorated with gold fringe and silver tassels, were almost as regal as King Shalaaman's crown, their robes multicolored and layered, their sandals encrusted with gems. They sat in highback chairs with wooden arms carved into lions. Behind them, the wall was incised with the images of Ugarit's many gods, and lined with columns of cuneiform script, proclaiming the authority of this court over all disputed matters in the land, and declaring the fairness and compassion of the justice that was dispensed here.

A man in a long blue robe and carrying an ebony staff took a place beside the dais and cried in a loud voice, "Listen now, citizens of Ugarit, and give heed to the gods of Ugarit! The blessings of Dagon and Baal and Asherah be upon the heads of these men of justice. Invoke the gods and be humbled!" He turned to Zira's lawyer and said, "You may now address this court."

"Blessings of the gods, my lords," Zira's senior lawyer said in a loud voice. He had brought two other lawyers with him, men equally as handsomely attired as himself, and looking very important. "Please accept the humble apologies of my esteemed client, Zira Em Yehuda, who would not waste your lordships' valuable time. It is not her doing, however, that we impose ourselves upon your very important time today."

The senior judge, Uriah, smiled at Zira and said, "It is always a pleasure and a privilege to see our friend again, Zira Em Yehuda. How is your son? We have not had a chance to break bread with him of late, times being what they are."

Zira bowed and said, "Rab Yehuda is well, your lordship. The blessings of the gods upon you for asking."

The High Court was open to the public, and so the crowd of onlookers who jostled for space were eager to be entertained. Some snickered when they saw that the woman standing against Jotham's infamous sister was barefoot. Many more expressed dismay that she stood alone against Zira who was flanked by three lawyers in handsome robes and jeweled rings. The dismay was not for Avigail herself but for the fact that with Zira so heavily favored the match would not only be boring but there was also no point in making wagers on the outcome.

Standing at the rear of the hall, in Nobu's watchful protection, Avigail's family feared this did not bode well for the outcome, and they watched anxiously.

Judge Uriah swiveled his head toward Avigail, slowly, as if his headdress were the weight of all the laws and punishments of Ugarit. "And who are you?"

"The blessings of Baal, my lords. I am the mother of Elias the vintner, whose house lies along the main road south of the city."

He scowled. "Where is your lawyer?"

"I cannot afford one, my lord."

"Then where is your male kinsman who will speak for you?"

"I speak for myself, my lord."

The three judges looked at each other. "This is highly irregular. Surely there is a distant kinsman, or a neighbor in good standing. It is customary for men to speak before this tribunal."

"I have no male protector, no man who can represent me, my lords," Avigail said, praying her voice did not betray her fear. "I stand alone. But I believe this is permissible, though irregular, for I am a full citizen of Ugarit."

They conferred among themselves, and then Uriah said, "There is precedence, although long in the past. Very well, good woman, although we would advise you to seek the assistance of a male relative or friend, or to hire a spokesman, for that would be in your best interest, we will nonetheless allow you to stand up for yourself." He turned to the court scribe who sat with clay and stylus. "Let it be so noted."

Uriah asked, "What case do you bring before this court?"

Avigail nervously cleared her throat and said, "My Lords, I am unused to speaking in public. I am a woman raised in the old ways, leaving these matters to men. You know my son, Elias, and you knew my husband, Yosep, both men of honor. And so I am a woman of honor. Yet I am forced to set aside all propriety and dignity so that I might fight for the rights of my family. I beg you to indulge my lack of experience in addressing this lofty court."

"Yes, yes," Uriah said. "State your case."

"My lords, this woman, Zira, and her brother Jotham defrauded my son by purchasing a loan contract he had with the bankers and then presenting my son with a collection note that is ten times the original amount. Now this woman has taken my home and threatens to sell me and my family into slavery."

Judge Uriah's thick black eyebrows arched. "This is a serious accusation. How does Zira Em Yehuda respond?"

"It is nonsense, my lords," Zira's lawyer said. "The accounting is honest and accurate. Elias could not pay the amount and therefore the holder of his note has the right to take his property. That is, his villa, winery, and family. His mother is acting dishonorably."

"It would seem so," the judge said sternly. "I advise you to tread carefully and invoke the gods, my good woman, for you impugn Zira's reputation and that of her brother, both of whom have high standing in this city. Have you proof of your accusation?"

"A record of the original loan transaction is in the bank archive." Avigail drew in a deep breath, praying that she recited to the judge exactly the words Faris had spoken to her. "I request the right to examine it and compare it to the collection note."

The judge frowned. "You do not have that right. No ordinary citizen does, and certainly no woman. Bank records can be examined only by a man who is head of a house. Otherwise the archives would be overrun with citizens who feel themselves cheated, which is most of the population of Ugarit."

The onlookers roared with laughter, and when the noise died down, the high judge said, "Where is your son's copy of the loan agreement?"

"It was destroyed, my lord, and the bank's copy, which Jotham purchased, is in Zira's hands, but she will not let me see it to compare it to the collection note. But I have been advised that the bank keeps a running account of all transactions that take place there, with names, amounts and the month the transaction took place. I wish to examine that record."

Avigail tipped her chin. "And I do have the right to examine official documents, my lord, for I am the head of a house. And I am no ordinary citizen. I belong to a family of high standing, as my lords well know."

One of the other judges leaned forward and said in an incredulous tone, "Of which house do you claim to be the head?"

"My own."

A stunned silence filled the hall. Zira spoke up. "You do not have a house, Avigail. You are part of your son's house. And besides, no woman is head of a house."

"I am now the head of my son's house, and, because he is absent, I have a right to call it my own house."

Zira could not keep from speaking, despite words of caution from her lawyer. "And who made you the head of his house?"

"You did, when you forced Elias to sell himself into slavery."

Zira waved an impatient hand. "You cannot be the head of the house, for Elias might still be alive and might come back."

"Nevertheless, I am the head of the house and therefore I claim it as my own."

When the hall erupted in heated talk and angry shouts, guards stepped forward and gestured for silence.

Zira turned to the judges and said, "My lords, must we waste time with this charade? Avigail is merely stalling the inevitable."

One of the other judges said, "Em Yehuda is right. This woman's claim is preposterous."

"And anyway," Zira snapped impatiently. "Elias left more than four years ago. If your claim is legal, why are you only just now making it?"

"Circumstances have changed," Avigail said. Recalling what Faris had told her, the second of the three things she must remember, she addressed the judges. "My lords, has the king not decreed that every male citizen is officially a recruit in the army? Has the king not declared a state of war?"

Uriah pursed his lips. "He has."

"And is there not an ancient law on the books that states, in times of war, when a house is robbed of its menfolk and only women are left, that the senior woman may claim that house and call it her own?"

He gave her a long, thoughtful look, his lips working beneath his moustache. "It is interesting that you should know this, Avigail Em Elias, for it is an old law and one that has not been invoked in a very long time. However, although we are not yet technically at war, the law pertains, for men are indeed being called to prepare for battle. It is an ancient law that dates back to the days when the cities of Canaan were constantly at war and many houses were lost when the men were killed. And so provision was made in such emergencies, that a woman could call herself head of a house so that bloodlines did not die out. What is the house that you head?"

"That of Avigail Isha Yosep."

Zira turned to her lawyer. "Speak up, man. These claims are ridiculous."

Her lawyer cleared his throat and said, "She is within her rights, dear lady. There is just such a law."

"And so I claim my right to inspect—"

"You are Habiru," Zira snapped. "You are not even Canaanite. You have no rights before this court."

Avigail leveled her eyes at Zira and said, "Why do you say that when all of Ugarit knows that I am a descendant of King Ozzediah? We can send to Jericho for the records if you wish proof. King Ozzediah was my mother's forefather."

Zira shifted on her feet. "But—but all of Ugarit knows you are Habiru!"

"Based on what?"

Zira opened her mouth but could not speak. The scandalous news of Rakel's deathbed confession had been leaked by the priest-of-the-dying, who was sworn to confidentiality. She dared not reveal that he was her source. "It's just well known, that's all," she said peevishly.

Avigail turned away from Zira and said to the judges in a loud, confident voice the third demand which Faris the dissolute lawyer had given her, "As the head of my own house, and as a descendent of a king, I claim the right to take my case before King Shalaaman."

Zira gasped. "You dare!"

The crowd erupted in cheers and money began to change hands in eager bets. The guards stepped forward with spears and clouted those in the front, while at the rear, Nobu exchanged smiles of encouragement with Esther.

Zira turned to her lawyer. "Say this cannot be!"

He cleared his throat again, nervously. "This is all true, my lady. Avigail has these rights. My lords," Zira's lawyer said. "May I have a moment with my client?"

They stepped away and engaged in urgent whispering. Avigail caught a few words. The lawyer: "You said . . . no challenge . . . Habiru . . ." Zira: "I did not think she would . . ."

"May we continue?" Uriah called out, bringing Zira and her

lawyer back before the three jurists. "Avigail Isha Yosep, have you anything else to add to your claims?"

"I do, my lords. When the bogus collection note is examined, it will be discovered that the man who forged the illegal tablet is Zira's own son, his seal is affixed to it."

The judges gasped and looked at one another in shock. "My good woman, do you realize you are accusing the Rab of the Brotherhood?"

"I do."

Again, the crowd burst into cheers for the woman who stood alone against a powerful woman and her three lawyers.

"How dare you!" Zira cried, and Avigail saw that she had gone pale.

Calmly, Avigail said, "I will drop my claims if you give me back my house and leave me and my family in peace."

The paleness was suddenly flushed with a red tide that rose from Zira's neck to her forehead. She turned to the judges, "She has no right to impugn my son's reputation. She has no right to take her claims to King Shalaaman. My lords, would you make a mockery of this court? Would you appear weak before all these people? Pass your judgment upon this slanderous woman here and now. Perhaps if I were to ask my brother to support me," she added pointedly and no one missed the veiled threat, Uriah in particular.

As he and Zira locked eyes, Avigail remembered what Faris had said about Zira and her son holding secret, damning information over the senior judge of Ugarit's High Court. Silence filled the hall as everyone held a collective breath. Uriah finally tore his eyes away from Zira and scanned the faces in the crowd, the guards lining the walls, the scribes and clerks, and finally Avigail herself. He seemed to everyone to be weighing something in his mind—something beyond the legalities presently laid before him—and when he finally spoke, the spectators detected an unusual tightness in Uriah's voice. "This woman's claims are legitimate. She has the right to be heard by the king. We will summon the bank record and we will transfer this case to the throne of Ugarit."

"But my lords," Zira pleaded.

Judge Uriah did not meet her eye as he said, "The gods have spoken."

Out in the colonnaded hall, Zira wore a thunderous expression on her face. She argued with her lawyers that Avigail had not earned the right to stand before the king. When they assured her it was all fair and legal, she said to Avigail, "Apparently old judges are determined to live by old laws, and there is nothing I can do about that. But do not think you have won a victory. I will state my case very plainly to Shalaaman, and I will send for more lawyers if I must."

Zira was determined not to have the extortion exposed, or her son's involvement in it. But she was confident that, although Shalaaman might favor Avigail because her granddaughter was his demon-charmer, not even he would dare to flout the law for his own interests. And he especially would not do so in a crowded throne room. "We will go at once to the palace," she said archly to Avigail, "and take our place in the outer hall. I will stand there for seven days if I must, to clear my family's name of this dirt you have smeared on it."

As Zira hurried off with her counselors in tow, Avigail waved to Nobu and he brought the family through the crowd. "Audiences before the king begin at noon," she said quietly. "I will stay and wait to be called with Zira. Nobu, take the others home and await word from me. Take heart, the gods are with us."

As they neared the villa, Daveed and Leah watched for soldiers who might be patrolling in the area. They had ridden steadily and swiftly for days, but now they slowed and approached with caution. Daveed might have been branded a deserter, which in times of war meant execution without a trial. And judging by the military camps and troops drilling outside the city walls, King Shalaaman was clearly preparing for war.

They were alone with only their horses and a pack animal. The Egyptian escort had abandoned them outside the town of Kadesh, grousing that they did not want to be soldiers any more and would seek passage on a ship bound for islands in the Great Sea.

A quick search inside the house found no one home. Fearing the worst, Leah said to Daveed, "I will go to the slave market. You go to the palace and tell the king of the Egyptian fleet."

To minimize the risk of drawing attention to themselves, they left the horses at the villa—as few private citizens rode horses—and joined the foot traffic streaming toward the gate. Judging by the numbers of people carrying all their possessions, many bringing children, Daveed and Leah realized families were seeking safety within the city walls.

When they saw that soldiers were stopping everyone at the gate to check identities and search bundles and packs, Daveed and Leah continued around, taking a road that followed the city wall to the eastern gate. Here they saw more people—but they were leaving the city rather than entering. "The people fear that war is coming," Daveed observed. "These are heading for cities in the east, hoping to find safety there."

"We have to get inside," Leah said, noting that soldiers guarded this gate as well. There would be soldiers at the northern gate, too, and most likely sentries watched the streets that came up from the harbor. "I will tell them who I am," she said as they neared the great archway that could be sealed with towering wooden doors in the event of attack. "I will tell them that King Shalaaman will wish to see me at once."

But when she gave the guard her name, a scribe consulted a clay tablet containing a list of names and informed the officer in charge that the two were to be arrested.

Four guards with spears and shields escorted them through the crowded streets, where Leah heard talk of war on everyone's lips. How far away were the Egyptian forces? they asked one another. Did Ugarit have enough manpower guarding the southern road? Leah saw in alarm that people were streaming toward the docks, where she suspected they hoped to find refuge on boats anchored there. And it made her blood run cold to think of the mighty armada that sailed the seas closer and closer to Ugarit's vulnerable harbor.

The prison, like that of Megiddo, had been built long ago beneath the palace, with dark stone stairs leading down to a dank subterranean maze of corridors and cells. Daveed and Leah protested their innocence, demanded to speak to a higher authority, and tried to make the guards understand that they must be taken to Shalaaman at once. But the prison was crowded with men who had been arrested on charges of espionage, treason, sedition, insubordination, fomenting revolution.

The imprisoned called out from their cells, creating a nightmarish cacophony of wails, shouts, protests of innocence. Daveed's voice was barely heard above the din as the wooden door closed in his face and they heard the bar fall into place to lock them in.

Leah pressed herself to the door and called out through the small opening, while Daveed made a swift inspection of the cell, feeling his way along the moss-covered walls, hearing rats scurry from his feet.

He came back to Leah. "There is no way out."

She could barely see his face, so little torchlight came through the small window in the door. Daveed took her into his arms and held her tightly as she trembled with fear.

Daveed was a deserter. In war times it was an offense punishable by summary execution, but only the king could give the order. "Shalaaman will not give the order," he said, "when he understands that I left the city in order to bring you back."

W hat news from Pharaoh Thutmose?" King Shalaaman asked sharply when Rab Yehuda entered the chamber.

His Highness was getting ready for his daily audiences in the throne room. But as slaves oiled his hair and beard and helped him into purple robes, he was in ill-humor. He had not slept well and there was a familiar tightness in his chest.

"Where are my sons?" Shalaaman cried. "Where is my demon-charmer, Leah? Why has the Egyptian not sent ransom letters?"

Yehuda bowed respectfully and said, "All royal couriers have arrived, Your Highness, and there is still no correspondence from Megiddo."

As he watched a darkness flush the king's face, Yehuda decided that there were many benefits to being Rab of the Brotherhood. It certainly made the climb to the throne much easier. Reading and crushing tablets from Pharaoh Thutmose, who had sent numerous offers of a peace treaty in exchange for the princes and the demon-charmer, was a luxury only Yehuda himself could enjoy, as a lesser scribe would not dare such an audacious intervention. "I am sorry, Your Highness. Perhaps a letter will arrive tomorrow."

"I want my sons back!" Shalaaman shouted, startling his slaves and attendants who knew him to be an even-tempered man.

"My king," Yehuda said, "you must calm yourself. The demons are always waiting, they wait for your weakness."

"I am not a man to be ignored or slighted! That devil who sits on the throne of Egypt will pay for these insults—" Shalaaman grabbed his chest and struggled to draw breath. His face turned red. His eyes stretched wide. "I cannot—" He thrust out his chest and made a wheezing sound. "I cannot—"

Doctors and magicians were summoned at once. And Jotham, who had had a private meeting with the king, was immediately at his sovereign's side. When the healers and wonder-workers arrived, they set fire to candles and lamps and torches and incense, pumping acrid smoke into the air, filling the chamber with eye-stinging fumes.

Servants helped Shalaaman to his bed, easing him down as he fought to breathe. Physicians began to chant, their drone mingling with the heady aroma of sandalwood and frankincense.

Yehuda stood back in the shadows, watching. When a servant came from the outer hall and whispered something to him, the Rab turned on his heel and hurried from the chamber.

Hearing footsteps in the corridor, Leah went to the window in the door and called out. "Please let the king know that his demon-charmer is here!"

To her shock, the melancholy visage of the Rab of the Brotherhood appeared in the torchlight. Yehuda's smile was unsettlingly cold. "You should know that Shalaaman has fallen ill," he said. "It is only a matter of time. Once he succumbs to the demon, I will be king, and my first order will be your execution."

Daveed said, "You must let me speak to him. I have vital information regarding the Egyptian forces."

"There is nothing you have to offer that is of any consequence. When I am in command, which will be soon, I will see to it that Ugarit is well protected. My first order as supreme commander of this city will be to recall the troops Shalaaman is foolishly wasting in places they are not needed—on the cliffs over the coast and guarding the harbor and waterfront. As soon as I am proclaimed king, I will order the immediate recall of those troops and deploy them to the south of the city."

"You must not do that! Listen to me—"

"Of course, we are all praying for Shalaaman's recovery. My uncle Jotham is at the king's side, asking mercy of the gods."

Leah exchanged a glance with Daveed, and an idea came to her.

"Rab Yehuda," she said, "Please tell your uncle I have vital information for him."

Yehuda's eyebrows rose. "What information could you possibly

371

have that would interest my uncle?" His lips lifted in another cold smile. "Do not think that offering yourself to Jotham will get you released from this cell. He lost interest in you long ago."

"Daveed and I were given secret intelligence regarding Egypt's new iron-smelting process."

When Yehuda said nothing, Leah added, "You did not think the Egyptians would learn the secret? Once the word was out, that the Hittites had found a way to extract metal from iron ore, a metal superior to bronze, that Egypt would not hear of it? But there is something in their process that Jotham does not know about. Something that makes Egyptian iron far stronger."

"You can tell me. I am, after all, soon to be king of Ugarit."

"I will tell only Jotham."

Yehuda laughed mirthlessly. "It will not buy you your freedom. And do not try to bargain with my uncle. He will extract your knowledge by means of torture. Which," Yehuda added before turning away, "might be amusing."

The royal bedchamber was mayhem. Military scouts came and went with reports. Courtiers milled about and wrung their hands. Physicians and wonder-workers raised their voices in loud chants as incense filled the air with dense smoke. Shalaaman lay in bed gasping and wheezing, his chest making strange whistling sounds when he exhaled, while the priests prayed and shook rattles to frighten the demon from Shalaaman's chest.

Jotham was there. He had seen his nephew receive a whispered message from a servant and then leave the royal bedchamber. He wondered what could be so important to take Yehuda away at this critical hour. Jotham knew his ambitious nephew was praying that Shalaaman would be taken by the choking demon. Others in the bedchamber felt the same way—men who would profit if Yehuda were crowned king. For himself, Jotham did not care who sat on the throne; war was good business. Even if Egypt were not to attack, Ugarit would continue to make iron weapons and stockpile them against such a threat. His allegiance would be to any man who wore the crown.

"Bring more sacred incense!" cried the senior physician, and attendants hurried in with censors, to clog the air with more clouds of acrid, stinging smoke.

Yehuda slipped into the royal bedchamber and asked one of the lesser physicians about the king's progress. "He is worsening, my lord."

The Rab looked across the smoky room at his uncle, who stood with Shalaaman's military advisers. He thought about what the girl Leah had said in her prison cell. Although Yehuda expected soon to be king, Jotham was still a very powerful man in Ugarit. Perhaps it would not hurt to curry a little of his uncle's favor at this crucial point. And knowing the Egyptians' metallurgy secret would only help Ugarit.

"Uncle," Yehuda said, walking up to Jotham and the officers. "There is something you should know."

As he listened to what his nephew had to say, Jotham's expression went from one of displeasure—he did not like standing about waiting for a king to die—to one of surprise and then curiosity. With a word to his companions, the fat shipbuilder turned on his heel and hurried out.

At that moment, the king took a turn for the worse, noisily sucking for air as his eyes bulged, making everyone think of a fish flopping on a boat deck. The generals held a brief conference in low voices. Thinking of Egyptian spies who must already be speeding their way south with news of this turn of events—Ugarit's king suddenly ill, leaving the city vulnerable—they sent orders for the lookouts and troops to be recalled from the coast and the harbor, to be deployed along the city's southern wall.

Yehuda smiled. It was precisely the command he himself would have given.

I am afraid, Daveed," Leah said in the darkness of their cell. "Yehuda will not let me near the king. He will allow Shalaaman to die!"

He held her close, and she drew comfort from his strength. "Shubat did not bring me this far—he did not save me from the arrows and slings of the Habiru—to die in a prison. The gods have a purpose for us, my love. Of this I am certain."

In the outer corridor, they heard a familiar voice suddenly calling for attention. Footsteps echoed along the stone floor, and presently a round face appeared in the small square opening of the cell door.

"What is it you wish to tell me?" Jotham barked impatiently.

"Let us out of this cell," Daveed replied, "and you will find out."

"I will not bargain with you. My nephew said you have information about the Egyptians' iron ore process. Tell me or I will leave you to the rats."

Before Daveed could reply, Leah went to the door and said, "Jotham, you know me."

"Hmmph! Dagon save me from you. I wish I had never set foot in Elias's house seven unlucky years ago."

"Jotham, Daveed and I made friends with Pharaoh Thutmose."

"Bull dung! Do you think me stupid? Dagon protect me."

"I was abducted and held hostage, as you well know. Daveed came to Megiddo to rescue me, and through a series events, he won the confidence of Egypt's king and was given the opportunity to witness Egypt's might with his own eyes, that he could report back and convince Shalaaman to surrender peacefully."

Jotham pursed his lips. "Go on."

Now Daveed stepped forward and described what he saw from the peak of Karmel, the mighty fleet anchored in a bay on the coast of the Great Sea. As soon as he mentioned ships, he had Jotham's interest. And as he described their unique design, adding that they were the first of their kind in the world—ships built specifically for combat— Jotham's interest was complete.

"Warships!" he declared, his small eyes glinting with fresh new ideas. War was indeed profitable business.

"But that is not all, my lord," Daveed said. "Thutmose gave the order for the fleet to sail to Ugarit. The ships are due to arrive and the admiral has orders to set fire to all vessels in Ugarit's harbor. Jotham, all your ships will be torched."

"Halla!" Jotham hissed. "Pray for me! I have few vessels out of Ugarit at this time. Egypt will destroy nearly my entire fleet! My precious beauties!" His eyes bugged out. "And the generals have ordered all military protection withdrawn from the port!"

"Then take me to Shalaaman," Leah said. "If there is still a breath in his body, there is a chance I can save him. If Shalaaman is restored, he will rescind the order and deploy heavy protection to the harbor."

* * *

O nce word of the king's illness left the palace, it spread through the city with a life of its own. In the great audience chamber, where foreign dignitaries awaited Shalaaman's appearance, as well as ambassadors bringing gifts and treaties, and ordinary citizens with claims before the throne, Zira and her lawyers stood anxiously with Avigail near the front of the waiting throng. The message was passed from one person to the next until the murmured rumor became a dull roar. Now even the courtiers arranged around the throne exchanged worried glances.

The king was ill.

When the doors to the bedchamber swung open, and Jotham marched in, the two prisoners behind him, Yehuda bellowed, "Arrest those two!"

But Jotham stepped forward and held up his hand. To Leah he said, "Quickly, go to the king."

She ran to the bed and saw in alarm Shalaaman's distressed state. His face was red but his lips had turned blue. Swollen veins stood out on his neck and forehead. She saw that every time he tried to inhale, the skin behind his collar bones was sucked in. "Remove all this incense," she said to the priests and physicians. "Bring ostrich feather fans to clear the air around the king."

When no one moved, Jotham shouted, "Do as she says! The demon-charmer will once more save the king!"

"Do not move, any of you," Yehuda cried. "This man is a deserter and is to be executed for treason. And this girl ran off with her lover, abandoning our beloved king."

Among those gathered in the bedchamber to pray for Shalaaman was Chief Judge Uriah, and he stepped forward now in his impressive robes and tasseled headdress to say in a sonorous voice, "Shalaaman has not yet gone to the gods, Yehuda, and you are not yet king."

Uriah strode across the room and people fell back to open the path. When the Chief Judge reached the Rab he leaned forward and said quietly, "Your days of blackmail are over. I will no longer be intimidated by your threats to expose my shameful secret. And I will see to it that should our beloved Shalaaman go to the gods this day, you will never sit on the throne of Ugarit."

Judge Uriah turned to the wonder-workers surrounding the bed and said, "Remove the incense and bring the fans."

As the others hurried away, carrying censors and braziers and smoking candles, Leah sat on the edge of the bed and took the king's hand. She spoke soothingly to him as he struggled to suck in air. Ostrich fans were brought and soon the air began to clear. "The demon will leave your chest, Your Majesty," Leah said in a calm voice, pressing his hand between hers.

Soon, before the staring eyes of the onlookers, Shalaaman's respirations grew less strained. They watched in wonder as the king they so loved began to improve.

Leah asked the priests to help the king to sit up and to help him lean slightly forward. "Pray with me, Your Majesty," she said soothingly. "Let the gods hear your prayer."

But he still fought for breath, his chest making alarming hissing sounds. Everyone knew it was the demon fighting Leah's charm.

"Open the drapes and bring a chair so the king can be taken to the balcony."

Six eager courtiers brought an ornate gold chair, and a wheezing Shalaaman was helped into it. They carried him out onto the balcony where a golden morning sun bathed all of Ugarit in a warm, blessed glow.

Shalaaman's respirations grew calmer, his color returned. Leah sat with him, assisted him with a slow, rhythmic cadence, saying, "Fill your lungs slowly, now empty them slowly. Take control of your body, Your Majesty. Take mastery over yourself. Show the demon that you are the king."

Gradually, the wheezing and hissing subsided, and Shalaaman was breathing normally again. The physicians examined him and declared the choking demon to be gone. The majority of those in attendance shouted loud praises to the gods, while a few quietly slipped out of the room.

"I thank Dagon," Shalaaman said as he soaked in the warm sunshine and inhaled the fresh air from the sea, "that he brought you back to me, Leah. How was it Thutmose let you go?"

"It is a long and interesting story, Your Majesty, but first we have urgent news for you."

Daveed stepped forward and gave his report on the Egyptian fleet. Yehuda protested that it was a lie, but the generals became nervous.

Daveed's details of the ships were too accurate. How would a scribe know such things? They agreed that Egypt posed a great threat from the sea, and that Ugarit was woefully vulnerable on its unprotected shore. Several officers hurried out to redeploy the troops along the shore and to see that the harbor was watched by sentries.

Though greatly weakened and in need of rest, Shalaaman called for Jotham to stand before him. "Take your fastest ship and sail out to meet the Egyptian fleet. Fly a flag of truce. Do whatever you must to prevent the burning of our harbor."

As Jotham hurried out, he sent a look Leah's way. It startled her. It was a look of . . . admiration.

Leah ordered cups of cold water brought to the king, and when the wheezing threatened to start up again, she calmed him with a soothing voice and his panic subsided. "Your Majesty must periodically leave this smoke-filled chamber and inhale the fresh air on the roof. You must expose your chest to the blessed rays of the sun, for the choking demon cannot resist its light and heat. In this way you will stay healthy for many years to come, and if I am needed, you have only to call and I will be at your side. Asherah is with us."

The sun was near its zenith when a breathless messenger came running into the bedchamber to drop to his knees, hail the great King Shalaaman, and cry in a panicked voice that Egyptian forces were taking possession of the harbor and commencing a march into the city.

Panic erupted in the bedchamber, but Shalaaman had the strength to call for order and to calm his courtiers and physicians. To Leah he said, "I will receive the Egyptians in my audience hall. I cannot let the enemy see me in this state. Help us, Leah."

More rumors flew through the audience hall so that Avigail no longer knew what to believe: the king had recovered, the king was dead, the king had run away to an eastern province. The guards kept the mob in order, but tension was building as the noon hour came and went and the king did not make his daily appearance. Avigail was wondering if she should go home and make sure Nobu and the family were safe, when the air was filled with the brassy blare of trumpets. All heads turned to the draperies on the right of the throne, heavy purple fabric through which Ugarit's kings had always made their grand entrances.

The hall fell silent. Zira and Avigail held their breath as they watched the drapes. And then they saw Judge Uriah, with his impressive gold and silver headdress and multicolored robes, enter through the drapes. Behind him marched two royal guards, whose shields were covered in gold, then came the king's familiar courtiers, and presently Shalaaman himself. The audience erupted in cheers at the sight of their beloved monarch who, although walking slowly and pale-faced, was nonetheless splendidly arrayed in purple garments edged in gold, the ancient gem-encrusted grown of Ugarit on his lofty brow. He marched with dignity and poise toward his throne, and when he stopped and turned, all of Ugarit forgave him for faltering a little. He had just come from one of his demon-seizures.

Then they saw the young woman at his side, known to many as his demon-charmer. And a few saw a familiar face in the man walking with her—Daveed the scribe from Lagash. Behind them came Yehuda, famed Rab of the Brotherhood. They took places around the throne and Shalaaman slowly lowered himself onto the mighty chair from which generations of monarchs had ruled Ugarit. He raised his hand to call upon the gods to bless this assemblage, but before he could say a word, the great towering double doors of the audience hall swung open and a most impressive man strode in.

Avigail whispered, "Halla!" and traced the sacred sign of Asherah in the air when she recognized the man as being Egyptian—and someone of high rank. It soon spread through the crowd, as everyone whispered at the man's passage over the marble floor from the double doors to the throne, that this was Admiral Hayna, commander of a fleet that was rumored to be the greatest in the world.

And he had come to conquer Ugarit for Pharaoh Thutmose.

At his side was Jotham the shipbuilder who walked as sedately as his corpulence would allow, and behind them strode what could only be the admiral's understaff, men in linen kilts and white cloth head-dresses, like Hayna himself. Underdressed, in the eyes of Ugarit which enjoyed a much cooler climate than the land of the Nile. And with the leathery tanned skin of men who spent their lives at sea.

The hall was so silent one could hear the soft whisper of the Egyptian's sandals on the floor. All eyes followed the impressive visitor, who despite a lack of colorful and formal dress, nonetheless struck awe in the hearts of the onlookers—if only for the threat he personified. He came to a halt before the throne, stood for a long moment, silent and unmoving, and then, with poise and grace, inclined himself from the waist—not subserviently, everyone was quick to note, but in a manner of respect—and called out, "The gods of Egypt bring blessings to the gods of Canaan! The living god of Egypt, Pharaoh Thutmose, brings greetings to the King of Ugarit, King Shalaaman, one whose name means 'peace.'"

The crowd was stunned. Admiral Hayna spoke Canaanite. He had also addressed Shalaaman in friendship. He also carried no weapon, everyone now noticed. In fact, he did not seem to have come to conquer the city at all.

Still, everyone waited for Shalaaman's reaction. The moment stretched as a warm afternoon breeze wafted into the magnificent hall, stirring ostrich fans and the hems of gowns and cloaks. Near the front, Zira and Avigail stood in awe, briefly forgetting their personal conflict in the face of what they knew was an encounter to be talked about for many years to come.

They had lived in fear of the Egyptian threat for so long that a peaceful resolution had not occurred to them.

Only Jotham knew the truth: that Hayna had given his ship captains the order to volley fire at the city when Jotham showed the flag of truce. Hayna boarded Jotham's beloved *Edrea*, as if taking possession of the vessel, and had listened to the shipbuilder's passionate plea to spare Ugarit, delicately reminding Hayna that a city full of riches was more profitable to Pharaoh than one razed to ashes—subtly pointing out that admirals could profit as well. And so Hayna had accepted Jotham's invitation to pay a diplomatic visit to King Shalaaman.

The king now rose, under Leah's watchful eye. He was shaky but in control, and his voice was strong as he called out over the heads of the gathered throng, "We welcome our honored Egyptian guests, and we offer the blessings of our gods upon our brother in Egypt, Pharaoh Thutmose. Truly this is a day of days!"

Low murmurs began, and then people grew brave and spoke more loudly, until shouts rose to the ceiling calling upon the blessings of the gods in this momentous hour. While the citizens of Ugarit gave themselves up to intense relief and started making plans for feasting and sending for relatives and family members who had fled the city, while strangers embraced one another, and even Zira and Avigail exchanged a sigh of relief, Shalaaman and Hayna—Canaanite and Egyptian—eyed one another in the unspoken understanding of kings and military men everywhere: we will make a good show of friendship, but later we will argue the terms of our new treaty. We are not your vassals, Shalaaman's regal stare said, and Hayna's eyes, heavily rimmed in black kohl, sent the silent assurance that Egypt and Canaan were never going to be "brothers."

It was a shaky peace, but peace nonetheless. And even though everyone knew the Egyptian fleet would sail into the harbor and anchor there, showing Pharaoh's presence, Ugarit could look forward to a new era of alliance and prosperity.

Judge Uriah, Jotham the shipbuilder, and Shalaaman's generals and high council gathered together to escort the esteemed guests from the throne room to the special chambers within, where negotiations and politicking would begin. But the crowd did not care. Danger came, danger went, and the cheering did not stop.

And so no one heard Yehuda give a sudden cry, or see him fall to the floor. But when Zira ran to him and took him into her arms, those around him stared in revulsion at the flailing limbs and foaming mouth. No one moved as they witnessed the seizure that many had thought only to be rumor.

When Yehuda finally lay still, guards picked him up and carried him out, Zira and her lawyers following.

Leah spoke briefly to Shalaaman, who gave her a nod, so that she ran from the dais to take Avigail into her arms. "Praise the gods," her grandmother said, "I thought I would never see you again!" They kissed and embraced, and tears flowed down their cheeks.

And then King Shalaaman called for silence and commanded Leah to stand before him. "The gods smile upon you, daughter. They have restored you safely to my presence. Once before I rewarded you for ridding me of the demon, and so again I reward you."

But Leah said, "Asherah is my witness, I will serve you, Your Majesty, and help you with your affliction. But I will not be your prisoner again. I must be allowed to go home. That is all I ask in reward."

The crowd was stunned by her tone and manner—that a mere girl should stand up to the king in such a way. But they did not know that Leah had stood in the presence of the mighty and powerful Hatshepsut, and had seen how the mere presence of the queen instilled respect, admiration, and confidence in her subjects. For this, Leah sent a silent prayer to the gods, thanking them for granting her that brief sojourn in Megiddo.

They were gathered in the front garden of the villa, enjoying the summer day. Hannah and Saloma, in nice clothes again, laughed as Baruch and Aaron ran in and out of the flowers while Avigail sat contentedly in the sunshine watching Daveed and Leah walk among the grapevines. The property was theirs again. Zira had returned all deeds and the forged collection note.

The soldiers were gone from the fields outside the city as a peace treaty had been signed between Ugarit and Egypt. Everyone had heard that Thutmose had departed from Megiddo to return to Egypt and commence his new works project, using the labor of thousands of prisoners of war. Admiral Hayna was gone, having taken much of his fleet back to Egypt, while leaving three armed vessels and a group of Pharaoh's representatives. King Shalaaman sent a diplomatic mission to Thebes to negotiate for the release of the twin princes. In exchange, King Shalaaman promised to erect a temple in Ugarit to the devotion of Pharaoh Thutmose, Egypt's living god.

Avigail no longer feared the Egyptian presence in Ugarit. She realized now that change was not something to be feared because change was not necessarily bad. She had won her court trial by finding the courage to step outside her traditional role and flout old-fashioned ways. One can change with the times and still hold cherished traditions, she thought. In fact, the melding of two cultures might even bring out the best in those cultures so that the sum is greater than the parts. A richer culture emerges, and all citizens benefit. Just look at Hannah and Saloma, looking so elegant and cool, Avigail thought, despite the summer heat, in their new dresses of imported linen. So much better than wool!

Not everyone had fared as well. Yehuda's practice of forgery and bribery had been exposed and he was arrested. But because of his high status, and because King Shalaaman was in a forgiving mood, Yehuda was allowed to stay under house arrest for the rest of his life, with his mother Zira reportedly tending to him night and day. Jotham, on the other hand, was seldom at his oceanside villa, preferring to oversee the rapid growth of his ironworks outside of town, and now a new endeavor: building warships.

Avigail smiled and closed her eyes in the sunlight. *Never again will our home be taken from us.* In a few days, Ugarit would be celebrating the new year. The house of Elias would be open to all friends in a grand feast. Avigail thought: *we will serve pork chops and suckling pig and blood sausage.*

She sighed in contentment. Events set in motion long ago, the night Jericho fell, had brought Avigail and her family to this wondrous moment of joy, peace, and security. The world was almost perfect again. With Daveed's help, she had sent letters of inquiry to Babylon, asking after a vintner who had purchased a slave named Elias. Soon, Avigail was certain, they would receive news.

Esther came out of the house then, dressed in shades of pink, and went straight to the front gate to look up the road toward the city. Avigail knew whom her youngest granddaughter was watching for. She had seen the gentle friendship bloom between Esther and Nobu, who was no longer a slave. Daveed had gone to the courts and drawn up documents declaring Nobu a freed man, and now he was looking to establish himself as a barber in the city.

Avigail smiled and shook her head. The gods never ceased to amaze her with their plans—she would not be surprised if another wedding were soon to take place in this house . . .

Daveed and Leah walked among the vines, talking about all the things they had seen, and the life together that lay before them. Daveed was now the Rab of the Brotherhood, and he knew it would be a monumental task restoring honor and righteousness, and that it would perhaps take years or even generations before his new writing system was accepted. But gradually, he knew, students would come back to the Brotherhood and embrace the swifter, easier, and more efficient script.

In order to teach my new code, he thought as he walked hand in hand with Leah, I must name the symbols so that they are easy to remember. I will begin with the first, and because it is the sound A, I will name it alep. The second, because it represents B, I will call bet . . .

Esther called out, and Daveed turned to see Nobu arriving at the gate, puffing beneath the summer heat. The former slave paused to greet Esther and give her a small gift he had purchased in the city, and then he joined Daveed and Leah under the shady vines. "It was ready, as you said, Master," Nobu said as he handed a small leather pouch to Daveed. "I dared to take a look. It is worthy of the highest gods!"

Daveed smiled and handed the pouch to Leah. "You have the honor."

He had told her his plans, but Leah had not seen the final design, or what extra quality the silversmith's own skills and talent would bring to it. In excitement she opened the purse string and upended the pouch's content into the palm of her hand.

"Halla!" she whispered at the sight of the silver flashing in the sun. The pendent filled her palm, a fine piece of delicately worked silver, each facet of the design shining clearly and distinctly: the staff, the wings, the serpents coiling up. The ancient symbol of Shubat and of Ningishzida, the gods' own symbol of writing, wisdom, and healing, handed to humankind back in the mists of time. Revived in this bright summer of a new prosperity for Ugarit to bring new life to an ailing Brotherhood—the result of Daveed's epiphany on a bloody battlefield.

"By Asherah," Leah whispered. "It is beautiful."

Daveed laid his hand on Leah's cheek and kissed her. "It is a good symbol, my love, and when I create it on clay, and have it painted over doorways, and inscribe it in stone, then the power of the wings and the serpent and the tree will be called into existence, to fill the rooms and hallways and hearts and minds of the Brotherhood. Righteousness and honor cannot help but return to my brothers."

Taking the piece of jewelry and slipping it back into its protective pouch, Daveed said, "I realize now, my beloved Leah, that everything happens for a reason. Even tragedies can end in positive results. The purpose of my new script, I know now, is to be an instrument for reform. Just as the Brotherhood needed a new symbol, they needed a new way of writing. This was why the code came to me on the dawn of the rising of the White One. Without my new script the brothers would have remained tied to the old ways and therefore be vulnerable to a return to corruption. For this reason I will lift Shubat up to be the patron god of scribes and writing."

But no, he thought suddenly, recalling that dawn, four years ago, of remarkable revelations. It was not Shubat who spoke to me. It was the older, more powerful El Shadday—the Almighty—and his elohim who revealed the new script to me. When he had said the Day of the Book is coming.

What is the Book? Daveed wondered, imagining it to be something like the Tablet of Destinies, or the Scroll of the Ancients. When Shalaaman had completely recovered from his ordeal with the choking demon, and was meeting with Egyptian emissaries to work out a peace treaty, Daveed had informed him of the secret cache of treasures he had created in the archives, to protect priceless relics and tablets from being stolen or destroyed: slivers of wood from the Ark, that granted eternal life; a blue stone from the heavens that revealed the future; a dagger of mysterious metal that always pointed to the north—all the miraculous and wondrous treasures Daveed offered to Queen Hatshepsut in exchange for Leah's life. Shalaaman had marveled over the astonishing collection, and then had commissioned a special, secret vault to be built to hold it all. When demands came from Hatshepsut, reminding Shalaaman that the treasures were rightfully hers, Shalaaman responded with polite but evasive diplomacy—a dialogue, Daveed knew, that could continue for years. The treasure, Shalaaman had assured him, would always belong to Ugarit.

And perhaps someday, Daveed thought now, the Book promised by El Shadday, whatever it was, would join those ancient treasures.

Pausing beneath an arbor of healthy grapevines, he took Leah into his arms, and as she held tightly to her strong and handsome, brave and smart Daveed, her gaze went over his shoulder and past the white walls of the villa. And she saw a familiar figure coming up the road. A broad-shouldered man in a knee-length tunic and cloak, walking with a tall wooden staff and carrying a pack on his shoulder.

She stared in disbelief. "Father!"

Daveed turned around. "By Shubat! It is Elias!"

Now the others saw him, and as they all rushed to greet him, the laughing Canaanite was nearly pushed off his feet. "The gods are great!" he cried. "For they have restored me to my family."

But Avigail quickly drew back and said in horror, "My son, did you run away?" Runaway slaves were executed without trial.

"The man who bought me is fair-minded. When I made colorless wine for him, and his friends were eager to buy it, he asked me to show him the process, I said I would teach him my secret in exchange for my freedom." He showed her a tablet. "This is proof of my manumission."

The boys came shyly up. "This is Aaron, your son, and Baruch, your grandson."

Elias dropped to his knees and wept as he embraced them.

As Leah watched her family take turns kissing and embracing their returned loved one—father, grandfather, husband, son—she thought how seven years ago her perfect world had been thrown off balance by Zira's bad-luck words. They had triggered the preterm labor, which caused Leah to be disobedient, which enraged Jotham and set him on his path of revenge. Even Daveed's coming to Ugarit had stemmed from that fateful night.

But perhaps it was not entirely because of Zira's words, Leah thought now. Really, it was she herself who had set off the remarkable chain of events that brought them to this hour. One small act of disobedience. Had she turned back when her father commanded her to, had she not run out of the hospitality hall, none of the events that followed would have happened. Leah would have married Jotham. Daveed would never have come to Ugarit. Pharaoh Thutmose would have launched his attack, and Ugarit would have been reduced to ashes because she and Daveed would never have met Egypt's king, and ultimately saved the city and citizens of Ugarit.

Leah thought: But my strange and happy road does not end here. Per Hatshepsut's order, Chief Physician Reshef gave me the recipe for a medicinal eyewash that prevents blindness, as well as the spell that is to be chanted with its administration, and the protective Eye of Horus that Daveed will wear for the rest of his life. I will continue to collect such cures and healing formulas. I will search far and wide, and I will inscribe them on clay with Daveed's new script, to be stored away for future generations. And because the image of the serpents on a winged rod was the symbol of Ningishzida, Sumerian god of medicine, I will imprint that symbol onto my formulas so that people will know that the tablets contain the answers to good health and long life.

Thinking of the new symbol, she thought: I will have one fashioned of ivory and send it to Chief Physician Reshef in exchange for the gift he gave to me.

Thoughts of the Egyptian doctor made Leah turn to face the sea, and she knew beyond a doubt that soon more of Pharaoh's ships would be anchoring there for the first time in man's memory, a sign of the largest empire the world had ever known—a sign that more empires would rise and the world would never be the same again. And then she turned eastward and saw the great cloud of black smoke pluming up from the iron factory, and she thought of the new weapons being forged there, a sign of the new warfare to come. And she thought: Daveed's new emblem is not just about the Brotherhood or his new way of writing. It is a sign of the times.

We were born to see the sunset of the old world, and the sunrise of the new one. It frightened her a little, to wonder what new marvels lay ahead, but it excited her, too, to think of facing them with Daveed, and her family, at her side.

AUTHOR'S NOTE

Three fascinating historical mysteries inspired me to write *The Serpent and the Staff*.

The first is the namesake of the title: the Caduceus. The origins of this familiar symbol is lost in the mists of time. A snake, or two snakes, coiling up a tree or a rod, sometimes with wings, or flanked by angels or gryphons with wings, is very ancient and universal, found in Egypt and Mesopotamia long before the Greeks adopted the winged staff as the symbol of the god Mercury. The oldest-known image dates back four thousand years to ancient Sumer, where we find it carved into stone walls. No one knows what the symbol originally stood for, but it has come to represent healing and medicine (a bronze staff with serpents is found in the Old Testament when Moses used such an image to treat venomous snakebites). Today we see the serpent and the staff in hospitals, on ambulances, medicine bottles, oxygen tanks, prescription pads. I wonder what Daveed and Leah would make of it!

The second is the origins of the alphabet. Generally believed to have begun in ancient Egypt around 2,000 B.C.E., the first consonantal alphabet (that is, symbols standing for sounds rather than objects or ideas) is thought to represent the language of Semitic workers in Egypt. Biblically, this would mean the Israelites of Joseph's time. A thousand miles north, however, in the Syrian city of Ugarit, a secret alphabet emerged, known only to a handful of scribes in that ancient town. No one knows why this alphabet was developed or by whom, or why it was kept a secret. Both in Egypt and Mesopotamia, the traditional writing systems of the time were cumbersome and difficult to learn, being made up of thousands of symbols that each carried a variety of meanings. The alphabet seems a convenient and streamlined method of communicating—why keep it a secret?

My theory is that the scribes were jealously guarding their power over the rest of the population—after all, the man who can read and write has a vast advantage over those who cannot. But the new alphabet could not realistically remain a secret for long, and once that secret was out, once the ordinary citizens of Ugarit discovered that they, too, could obtain the power of reading and writing for themselves, word of the new code would have spread quickly, far and wide, being snatched up as if it were gold being tossed into the wind.

A few centuries later, a race called the Phoenicians would refine the new code even further, leading to the modern alphabet we use today.

One last note of interest regarding the invention of the alphabet: I find it significant that the first fragments of the new code were medical texts, cures, recipes for remedies. Recalling the old adage that necessity is the mother of invention, it makes sense to me that the first people to devise a cleaner and more streamlined way of writing, especially a way that left little room for error, would be in the field of medicine. Recording who owns which olive grove, or tallying up the number of goats a man owns—even the terms of a marriage contract—are not as vital or urgent as giving the right medicine to a sick child.

The third inspiration for this novel comes from people. Although Elias and his family, Daveed, Jotham and Zira, and King Shalaaman are all inventions of my imagination, two people really existed: Pharaoh Thutmose (whom Egyptologists call "the Napoleon of ancient Egypt") and his formidable aunt, Hatshepsut, known for her magnificent temple at Deir el-Bahri in Egypt (and yes, she did insist on being called "His Majesty"). While these two personages blaze across Egypt's history in grand proportions, they present a mystery that has intrigued Egyptologists for decades, and remains unsolved to this day: the question of why, when Thutmose was the legitimate heir to his father's crown and throne, did he allow his aunt to take over the rulership of Egypt until her death? An even bigger question (which might answer the first) is how did Hatshepsut die? So much is known about these two historical giants and yet, paradoxically, so little. Did her ambitious nephew, upon reaching the age of twenty-two and tired of being under Auntie's thumb, assassinate her? Archaeological evidence indicates that Thutmose was held in a kind of bondage during Hatshepsut's reign; what finally liberated him? Thutmose III was one of Egypt's mightiest kings. What kept him silent and inactive for twenty years while a woman ruled in his place?

Finally: Pharaoh Thutmose did indeed abduct the sons of enemy rulers. They were well taken care of and raised in a foreign palace, given high positions. Their kingly fathers seemed to take this practice in stride, but history is silent on how the princes' mothers felt about it.

Barbara Wood is the international bestselling author of 26 acclaimed novels, including the *New York Times* bestseller *Domina*. Her work has been translated into over 30 languages. Barbara lives in Riverside, California.